WARSAW
FURY

WARSAW
FURY

MICHAEL REIT

MICHAELREIT.COM

Published by Michael Reit.

ISBN: 978-3-9505033-3-3

Cover design, illustration and interior formatting:
Mark Thomas / Coverness.com

Image sources:
Couple: © Magdalena Russocka / Trevillion Image
Heinkel He 111 bomber: Bundesarchiv, Bild 101I-385-0587-07 / Wanderer, W. / CC-BY-SA 3.0
via Wikimedia.org
Changes to image: The bomber image was edited to remove tail and squadron markings.

To the brave men, women, and children of Warsaw under Nazi occupation.
Your sacrifices will never be forgotten.

PART I

WARSAW,

29 AUGUST 1939

CHAPTER ONE

The tram skidded a few extra paces before it screeched to an angry halt. Natan Borkowski jumped on board the tram with his fellow students, relieved to escape the pouring rain that started as they left school.

The conductor looked disapprovingly at the group of two dozen boys piling into the car, instantly fogging the windows.

"You boys better show me your tickets, or you're off before the next stop," he said menacingly as he shuffled down the car.

Natan grinned as he brushed the rain from his jacket—Warsaw tram conductors were hired for their moodiness. He rubbed the fog off the window and looked out at fellow Varsovians huddled close to the colorful, majestic buildings of the Old Town—overhanging roofs provided just enough escape from the raindrops clattering down. The streetcar clanged its bell as a horse-drawn carriage blocked the intersection, its driver shouting obscenities at the soaked beast.

As they made their way out of the city center, the car emptied until it was only Natan and a handful of others. He enjoyed the rhythmic drumming of the wheels as they crossed the Vistula River. On a typical summer day, the river would be dotted with an eclectic mix of small pleasure vessels and riverboats ferrying tourists. Today, only a few old river barges struggled through the surprisingly high waves.

Natan skipped off at the next stop, careful not to slip on the cobblestones. The rain was still coming down hard, and he jogged the last two blocks along the deserted streets to Borkowski Leather Works in record time. A tattered old sign that creaked in the rain betrayed the factory's purpose; he entered the yard through the broad archway between two large houses. On either side of the space, workers hauled overloaded pallets toward two trucks. Natan spotted the drivers having a smoke under shelter, oblivious to the men outside getting soaked.

Papa better not see them standing around doing nothing, he thought with a chuckle.

He crossed the yard, the muddy ground tugging at his shoes. When he opened the door to the factory, the sweet smell of new leather filled his nostrils. Natan brushed most of the mud off his shoes as he entered the factory. Even though the floor wasn't spotless—it was a factory, after all—his father was a stickler about bringing in dirt.

He ascended the stairs to the offices and waved at some of the men on the floor below—the hum of the machines drowning out their hoots. Natan opened the door to the offices, momentarily interrupting the silence—it always struck him how quiet it was, compared to the constant cacophony of the factory floor.

Natan headed straight for his father's office, nodding at the other clerks in the main room. Jan Borkowski stood near the window of his office. He appeared deep in thought, and Natan cleared his throat. His father turned and gave him a measured smile.

"Do you see that?" His father pointed at the trucks in the yard. "Where do you think the drivers are? I don't see them anywhere."

Natan suppressed a smile. "Probably taking a break."

"No, no. I've checked a few times now, and all I see is our men coming out of the factory, loading box after box, but the drivers are nowhere to be seen. Lazy bums. I'll have a word before they head out. How was school?"

Natan shrugged. "You know, like any first week back, although it's nice to be a senior since there's no one left to push us around. What would you like me to work on today?"

His father raised an eyebrow as he sat down behind his large mahogany desk. "Got somewhere else to be?"

"No, it's fine," he said with little enthusiasm. *Maybe I can join my friends later this evening.*

His father handed him a thick folder. "Process these invoices and let me know when you're done. I'll have some more work for you by then."

Natan sighed inwardly. *This is going to take a while—better get on with it.* Turning toward his desk, he saw Kasia Nowak walk in—her face creased with worry as she brushed past him.

"Mr. Borkowski, I was preparing the paperwork for the shipment downstairs, but we're missing the final approval from customs," she said, her voice an octave higher than usual. Natan stopped at the door.

His father stared at his assistant and offered a frown. "How is that possible? I signed that form over a month ago."

Kasia nodded, concern in her eyes. "And I remember marking these to be mailed out right after. I called customs, and they have no record of receiving our request. It must've been lost along the way."

Mr. Borkowski slumped back in his chair. "Can we get them to expedite? This is our biggest shipment of the year. We can't have any delays."

"They said we need to refile, and then they'll process it in due time," she said, quickly adding, "their exact words."

Natan felt his stomach turn. He knew what they were talking about—those papers were still on his desk.

His father got up, grabbed his coat, and made for the door. "If we wait for them to go through their usual process it'll take another two weeks. We can't wait that long; they're almost done loading up the trucks." He pointed at the window. "I'll go down there myself and get this fixed."

He stormed out of the office, leaving Kasia and Natan behind.

Natan was turning to leave when Kasia's voice cut through the silence. "Natan."

He turned back hesitantly.

"Did you forget to deliver those papers to the post office?" Her voice was soft, but her eyes bored into him.

He nodded. "They're on my desk, but you already knew that, didn't you?"

"I did, but your father has enough to worry about as it is."

Kasia looked more disappointed than angry, which only made him feel worse. "Is there anything I can do to make this right?"

"Yes," she said as she walked toward the door. "Go with your father. I doubt there's much you can do, but he'll appreciate having you there." Mr. Borkowski was already storming down the stairs, and Natan headed for the door. "Should I tell him?"

"That's up to you, but don't just stand around here."

Natan sprinted down the stairs, catching up with his father as the driver closed the back door of his father's car. He opened the door himself and sat down next to his father in the back seat. His father looked surprised to see him.

"I'd like to help, Papa."

*

The customs office was bustling with activity as the Borkowskis entered the crowded waiting room. Simple wooden chairs lined the walls, each taken and another half dozen people standing around. Two clerks sat behind modest desks on the far side of the room, surrounded by filing cabinets. They looked bored as they rummaged through the paperwork.

"They don't look like they're too bothered," his father mumbled, his cheeks reddening a little.

One of the men standing nearby overheard him. "Oh no, they have all the time in the world," he said with a thick accent from somewhere south of Warsaw.

Mr. Borkowski looked around impatiently, scanning the room. "How long have you been waiting?" he asked without looking at the man.

"Over two hours."

Natan checked the time. It was almost four. *They'll be clocking out in an hour sharp, no doubt.*

"Let's go," his father said as he crossed into the hallway and turned toward the staircase.

"Where are we going?" His father took the steps two at a time, and Natan struggled to keep up with him.

"There's no sense waiting for those clerks. I know someone who can help us right now."

They entered a narrow hallway on the second floor, where it was noticeably quieter. A young woman shuffled past them without as much as a glance. His father marched down the hallway before stopping in front of one of the closed doors. He rapped his knuckles loudly.

A groan came from the other side, and Mr. Borkowski opened the door. They stepped into a cramped office filled with filing cabinets. Squeezed in between was a simple desk with a small, stout man seated behind it, his hair combed over in a futile effort to conceal his bald crown.

The man stood and drew a sappy smile. "Mr. Borkowski, what an unexpected surprise." His voice dripped with irony as he emphasized the last word.

Natan's father didn't return the smile, although he shook the man's outstretched hand. "It appears there's a problem in your organization, Anton," he said curtly.

Anton waved him to the only other chair in the room, leaving Natan hovering around awkwardly.

"What seems to be the problem?" Anton said as he sat down. The old office chair squeaked as he readjusted himself.

"I can't have my largest shipment of the year sitting around for another two weeks," he said with determination, his cheeks flushed. Natan hardly recognized his father like this; he was generally calm and composed.

Anton sat shaking his head, a deep frown creasing his face. One of the longer strands of hair threatened to slide out of position, but he managed to catch it just in time. "I'm sorry about this, we rarely lose paperwork around here. But if you've been advised to reapply, there's very little else the department can do. You'll have to wait," he offered. Natan winced at his insincere tone.

"Well, that's simply not an option for me. I can't explain this to my German customer. He's expecting the boots this week."

Anton held up his palms and said nothing—silence hung in the air.

He wants something.

After a moment, Natan's father leaned forward. "Say, Anton. I know *the department* can't do anything for me, but is there any chance you could do me a personal favor?"

An unmistakable twinkle of greed appeared in Anton's ratty eyes as he lowered his voice. "Well, the issue is with the border patrols between Germany and Poland these days. You know how it is—people are nervous. Last I heard, soldiers were crawling about on both sides. We need to grease the wheels of the machine a little, if you know what I mean?"

Jan Borkowski nodded. "How much?"

The man scribbled a number on a piece of paper and slid it across the small desk. Natan saw his father's shoulders tense.

Mr. Borkowski stood up, stuffing the piece of paper in his pocket. "And this will get it done?"

"Absolutely," Anton said, getting up as well. The small man's demeanor had changed—now he was eager to help. "I will take care of it myself, and the papers will be in order within a few hours."

His father's eyes lingered a fraction longer than necessary on Anton, who shifted on his feet. "Then I'll have the money delivered to you tomorrow morning," Mr. Borkowski said, "and I expect to have the papers in time for my men to start driving tomorrow afternoon." Anton turned back to his work as father and son quickly left the office.

Back in the car, Natan couldn't contain his curiosity any longer.

"How much does he want?"

"Too much." His father handed him the crumpled piece of paper and tapped the seat to signal the driver. "Factory," he said.

Six thousand zloty. Natan swallowed hard—that was enough to pay all the men in the factory for a month. He looked outside the car as Warsaw's wet, slippery streets slid by. Even though it was only late afternoon, rain clouds hung overhead, casting a wet, gray blanket over the city. *Should I tell him?* Natan had been careless with the papers, and he remembered pushing them aside on his desk when he'd left that particular afternoon over a month ago. He'd been too anxious to get out of the office to meet his friends, and he had then simply forgotten about it. He glanced at his father, who looked like he had the weight of the world on his shoulders.

"You know, if we don't get this shipment out this month, we'll have to shut the factory down for a while," Jan said as he gazed through the window. In the Old Town area, the small streets meant the traffic moved slower. Their driver honked at a group of pedestrians blocking their way.

"But if you pay that customs man, we should be okay, right?"

His father nodded slowly. "Yes, but I don't have that kind of cash."

Natan pondered his response before asking, "Do you think it has something to do with the recent German-Soviet treaty?"

"I'm sure it's because of that, and, for what it's worth, I think Anton will have to use quite a bit of that money to secure the passage of our trucks."

"Can't you take out a loan with the bank?"

Jan didn't answer immediately but soon turned toward Natan.

"I can't. We've already overextended our credit. This shipment is our lifeline." In the semidarkness of the car, Natan could see his eyes glisten.

The traffic moved again, and they turned onto one of the larger throughways, heading toward the Vistula. His father spoke to the driver. "Max, change of plans. Let's drop Natan off at home, then head to Ochota."

Max nodded and merged to the left lane, quickly overtaking the other cars.

Natan was surprised. "Where are you going?"

His father gave him a weak smile. "To take care of this problem."

"I want to go with you."

"Out of the question—you're going to do your homework and have dinner with your mother. I'll be back a little later."

Natan wanted to protest, but his father silenced him with a stern look. "I don't want you anywhere near the people I'm meeting. You're going home, and that's final."

Natan opened his mouth, but his father had turned away. He caught Max's gaze in the rearview mirror, and the man shook his head almost imperceptibly. There was little sense arguing with his father. Natan brooded silently for the rest of the ride.

They stopped in front of their house. As Natan opened the door, his father placed a hand on his shoulder. "Not a word of this to your mother. Tell her I'm taking care of an errand at the office, okay?"

Natan nodded and got out. As the car sped away, he stood in the rain for a minute, cursing himself.

Chapter Two

Try as she might, Julia Horowitz found it impossible to get back to sleep. She could hear her mother shuffling plates and cutlery in the kitchen, and she glanced at the clock on her tiny bedside cabinet—half past five. Finally, she sighed, surrendered, and swung her legs out of bed.

The two other beds in the small room were vacant, which meant the rest of the family was already at the breakfast table. She quickly dressed and joined them.

"Look who finally decided to get up as well," her brother Olek said, grinning. He spoke in Yiddish, as they all did at home.

She shot him a look but didn't say anything. *Why bother.*

Their mother placed a small skillet of scrambled eggs in the middle of the table, and Olek and her father scooped most of it onto their plates. Julia and her mother waited until they finished before taking what little remained for them to share.

The little room doubled as a kitchen and living room. Julia nibbled at her eggs and took a small piece of dark rye bread—already stale, but she didn't complain. Her mother did her best to make sure there was something to eat at least twice a day. On the Sabbath, they would have a hearty but straightforward midday meal as well. She glanced at Lea Horowitz, who was eating quietly, her eyes focused on her plate.

As Olek scraped the final pieces of egg from the pan, Julia took a deep breath and turned to her father. "Papa, there's an exciting project at school today."

Wojtek Horowitz looked up from his plate with a frown. He preferred breakfast to be a quiet time.

"There's a selection round for an extra class on law," Julia said, speaking quickly before her father could silence her.

Olek interrupted. "A class on law? What's that to you?" A few crumbles of bread flew from his mouth.

Why must you be such a pig? Julia grimaced, ignoring her older brother and turning her eyes toward her mother. "I've been selected to apply. Mr. Lewandowski says I would be a great student."

Her father wiped his mouth and said, "Why would a girl need to learn anything about the law?"

She tried to hide her disappointment—he sounded annoyed. She had anticipated this and swallowed before responding.

"Papa, you know I'd like to be a lawyer when I'm older, right? I'd really like to—"

He silenced her with a quick hand gesture. "What time is this class?"

"Right after the morning classes, at one."

Wojtek shook his head resolutely. "Out of the question. I need you in the shop." He returned his attention to his plate. That was the end of the matter for him.

Olek looked across the table with glee, and Julia felt her frustration growing. She turned to her mother, who also shook her head.

She couldn't resist another try. "But Papa, the man teaching the class works for one of the biggest law firms in the whole of Poland!" *Why doesn't he understand?* "I've worked so hard for this!"

Her father's head shot up quicker than she'd expected. The annoyance gave way to anger as he put his fork down with a clang. "Julia Horowitz, I don't care for your tone. You won't question me. The law is nothing for a girl, and certainly not a Jewish girl like you. Your teacher should know better than to encourage it."

Her cheeks burned with indignation. Olek's grin was only widening. She wanted to punch him.

Wojtek Horowitz wasn't done. "Look around. Who do you think you are, chasing silly academic dreams? You should take after your brother. He's got a steady job, he's helping put food on the table. The very least you can do is help out in the shop."

It was true. Olek, two years her senior at 18, had recently dropped out of his last year at school to find a job in construction. He was contributing a large amount of his salary toward the very meal they were having now. And her father had a point—she had bigger aspirations than to become someone's wife and wither away as her mother had. She immediately regretted her thoughts as she looked at Lea, whose eyes were sad—silently pleading with her to stop.

Julia glared at her brother and nodded. "Okay, Papa, I understand. I'll come straight back after school."

She silently finished her breakfast.

*

Julia's best friend, Helena, was waiting for her outside the school. She raised her eyebrows as Julia came closer and smiled cautiously as they made their way up the stairs.

"What's wrong?" she asked without preamble.

Julia waved it off. "Nothing—just my father."

They hurried through the crowded hallway, avoiding the other kids rushing to their first classes.

"Come on, what happened this time?"

Julia sighed. "He won't let me go to the law class today. He says it's not for girls, especially Jewish ones."

"But you must go!" Helena exclaimed as she stopped abruptly in the middle of the hallway. The other kids glided past them as she turned to Julia, her face serious. "You're the only girl invited, and you're probably the smartest person in the room there."

Julia pulled on her friend's arm. "Come on, we're going to be late for math."

"Never mind math. This is a big chance, Julia. You have to go."

She smiled at Helena. "Okay, okay, I'll go."

Helena looked triumphant as they took their seats at the back of the classroom. Of course, there would be trouble waiting when she got to her father's shop. *I'll worry about that later.* She opened her textbook and tried to focus on algebra.

*

After lunch, Julia walked into the classroom set aside for the law class and was surprised to find she wasn't the first student there. She scanned the faces, all of them boys, for one that was familiar. Mr. Lewandowski sat behind the desk in the front. He glanced up, saw her, and stood as she came near.

"I'm glad you decided to come," he said softly, as the boys around them chatted, oblivious to Julia. "I think this will be perfect for you, and I'd like to see more girls pursuing a career in law." He winked at her.

Mr. Lewandowski always encouraged her to follow her dreams. When he'd asked her what she wanted to become at the start of the year, she'd been hesitant to share her ambitions. He pushed her, and that's why she was here today.

"Thank you," she said, scanning the room. "The lawyer's not here yet?"

Mr. Lewandowski shook his head. "He's a busy man, and from what I know, extremely punctual. He'll probably show up right on—ah, there he is!"

A tall man confidently entered the room. He wore a fine suit and had an expensive-looking raincoat draped over his arm. As he passed the desks, his eyes were focused on Mr. Lewandowski, approaching him with enormous, purposeful strides. They shook hands, and the man put down his leather briefcase.

Mr. Lewandowski introduced him as Mr. Kaminski. His gaze lingered on Julia a little longer, and she offered a smile he ignored. Then, finally, after what felt like a full minute of silence, he spoke.

"It's great to see such a large interest in the fine craft of the law," he said without enthusiasm, his voice a monotone baritone that sounded like a hum. "In the next few hours, I hope we can select the best students for my firm's internship." He looked serious as he wrote a few words on the chalkboard behind him. "I'll start with a short introduction about what we expect from you and what the course is like. Then, you'll all write a short essay detailing why you should be accepted into the course." He looked around the room. "Any questions?"

Silence.

Mr. Kaminski clapped his hands together. "Excellent. Then I'll start with a question for you. Who here has any experience with the law?"

No hands went up. For a moment, Mr. Kaminski looked disappointed, but he quickly recovered. "Anybody who knows someone working for the law?"

One of the boys raised his hand. "I know a policeman."

Mr. Kaminski smiled dismissively. "Very well, but that's not what I'm looking for. Anybody else?"

Nobody could come up with even a far-fetched connection to someone working in the esteemed field of law. Julia was unsure if she liked Mr. Kaminski very much. He then launched into a droning description of the inner workings of the law. Or, more specifically, his courtroom victories. He seemed to love the sound of his voice; his lecture went on for more than an hour. Julia glanced around the room and saw most of the other students' heads drooping. She stifled a yawn of her own. *How much longer is he going to be?*

When he mercifully finished his lecture, the air in the room felt heavy, and they took a short break. She was glad to get a bit of fresh air outside before returning—determined to ace the essay part.

Mr. Lewandowski handed out the papers while the lawyer offered instructions. They were required to write about the defense of a fictional case. "Make sure you're concise. We don't like wordiness."

For the next hour and a half, the classroom was silent but for the occasional rustling of paper. Then, when it was time to hand in their essays,

Mr. Lewandowski quickly glanced at Julia's small pile of papers. He nodded approvingly at her neatly written words.

As everyone filed out of the room, Mr. Kaminski was placing the essays in his briefcase. Julia gathered up the courage to approach him.

"Excuse me," she said, keeping a distance.

He looked up with the same impassive face he'd had throughout most of the class. "Yes?"

"I wanted to thank you for the interesting class. Can I ask you something about your firm?"

He closed his briefcase and nodded. "What would you like to know?" He looked like he was in a hurry, and Julia feared she was keeping him.

"How many lawyers work there?"

He thought briefly and answered. "There are about 20 of us."

"Are any of them women?"

"No," Mr. Kaminski said immediately. "We have plenty of women working as assistants and receptionists, but none are lawyers." He snorted a little, and a frown appeared as it dawned on him. "You want to become a lawyer?"

Julia nodded and opened her mouth to reply, but he cut her off.

"Let me tell you something. I haven't read your essay yet, and I'm sure you've tried your best, but I'm going to be honest. There's no chance we'll take on girls—it's simply not a job for women, certainly not in our firm."

She stood silent, stunned.

He wasn't done yet. "I noticed your name on the class list earlier. It's Horowitz, right?"

Julia nodded and said nothing. She knew where this was going.

"Jewish girl, then." She thought his frown couldn't become any deeper, yet it did. "I can't imagine your parents are happy about your ambitions." It wasn't a question, and he only paused long enough to pick up his briefcase with a sigh.

Julia felt her eyes sting but was determined not to show how much his words hurt. She swallowed hard and tried to keep her composure. "I understand," she said softly.

Mr. Kaminski grunted something unintelligible as he turned away from the desk. Then, he strode toward the door, leaving Julia in front of the classroom on her own.

*

She took quick steps through the narrow streets adjacent to Nalewki Street. The sun was doing its best to break through the clouds overhead; it did little to lift Julia's spirits. She kept her head down, and she prayed she wouldn't run into anyone she knew.

The lawyer's words had shaken her more than she cared to admit. Julia knew she was dreaming above her station—daughter of a simple shoemaker, after all—but nobody had ever told her in such bold terms. Well, her father and brother did their best to belittle her at every opportunity, but she had decided not to pay too much attention to them a long time ago.

When she had stepped into the classroom earlier, she'd felt energized, ready to take her chance. A door had opened, only for Mr. Kaminski to slam it shut only hours later.

She reached a busy intersection and paused for the traffic. A streetcar raced by, clanging its bells loudly as two street urchins crossed dangerously close. The people around her were busy doing their afternoon shopping, frequenting the small shops lining Nalewki. She passed her favorite store on the street, Elbaum Ladies' Clothing. Even though she'd never dared set foot inside, she loved to gawk at the luxurious clothing in the shop window. Julia stopped and noticed they were changing the dress display. She caught her reflection in the shop window, and her tattered shoes stared back. She sighed and walked on.

Julia neared her home, her father's workshop on the ground floor. The rusted signboard hung overhead really ought to be replaced or removed. Her father didn't seem to care—he said his customers were loyal and knew how to find him, regardless of the sign.

Julia stepped into the little shop that smelled of shoe polish and leather. She was glad to find her father occupied with a customer, and she squeezed past the man, her father giving her a thunderous glare. She quickly made her way to the small storeroom in the back, where she picked up a broom and started sweeping dirt out onto the pavement. As she stepped into the street, she suddenly felt a jolt of indignation rise up. *Who do these men think they are, telling me I won't make it? One day, I'll prove them wrong.*

Chapter Three

Jan Borkowski was already gone by the time Natan came down for breakfast. It started the day off badly, and Natan had struggled to keep his concentration through the morning classes.

As the boys walked down to the field for gym class, the sun was high in the sky, somewhat lifting his spirits. Surely his father had succeeded in getting the money? The coach handed out bibs, and Natan found himself on the much weaker side—he'd simply try a bit harder.

As the game started, he found his place up front. As expected, his team was down by a couple of goals within minutes. Natan made his runs and waited for his chance. It finally came after about ten minutes, when one of the better players in the midfield passed the ball perfectly between two defenders.

Natan seized his chance and chased the ball. The other boys weren't fast enough to keep up with him as he raced toward the goal. He set himself up for the shot—ready to pull the trigger—when his feet were hacked away from underneath him. He hit the ground with a loud thud, his head banging into the grass.

It took him a few seconds to recover, and he felt a little groggy as one of his teammates helped him up. His assailant strolled away without as much as a glance. Szymon Bacik. When Szymon turned around and winked at Natan, something snapped. Before realizing what he was doing, Natan dashed over to the smug bully and landed a punch square in Szymon's face. He heard a loud crack, and at first, he thought he'd broken a bone as a jolt of pain spread through his hand. But when he looked at Szymon, struggling backward and grasping his nose, the other boy's face was covered in blood.

Szymon's expression changed from surprise to anger as he looked at his bloody hands.

"Are you crazy, Borkowski?" he howled. "You broke my nose!"

Szymon launched himself at Natan and was on top of him, pummeling him with his fists. Natan put his arms up, shielding his face. He couldn't catch a breath as Szymon pushed his knees down into his chest. He struggled to break free, but Szymon pinned him down, and he could not avoid the punches.

The other boys rushed to the fight. Some were excited and shouted encouragement; others were looking on. As the two boys struggled on the grass, their teacher pulled them apart.

"Stop it, both of you!" he shouted as he pulled Szymon off Natan, who sucked in a deep breath of air.

He saw the face of his teacher, concerned yet stern. "Can you breathe, Natan?"

Natan nodded meekly.

"Good. Let's get you on your feet."

He took the man's hand and stood, feeling dizzy and a little nauseous.

His teacher inspected him. "Looks like you're fine, other than a few bruises. Too bad we can't say the same about him." Szymon stood glaring at Natan from a distance, holding his bloody nose.

"Well, that's it for the game, boys. Everybody can go grab a shower." Their teacher turned his attention to the two brawlers. "Except for you two—you're coming with me."

Natan sighed. He knew where he was going, and it only meant more trouble.

*

Natan struggled to keep up as Jan Borkowski strode down the steps of the ornate school building in a hurry, heading straight for the waiting car. His father got in and quickly closed the door. Natan walked around the car, his head hanging low. Then, dreading the ride home, he sat down next to his father.

"What were you thinking?" His father spoke calmly as the car pulled away. "Getting into a fight over a football game? What are you, 12 years old?" He shook his head in disappointment.

He's not going to yell at me? Natan lifted his eyebrows.

"And now you've got a suspension hanging over your head. Don't you realize how bad this will look on your university applications?"

Natan was silent. The same thoughts had dawned on him as he walked back from the headmaster's office. His grades were good—no, they were excellent—and he'd been involved in many extracurricular activities over the years. He'd done all of that to make sure his chances of getting into Warsaw's top universities were as high as possible. *Did I blow it with a single punch?*

"I'll try to talk to the headmaster again before they make a decision. You've always been a good student, so I hope we can reason with him." He looked at Natan, forcing him to meet his eyes. "Why did you do it?"

Natan shrugged. "He's always picking on people. I'd had enough."

His father held his gaze for a moment and nodded. "I hate bullies, too. But you can't go around picking fights with all of them. It's going to come back to haunt you."

"I know, Papa. I just couldn't stand his face. He looked so smug."

Jan Borkowski's eyes softened. "You're 17 years old, and you need to think about your future. If all goes well, you'll take over the business. I need you to focus, Natan. We have enough going on without you getting suspended. Don't you remember how hard it was to get you into this school in the first place?"

That shook Natan back to the reality of the previous night. The fight and its aftermath had taken his mind off the problems at the factory. *Another one of my screwups.* He bit the inside of his cheek.

"Did you get the papers?" he asked cautiously.

His father shook his head. "It hasn't been confirmed yet. Kasia is waiting by the phone for news."

"But you got the money for Anton?"

A quick nod. "I did."

Natan was relieved. If the money had changed hands, surely the paperwork would be a formality. He looked outside and was surprised to see Max turning onto the Kierbedź Bridge crossing the Vistula River. "You're not dropping me off at home?"

"No, let's not bother your mother with what happened at school. Hopefully, I can make this suspension go away before we have to tell her. She will not be pleased."

That's putting it mildly.

"We're going to the factory," his father said. "There's plenty you can do there, and it's better than having you sit at home."

It took another ten minutes to get to the factory, and Kasia burst through the door to greet them even before Max had killed the engine.

"Good news!" she called, her face flushed from the sprint down the stairs. "The papers are ready at the customs office. I'm on my way over there now."

Jan looked at his watch. "They took their time. Anton promised to have the papers ready before noon. You'd better hurry."

Kasia nodded, then noticed Natan. "Shouldn't you be in school?"

"Got in a fight."

She frowned in surprise. "Well, you can make yourself useful and join me."

Natan was keen to help and was following Kasia toward the street when his father called after them.

"Take the car—it'll be faster!"

The ride to the customs office was frustrating, as they hit the early rush hour traffic. Kasia fidgeted but didn't ask Natan anything about the fight. He liked her—Kasia knew when to leave him be, and now was definitely a time he needed to collect his thoughts.

As Warsaw crawled by outside, Natan pondered his future. He was cautiously optimistic his father would get him out of a suspension. Perhaps some of the other students could back him up. Szymon had provoked him with that tackle—he started it. There were fights at his school all the time, but few involved broken noses. There was little he could do about it now; he was determined not to let his father down a third time. They had to get those papers. The trucks were loaded and ready to go.

He looked at Kasia as they slowed down again. Her eyes shot back and forth as she tapped her foot. "We're going to be late—this traffic is horrible."

"It'll be fine. We still have time." He tried to sound more confident than he felt.

She looked at him. "Looks like the other kid got you pretty good."

He rubbed his throbbing left cheekbone, where he could feel a bump forming. "Well, I did break his nose, so I think I won."

She chuckled, and Natan thought he saw the hint of a grin. "You should be more careful, Natan."

They started moving again, and they had clear roads for the rest of the way. Max sped through the city, taking shortcuts only he knew, and they arrived at the customs office a few minutes before five.

"Shit." Kasia's face crumpled as she looked out the window. A clerk stood in front of the building.

They jumped out of the car and hurried toward him. He shook his head as he blocked their passage.

"We're closing," he said. "A few people are waiting inside, but we're not letting anyone else in. You can come back tomorrow."

"Can you please make an exception?" Kasia pleaded. "We were only just called with the message that our papers were ready, and we have our trucks waiting to go."

The man shook his head again, this time more persistently, as he folded his arms. "We open at nine tomorrow."

Natan took a few steps toward the man, but Kasia pulled him back and away from the building.

"What did I just say? Are you going to make another scene?" she whispered savagely. Her eyes shot fire.

"But we can't wait another day! Papa made it very clear that things are not good with the company."

Her expression softened. "He told you that, huh?"

"Yes, and it's all my fault. Those trucks would be in Germany by now if it weren't for me." Natan sat on the steps leading to the building.

Kasia sat down next to him and put her hand on his knee. "We all make mistakes, Natan—it's part of life. It's how you handle them that matters."

"I'm not handling this one very well," he said as he kept his head down.

She smiled. "Sure. But you know what? There might be something we can do, after all."

He lifted his head. "What are you talking about?"

"I've been here many times, and I know where they keep all the papers. It's that little room in the front where the clerks hand them out when you come in."

Natan nodded. He remembered the room with the filing cabinets. "But how will we get in?"

There was a twinkle in her eye. "We're going to take the other entrance."

*

They stood in the alley behind the customs office. The sun was still high in the sky, and it was a pleasant afternoon. Natan felt conspicuous, but Kasia looked quite at ease as she lit a cigarette.

"They'll be done soon enough," she said while she blew out a puff of smoke. "Most of the clerks can't wait to get home once it's five. I'm sure they're annoyed at those people keeping them on duty."

Natan kept his eyes fixed on the top floor windows' lights. *Anton's probably not the only one making some cash on the side.*

When the lights finally went out, they waited another few minutes. Kasia dropped her cigarette and crunched it under her shoe. "Okay, let's do this."

The wall to the small garden of the building was three, maybe four meters high. They'd need something to scale it. Kasia pushed a garbage bin to the wall.

"There. You can go first, and I'll be on the lookout," she said, her eyes scanning both ends of the alley.

Natan did a quick scan himself before he mounted the bin, grabbed the top of the wall, and effortlessly swung his legs over. It was surprisingly easy, and he was glad the other side was grassy ground as he made a soft landing.

He waited for Kasia to appear. Nothing. Then, the rasping voice of a man who'd smoked too many cigarettes. *Does Kasia need help?* Natan scanned the small garden but found nothing that would help him scale the wall from his side.

"No, I'm all right, thank you," he heard Kasia reply.

"What's a pretty lady like you doing in an alley like this?" Then the man launched into a coughing fit. Kasia said nothing.

"I'm fine, really," she said after a moment. "Maybe you should move along. I'm just taking the garbage out." Natan heard her knuckles rapping the bin.

"I have nowhere else to be," the man responded.

Kasia sighed loudly. "Well, perhaps you could spend your time somewhere else, rather than around me?" There was irritation in her voice.

Even without seeing her, Natan could tell she was getting impatient. But she didn't sound distressed. In fact, she sounded confident and in control.

It was silent for a moment until Natan heard footsteps receding on the other side. Kasia's face peeked over the wall a few seconds later before she swung herself over and gingerly dropped down next to him.

"What was that all about?" Natan asked.

She shrugged. "A bum with nothing better to do. He was harmless, especially after I showed him this." She flashed a small pocket knife.

Natan smiled. "You're a woman of many surprises."

"I know how to handle myself on the street. Plenty of odd people in this city. Girl's gotta protect herself." She walked to the back door of the customs office. "Let's get inside. I don't want any other people seeing us hanging around here."

The door was locked, as expected. Natan tried to force it without success.

Kasia stood by, a look of amusement spreading on her face.

"What's so funny?"

She gently pushed him aside and took a small piece of metal from her pocket, which she inserted into the lock.

Natan was stunned. "You carry a lockpick around?"

Kasia didn't answer but leaned her ear closer to the lock. Her tongue stuck a little out of her mouth as she concentrated. Natan kept quiet and looked up. The buildings were built close to each other, about four to five stories high—he suddenly felt very exposed.

In the silence of the garden, the click of the door unlocking was almost loud enough to unnerve him.

Kasia looked up triumphantly and tried the door. "I haven't lost my touch," she said with a hint of false modesty.

She opened the door, and as they walked in the semidarkness of the hallway, he said, "I'm not sure what amazes me more—that you carry a lockpick around or that you actually know how to use it."

Kasia continued ahead of him—evidently knowing where to go—before she responded. "The lock of my apartment is a bit iffy. Sometimes the key doesn't work, and I need to pick it. It's been a while, but it's good to have an alternative on me."

Natan laughed out loud. "You need to pick your house door? That's ridiculous."

"We don't all live in mansions," she quipped.

Touché.

At the front, Natan recognized the main entrance, and they paused to make sure they were alone. Then, when all remained quiet, they walked into the main administrative room and went straight for the two desks at the back. The desks were neat, orderly, and—to Natan's dismay—devoid of any paperwork. But for a few stamps and pencils, there was nothing of value. *Great. We broke into this place for nothing.*

Kasia seemed less anxious as she ignored the desks and went for the cabinets lining the wall. The drawers were labeled alphabetically, and she reached for the one labeled "A–C." Much to Natan's relief, it opened, and

Kasia quickly leafed through the different papers.

"I think I've got it." She held out a thin folder with his surname. She opened it to reveal a thin manila envelope. Natan held his breath as she ripped the top and retrieved the papers inside. She smiled as her eyes scanned the documents. "This is our permit, Natan."

She handed him the papers triumphantly, and he nodded. "Let's get out of here."

CHAPTER FOUR

Julia's father had been oddly quiet after the customer left. She'd braced herself for a verbal lashing, but her father had simply ignored her and left her to do her chores. Today she decided to head straight to the workshop after her morning classes, and she found a stack of shoes ready to be polished.

She sat in the back room, trying to rescue an old pair that had seen better days. It wasn't an uncommon sight in their little workshop: her father's clientele struggled to get by.

Julia finished polishing the brown pair and inspected her handiwork; it would have to do. She picked up another ragged pair and continued her menial task. As long as her father left her alone, Julia was content. She knew his anger was brewing, and there would be a lecture sometime soon.

Julia walked into the front to find her father looking outside to the alley. He turned when he heard her. "You're done polishing?" It was half past four, and she looked forward to meeting Helena to practice their German together. A lot of business these days was done with German companies, and she imagined if she wanted to have a future in law—or anything meaningful, for that matter—it would help to speak more than just Yiddish and Polish. German would be a good start.

She nodded. "I'd like to go to Helena's now." She took a few steps toward the door, but her father cleared his throat. *What is it now?* She reluctantly turned; he was shaking his head.

"Actually, I'd like you to clean the front room as well."

Julia groaned inwardly and considered arguing with him but bit her tongue. She was already on thin ice—no need to make it worse.

He looked at her, waiting for her challenge.

Instead, she turned and sullenly went back into the storeroom.

*

Half an hour later, mercifully, her father hadn't come up with any other tasks. She made a fast exit onto Nalewki Street before he could change his mind. As she merged onto the crowded sidewalk, her breathing relaxed. The bustle of the street made her anonymous as she mingled with the people around her.

Nalewki Street had everything, from small, family-run grocery stores to industrial-sized department stores. It attracted a varied mix of people from all walks of life. Julia walked behind a woman wearing a colorful dress in a lavish flower print. The lady went into Baumgartner's Bakery, and Julia slowed her pace a little to catch the waft of freshly baked *pączki* coming from the store. They never had the delicious deep-fried treat at home; it was an indulgence her father wouldn't allow.

Julia continued without further delay, for she was already late. Helena wouldn't mind, but Julia hated being tardy. She checked the giant clock of the Borzech department store on the corner—a quarter past five. It would take her at least half an hour to get to Helena's, and that was if she hurried. That would leave them only a very short hour to practice. She grumbled as a tram stopped next to her, and, on impulse, she decided to jump on board. Julia found a seat in the back, behind a large man wearing a bowler hat. As she didn't have money to pay the fare, she peeked to the front, but she didn't see a conductor. *Lucky.*

She looked around as the tram cut through the city at a steady pace. *Maybe I can sneak onto trams a bit more often if it's this easy?*

"Excuse me, young lady." A harsh voice interrupted her thoughts, and she looked up to see the stern face of the conductor. She hadn't heard him approach. "Can I see your ticket?"

Julia felt a cold shiver run through her body and managed an awkward smile. "Of course, sir." She made a show of fumbling in her pockets and hoped the man would move on. Meanwhile, the conductor had all the time in the world, and drummed his fingers on the seat next to her.

With as much innocence as she could fake, she looked back up. "I must've lost it."

He nodded, and for a moment, Julia thought she got away with it. "Well, then I guess you can buy a new ticket."

She looked downcast. "I don't have any money."

His face remained the same as he calmly spoke the following words: "Then you're going to get off at the next stop, and we'll call the police. It's illegal to ride the tram without a ticket." He walked to the front of the tram to let the driver know.

His words chilled her to the bone. The police? She felt a wave of panic. Her father would be furious.

She looked around the tram. It was going too fast for her to jump off now. The conductor sat close to the exit, so he would probably beat her to it if she made a dash for it. As her eyes darted around, she saw a man sitting near the exit, facing her. He held her gaze and smiled.

Julia raised an eyebrow. He must've overheard the conversation. The tram slowed down to let other traffic pass, and the man made an almost imperceptible movement with his head toward the open exit. *Make a run for it? Really?* The man cleared his throat and repeated the gesture, now signaling with his hands as well.

She did a quick double take. The conductor sat with his back to her and was oblivious to what was going on behind him. The tram now stood almost completely still as they waited for a cart to clear the road. *Now or never.* She got up, taking quick strides to the exit.

The conductor must've heard the commotion as he turned and shouted. "Where do you think you're going?"

Julia kept moving, ignoring him—her heart in her throat.

She was almost there, but the conductor had also gotten up and moved quickly toward the exit. She wasn't sure she would make it until the man near the exit dropped his hat in the aisle. As he reached for it, he pushed it farther away from himself, forcing him to get up, blocking the conductor's path.

Julia shot him a thankful look as she reached the exit, and he winked at her as he picked up his hat.

"Stop right there!" the conductor shouted as she jumped off. She didn't look back as she landed on the sidewalk and sprinted into an alley.

*

When she finally arrived at Helena's, it was well past six, and she found the family at the dinner table. They insisted she join them for the evening meal. She gratefully accepted, and Helena's mother served her a generous portion of beef stew with a thick slice of fresh bread. She tucked in with relish and only then realized how hungry she was.

"This is delicious, Mrs. Kowalczyk," she managed to utter between bites.

Helena's mother smiled. "Help yourself to some vegetables as well, dear."

As they ate, Helena asked, "Can we study in your office, Papa?"

"Of course—what are you working on?"

Julia liked Helena's parents. They were so supportive of their daughter, and Julia always felt at home with them. She wished her father would encourage her to study the way Mr. Kowalczyk did. Maybe it had something to do with Helena being an only child.

"German—I told you about this earlier, didn't I?"

Helena's father put down his fork. "Of course. How are you two doing?" He looked at Julia.

She smiled. "Well, it's all very basic, but I think we could have a simple conversation in German."

He nodded and looked sad. "Unfortunately, you might get to practice your German sooner rather than later."

"How do you mean?"

"The news is saying there's more activity on the border today. It appears the Germans are moving more troops toward us."

Julia stopped chewing.

"But that would violate the treaty, wouldn't it?"

Mr. Kowalczyk nodded. "Somehow, I don't think Hitler cares too much about Versailles and its rules. He's probably feeling more secure now that he doesn't have to worry about Stalin."

Julia pondered that for a moment.

"What about the British and the French?" she asked. "They'll help us if anybody attacks us, right?"

"I hope so," Helena's father said. "But they're far away. If Hitler decides to attack with his powerful army, we might be overrun before they can make it here."

Julia suddenly didn't feel hungry anymore, and she put down her fork. Helena was getting restless, and she asked if they could be excused.

As they sat in the study, Julia found it hard to concentrate. She didn't like the sound of German anymore.

"Are you okay?" Helena asked. "I've asked you twice what your address is in German."

Julia, feeling a little dazed, turned to her friend. Helena looked concerned but also a little impatient. Julia nodded. "I'm all right. Aren't you worried about Hitler?"

Helena thought about that for a moment. "I don't think he's going to attack us. Besides, our army is already there as well. I'm sure they'll stop the Germans before they can get to Warsaw."

Julia wasn't so sure. "From what I've heard, the German army is much stronger than ours."

"Then the Brits will come to our aid," Helena said with confidence.

Julia was getting a little frustrated. "Haven't you heard about what the Nazis are doing in Germany? About what they're doing to the Jews?"

Helena pulled a face. "But that's only because they're blaming the Jews for their problems in Germany."

Julia realized Helena wasn't going to understand. She loved her friend, but she wasn't Jewish. She'd never experienced the subtle mannerisms some people in Poland exhibited when they realized a person was Jewish. Julia had heard what happened in Germany, and she feared the feelings of antisemitism were bubbling under the surface in Poland as well. All it took was someone scraping away the thin layer of civility, like in Germany.

"Helena, do you mind if we continue some other time? I'm tired." She stood and started packing her books.

Her friend walked her to the door, and they hugged. "I'll see you at school tomorrow," Helena said.

It was still light outside, the sun low on the horizon. Julia decided to walk and not chance another encounter with an angry conductor. Besides, she had plenty to occupy her thoughts on her way home.

CHAPTER FIVE

Natan's mother scooped some more eggs and sausage onto his plate. "Come on, Natan, you've hardly eaten anything."

Protest was futile, so he forced down another bite. Natan was still hopeful his father would be able to convince the headmaster to reconsider the suspension. They hadn't told Vera Borkowski that Natan wasn't going to school today but would join his father at the factory.

Jan Borkowski walked into the breakfast room and sat down. Almost immediately, Zuzanna, one of their servants, appeared to pour him a large cup of coffee before offering him some pastries from a polished serving tray.

Zuza disappeared back into the kitchen, and Jan took a bite of his croissant. "Are you about ready to go?"

Natan nodded, relieved he wouldn't have to finish the whole plate in front of him.

"Are you dropping him off at school?" his mother asked.

"I'll give him a ride," his father said, avoiding the question.

Natan pushed eggs around his plate as he recalled the night before. When he and Kasia returned to the factory, Mr. Borkowski had quizzed them about why it had taken so long. He'd even seemed a little cross until they told him how they'd secured the papers. Then, he'd laughed out loud when Kasia told him about her run-in with the bum.

The trucks had left early in the evening, and they should be near Germany now. Natan wondered if there would be any trouble at the border, and he suspected his father was far more nervous than he made himself out to be.

The kitchen door opened, and Zuzanna rushed back in, looking worried.

His father looked up. "What's wrong, Zuza?"

"Sorry to disturb you, but Max and I just heard something on the radio, and we think you would want to know this."

Max and Zuza had probably been chatting in the kitchen as they waited for the family to finish their breakfast.

"Yes, go on." His father sat up straight.

"Well, we were listening to some music. But then it was interrupted by a news bulletin. They say the German army has invaded Poland."

All was silent as her words faded away. Zuza's eyes shifted nervously between Natan and his parents.

His father kept his composure. "Thank you, Zuza. Please tell Max to get the car ready, and I'll be out in a few minutes." He finished his coffee with a big gulp as his eyes remained fixed on the door Zuza had closed.

Natan sat silent and worried about what this meant. Would the Germans break through the lines quickly? He knew the Polish army had been mobilizing and were expecting something. And would they make it all the way to Warsaw? How long would it take?

"Natan." His father interrupted his thoughts as he stood. "Let's go. This changes everything."

*

Max sped through the busy Warsaw streets as they rushed toward the factory. Jan Borkowski was scribbling furiously on a piece of paper, but Natan couldn't see what he was writing.

On the car radio, the government was instructing people to stay indoors and await further news. They said there had been no official declaration of war from Nazi Germany, but confirmed there had been skirmishes on the border. The news didn't mention how many, but Natan didn't think it would take long for the announcement of war to come. Outside, other people appeared to feel the same, as long queues formed outside various stores.

His father closed his notepad and looked outside. He seemed on edge, which was unusual for Jan Borkowski.

"Do you think the trucks made it in time?" Natan asked the question that had been on his mind ever since Zuza brought the news.

His father pursed his lips. "I don't know. Judging by the time they left last night, they might have managed to sneak through before the firing started. But with any bad luck or holdups along the way, the chances are they're stuck near the front lines."

That would be the worst possible place, Natan thought. Then, no matter what happened, they'd either lose the shipment or the trucks would return later that day.

His father echoed his thoughts. "I hope they managed to get past the border. I would hate to see the trucks pull back into the factory today. There's no way we can resend the shipment anytime soon—that's for sure."

And it's all my fault. He looked at his father, who almost seemed to have shrunk from anxiety. Natan made an important decision.

"Papa, I need to tell you something about those shipment papers."

Jan turned to him, his eyes focused.

"I forgot to post the papers. I meant to do it the next morning after I got them, but then they got lost in all the other paperwork on my desk. I'm so sorry."

His father looked at him silently for a minute, and Natan saw a hint of disappointment in his eyes. He then spoke in a surprisingly level voice. "The most important thing about making a mistake is owning up to it, and doing everything you can to fix it, Natan. It's tough for people to admit they've made a mistake, and by then, it's usually too late."

Natan was silent. *I should've fixed this sooner.*

His father looked outside. "And you did everything you could once you found out about the mistake. It would've probably been okay if not for what happened today."

"I wish I could go back and fix the problem, Papa." Natan dropped his head.

His father turned to him and put a hand on his shoulder. "What's done is done. There's no sense torturing yourself over it. It took courage for you to admit this. Let's make it better now. We have over a hundred people in that factory who depend on me—no, on us—to come up with a plan now that we appear to be at war."

They approached the factory, and Natan felt like a weight had fallen off his shoulders. His father had forgiven him and now asked for his help. He would do everything he could not to disappoint him.

As Max pulled the car into the yard, they saw Kasia standing outside. That usually meant bad news. Natan looked at her face: it was creased with worry.

His father practically jumped out of the car, and Kasia approached him, holding a piece of paper.

"This order was delivered only a few minutes ago," Kasia said, handing Jan the piece of paper. "The factory is seized by the government."

Jan's eyes scanned the page without a hint of surprise and he handed it back to Kasia. "It was to be expected that they should seize all industry to help their offensive, but they're moving very fast. A lot faster than normal. That's not a good sign."

Kasia nodded. "The radio says we're not officially at war, but this proves otherwise, don't you think? Do you want me to assemble the workers?"

"Not just yet; let me think about the best way to handle this. Have you heard anything from the drivers?"

She shook her head. "No, the last I heard from them was when they took a break near Poznan, at around nine last night."

Natan calculated their pace. Poznan was about halfway to the border. They might just have made it. But only if they were let through. He decided there were too many unknowns.

They entered the factory, where the workers stood at their posts. Most of them looked up as Kasia, Natan, and Jan mounted the stairs. Their faces showed they shared Natan's anxiety.

In his office, Jan Borkowski went to work, dictating instructions to Kasia. "Let's make sure we keep our people safe. The order from the government says we'll need to keep the factory in operation and that they will place orders within a few days. I expect they'll need shoes, most likely army boots. We can produce those, but let's focus on getting our materials stocked up."

Kasia penned down the instructions, although Natan knew she would rattle this off from memory later. His father's assistant had been with the company for over 20 years now, and she knew exactly how everything worked.

"And let's make sure we're not putting anybody in danger. We will work only in daylight for now unless they tell us otherwise. So make sure we get the whole factory blacked out. I don't want us to be a target of any bombing raids."

Natan swallowed hard. It was difficult to imagine bombs dropping on Warsaw, but he also knew they were well in range of the German *Luftwaffe*'s bombers. As his father continued, Natan suddenly felt very useless—the thought of doing his paperwork in the office seemed futile.

"Papa, anything I can do?" he asked at a short break in the stream of instructions.

His father thought for a second. "Yes, go home and help your mother prepare the house. We need to be properly blacked out there as well."

Natan nodded and turned toward the door.

"Oh, and Natan, don't forget to buy tape for the windows. We don't want splinters of glass flying around the house when the bombs drop."

Natan nodded and pretended taping the windows was the most normal thing to think about right now. His hands were shaking as he left the factory.

*

Max was instructed to stay at the factory in case Jan needed to go somewhere, so Natan walked toward the tram stop a few blocks down. This neighborhood was as busy as the other streets they'd crossed earlier. People were using tape and all sorts of paper to cover their windows—nobody was taking any chances.

The queues for the stores snaked around street corners, the line for the grocery store beaten only by the one for the tobacconist. As Natan turned onto the main thoroughfare and sat down at the tram stop, the piercing sound of a siren rang in the air.

Natan instinctively looked down the street, but he saw nothing out of the ordinary. It took him a few seconds to realize this was no common siren. It was the air raid alarm.

All around him, people responded similarly. Surprise made way for confusion as the queues dispersed. The people in the front squeezed into the stores, while others rushed into nearby apartment buildings. Natan was in the middle of the street as panic erupted around him. The street—orderly moments ago—was now a pandemonium as people jostled for shelter.

Fear gripped his throat when he realized he had no idea where to go. The factory was too far if planes were approaching. He looked around and was surprised to see a group of four older men huddled around a newsstand, looking up into the gray sky.

Natan approached the group. They didn't look concerned, one of them even sipping something from a flask. Another nodded at him. He looked to be in his seventies, a bundle of white-grayish hair pointing in all directions.

"No need to panic, young one," he said with a deep voice. "It's important you listen to the other sounds, not only the siren."

Natan didn't understand, and it must've shown, as the man continued. "Listen to the sound in the sky. Do you hear any engines? Do you see any planes?"

He looked up and strained to hear anything beyond the blaring siren.

The man smiled knowingly, displaying crooked teeth. "I don't think there will be any bombs near us today."

"How can you be so sure?"

"Because we've lived through this before. The last time it was the Soviets. There will always be someone to fight. They still teach you this in school?"

Natan nodded.

"Well, then take it from me. If you can't see or hear the planes, there's no danger." He nodded to the last few people fleeing into buildings around them. "You find a proper shelter, a basement even, and you ride out the storm there."

The street was now deserted, and while the howling of the siren still cut through Natan's bones, he felt his initial fear ebb away somewhat. The man and his compatriots casually scanned the sky.

Natan mustered up the courage to ask another question. "Aren't you afraid of the Germans and their planes?"

"Of course I am. Hitler is a dangerous man. He doesn't care about the rules or other countries. He will do whatever he thinks is best for Germany. It's no surprise they're invading us now, and they will probably succeed. But I'll tell you one thing, young one. They will not take Warsaw just like that. No, they won't." He shook his head resolutely. "I fought the communists when they thought they could take our city in 1920. They never did. We Poles, we're defiant. We always find a way. And Hitler won't beat us down, either."

His bright green eyes were filled with fury—a passion burning strong. Natan found it impossible not to feel a little patriotic. As he was about to speak, the sound of the siren abruptly stopped. A heavy silence hung in the air, and for a moment, nothing happened on the street. Then, a long burst from the siren cut through the silence.

"The all clear," the old man said.

After a minute or two, people cautiously emerged from their shelters. Slowly but surely, the street came back to life, the queues reforming, the sound of cars returning. Natan looked at the old man, who simply smiled at the scene in front of him. He turned to Natan with a look as if to say, "I told you so."

Natan heard a familiar clanging of a bell and saw his tram approach in the middle of the street. He nodded at the old man and hurried toward it.

CHAPTER SIX

O n the other side of the city, Julia exited an apartment building. She had been relieved to hear the all clear and hurried onto the street, carrying a small bag containing Mrs. Kachinski's shoes. She'd spent her Friday helping her father, and he'd asked her to run this errand on her way home. He would work a bit later today, determined to finish all his work before the Sabbath.

When the siren sounded, Julia had rushed into the first building she saw. She and several others had found shelter in the hallways, and they had spent a good fifteen minutes anxiously waiting for the sound of bombs. When the all clear sounded, she was keen to be on her way, and the other people had followed.

Mrs. Kachinski lived a little outside Warsaw's Jewish Quarter, and it took Julia twenty minutes to get to her. She was happy with the delivery and handed Julia a modest tip of a few *groszy*.

Julia was now on her way home but stopped for some groceries along the way. She joined one of the queues that didn't seem quite as long as the ones she'd seen earlier. She hoped they still had the vegetables her mother needed for dinner.

Two ladies in front of her chatted amiably. "I hear we were lucky not to have been hit this morning," one of them said, speaking loudly enough for everyone in the queue to hear. "My son told me they spotted German bombers on the other side of the city."

The other woman peeked over her tiny, round spectacles. "I can't believe it!"

"They dropped quite a few bombs, but apparently, we had fighters in the air, and they chased them off. We should be proud of those boys, or it could've been much worse!" Her voice rose an octave, her cheeks flushing. Julia wasn't sure whether she was afraid or simply excited to share the news.

The line moved slowly, and as the ladies continued to chatter, Julia averted her eyes. She didn't care for gossip, but she was concerned that the bombers had already reached Warsaw. Surely the Germans wouldn't give up so easily. She needed to find out where she and her family could hide the next time the siren sounded. *Hiding in apartment hallways won't do.*

Most of the good vegetables were gone when it was her turn, and Julia had to content herself with a small cauliflower and a handful of potatoes. She complained they looked a little withered, but the lady behind the counter had simply shrugged.

She returned to the family's tiny apartment, where she found her mother and Olek at the kitchen table. Lea looked up, her eyes red and puffy. Julia dropped the bag of groceries and rushed to her mother. Then her brother lifted his head, and she saw the reason for her mother's grief. Olek's face was battered and bruised. His left eye was shut, and his cheeks were puffy. Julia was dismayed.

"What happened?" She knelt next to them. Olek looked horrible, pale as a ghost.

He tried to wave it off. "It's okay, I'm all right. It'll heal in a few days."

"You look like you were hit by a truck and then run over by a second one," Julia said. Her brother could be an absolute pain, but he was still her blood, and it distressed her to see him like this.

Lea took over. "Be quiet, Olek—you need to rest." She handed him a wet towel. "Here, press this on your face—it'll help against the swelling."

Julia sat down across from her brother. "Who did this to you? This is the second time in two months. Next time they might finish the job, you know."

"It was those boys from Nelek's firm," Lea said, her cheeks red with indignation. "They attacked Olek and a colleague after they left the building site. Said they're stealing their business. Said they're good-for-nothing Jews."

"Are you going to report it?" she asked, but she knew the answer.

Olek raised his hands. "It won't do me any good. Even if the police do something, which they won't, it will only put a target on my back. They'll find me again, and the beating will be worse."

The police won't lift a finger. They'd tell him to toughen up.

She looked at her brother and mother. With the war on their doorstep, they had bigger things to worry about. The Polish brutes would pale in comparison to the Nazis if the stories from Germany were true. Deciding she needed to have something to do, Julia volunteered to cook dinner. Her mother gratefully accepted as she fussed over Olek.

After she'd finished preparing the pitiful dinner, Julia helped prepare for the Sabbath. Her mother lit candles in their modest living room, saying the usual prayers for the two of them before they ate, since Olek was already in bed. When Wojtek came upstairs after working late, they all whispered soft prayers for a swift recovery for Olek. Julia also slipped in a prayer for the defense of her country. They needed all the help they could get.

*

The following day, all four of them went to the little synagogue in the bright morning sunshine, Lea walking beside her daughter, holding her hand. The men followed closely, Olek with a wet cloth wrapped around his head to cover his left eye. The swelling had increased overnight, and the pain had become almost unbearable.

The service was short, and the rabbi avoided talking about what was going on at the border. *Isn't he worried about the clear danger from the west?*

As the congregation gathered in the street afterward, she was relieved to find she wasn't the only one worrying. All the talk was about the war. Nobody cared about an official declaration of war; the Nazis were coming.

"The only thing that matters now is that the Brits and French keep their promise," a tall young man said with conviction.

Another man interjected, "So far, they've been quiet." He wagged his finger at the younger man. "I bet you they're going to leave us to fight our own war. Can't trust 'em, I tell ya."

The other men crowding around murmured assent while some wandered off.

"And when they do, they're going to overrun the Polish army, and they'll start persecuting us just like they do in Germany." The loudmouth wasn't done yet. "Don't you remember them smashing up all those houses all over the country?"

Julia shuddered to think something like the Night of Broken Glass could happen in Warsaw.

Her mother tugged at her dress. "Shall we go home? Olek needs to rest."

"Of course." Julia turned, and they slowly walked away from the synagogue, Olek supported by his father. Some people offered wishes for a speedy recovery, others from the congregation simply shared looks of pity. Lea Horowitz thanked them as they headed toward the street.

They were only a short distance from the synagogue when the wail of the air raid siren cut through the sky. Julia—and everyone else around her—froze. It felt like time stood still, and for a moment, people seemed unsure what to do. Then there was another sound, one Julia couldn't immediately identify. It started as a low, soft hum, like a swarm of bees. Then, it grew louder.

When someone pointed at the sky, Julia looked up, and her blood ran cold. A few hundred meters away from them, there was no mistaking a German Luftwaffe bomber squadron. They flew low enough for Julia to make out the black and white cross insignia on their wings and tails. On their flanks, they were escorted by smaller planes. *Fighters.* The Germans had learned from their setback the day prior.

Panic quickly ensued as everyone scrambled to find shelter. People near the synagogue entrance rushed back inside, while others fled into nearby buildings. The street was suddenly crowded as people appeared from all over. Then, someone bumped into Julia, and she tumbled to the ground. As she got up—her head spinning—she caught sight of her mother's hat disappearing into the synagogue.

The entrance to the synagogue was crowded as people jostled to fit through the doors of the little building. Julia tried to follow her mother, but it was no use—the crowd was too dense. Across the street, a few heads disappeared into what looked like a cellar. The engines of the bombers roared directly overhead. She glanced up as she ran across the street toward the basement. A man holding the hatch gestured impatiently. "Come on, quickly—get in!" he shouted urgently.

Julia hesitated only for a moment, then quickly descended the rickety stairs into the darkness as the hatch fell into place behind her.

As her eyes adjusted to the darkness, someone lit a candle. The people who owned this cellar had made preparations. There were about a dozen people crammed into a space where only half could sit comfortably. The smell was musty, the air damp, but Julia didn't care—she felt a lot safer than she had only a moment ago.

Four children huddled in the corner. They looked frightened, their eyes shifting back and forth between the candle and the cellar hatch—where a sliver of light broke through one of the cracks.

The street above had gone quiet but for the wail of the siren. Julia strained her ears and could just about hear the sound of the planes' engines overhead. Some people shifted themselves to get a little more comfortable, but the tension in the enclosed space was palpable.

Then the ground shook with a great impact, and sand filtered down from above them. Julia's ears rang, and the children started crying. She looked around, relieved there was still light filtering through the door above them. Another explosion sounded nearby, and Julia felt the ground move under her. She covered her ears and closed her eyes with her hands, and tried to soothe herself.

The sound of the siren was drowned out by the ringing in her ears, and for a moment, she thought it was their cellar that had been hit—she momentarily felt the ground underneath her fall away. When it returned, she realized the force of a nearby explosion had lifted her.

Her eyes immediately went to the door again. There was still light. *We can still get out.*

One of the men in the back suddenly stood up and dashed for the hatch. He was halfway up the stairs when the man who let Julia in grabbed his legs.

"What do you think you're doing?" he shouted over the roar of the planes. They were now directly overhead and must've descended even lower, for it sounded like they were almost on the street level.

The man on the stairs looked back, his eyes wide with terror—he'd clearly lost his mind. *Was this what it meant to be shell-shocked?*

"We need to get out, or we'll be buried alive!" He kicked out to break free from the other man's grasp. It was useless, as the one holding him was much stronger and tightened his grip.

"Get ahold of yourself—you're scaring the children," he said firmly but without menace.

The sound of the crying children was now wholly drowned out by the planes' engines, and Julia tried to focus.

The man on the stairs seemed to have calmed down as the more muscular man had his arms around him in a bear hug, making it impossible for him to move.

Julia didn't know how long they'd sat like this, but suddenly the sound of the planes was gone. The siren still howled, but something felt different. *Was this it?* The other people in the shelter stirred, some eyes hopefully turning toward the hatch.

The sound of the siren changed; it was no longer howling but made a continuous sound. Then silence. The all clear.

The hatch creaked as the large man struggled to lift it. Julia worried something was blocking it, but as he strained, it gave way, and bright sunlight streamed into their dark shelter. Julia shielded her eyes as she climbed up and into the street.

She blinked hard, struggling to comprehend the scene in front of her. The air in the street had an odd glow, and at first, she didn't understand what she was looking at. Then she saw it was floating gray-white dust, giving the street a surreal atmosphere.

Julia slowly stepped into the street, where people emerged from buildings in a haze. Her steps made markings in a dirty blanket of dust-snow.

It quickly became apparent where the dust came from. Across the street, next to the synagogue, was a large crater. The building had taken a direct hit, and only an outer wall remained. Several men were already going through the rubble, seeking survivors.

As she crossed the street, stunned, she saw people streaming out of the synagogue. They looked as perplexed as everyone else, struggling to make sense of the apocalyptic scene. Julia ran toward the synagogue in search of her family. Surely they were among the group coming out now—she'd spotted her mother's hat going in.

It was impossible to get in, so she waited impatiently. As the last people came out, she had a quick look inside. Empty. She turned around and scanned the faces in the street. Everywhere people searched for their loved ones, falling into each other's arms as they found each other.

Julia suddenly felt dread wash over her. *Where are they?* She looked back at the rubble next to the synagogue. *They can't be.* She felt an uncomfortable tension build in her stomach as panic threatened to take over.

She rushed to the men going through the rubble. They looked at her with sad eyes. "Are you looking for someone?"

Julia nodded. "I can't find my parents. They were close to the synagogue when the bombs started falling, but now they haven't come out." She sputtered, not sure what she should do.

One of the men came over and gently took her hand. "I'm sure they're in the street here somewhere," he said. His eyes were soft, but his touch was firm—he wanted her away from the building. "They're probably looking for you, too. Now, what do they look like?"

Julia hardly heard him as she kept scanning the faces on the street. Then, she saw something familiar in the road. Her mother's hat. She tore herself away from the man and ran to pick it up. There was no blood, and it wasn't damaged.

Julia looked around feverishly—they had to be here somewhere.

She avoided looking at the destroyed building and was startled when she felt a hand on her shoulder. She turned around, and her knees almost buckled.

It was her father, his face white as a ghost's from the dust. Behind him were her mother and Olek. She fell into her father's arms and sobbed uncontrollably.

CHAPTER SEVEN

Zuza came down the stairs of the cellar with a tray of tall glasses of lemonade. She handed them to Natan, his father, and the two men helping out, who took their drinks and ascended the stairs for a cigarette. Natan and his father stayed behind, inspecting their handiwork.

"It looks pretty solid, Papa," Natan said.

"Solid? I'd say this has never been more robust." He slapped the piece of wood.

They'd spent the morning reinforcing the ceiling with makeshift wooden pillars all around the cellar. The cellar ceiling used to move a little when Natan's mother walked on the floor above. Now, they heard Zuza and the men walk above their heads; the ceiling seemed stable. They were about halfway done, and determined to finish the job today.

This was the third straight day of bombings, and there had been no news from their supposed British and French allies. The bombs started falling closer to their home, and Jan Borkowski had suggested they'd better prepare for the worst. Natan agreed—it didn't look like this would end soon. He remembered what the men on the street had said the other day, but he felt a lot safer knowing he could find shelter in the cellar.

The news service on the radio reported that the Polish air force had put up a good fight, and they cautiously predicted the Germans might be discouraged from continuing their aerial assaults.

"I doubt they're going to give up so easily," Natan's father said. He hammered another nail into the wooden pillar. "The boys on the radio seem to forget the Germans have sent their own fighter escorts as well. I doubt our fighters can keep them at bay much longer."

Natan shared his father's view. "From what I've read, the German air force is much larger than ours."

"And more advanced." His father shook his head and wiped the sweat from his brow. "No, I think the worst is yet to come. Once they've crushed our resistance, then the real storm will hit."

He reached for the box with nails and held it upside down. "Can you get me some more?"

Natan grabbed the toolbox and frowned. "I think we're out."

"Ah, damn it. I thought we had another box. Do you mind running to the store?"

Natan could use some fresh air, and he was already at the stairs. "I'll be back before you know it."

The store was only a few minutes away, and he arrived to find it empty. Outside, there was the rumble of explosions in the distance. *It's strange how quickly we've gotten used to the sound of war.* He found the nails and went to the cash register.

As the clerk handed him his change, a tremendous explosion shook the store windows. Natan and the clerk instinctively ducked. Perhaps they weren't that used to the sounds, after all. They stayed on the floor for another minute to ensure there wasn't a second or third bomb, but all remained quiet. *Why weren't there any sirens?*

"Perhaps it was another lost bomb," the clerk said nervously as they both got up.

Natan nodded and left the store. Scanning the horizon, he saw a dark plume of smoke from where he was headed. He felt a shiver down his spine. It had been even closer than he thought.

Natan instinctively picked up his pace to make sure his parents were okay.

As he approached his street, the smell of fire and smoke intensified. There were more people outside, heading in the same direction.

He turned the corner into his street and stopped in his tracks. He dropped the box, nails spilling on the ground.

It can't be.

The spot where his house had been minutes ago was reduced to burning ruins of rubble and smoke.

Forgetting everything, Natan sprinted toward his home. A crowd had already gathered and kept a distance from the blazing inferno. He pushed through the people, his mind in a haze, his vision blurred from the hot tears streaming down his face. Someone resisted as he tried to get past, and he roughly pushed the man aside.

"Hey, watch where you're—" The man stopped abruptly as he recognized Natan.

Natan didn't hear him, and as he reached the front of the group, continued walking toward the burning remains of his home. The heat scorched his eyebrows, but he didn't care. If his parents were still there, he needed to get them out.

Just as he was about to get too close, someone pulled him back. As he did, one of the walls collapsed outward and crashed down centimeters from where Natan had stood only a moment before.

He tried to focus on the face in front of him, but his vision blurred, and the heat made it hard to breathe.

"Natan, are you trying to get yourself killed?" He recognized the voice of his neighbor, Marek Piotrowski.

Natan felt numb as he looked toward the man who'd lived next door for as long as Natan could remember. *This can't be real.*

Marek sat him down on a garden wall and peered into his eyes. "You need to wait for the fire brigade. You can't do anything."

"But my parents!" he started. His voice was oddly high-pitched, and he felt like he was looking at himself from above, not really in control of his body.

A shadow crossed Marek's face. "They were inside?" he asked softly.

Natan nodded. "We were—" He paused, and his throat constricted. He couldn't breathe, and then he coughed violently.

His neighbor patted his back, and air flowed into his lungs.

"Papa and I were working on the cellar. I was only away for ten minutes." He looked to the ground.

Marek knelt next to Natan and was silent, agitated. "I'm sorry, Natan," he finally managed.

Sirens approached from a distance, and it didn't take long before fire trucks raced around the corner. The crowd moved back a little as the firemen opened their hoses. Natan sat on the wall, his eyes fixed on what used to be his home. But then a thought snapped him back to life. He rose quickly and approached one of the firemen.

"When can we get to the basement?"

The man glanced at him with annoyance. "With the bomb that landed on this house, there's little chance there's anything left." He continued spraying the dying flames as the smoke billowed.

Natan's sorrow turned into anger, and he shoved the man. "Don't tell me there's nothing left! My parents are under that rubble!" The man was a lot bigger than Natan and didn't flinch. His features softened as he held up his hand for Natan to stop. But Natan couldn't, and he continued to lash out at the fireman. The man put down his hose and grabbed Natan's hands. "Son, I know this is very hard for you, but let us do our job. We need to make sure the rest of the building won't collapse any further before we can check the basement."

Natan felt any remnants of strength sapped from him. "W-we were reinforcing the basement," he stammered through tears of frustration. "Maybe they were in the basement when the b-bomb hit—"

The fireman looked at him compassionately as Natan slumped to the sidewalk. "As soon as we know it's safe enough, we'll go check."

Marek returned and led Natan away. "Let them do their job, Natan. Let's get you something to drink."

Natan nodded. He suddenly felt drained and followed Marek away from the crowd of onlookers.

It took the firemen an hour to douse the flames. Natan had watched them through a window of Marek's house for most of that time before he went back to lead the firemen to the basement entrance. As the rubble crunched under his feet, he struggled to accept this was all that was left of the place he called home.

The five firemen took out their shovels and started to clear the rubble without another word. Natan helped them, and together they labored at the arduous task. In the remains of the building, he saw pieces of furniture, and he swallowed hard when his shovel was filled with torn clothing. He recognized some of his mother's dresses.

After an hour of hard work, they reached the outline of the cellar entrance. Natan dropped his shovel in a wave of nausea. He walked away and vomited what little was in his stomach. When he returned, the firemen were waiting— they had halted their efforts.

The foreman approached Natan, his hard hat in his hand. He looked at Natan with sorrow in his eyes. "I'm sorry, son. I know you were hoping for something else."

The words hardly registered, but Natan nodded slowly. He walked back to the spot where he'd dropped his shovel. The firemen gave him some space.

Natan knelt, hardly feeling the debris cutting into his knees. The entrance to the basement was no longer there. The entire building had collapsed into the cellar, filling it with ash, wood, books, draperies, and other debris. Even if, by some miracle, his parents had been in the basement, they wouldn't have stood a chance.

The bomb had come a day—no, mere hours—too soon.

Natan buried his face in his hands and wept as he collapsed on the ruins of his home.

CHAPTER EIGHT

Julia stood in one of the narrow streets near her home, using the back of her sleeve to wipe sweat from her forehead. She inspected the pile of rubble in front of her, twisted metal, rocks, and concrete. One of the men dumped another bucket of debris on the far side of their makeshift barricade, then walked back to one of the collapsed buildings less than a hundred meters away.

It was the fourth day of the German attacks, and things were getting worse by the hour. The Luftwaffe continued to send their bombers, escorted by more fighters. Resistance by the Polish Air Force was waning, and the bombings became heavier, hitting targets all over the city. News from the western front wasn't very encouraging, either. The German army had broken through the Polish defenses and made steady progress east.

"Won't be much longer until they're in our streets," Pavel said as he stepped closer to her. The tall man had taken responsibility for their little barricade, and when Julia had seen him hauling rocks earlier that day, she'd asked if she could help. Julia didn't know if their efforts would matter, but it felt better than doing nothing. And she had nothing else to do, as schools had closed, and Warsaw had gone into survival mode.

It had been easy to find the material for their barricade, as every bomb supplied them with more debris. Some neighborhoods had been hit so heavily that buildings had collapsed into streets, blocking any passage without their efforts.

She walked to the bakery across the street, which was still open. The owner had been so impressed with the volunteer workers that he offered them free rolls and said they were welcome to refill their water canteens as much as they wanted. Now, however, he shook his head as she walked in.

"I don't know what's going on, Julia, but the tap isn't working anymore," he said with a puzzled expression. "Normally, I would've called on the water company, but . . . well."

"They must've hit the waterworks," a voice behind Julia said, startling her. Pavel had followed her into the bakery. "I've heard the Germans have been targeting them all over the city. We're not the first district to be without."

Julia was incredulous. "Isn't it illegal to target civilians?"

Pavel nodded. "Sure is, but the Nazis don't care. My wife said she heard they also hit several hospitals in Ochota yesterday. Looked to be deliberate, too."

"They don't seem to mind bombing our entire city," the baker added.

Julia stormed out of the store, forgetting her thirst as she set on the task of strengthening the barricade. She filled her bucket from one of the buildings across the street. It was hit the day before, and thankfully nobody had been inside at the time. The occupants had returned a few hours later to find they had no longer had a home. Julia had felt sorry for them as they dug around in the ruins, finding very little of value.

When she sat down to take a breather, a tall, slender man approached her. He had dark brown eyes framed by oversized glasses, and he wore what looked like an old army uniform.

"Not bad," he said as he inspected her work. "Plenty of cover, and the Germans would not be able to approach it so easily. However . . ."

Julia looked at him as he paused. "What?"

He shook his head as if he'd suddenly forgotten what he wanted to say. She waited, not sure what to make of him.

"Ah, yes." He seemed to remember. "If a tank were to approach this, one shot would probably be enough to tear it apart."

Julia was slightly offended. She'd worked on the barrier for almost the whole day. She thought it was pretty good.

"What would you do differently?"

He smiled. "Me? I wouldn't know—I'm not an engineer. But the people I work with certainly would." Glancing up to notice the confusion on her face, he continued. "I'm with the Civil Guard, and we're in a bit of a pickle. Most of our young men have left the city, either to fight the Nazis in the west or prepare to fight later. We need all the help we can get as we prepare for the Germans to show up at the gates of the city."

Julia swallowed hard. If the army thought the Nazis were close to Warsaw, there was little time left.

"Look," he said, "if you want to make a difference, you should join us." He pulled out a pencil and scribbled something on a small piece of paper. "We meet here tomorrow morning"—he tapped the address.

She took it from him, and before she could say another word, he was off.

*

Unsurprisingly, Julia's father had been less than thrilled about her plans to attend the meeting. Breakfast had been a tense affair, with her mother standing up for her. She had argued Julia could certainly help in the mornings, and there would still be plenty of time in the afternoons for her to assist in the shop, even though business was almost nonexistent. In the end, Wojtek Horowitz decided Olek would accompany her. He wasn't allowed to go back to work yet, but he had sufficiently recovered from his injuries to join her at the meeting.

It was only a short walk, but enough time for Olek to get on her nerves.

"What do you think you're going to do there, anyway? I bet they need strong men, not little girls."

"Which makes me wonder why you're coming along," Julia retorted.

Olek pulled a face. "They need me back at work tomorrow—I'm only joining because Papa told me to. Trust me, I would much rather be working, making a difference."

She looked at him in disbelief. "Make a difference? Look around you. There won't be a job left for you if this continues."

He shrugged. "Who do you think is going to rebuild the city? People like me, Julia. There will be plenty of work for me. The only difference is who's paying for it."

Julia couldn't argue with such ignorance, so she increased her pace, staying a few steps ahead of him until they reached the address the man had given her.

A bulky man stood in front of the building and looked at them suspiciously as they approached.

"Can I help you?" he said curtly. His tone suggested he'd rather not.

Julia was a little intimidated but said she was invited and was there to help.

Olek chuckled and said, in Yiddish, "See, I told you this is useless."

The demeanor of the man changed from indifferent to hostile. He glared at Olek. "We don't want your kind here. Get out of here, both of you. We don't need any *kikes* in the Civil Guard." The man took a step toward them.

Olek, despite his indifference on the way over, was now in his element. He wasn't going to be bullied, even if his left eye had only partially healed. He took a step toward the man.

Julia recovered and quickly stepped between the two. "Please, I want to help, and your boss invited me."

The man scowled at her. "I have no boss." He shot a look of hate at Olek, who stepped back a bit and squared himself—fists formed, ready to brawl.

Julia was about to turn away when her friend from the day before appeared in the door opening. He was in that odd uniform again. "What's all the fuss about?"

His eyes scanned the situation, and his face softened as he spotted Julia. "Barricade builder, you came!"

The man at the door protested. "You're gonna let in these kikes?" He spat out the slur.

"They're as Polish as you and me," her friend said, his eyes shooting fire at the other man, who seemed to shrink at the dressing down. "We're not at war with our own people now, are we? The bloody Germans are at the gates."

The man opened his mouth reluctantly, and Julia wondered what he could possibly say. For a moment, he stood gaping, the uniformed leader glaring at him. Then the man thought better of it and stepped aside.

Julia strolled past him, resisting the urge to shoot him a triumphant look. Olek had no such qualms, making sure he brushed the man's shoulder on his way in.

They walked through the nondescript hallway of the building, climbing a flight of stairs as they followed the man in uniform.

Reaching the top of the stairs, he turned back. "I'm sorry you had to experience that. I want you to know we don't all think like that."

Julia simply nodded. *I'm used to it.*

Olek spoke up, much to her chagrin. "What is this organization, anyway?"

"We're the Civil Guard of Warsaw."

"What does that mean? Don't we have the police, the army?"

"We do, but in case you haven't noticed, most of the army has left the city. They're on the outskirts, waiting for the Germans. The police have joined them." He waved his hands at a door down the hall. "That leaves us. Join me, will you?"

He didn't wait for an answer and strode down the hallway. Julia gave her brother a reproachful look. *Why does he have to be such an ass all the time?*

They followed the man into a cramped room where 20 other people were sat on simple chairs and stools. Julia and Olek had to stand at the back of the room. They leaned against the wall as their escort found his way to the front, where he faced the crowd and started without ceremony.

"First of all, thank you all for being here. My name is Maczek." He spoke clearly, his voice booming through the small room. Julia looked around and noticed he had the attention of everyone in the room—primarily young people.

"Poland is under attack. We've all seen the destruction in our streets, and we know we can't hide behind our doors. The Germans will be here any day now."

He paused for a moment. The sound of explosions coming through the open window added weight to his words.

"The Polish army has retreated from the border. Make no mistake about it; the German army is much, much stronger than ours. We were overrun in open battle." Maczek looked around the room. "But all is not lost. They haven't taken our cities yet. They haven't taken Warsaw. We are still here. Their planes might be overhead, cowardly dropping bombs on our hospitals and schools, but there are no German boots in this city. And as long as I'm alive, I will do everything to keep them out."

Julia felt her pulse quicken, and others stirred in their seats. Maczek was saying what she'd felt ever since the bombings had started.

He turned to a map of Poland behind him and pointed at Warsaw, drawing an imaginary circle around the city.

"This is the perimeter of Warsaw where the army will focus its efforts. We expect the Germans to attack from the west, avoiding the river. Now, you may wonder what *we* are going to do. You're not trained fighters; you're not soldiers. But we, the people of Warsaw, can do our bit. Some of us have already started by building barricades in the streets." He looked at Julia and gave an almost imperceptible nod. "Others can help carry supplies between the city and the front lines."

There were some murmurs as the youngsters took in the message. Julia's heart swelled with pride; they *could* make a difference.

"So, I ask all of you," Maczek said, his voice rising a little. "Will you join us in the Civil Guard?"

The murmurs ebbed away as everybody waited for the first person to speak. There was a note of excitement in the air, and Julia was about to speak up when a familiar voice beat her to it.

"But if the Germans are so much stronger, what's the point of even trying this? Why don't we let the army do their job? It sounds like we're going to be slaughtered."

It was Olek, of course, with his usual petulant look, his arms crossed in front of him defiantly. Julia wished she could disappear. *Why can't he keep his big mouth shut for once?*

Maczek remained calm, his face not betraying a hint of hostility at Olek's words. Instead, he nodded and spoke calmly: "How old are you?"

"Twenty," he answered, adding a couple years. Julia bit her tongue.

"And what do you do?"

"I'm a carpenter—I build houses." There was a hint of pride in her brother's voice.

Maczek smiled. "Then you know how important it is to have the right supplies for your job, don't you?"

Olek looked unsure. "I guess so."

"But surely, if your foreman doesn't supply you with your hammer, your nails, your wooden planks, you have no way of doing your job, right?"

The energy in the room seemed to shift, and Julia reflexively took a step away from her brother.

Instead of accepting what the man had said, Olek retorted, "What difference are we really going to make? Look at the people in this room. They're all kids!"

Some of the others turned around now, shooting angry looks at Olek. He continued, undeterred. "I'm certainly not going to be part of this! You should leave this to the army." He pointed at Maczek, who stood at the front, unmoved. "And it will be your fault when these kids are torn to pieces on the front lines."

Olek turned and took a few steps toward the door before turning back. "Come on, Julia, let's go."

Julia glanced at her brother, not hiding her contempt. She was furious with him, and she felt her cheeks flush. She shook her head resolutely.

"No." She spoke softly but loud enough for everybody in the silent room to hear.

There was a hint of surprise in her brother's eyes, but only for a moment. "Papa won't allow this. You know this, right?"

I know, but I'm going to do it anyway. She took another step away from him.

"Suit yourself," Olek said gruffly before storming out. His footsteps echoed in the hallway.

When Julia turned back to face Maczek, all eyes were on her. She looked down and fumbled with her hands, not sure what to do with herself.

From the front, breaking the silence, Maczek spoke: "Well, I guess the Civil Guard isn't for everybody."

That broke the tension as they all laughed, and Julia looked up with a smile. Maczek was looking back at her in admiration.

Chapter Nine

Natan was still in bed when there was a knock on the door. Kasia peeked her head around the corner without waiting for a response. "It's almost nine—breakfast is ready."

"I'm not hungry."

She pushed the door open a little farther and stepped inside. "You haven't eaten since yesterday afternoon. You have to eat."

"I had some cookies last night."

"Doesn't count." She walked to the window and opened the curtains, the bright light of the late summer sun blinding him.

"I don't feel like eating." *I don't feel like anything. Leave me alone.*

It had been almost a week since that dreadful day. He'd collapsed onto the remains of his house, and later Kasia had picked him up from the fire station. She'd taken him to her small apartment in the Old Town, where he'd hardly slept the first night. Outside, the rumble of the bombings continued, and he could not sleep—convinced the next one would hit his new home and end it all.

Natan felt safe with Kasia, but he didn't want to talk. After the small funeral—it was dangerous to be out in large groups—he'd spent his days alone in his room, curled up in bed. Every few hours, Kasia would check in and bring tea and cookies. He declined all regular meals but nibbled on snacks. She had let him be.

Today, she was not going to be so accommodating. "I think you need a change of scenery, Natan. I need your help."

As his eyes adjusted to the brightness, he sat up in bed. "My help with what?"

"At the factory."

The factory. He couldn't imagine walking into the offices and not finding his father. His Papa. He swallowed hard and felt his eyes sting.

Kasia sat down on his bed and looked at him with compassion. "Natan, I can only imagine what you're going through. When my Piotr didn't come back from the war, I didn't want to believe it."

Natan looked at her. He knew she'd lost her husband in the Great War, but she'd never spoken about it.

"I was like you. I locked myself away from the world. I sat in my room, looking out of the window into our little street, waiting for him to appear around the corner. I was sure he must've lost his battalion somewhere along the way, and he would make his way home."

Her eyes were damp as she continued. "But after a week, or maybe two weeks, my mother told me I couldn't continue to live like that. She didn't remind me Piotr was gone, but she told me he would want me to carry on with my life no matter what. I was only a few years older than you, Natan." She gave him a weak smile as she wiped her eyes. "Piotr was the love of my life, my rock. We were going to move to Warsaw together. We were going to have children."

Natan was silent. Kasia stared out of the window as she paused—transported back to her home in Łódź.

"And then the war took it all away. Just like that"—she snapped her fingers. She turned her attention back to Natan. "They took your parents like they took my Piotr."

He nodded but said nothing. He didn't know what to say.

She took his hand. "But listen to me. We have each other. We will take care of each other, and we won't let them win." There was determination in her voice. "And we will live, Natan. We won't let them destroy our lives like this. I know your parents; they would want you to continue their legacy. Your name is still on the factory. It needs a Borkowski."

"I know nothing about running a company, Kasia," Natan said, finally finding his voice. He was relieved they could talk about something other than what had happened a week ago.

She looked at him with fierce eyes. "But I do. And I will teach you everything there is to know."

Her determination was infectious, and Natan felt a flicker of fire in his belly. *She's right. Papa would want me at the factory. Mama would be proud.* He swung his legs out of bed, setting his feet on the cold wooden floor.

When they arrived at the factory an hour later, it was clear something was amiss. The yard was deserted, and it was oddly quiet—the clanging and hissing of machinery inside should have been audible from where they stood. They exchanged a look.

Natan opened the factory door, confirming what they both suspected—there was no one there, and the machines were idle.

As they turned to the stairs, the door at the top opened, and a man in a Polish army uniform looked down on them.

"Are you Miss Nowak?" he asked as he came down the stairs.

"Mrs.—yes," she answered curtly.

He ignored her correction and continued. "Good. I've been waiting for you. Are you always this tardy?"

"I wasn't aware we had an appointment." Her tone was frosty. "Who are you?"

"Lieutenant Radej," he said without extending his hand. Instead, he brushed past them and onto the factory floor. "I'm here to relieve you of your duties."

Kasia looked cross now. "I'm sorry? I didn't know you were in charge."

Natan felt his stomach turn.

Radej waved his hand dismissively. "The paperwork is in the office—you're welcome to take a look. Short of it is, this factory has been assigned to the army, and we'll start producing essential war supplies here. I've been assigned to make sure it runs smoothly. You'll report to me now."

Kasia ignored him and quickly ascended the stairs, two steps at a time. She returned with a small stack of documents. Radej hadn't bothered to wait and was inspecting some of the machines. It was clear to Natan the man hadn't the faintest idea about leatherworking.

"Is it true?" he asked softly, making sure the lieutenant couldn't hear.

She nodded without replying, her eyes scanning the words on the paper before raising her voice: "Where did you send the men?"

Radej returned to them. "They've been ordered to help with the fortifications outside the city. They'll return when we've driven the Germans back."

Natan wasn't so sure about that, but he kept his thoughts to himself. Radej looked at him for the first time. "And who are you?"

"Natan Borkowski, my father owns"—he corrected himself—"owned, this factory. I guess it's mine now."

Radej shook his head. "If you thought you'd take over now, you're mistaken." *He didn't even bother asking what happened to Papa.*

"You can take those papers with you," Radej said. "For as long as we're at war, this factory no longer belongs to you."

The outer door opened, and more soldiers entered. Radej directed them to the offices. He looked impatient.

"Now, if you don't mind, we have work to do. Please leave," he waved them to the door. It wasn't a request as much as an order. "I'll call for you when we need you, Miss Nowak."

Kasia glared at Radej as she stuffed the papers inside her jacket. Finally, they opened the door, and Natan took one look back at the factory floor before stepping out.

*

Natan needed some time to himself. Kasia would go through the paperwork at home and see if there was anything they could do. Natan wasn't too optimistic as he strolled the streets near the factory. That morning, he'd felt a purpose for the first time since losing his parents—he'd honor their memory by continuing his father's lifework. He felt more lost than ever. As he walked toward the river and found a seat on a small bench, he failed to see the approaching old man until he sat down next to him.

"If you don't mind, I'd like to be left alone," Natan said curtly.

The man nodded but made no move to leave.

They sat like this for a while, and Natan found it hard to concentrate. *Why does he have to sit next to me?*

"You know," the man started, his voice clear despite his age. "I've taken a walk down the river every day for over ten years now, and I always sit here."

Great—I'm on his bench.

"And I'm usually the only one here at this time. And with the city under attack, it's rare to find someone else here." He looked at Natan, who kept his gaze firmly on the water. "Especially a young man like you. What are you doing here?"

Natan realized the man wouldn't leave him alone and answered reluctantly, caught off guard by the question. "I needed some air myself."

The man nodded. "It's good to be alone sometimes."

Natan nodded, and there was another moment of silence.

"I guess I'm surprised to see an able-bodied man like yourself here. Most of the others have left the city, either to family in the countryside or to join the army."

Natan sat up, surprised. He hadn't seen a newspaper in a week. "Really?"

"It was an order of the new commander of Warsaw. Not everybody listened to him, though. People who stayed behind are helping with the defense of the city. Why didn't you go?"

"I have nowhere to go." It was true—his life was in Warsaw. Or, it had been. He wasn't sure what or where his life was now.

"Then why don't you fight the Germans?" There was no malice in the man's voice, no judgment. It was simply a question.

Natan shrugged. "I don't know anything about fighting. I'd be useless."

The man shook his head as his gray hair was caught in the wind. "Nobody does. But don't you want to keep the Germans out? Don't you want to fight for your freedom?"

Of course I do, but what am I going to do?

The man stood up with a groan. "Everybody can make a difference, young man. Even if you've never lifted a finger in anger, your country needs you now. Warsaw needs you."

A Stuka plane passed overhead, and the man's gaze fixed on it as it crossed the Vistula. "They're at the gates, and we need all the help we can get."

With that, he stood up, took his walking cane, and left without another word.

Natan spent his walk back to Kasia's apartment with the old man's words ringing in his ears.

As he crossed into the Old Town, a large crowd blocked his passage. But as he looked closer, he saw this was no regular gathering. People rushed through the streets, carrying uniformed soldiers on stretchers. As he approached the procession, he saw many were only a few years older than himself. Some looked close to death, their eyes closed, their faces pale. The stretcher-bearers varied in size, and he saw they weren't wearing army uniforms. These were civilians—like him—carrying the wounded to the hospitals. A woman around the age of his mother struggled with her end of one of the stretchers.

On impulse, Natan rushed over. "Please, ma'am, let me take this end."

She looked grateful, and he took over as she sat down on the side of the street, catching her breath.

Natan and the man in the front hurried through the Old Town's narrow streets. They didn't talk and simply followed the people ahead of them. Natan wondered where they were going as they turned east, away from where the hospital was.

After five minutes, they were abruptly stopped and directed into an apartment building. Above its door hung a tattered, homemade Red Cross banner. They stepped inside and were directed to the second floor, carefully carrying their soldier up the stairs.

As they put him down in a room with a half dozen other soldiers, Natan couldn't help but wonder what was going on. The hospital was crowded, and he'd seen some of the other stretcher-bearers make their way to another building.

He knelt next to the soldier. The man looked back at him and mumbled his thanks, his eyes unfocused.

"Please, can you tell me what's going on out there?" Natan asked softly.

The soldier swallowed. "We're completely outnumbered. The Germans are everywhere. We thought they'd attack from the west, but they also came from the south. We're overrun."

Natan nodded but said nothing.

"It will be a matter of hours until they break through . . . the outer defenses," the soldier continued with ragged breath. "It's like in Lwów—" He stopped abruptly as his head fell back on a small pillow. Natan looked around for a nurse as he checked the man's pulse. It was weak, but he was still alive. Natan rushed into the hallway and clutched onto a passing nurse. She nodded calmly. "Don't worry. We'll look after him, just like we do the others. If he's in that room, he's probably completely exhausted, with minor injuries. Best let him rest."

She hurried by him, and Natan stood in the hallway. He looked back into the room where soft snores came from some of the soldiers. He realized he couldn't stand by any longer. He was going to help. If the Germans were approaching the city, there must be more soldiers like these men. He bolted down the stairs and looked into the street. Another group of stretcher-bearers stood outside, and he rushed to join them.

"Where are you going?" he asked.

"Ochota," the man replied. "The Germans have breached the city perimeter." He looked at Natan and nodded at the other side of the stretcher. "Want to make yourself useful?"

Without hesitation, Natan picked up the stretcher.

CHAPTER TEN

Olek had been wrong about their father. When Julia came home from the meeting, she'd expected Papa to be waiting with a lecture. There had been none. He'd simply told her she could help out with whatever the Civil Guard needed, as long as it didn't get in the way of her work.

As soon as the bombings started, the schools had been closed, so Julia had plenty of time in the mornings. Business at her father's workshop had slowed down even more after nine days of German attacks. So when Julia heard they'd broken through the southern perimeter of the city, she pleaded with her father to allow her to spend the whole next day strengthening the barricades. He'd been quick to agree, much to her surprise.

That's how Julia found herself working in one of the narrow streets in Mokotów, one of the city's southern districts. It lay between the fallen southern districts and the city center to the north, and the Civil Guard and army knew the next German assault was likely to be on Mokotów. They'd finished their barricade earlier that morning and were now laying the final touches on a booby trap some hundred meters farther down the street.

Julia sat behind the barricade when Lazor, a friendly young man of about twenty, sat next to her and took a sip of water from his canteen. "They're quite confident the Germans will make their way through our street," he said, pointing at the men farther up the way. They were covering their jerry can—filled with lighter fluid—with debris from nearby buildings.

Julia nodded and took a small bite from the piece of bread given to her that morning. "I hope they do—this is a strong position. I can't wait to see the explosion."

The men had finished covering the jerry can, and one took out a piece of string and doused it in lighter fluid, too, then started unrolling it as he moved back to the barricade. Once the Germans were close enough, they could quickly light the string and hopefully set off an explosion.

"Do you think that will work?" Julia asked. She had her doubts about the little piece of string that held their hopes.

Lazor looked more confident as he smiled. "It has to. We don't have enough weapons to hold them off. If that bomb doesn't stop them, we'll have to abandon this position, and they'll take even more territory."

As the men were about to return to the barricade, the unmistakable sound of gunfire rattled through the air. Instinctively, Julia peeked over the barrier and saw the shots were coming from the other side of the street. Lazor pulled her back down.

"Keep your head down! Are you trying to get yourself killed?" he said, his eyes wide with fear. She'd never seen him like this before. But then again, they'd never been this close to the enemy before.

The men in the street dropped what they were doing and sprinted back to the barricade. Some of the men next to Julia fired a few shots to cover them. They all made it as the German fire stopped for a few minutes. *Why did they stop?*

The answer came soon enough. She'd found a small gap in the barricade where she could look out into the street. At first, she only heard it, but when the barrel of a tank came into view, she knew they were in big trouble.

A German Panzer tank turned the corner, its turret now pointing straight at them. She felt her heart stop for a moment and considered running away. Then she looked at the faces of the men around her—set in grim determination, gripping guns tightly.

"We need to set off that trap," one of them said. "There is no other way to stop the tank."

The tank started rolling toward them, slowly and carefully. Some other barricades had had antitank weapons, and the Germans had become more cautious. They didn't know how poorly Julia's small group was equipped. German soldiers on foot followed the tank, ducking to keep their cover.

"If only we could get close enough to light the piece of string on the ground, we could take it out," Lazor said.

The man who spoke earlier nodded. "But it's suicide to run the whole distance there, even with cover fire. If the men in the tank don't take you out, one of the soldiers will."

Julia looked around. Most of the buildings lining the street were in bad shape. The Germans bombs had found their targets in this neighborhood. A thought struck her. "What if we approach the trap from one of the buildings?"

The men looked at her. "How so?" Lazor asked.

"The buildings on the one side of the street have all collapsed or have most of their sidewalls blown away by bombs. Maybe there's a way around to get close enough to the bomb to light the fuse without the Germans noticing?" Her eyes scanned the street. "That red one is even with the bomb, isn't it?"

They looked at her in surprise for a moment.

"Who would do it? It's a long shot, and chances are any passages are going to be narrow."

"I will," she said resolutely. She'd already made up her mind.

Lazor looked at Julia, and his eyes registered surprise.

*

There had been no protests, and Julia now carried a handmade torch—nothing more than a piece of wood with a turpentine-soaked rag wrapped around it—and a box of matches as she sprinted away from the barricade to the street adjacent to theirs. Unfortunately, the tank was still rolling forward, and time was not on her side.

She approached a corner and prayed there would be no Germans there. The street was empty, and she ran on, keeping her eyes peeled. Another building blocked her passage, and she cursed silently. Her frustration quickly turned to relief when she saw this building, too, had been gutted by bombs. Julia hurried in, ignoring the idea of it suddenly collapsing onto her.

She reached the back door and was relieved to find it opened into a narrow alleyway. Facing her was the red building. There would be no problem getting into it, as all the windows had been blown out on this side as well. She climbed inside and hurried toward the street side. There, she heard the creaking of the tank's tracks as they crunched through the debris on the street. She got on her knees and crawled to the nearest window.

The tank was now only ten meters away from the booby trap, and there was no time to lose. She fumbled with the matches and dropped the first one. *Come on, Julia, focus.* She struck the second match, and it caught fire, the faint smell of sulfur a delight to her senses. She held the torch to it, and it came to life with a satisfactory whoosh.

Julia knew she had very little time to get the torch near the bomb and even less room for error. If she missed, that was it—she would probably not make it away from the tank alive. If the bomb didn't go off, it would be the same. *But I have to try. They're counting on me.*

The drop from the window was only two meters, and she could easily jump out. She wouldn't have time to climb back in, though. Instead, she would need to run back to the barricade. Julia took a deep breath and stood up, approached the window, and said a quick prayer.

She held the torch out of the window a second before she jumped. *I hope they're ready.*

Julia hung in the air a little longer than she'd expected but made a solid landing, and as soon as she did, her surroundings blurred. All she heard was her own breathing and heart pounding in her ears as she focused on her target. After what felt like an eternity, she saw the piece of string only a few meters away. She considered tossing the torch right away but decided the risk was too great: What if she missed?

Julia felt as if she floated on the street as she covered the short distance to the middle. As she reached the bomb, she paused and turned to face the tank. It was even closer than she'd expected, and she thought she made out the eyes of the driver peering through an observation slit. She saw the soldiers behind the tank, but they hadn't spotted her yet.

Without another thought, she dropped the torch onto the ground. As she did, all her senses suddenly returned, and she heard voices shouting. German voices.

Julia turned away, not checking if the piece of string had caught fire, and ran toward the wall on the side of the street, crouching down to make herself a smaller target. As she felt the wall on her left, the sound of gunfire erupted. She had no idea who was shooting, but her whole body tensed. She expected to feel the impact of a bullet any moment now.

Julia ran like never before. Her lungs felt like they were about to burst as she got closer to safety. The flashes near the barricade assured her that her friends were providing covering fire. But she heard nothing behind her. *Did it not catch fire? Did I mess it up?*

At that moment, a loud whoosh drowned out all other sounds. Almost instantly, a blast of heat scorched the hairs on her neck, its force almost knocking her down. For a few seconds, all air was sucked from the street, and Julia gasped for breath as her oxygen-deprived lungs protested. Then, there were merely sounds of anguish.

The screams and panic cut through the street behind her, but she wouldn't— couldn't—look back. She had only a few more meters to go. As she climbed the barricade, strong arms lifted her up and over.

"Did it work?" she gasped out.

Lazor stood facing her, his face beaming. "Why don't you take a look?" She took his arm as she turned around behind the safety of the barricade. The tank, charred black, with a fire blazing from within, stood in the middle of the street. The area around it was a raging inferno strewn with bodies. Some still moved, and she heard cries and moans of pain, stifled by the roar of the fire.

Behind the tank moved the shadows of the retreating soldiers, a number of them limping as they ran.

Julia turned her back to the gruesome spectacle and suddenly felt exhausted. She grabbed onto something as her knees buckled. Her head started to spin, and the last thing she remembered was Lazor catching her as the ground moved toward her.

CHAPTER ELEVEN

Natan called out, "I'll be right back!" as Kasia stood at the kitchen counter, measuring small portions of the last of the porridge for their breakfast. He stepped out of the apartment to make his customary early morning walk to the well a few streets down. It was a little before six when he joined the relatively short queue. It would be an hour's wait if he'd arrived half an hour later.

It had been like this for the past week; bombings had intensified, targeting waterworks and hospitals. Wells—both new and ancient—were back in operation as Warsaw's citizens found ways to survive. Now that the city was surrounded, food was scarce. All roads into the city were cut off, and Natan wasn't sure how much longer they would be able to hold out. The news on the radio told them to be strong—help was on the way. But their British and French allies had yet to send their armies to Poland, even though it had been almost a month since the Nazis invaded.

Natan took his bucket—filled close to the brim—and started his walk back. For the past two weeks, they'd seen casualties rise steeply—both military and civilian. He reported for duty every morning and spent his day hauling their shrinking stock of supplies across the city. The front lines moved closer to the city center every day.

The sound of the cannons had become a constant drone in the background. Natan was used to it; there was nothing they could do but pray.

As he pondered the day ahead, he noticed the thunder of the German artillery was more frequent than usual. He stopped and listened, and before his eyes, a building exploded only 200 or 300 meters away. He instinctively took a step backward, even though he was well out of range of any direct debris. Another explosion rocked the ground behind him. A shell had hit the building next to the well.

He dropped his bucket and sprinted back—the building had collapsed onto the well, and the people waiting their turn. The pile of rubble was over five meters high. They hadn't stood a chance. More explosions erupted around him. It could mean only one thing—the Germans were getting ready to finish them off.

Natan looked up and down the street and spotted an open gate. He took a chance and ran toward it. The street traffic thinned quickly as people found their shelters.

He turned into the courtyard and almost bumped into a young boy.

"Do you have a basement?" Natan asked, panting from his sprint.

The boy nodded. "Follow me."

They ran across the yard to where the boy opened a rickety side door. Natan followed him down a dark flight of stairs. He felt for a railing but found none, and he prayed the steps were even.

They reached the bottom, and Natan saw the faint glimmer of candlelight. As his eyes adjusted to the semidarkness, he found himself in a small room with about a dozen people. They looked at him as the boy sat down next to a woman Natan assumed was his mother.

"Who are you?" a voice asked from the darkness.

Natan couldn't make out a face. "I was collecting water at the well when the bombs started falling. Can I stay with you until it quiets down?"

His words were met with silence and a few blank stares. *I'm not welcome here.* It took a few seconds for the same voice to respond.

"As long as you don't touch our supplies, you can stay."

Natan nodded.

They sat in silence for what felt like hours while explosions outside continued without respite. Nobody in the basement spoke, but for a few children crying as their mothers whispered soothing words.

Natan suddenly felt restless. *I need to be up there. I can't hide down here while others fight.* He stood, a dozen pairs of eyes looking at him in the flickering light.

"Thank you for letting me take shelter here," he said softly. "But I must go and fight."

The young boy got up as well and said, "Can I come with you? I also want to help."

Natan smiled. He was no older than ten but lacked no bravery.

He ruffled the boy's hair. "Maybe next time. Best to stay down here. I'll come back for you if we need more help."

The boy looked disappointed and relieved at the same time as he curled back into the safety of his mother's lap.

Natan ascended the stairs and stepped back into the courtyard. The sound was much louder now, the screeching of the dropping shells tearing into his eardrums. He heard the constant drone of Luftwaffe bombers in the sky overhead and saw them delivering their deadly cargo.

The Civil Guard post was a good ten blocks down. There was no time to waste; maybe he could help somewhere, somehow. He sprinted down the street and was shocked to see how much had changed in only an hour.

The street was strewn with fresh rubble, and he skipped over stones as he navigated electrical wires. Destruction was commonplace, but what the Nazis had unleashed in the past hour was beyond comprehension. He ran into the street of the outpost, then stopped in his tracks and blinked hard. Only a few meters ahead of him, in the middle of the road, lay a group of people—motionless. *Why haven't they taken cover?* As he got closer, it became clear. They were dead. A man's legs had been ripped away from him. A woman's face was barely recognizable as such, and two young boys had been perforated by shrapnel. *A family.* Natan swallowed hard and silently crossed himself.

Natan was lucky. Slowly he made it to the Civil Guard outpost, without further incident, relieved to see about half a dozen men milling around.

"Did you come in from that hell storm?" one of them asked, surprised. Natan didn't recognize him but nodded.

"I can't quite believe it myself that I made it here." He looked around the room. The men looked despondent. "What can I do?"

More surprised looks.

"What do you mean?" the same man asked. "There's nothing we can do right now but wait it out."

Natan didn't understand. "We do nothing?"

The man, who appeared to be the leader of this outpost, glared at him. "Not unless you want to get yourself killed. Go down to the basement with the others—we'll get you when you're needed." He gestured toward a door on his left.

Natan did as he was told and joined a group of men playing cards.

*

Natan felt like he'd slept for only a few minutes when someone roughly roused him. "Let's go, it's time," the man said before hurrying up the stairs.

He looked around, and for a minute, he was unsure where he was. Then he remembered and quickly got up. After spending the previous day in the basement, he'd gone to sleep on the floor. Unfortunately, there had been no blankets, and Natan felt stiff all over as his legs protested the short ascent up the stairs.

The first thing he noticed was many more men than on the previous day. The morning sun was making its way up into the sky, and there were no more bombers outside. It was almost silent, but for the sound of not-so-distant gunfire.

The same man who'd sent him down to the basement now stood near the window and cleared his throat.

"Sons of Poland, the time has come. The Germans sent their troops in less than fifteen minutes ago, and we're going to help the army at the riverside."

There were murmurs in the room as about 30 men took the news. All part of the Civil Guard, like Natan. They didn't fight on the front lines but helped wherever they could. Despite this official assignment, Natan had seen his share of the front, often needing to run close to the fighting soldiers to retrieve a fallen comrade. His hands shook, and he tried to calm himself. If the Germans were attacking from all sides, how would the famished and exhausted soldiers stop them?

He was assigned to a stretcher along with a bulky man called Pietrek.

"How long have you been doing this?" Pietrek gruffly asked as they picked up their stretcher.

"A little over two weeks. Every day, though." *I'm no rookie.*

Pietrek seemed satisfied, and they ran toward the riverside. The battle sounds increased as they moved closer to the Vistula. Natan felt his pulse quicken—this always happened when he approached the front.

They were stopped by a young soldier facing them. "We need you about a hundred meters over there, near the embankment."

Pietrek grabbed the stretcher and looked back at Natan. "You ready for this?"

"Yes." He followed Pietrek as they raced through a narrow alley. The sound of automatic gunfire was constant on their right side, where the army had set up machine guns in the buildings facing the water.

As always, it was easy to find their way. They only had to follow the screams. Sure enough, a minute later, they were on their way with a wounded soldier. They rushed through alleyways to yet another makeshift hospital. Natan had seen many of them over the weeks.

They continued these runs throughout the morning, and a disturbing pattern emerged. No matter how many runs they made, there were always more wounded waiting.

As they left the last medical outpost—Natan didn't consider them hospitals anymore—a terrifying sight met them. Hundreds of soldiers ran through the streets, carrying their weapons—some even holding parts of disassembled machine guns. They were running away from the riverside.

"Retreat, retreat!" the men screamed.

Natan and Pietrek stood gawking at the panicked men scrambling behind new barricades farther into the city.

One of the soldiers stopped long enough to warn them: "Get back—the Germans have broken through the lines! They're crossing the river!"

Pietrek hauled the stretcher over his shoulder as they joined the fleeing army. As Natan ran, he knew they could no longer stop the Germans.

*

And they couldn't. Only hours after the attack had started, news filtered through that the Polish military command had started capitulation talks. The Germans pushed on during the day until they had taken most strategic positions in the city. The fight looked hopeless, although those with arms still skirmished with the Germans.

After spending the entire day carrying wounded soldiers and supplies, Natan was exhausted. He finally made his way home after two grueling days. He was relieved to find Kasia there, her apartment somehow untouched by all the fighting. She looked at him and burst into tears. "Natan, I was so worried about you! When you didn't come back yesterday, I feared the worst."

She hugged him hard; tears welled up in Natan's eyes as well. They stood there for a minute, shaking with relief.

He told her about the past two days, and she listened without interrupting. Kasia made him a simple sandwich—it was all she had.

"We have nothing left," Natan said as he took a big bite. "The army is beaten, demoralized, and hungry. The Germans can finish us off anytime they want."

"I hope the peace talks go swiftly," Kasia said. "At least then we'll know what happens next."

Natan nodded. "I worry, though. Hitler has made no secret of wanting to make us part of the new Reich. What does that mean for us? Where does that leave us?"

Kasia shook her head and said nothing. Natan knew she worried about this, too. She'd lived under German occupation before, but he would ask her about that later.

As he finished his sandwich, he was overcome by exhaustion and made his way to bed. He took off his shoes and sat down, and as soon as his head hit the pillow, he was gone.

The next morning, Warsaw surrendered.

PART II

WARSAW,

12 OCTOBER 1940

CHAPTER TWELVE

Julia adjusted her scarf and pulled up the collar of her coat a bit. It was unusually chilly for an October morning. She turned onto Nalewki Street, no longer the busy thoroughfare of old. Ever since the Germans took over— now almost a year ago—business after business had disappeared. Sometimes they went quietly; the shops would be busy one day and vacant the next. Other times, they were forced out, the broken glass and empty shelves a testament to the previous night's plunder.

Thankfully, her father's little workshop and their home were tucked away from the main street, and they'd been spared such trouble. Nevertheless, business was slow like never before, and she shivered as she rubbed her bony hands together.

She arrived at the bakery and joined the long queue that stretched around the corner. It took her most of the morning to collect their meager supplies, and the small bag she carried would still be only half-full.

When it was her turn, she secured half a loaf of bread and some flour. She then crossed the street to collect their ration of milk, passing part of the wall that was being erected.

This part was finished, and a group of men worked on the next bit down the street. The wall was about three meters high, the top lined with barbed wire and—in some places—pieces of shattered glass. The Germans had started construction immediately after taking over Warsaw, and the wall was almost completed. Everywhere Julia went in the Jewish district, she saw that the wall had risen with surprising speed. Her brother had been forced into building it, as well. He would leave for work before dawn and wouldn't be home until well after sunset.

There were rumors about the purpose of the concrete partition, but nobody knew what was going on. Julia tried to ignore the gossip, but it was hard when she spent every morning in line with bored people with nothing better to do than chatter away.

She was relieved to leave with half a bottle of milk—it was all they could afford—and head home. She looked at the empty storefronts on Nalewki and wondered how long this would last. She was no longer in school—all schools had been closed permanently by the Nazis—and spent most of her time helping her father with his few cobbler assignments.

Before turning into her own street, she noticed a small crowd gathering around an information kiosk. The circular pillars were a common sight in the city before the war—used to announce events, plays, and community news. The Nazis had repurposed them to spread their propaganda and broadcast their ever-increasing restrictions on Warsaw's population.

An SS soldier stepped away from the pillar as the crowd parted for him. He looked at them with disdain, his hand subconsciously on the holster of the gun hanging loosely on his belt.

Julia stepped closer and heard the murmurs of the people deciphering the poster. Their faces betrayed shock, fear even. The Nazis insisted on posting these announcements in German, and someone was translating out loud as she joined the growing crowd.

"By order of the Governor-General, all Jews in Warsaw and the connected districts will report for relocation to the new Jewish section by 15 November," a man said, his voice trailing off as he finished the sentence.

A woman next to him spoke up. "What does that mean? What area?"

The man pointed at the poster. There was a crude map of Warsaw, a line running along the streets Julia knew well. The line was the wall, and it confirmed what she had expected. They were about to be shut into a ghetto.

She quickly stepped away as they all started speaking at the same time. She rushed home and opened the door to the shop, relieved to be inside. Her relief was short-lived. Her jaw dropped as she looked around. Her father was on his knees, collecting pieces of wood. Her mother walked in, a broom in her hands.

"They've destroyed everything and stolen your father's tools." Lea pointed at the spot where her husband's small tool cabinet used to hang behind the counter. It had been smashed up, as had the shelves lining the walls on Julia's side of the counter. That was where customers' shoes were displayed—waiting for collection after her father had repaired them. Some lay on the ground, and Julia picked up a pair. It was apparent why the thieves hadn't bothered to take them: the soles were peeling; her father had yet to start work on them.

Putting the pair on the counter, Julia asked, "Who did this?"

Her father got up with a groan. "If only I knew—they left before I had a chance to come down. I did see a group of four or five men running away, but I couldn't see their faces." He leaned against the counter, his face pale. "Without my tools, I have to close down. With the little business we had, I barely managed to keep the lights on. But I don't have enough money or paying clients to replace all my tools."

Poor Papa. Julia's heart ached for her father. Even though he could be tough on her, she knew the workshop was his life.

"I'm afraid there's more bad news," she started cautiously.

Her mother stopped sweeping the floor and looked up.

"The Nazis are almost done with the wall. They posted a new order that all Jews in the city have to move to within the new wall's boundaries."

Her mother gasped. "But there's not enough space for all of us to live in this tiny area! And what about the other people living here?"

Julia shrugged—she didn't know, either.

Her father walked to the window and said nothing for a minute or two. It was silent in the little shop as they gathered their thoughts. When he turned back to them, it looked like he'd aged a few years.

"The only positive thing about this is that we already have a home within the boundaries," he said. "But we will have a problem with money. I can still shine shoes, but nobody has money for that, and I can't support us on that. Olek is in forced labor, and they pay him a pittance."

Olek earned less than a tenth of what he had made before the Nazis invaded.

"What does that mean, Papa?"

He looked around the store, his thoughts seemingly wandering. Then he spoke. "We may need to find people to share our home. There will be a shortage of houses next month. Your mother is right—even when the non-Jews move out, there won't be enough room for everybody. We could charge rent for this area, the workshop."

"I guess a family of four, maybe five, could live down here," her mother said.

Her father nodded. "But even then, we will have very little money."

Julia looked at her parents, and her heart broke. They had always supported her and Olek, and she was used to being poor. But now, with her father's livelihood so cruelly taken from him, he could no longer do even that. Prices would only go up when more people moved into the area. She decided she wouldn't wait around—she turned to her parents, her face set in determination.

"I'm going to look for a job."

Before they could protest, she had left the shop.

*

The door to the grocery store closed with a thud behind her as Julia stepped into the street. She'd started the afternoon hopeful she'd find a job. But as the day progressed, her optimism dwindled as she got the same response everywhere: not interested. Business was slow in the Jewish district, and everyone mentioned it was bound to get worse soon.

It was getting dark when she decided to go home and try again tomorrow. She was quite a hike from home, and she wasn't very familiar with the current neighborhood. As she turned into what she thought was a street that would lead her back to Nalewki, her passage was partially blocked by a section of the ghetto wall. It was still under construction, and half of the street was still open.

Instead of turning back, she decided to take the longer route around the wall. She enjoyed the crisp October air—it cleared her mind.

The streets were quiet as most Varsovians had retreated into their homes. There was little life in the cafés and restaurants these days; the occupation wasn't merely hurting the city's Jewish population. As she passed the dark windows of the places that used to flourish at this time of day, she was surprised to see light and a low hum of sound emanating from windows farther down the street.

Intrigued, she approached what turned out to be a restaurant. She heard the sounds of laughter and the clinking of glasses. People were having a great time, and the place appeared to be packed.

On a whim, she opened the door, and the sound of many voices speaking simultaneously increased. Before stepping inside, she took off her white armband with the Star of David and stuffed it into her pocket. The warm, smoky air mixed with the distinct smell of frying oil hit her nostrils and her mouth watered. It had been a long time since breakfast, and the sights and smells of the restaurant made her stomach grumble.

The people at the tables were oblivious to her, and as she scanned the room, she knew she was in the wrong place. This was no ordinary restaurant. She should've known; only very few people had enough zlotys to go out these days. Julia instinctively put her hand in her pocket and fingered her armband.

The dining room was predominantly filled with men. They wore crisply pressed gray-green uniforms, although most of them had loosened their collars. At one or two tables sat women, most of them looking either bored or overly excited. But it wasn't the women Julia was worried about. The uniforms were a common sight around the city these days. The mix of German and Polish spoken at the tables confirmed she had stepped into an SS restaurant.

She turned to leave when a voice startled her.

"Can I help you? Are you lost?"

Julia turned to find a tall man wearing a spotless white shirt and black apron addressing her in German. He looked at her inquisitively, but he was not unfriendly. Without thinking, she answered, in the same language: "I'm here for the job."

He looked puzzled. "What job? We're not looking for anyone."

"I was told to ask for the owner," Julia said, hoping that would be enough.

The waiter hesitated for a moment but then shrugged. "Well, okay. He's at the bar—follow me."

Julia struggled to keep up as he strode through the dining room. The Germans cast their eyes over her, but she kept her gaze on the young man in front. Her heart pounded in her chest.

They reached the bar, and the waiter waved at an ordinary-looking man. He was busy pouring a round of beers, and Julia stood awkwardly as the other waiters went to and from the bar with large trays.

The man closed the tap handle and walked in their direction, looking inquisitive.

"This young woman says she's here for a job, Mr. Furmanski," the waiter said, nodding at Julia.

Mr. Furmanski raised his eyebrows slightly. "Is she, now?"

"I was told to find you," Julia said, feeling her cheeks flush. She wasn't really sure what she was doing and wondered if it was too late to head for the exit.

A smile formed on the man's face. He waved the waiter away. "I remember now—let's have a chat in the back." He gestured to a door behind the bar. Julia hesitated, but she knew she couldn't back out now. She followed him into what appeared to be a storage room. He closed the door behind them.

"What do you think you're doing just strolling in here?" he said with a look of concern. "You're Polish, aren't you?"

She was caught off guard and only nodded.

"You realize this place is only for Germans, right? Did you not see the sign outside?"

She hadn't and silently berated herself. She was always so careful, but the bright lights had drawn her in. "I'm sorry, I didn't think clearly. I've been out all day looking for a job, but there are none. Your place looked so warm and inviting."

The man nodded. "Well, that's the point of a restaurant. I'm lucky the

Germans decided to pick my place; business has never been better. But what's this about a job?"

"I made it up," Julia said, looking down.

"I don't have any jobs, either."

Julia nodded and looked up. "Of course, it was silly of me. I'll leave and not cause any trouble for you."

Furmanski met her eyes and looked her up and down. He was silent and made no effort to send her away. Instead, he leaned on one of the shelves. "How good is your German?"

Julia frowned. "Umm, passable, I guess." She was taken aback.

"Have you ever served drinks before?"

She understood where this was going and made a quick decision. "Yes, I've worked in some restaurants on the other side of the city. Never as glamorous as this one, though." She forced a smile.

Furmanski smiled back. "We can always use another pretty face in the room. You've seen how busy it gets here, and some of the others have been complaining about the workload. I can't pay you much, but why don't you come back tomorrow and see how it goes?"

He held out his hand, and Julia shook it without hesitation.

CHAPTER THIRTEEN

Natan was up early and strolled into an empty kitchen. It wasn't often that he beat Kasia to the breakfast table, and he put a kettle on the stove, a task she usually performed. As he waited for the water to boil, he looked out of the window. The street outside was quiet, as it always was this early in the morning. It was still dark, and that meant nobody was allowed to be out apart from German soldiers.

He looked at the prominent gap in the row of buildings across the street—the result of a direct hit from the bombings of last year's siege. Nobody had even considered rebuilding the ruins strewn across the city. Natan felt a sharp pain in his chest as his parents' faces suddenly flashed in front of him. Every once in a while, something would trigger the memory of that fateful day more than a year ago now. He drew the curtain, momentarily blocking out the ruins across the street.

The kettle whistled, and Natan made a pot of substitute coffee—there was no way they could afford the real thing.

Kasia walked in, no doubt awakened by the sound of the kettle or the smell of Natan's brew. "Good morning," she said and took a mug from him as she sat. She looked surprisingly awake as she met Natan's eyes. "You look like you've got something on your mind."

He did, and he bought himself some time by taking a sip. He wasn't sure this was the right time. But then, there really wasn't a good time. *She's not going to like it, whether it's now or later.*

"I've been thinking," he started, carefully watching her reaction as he continued. "Ever since the Germans assigned you to help run the factory, you've been working with the resistance as well, right?"

She tensed a little but quickly recovered. "Well, I've never actually been that explicit about it, but I guess little gets past you."

"Even for a woman who loves her shoes, there have been a lot in this house recently," Natan said.

"Okay, okay, I do take a few home and hand them out to people in need. It's a small bit of resistance. I hate working for the Germans and thinking they're wearing our shoes as they trample all over Europe." She looked up. "But that's not what you wanted to ask, is it?"

"I want you to put me into contact with them." *There, I said it.* He held his breath.

She looked at him with curiosity, and he found it impossible to read her beyond that. Kasia stood up and refilled her cup before turning back to him. "I don't like it, Natan. What do you think you're going to do?"

"Do my bit for Poland," he said without hesitation. He knew she'd ask him this, and he was ready. "It's been a year, and life is only getting worse. There's hardly enough food, and now they're shutting the Jews into a ghetto next month. All I do is study while other people are fighting. I want to fight."

"But going to class is an important bit of resistance as well, Natan," she countered. "We'll need educated, smart people when this is over. We can't let them win. You meeting with the professors is the best thing you can do right now."

After the Germans had banned Poles over 14 years old from going to school, Natan started attending clandestine classes every morning. He was halfway through his final year—the occupation had severely delayed his studies.

He banged his fist on the table, his mug jumping up a bit. "But it's not enough, I can do more!"

Kasia stepped back and said nothing. Her eyes betrayed concern and something else. *Understanding?*

They were quiet for a few minutes, sipping their drinks in silence. Natan looked at the window he had blocked with the curtain. Again, he saw his father's confident face, his mother smiling, and this time there was no pain, just sadness as their faces had already started to blur in his memories. The men responsible walked the streets of his city so carelessly—so arrogantly—like they were untouchable. The thought of doing something about it had been simmering in his mind for months now.

Kasia broke the silence. "Okay, I'll ask around."

His heart leaped. He wanted to speak, but Kasia silenced him with a quick raise of her hand.

"But you will continue your studies, and I can't promise they'll take you. If they don't, you'll accept that. You won't go looking for trouble on your own, you hear me?"

"Of course, Kasia, of course." Natan was ecstatic. He'd expected her to reject his idea out of hand, but instead, he might have a shot at joining the resistance. He quickly drained the last of his drink and grabbed his coat.

The walk was only ten minutes, and it took Natan through most of the Old Town's most picturesque streets. Or they had been before the Luftwaffe had reduced almost half the beautiful buildings to rubble. While he used to stroll through this area admiring the architecture—the colorful buildings with their sculptured window fronts—he now kept his eyes peeled for German patrols. They were especially suspicious about young men walking the street, and it was rare for Natan not to be stopped and asked for his papers.

He'd become good at spotting the patrols from far away and turning into a side street or, if that wasn't possible, casually crossing the street. He neared the street where his class met, but he paused as there was some commotion ahead. A dozen people stood on the sidewalk, their backs to Natan. As he got closer, he noticed a German soldier keeping them at bay. Behind the soldier, in front of a large apartment building, stood a compact German army truck.

Natan was relieved it wasn't the derelict building of his class, but one a little farther down.

He didn't have to wait long to see what they were there for. An SS soldier—holding a machine gun—stormed out of the building and down the front steps. His face was twisted in rage as he shouted at the people following him. Natan heard the panicked cries of children before he saw a group of six escorted out by another couple of SS soldiers. They, too, held their machine guns at the hip. There were two women in their 40s, a man of about the same age, and an older man in his 70s. They were followed by two young children, both no older than ten.

"*Schnell, schnell!*—hurry up!" screamed the soldier in the front. Not to be outdone, one of the other soldiers—a young man not much older than Natan himself—kicked the old man as he struggled down the stairs. He lost his footing and slipped down the steps onto the pavement. He was unable to get up, and the SS soldier kicked him in the chest. The old man let out a shriek and grabbed at his ribs. The rest of the group turned in horror. The younger man instinctively stepped toward what was probably his father.

"Get up, you old Jew!" the soldier yelled before noticing the younger man approaching him. He lifted his gun. "Step back, now!"

The younger man froze as he stared into the barrel. Another soldier roughly pulled him back to the rest of the group, away from the older man, who now lay motionless on the sidewalk. The soldier bent down, a scowl on his face.

"This one's no good anymore," he said to the other soldiers as he stepped over the man. They then herded the group to the side of the street, their backs to the very building they had been evicted from.

Natan was sickened at the sight of the old man on the street. The faces of the others showed nothing but fear, the children shaking and holding on to their mother's hands.

With a short nod by what appeared to the senior SS man, the others raised their machine guns. Natan looked away. The explosion of the guns and the impact of the bullets in the stone behind them echoed horrifically.

When all was silent, Natan slowly looked up. The bodies of the people who had stood there breathing only a few seconds ago were now mangled in grotesque positions on the ground. The two children lay under their mother's body—she had tried to shield them.

The street was quiet. A few of the people around Natan looked on in fascination, but most of them looked as horrified as he felt.

The soldiers slung their guns over their shoulders and walked back to the truck. The younger soldier was about to climb in but then turned and walked back to the old man on the ground. He unfastened his sidearm and—with an air of utter indifference—fired two rounds into the back of the man's head.

He got into the truck, and without another look, he ordered the driver to hit the gas, and they sped away. As the truck turned the corner, the crowd hurried on their way, keeping their distance from the corpses. Natan did the same. There was nothing he could do for these people. For now, anyway. But inside him, he felt his hatred for the Nazis burn even more fiercely. He couldn't wait to fight back.

*

Kasia had had good news for him when she returned from the factory: she had set up a rendezvous with the resistance. She didn't know who Natan would meet—it was always better to know as little as possible. Natan was elated, but Kasia had tempered his enthusiasm; this was only the first meeting, and they could very well reject him.

Despite the warning, he felt confident as he walked through the Old Town's narrow streets to an address only a few blocks away. Kasia had made it very clear she expected him to be home before curfew.

He arrived at an unpretentious building—painted in drab yellow—which had seen better days. He climbed the stairs to the third floor, where he quickly found Number 12 and knocked. He waited for a good half minute without an answer. He knocked again.

"Are you looking for someone?" A man carrying a small pouch approached Natan.

Natan responded with the passphrase he had memorized. "I'm meeting my uncle for dinner." It felt odd saying such a random thing, but the man nodded and nudged him aside as he unlocked the door.

They stepped into a sparsely furnished apartment, which smelled like a window hadn't been opened for weeks. It had only two rooms, and the kitchen was part of the living room. There were two single beds in the small bedroom, both unmade. The man sat down in one of the simple wooden chairs, and Natan followed suit.

"So, you want to make a difference?" the man said without preamble or introduction. Kasia had warned him not to ask for any names nor volunteer his own. It would not be expected nor appreciated.

Natan nodded and put his hands on the table. "I can't stand by and do nothing any longer. I'm 18 years old, no longer a child, and I want to avenge my parents' death."

The man held up his hand. "Hold on there, slow down. It's not about what you want. It's about what you can do for us." He lit up a cigarette and put the package back in his pocket without offering Natan one. "Do you know how to fire a gun?"

Natan shook his head.

"No experience with guns, then. Fighting? Engineering skills?" The man rattled off the options.

Natan kept shaking his head. *Come on, think of something.*

The man sighed. "Anything you're good at?"

"I'm really good at sports." He felt silly, but it was the first thing that came to his mind.

Now it was the man's turn to shake his head. "Well, there's little use for sports, don't you think?"

Natan felt his opportunity slip away and racked his brain for skills that would be useful to the resistance. "I'm also good with numbers. I've done a lot of accounting work in my father's"—he stopped himself—"I've done a lot of paperwork in offices in the past."

The man sat up. "Son, that's not what we're looking for. We need fighters, and you don't sound like one to me."

Natan was about to open his mouth when a loud screeching noise interrupted, followed by car doors opening and slamming outside.

The man across from him quickly got up and peeked through the window. He switched off the lights and put a finger to his lips. "Germans," he mouthed.

A million thoughts ran through Natan's head as he listened to the sounds outside. *Do they know about the apartment?* He looked at the man. *Or about him?* A cold sweat formed on Natan's brow.

It didn't take long until the sound of heavy boots ascending the stairs filtered through the door. He heard stressed voices shout in German. *They don't care that everybody hears them coming.* He looked at the man next to him, who had his eyes on the door.

Natan heard the distinct cocking of a gun. The resistance man held it close to his chest. *I hope he won't have to use it; there are too many of them.*

The soldiers were now on the floor below them, and Natan held his breath as he waited for the sound of boots to come up. It was oddly quiet for a minute, and then a loud crash broke the silence, followed by voices shouting in German and high-pitched, frightened voices in Polish.

"They're raiding the apartment downstairs," the man whispered. He uncocked his gun. "Don't move."

They sat in silence as they listened to the drama unfolding in the apartment below. The people were taken out into the street, and Natan feared he would witness his second execution of the day. He braced himself for the shots. They never came. The people were loaded into the truck before the sound of the engine faded away.

When all returned to normal, the resistance man spoke up. "It looks like I may have underestimated you."

Natan was surprised. He didn't feel like he'd done anything remotely brave.

It must've shown, for the man continued with a faint smile. "Many others would've panicked in that situation. They would've tried to run. You didn't. I watched you, and you didn't flinch."

The man walked toward the door. "It's getting dark. You better get home before the curfew."

Natan was unsure what to do, and he followed him.

The man put his hand on the door handle before turning back to Natan. "We'll be in touch. I think we may have a job for you after all."

CHAPTER FOURTEEN

Julia stood at the bar, waiting for Marco to finish pouring five generous shots of vodka. The day was winding down, and this was the last call for the only table still occupied. Even though the curfew didn't apply to Germans, it certainly did for most people working in the café. Julia delivered the drinks to the table, keeping the serving tray nice and steady. She'd struggled with that a few times on her first day but quickly got the hang of it. As long as she kept the taller glasses near her, she could glide through the packed dining room nearly as well as the other waiters. Thankfully, Marco had taken her under his wing and taught her a few tricks.

The SS men at the table greeted her with boisterous applause as she set down the glasses in front of them. *If only they knew a Jew is serving them.*

"We'll be closing up after this," she said sweetly in her accented German. "Shall I put these on your tab?"

"Sure thing, sweetheart, and this is for you." One of the men handed her a small bill, which she slipped under her apron. She thanked him and walked away from the table. When she got to the bar, her boss, Mr. Furmanski, gestured for her to follow him. She liked him, as he'd been patient with her on her first day when she had dropped a tray of drinks. He'd quickly seen how well she got along with the clientele, and at the end of her shift, he'd told her to come back the next day. She'd been at the café for a good week now, and she enjoyed the work, despite the questionable crowd.

He held the door for her as they entered the little storeroom behind the bar where she'd had her first interview. He turned to her, and she was surprised to see him looking a little cross.

"Julia, is there something I should know about you?"

She swallowed and frowned. "I'm not sure what you mean."

He sighed and reached into his apron. Julia let out a soft shriek as Mr. Furmanski held up her armband.

"I found this in the changing room," he said. "It's yours, isn't it? The others have worked here for years, and I know it's not theirs."

She hesitated for a moment but then decided there was no sense denying it. "It's mine," she whispered, her eyes downcast. *He's going to fire me, surely. Or worse.* Suddenly, she felt afraid. What if he walked back into the room and told the SS men to take her with them? They wouldn't be so friendly with her anymore. She looked up at her boss, who looked back at her with a curious expression.

"I always thought there was something odd about you showing up on my doorstep last week. It seemed so out of the blue. But really, I would've never thought you were Jewish. You look so . . . Polish."

Her blond hair threw a lot of people off—she didn't fit the stereotype. "I am Polish," she said. "And Jewish."

"Of course, of course." He looked uncomfortable, and he didn't immediately continue.

Julia wondered what was going through his mind. *Maybe I should tell him everything. If he's going to fire me, he should know the whole story.* "You know, I'm now the only one making any money in my family." She told him how her father's shop had been ransacked, how her brother was working on the wall without pay. He listened attentively without interrupting her. When she finished, his eyes were full of concern.

"I realize it's hard to support yourselves these days, and it will probably get even harder when you're moved into the ghetto." He looked thoughtfully, then paused. "You know what, Julia, I don't want to be the one that destroys your family's livelihood. Let's worry later about how we get you to work. The Germans seem to like you, and you never know, maybe we can arrange something when they finish the wall. But, for now, let's keep this between us, okay?"

Julia couldn't believe what she was hearing. She had been ready to hand in her apron and leave through the back door. "Th-thank you so much, Mr. Furmanski."

He waved his hand dismissively. "Please, you're doing me a favor. I've seen a lot of people start patronizing this place since you began working here." He winked at her. "I'm not saying it's all because of you, but, well, your tips speak volumes as well, right?"

She managed a smile. He was right—the Germans had been rather generous.

"Now, get out of here. I'll close up and see you tomorrow."

She didn't know what to say, and on impulse, she hugged her boss.

*

After she'd changed into her regular clothes, Julia stepped out into the cold, wet street. It was dark, and she had only half an hour to get home in time for curfew. Julia took large steps through the slippery roads. It would typically take her twenty minutes to get home, but the rain had her walking a little faster than usual.

"Julia? Is that you?"

She was surprised to hear her name and turned to see a man waving at her from across the street. *Who's that, and how does he know my name?*

He noticed her look of surprise. "You don't remember me, do you? It's Adrian from the barricade at Opaczewska." His clear blue eyes looked right into her soul.

"Of course, Adi, how are you these days?"

"I'm good. I still think of what you did back then. People talk about you all the time." His eyes lit up.

So much had changed since then. She forced a sad smile. "We kept them at bay a bit longer."

He looked behind her, at the café. "So, what were you doing in there?"

She thought she saw a bit of judgment in his eyes. "I work there."

"Isn't that a Nazi hangout?" Adrian looked at her incredulously. "How can you work for them, after everything they did to us? And you, especially."

Julia felt her cheeks flush. "I don't work for the Nazis—I work for Mr. Furmanski, and he's Polish." She crossed her arms. "I don't need to explain myself to you."

Adrian wasn't convinced, and he shook his head. "You're serving them their drinks, probably enjoying quite a bit of their attention as well. But remember that when they leave in the evening, they go back to their jobs of harassing innocent people on the streets. Or worse . . ."

"You're in no position to judge me," Julia said calmly, barely controlling her rising anger. "You have no idea what my life is like. I hate the Germans as much as anyone, but I need to support myself and my family. When I searched for jobs in my own neighborhood, nobody would hire me. They had no money for me. It's not by choice that I serve them; I have no other option." She met his eyes challengingly. *Who do you think you are?*

To her surprise, a smile formed on his face. "So they haven't turned you, then?" His eyes glistened.

"No, and frankly, I'm insulted that you would think so. How would I go from blowing up tanks to being in cahoots with them?"

"Do they talk about their work?"

"What do you mean? To me?"

He nodded. "Sure, to you, or do you overhear things they say?"

"Well, most of the time, they don't pay a lot of attention to me. They consider themselves pretty upscale. My boss likes to maintain that illusion, so we're encouraged to blend into the background."

Adrian looked thoughtful. "So you pick up a thing or two when you're serving the tables?"

"I don't really pay attention to most of the stuff they say."

"Would you understand what they said if you paid more attention? I assume you speak a bit of German if you're working there?"

"My German is pretty decent, and they're usually drunk, so whatever they're saying is usually not too complicated." *Where is Adrian going with the questions?* "Why are you so interested? What do *you* do these days?"

He gave her a sly smile and held up the palms of his hands. "Oh, nothing quite as interesting as what you're doing. I have no chance of getting a job, so I look after myself—you know."

Julia didn't like the answer and decided this was enough. "Okay, well, that sounds pretty mysterious. I must be heading home."

He stepped in front of her, blocking her way. "Sorry, I didn't mean to upset you. The truth is I needed to test you a little."

She raised an eyebrow. "Test me?"

"Look, I think you working there might be very interesting for some people I know."

She bit her lip. *So vague.*

He sensed her unease and quickly continued. "Let me just say that I'm going to have a chat with some people who look after our country's interests, if you know what I mean. I think they'd love to hear about your job."

Julia understood. "You knew I was working here."

He shrugged. "Maybe I did. But I'm glad I ran into you anyway. I'll be in touch." With that, he turned to cross back to the other side of the street. Then, over his shoulder, he uttered, "But don't tell anyone about this. We don't want the Nazis to know we talked."

Julia watched him disappear down the street to slip into a small alley. She stood in the rain and wondered what had just happened.

CHAPTER FIFTEEN

It had been two weeks since Natan's meeting with the resistance man in that stuffy apartment. He'd heard nothing until Kasia came home from work earlier than usual one day and handed him a scrap of paper with an address—the resistance wanted to meet him. Of course, he would have to skip school, but this would be more important. Were they going to accept him after all?

He hardly slept and finished his breakfast well before Kasia was up. As she came out of her bedroom, he was already halfway out the door.

"Keep your cool there, Natan—they haven't accepted you yet!" she called as he rushed out.

Natan had plenty of time to get to the meeting point. The walk would be fifteen minutes, leaving him with time to spare. It was a sunny morning, and Natan took a deep breath of the crisp winter air and felt confident. He would make a difference for his country; surely they wouldn't have invited him if they didn't want him? The man must have been impressed by him in the end, even though it had been a rough start. He'd make himself useful, he was sure of it. As he walked along, deep in thought, he failed to spot the two SS men heading toward him. When he did, it was too late to get out of their way—he knew they were going to stop him as they eyed him suspiciously. Sure enough, they blocked his passage.

"Where are you going?" one asked. He sported a thin mustache, making him seem older than he probably was.

Natan was caught off guard and didn't immediately reply. His hesitation only made them more suspicious.

"Lost your tongue?" The other one asked. He was a bit taller and stepped closer.

Natan instinctively stepped back, but then he recovered. "I'm on my way to work."

"Really, where?" The taller one asked, frowning.

"I work in a leather factory across the river."

"Aren't you going in the wrong direction?"

Natan had his answer ready and nodded. "I'm just cutting through to get to the tram—that way, it's faster."

The smaller soldier appeared bored. "Come on, let's go," he said, nudging his colleague, who ignored him and held out his hand.

"Show me your *Arbeitskarte*."

"Of course." Natan reached inside his jacket, where he kept the piece of paper that proved he still worked at his father's old factory. He hadn't been there for over a year, but Kasia had somehow secured one for him anyway. It made it much easier for him to explain why he was on the streets. When he fingered his pocket, his heart stopped. The Arbeitskarte wasn't there. He checked the other pocket: nothing.

An ugly grin started to form on the soldier's face. "That's what I thought." He turned to his colleague with a triumphant look.

Natan felt a trickle of sweat rolling down his back as he rechecked his inner pockets. As the soldier reached for him, he felt the piece of paper in a side pocket. He quickly pulled it out and handed it to the soldier, who looked disappointed as he inspected it. After taking longer than usual—this wasn't the first time Natan had been stopped—he reluctantly handed it back to him.

"Seems to be in order. Better not lose that. Next time we might not be so patient," the soldier said as he waved his hand dismissively. The men walked on, and Natan breathed a sigh of relief. That was way too close.

He took a slight detour—staying clear of the main streets, navigating narrow side streets. He found himself in front of an old school building and tried the front door. It didn't give way, the lock rattling in the doorframe. Natan then remembered Kasia told him he needed to go around the side of the building. He found the door there and entered a dark hallway that still smelled like a school—he caught a whiff of cheap detergent. Unsure where to go, he walked along the classroom doors lining the hallway. It was quiet, and his footsteps echoed off the walls.

He reached a flight of stairs where a faint glow of light flickered from below. A single light bulb illuminated the way as he carefully and slowly descended to a narrow corridor. At the end, he found another source of light and stepped into a small room, where eight youngsters—none out of their teens yet—sat on simple chairs scattered around the small, musky room. None of them acknowledged his presence.

Natan decided he was in the right spot, and he sat down on one of the vacant chairs. The other boys kept their eyes averted.

They sat for a few minutes until the silence was broken by a tall, muscular man who strode in with purpose, his eyes scanning the small group. As if on cue, they all stood up, and Natan followed.

"Sit down," the man said with a deep voice. "There's no need for that."

They quickly sat down, and Natan scanned the other faces—everyone seemed a bit nervous.

"Good. I'm glad you all made it. It's not the easiest place to find, and that's exactly why we picked it." The man looked around the room as he spoke, fixing his gaze on each of them as he did. Natan felt slightly intimidated when the piercing dark eyes focused on him. Nevertheless, he made an effort not to look away.

"You're all here because you were invited. Someone thought you were good enough to be part of this meeting. That means you passed the first two tests. But before I tell you more about what we do, I want to know one thing from you." The man stepped closer to the front row, where the two smallest members of the group sat. He stopped and looked up, his eyes not focusing on anybody in particular. "Why are you here?"

His question was met with silence. Most of the boys kept their gazes firmly fixed on the dusty floor. The muscular man in the front was motionless, looking like he had all the time in the world.

Natan heard himself say, "To fight the Germans."

The man's eyes were now on him. They no longer had the piercing gaze. Instead, Natan thought he saw approval and maybe a hint of a smile on the man's face. He pressed on.

"Actually, no," Natan added. "I want to kill them. I want to kill the Nazis."

The smile grew as the man slowly nodded. "That's the attitude. Who else wants to kill Nazis?"

All other arms shot up as the man walked through the small crowd toward Natan.

"We can use someone like you. Someone who's not afraid to speak up, to take action when others are hesitant." The man stopped in front of Natan and signaled for him to stand. "Let's see if you have what it takes to be part of the *Szare Szeregi*—the Gray Ranks."

*

It was well past noon, and Natan had spent the better part of the morning in the stuffy cellar. The cold street air felt good. He was excited about joining the Gray Ranks. He'd heard the stories of young men like him playing an active part in the resistance. It was hard to miss the threats to the Germans painted on walls across the city and thrilling to hear about another successful assault against the occupiers. The man in the cellar, Mischa, had told them how the young members of the Gray Ranks were involved, their youthful faces keeping the Nazis off guard until it was too late. The boys in the cellar had listened breathlessly, and at the end, Mischa had made it clear they could each play their part.

But not before they passed their first assignments, which were handed to them right away. It had come as a surprise, but none had rejected the mission. On the contrary, they were too excited, too worked up, eager to do their bit for their homeland.

Natan felt the five sheets of paper almost burning in his pockets. They were all handed five copies of the *Biuletyn Informacyjny*—the weekly bulletin printed by the resistance—and told to distribute them throughout the city. They had been overwhelmed to receive such pristine copies of this week's version. Natan was used to finding a copy tacked up at a street corner, more often than not torn and unreadable. Carrying five of these was a great honor.

Nevertheless, it was also hazardous. Possessing it could get a whole family hauled away. *I'd be shot on the spot if they found these on me.* He thought about where to leave his copies—Mischa had told them public places were best, preferably near public transport. The problem—especially at this time of day— was that it was easy to get caught in crowded areas. And it wasn't only German soldiers he needed to watch out for. There were plenty of his countrymen who would have no problem betraying him.

His heart pounded in his chest, and he made an effort to calm down as he crossed into the Old Town. Natan ran for a stopping tram, jumping on board as it started moving again.

The car wasn't crowded, and he found a seat near the door. Nobody paid him any attention: an older man stared outside, and a woman shushed her baby. Natan looked for a conductor but was relieved to find none. He would be fine without a ticket, as long as he got off at the next stop.

He took a deep breath, reached into his jacket, and took out the bulletins as covertly as he could.

Quickly, and as silently as possible—the ruffling of the sheets sounded like thunder to him—he placed a copy of the *Biuletyn Informacyjny* on the wooden seat beside him as the tram slowed for the next stop. *Time to get off.*

Keeping his head down, Natan stood and moved toward the exit. He held on to the sides of the benches as the tram started braking more forcefully. Then, he felt a hand on his arm.

"I think you forgot something, young man." It was the man who—only moments earlier—had been entirely oblivious to what was going on around him. Now, he was pointing at the sheet of paper Natan had left on the bench across the aisle.

Natan didn't know how to respond. The man reached for the *Biuletyn Informacyjny*, and Natan's heart sank. His eyes scanned the tram, but none of the other people seemed to have noticed—nor cared about—their conversation.

The man's eyes widened when he realized what he was holding. He recovered and looked up at Natan with an expression he couldn't immediately place. Apart from surprise, the man's eyes were showing something else. *Admiration?*

The tram came to a stop, and new passengers climbed aboard. Natan inhaled deeply as two men in dark green SS uniforms boarded at the back of the tram.

Natan held his breath. *Should I dump the copies and run?* The man's grip on his arm became firmer. *Pretend they're not mine if he rats me out?* He looked at the man, who put the sheet of paper on the vacant seat next to him.

Outside, Natan saw two young women running to make the tram.

The man winked at Natan, released his grip, and said softly, "Good for you, son. There should be more like you. Now get out of here."

Natan restrained himself from running for the door but calmly stepped off as the two women boarded.

As the tram pulled away from him, Natan saw the caps of the SS soldiers in the back window disappear in the distance. His heart was still pounding.

CHAPTER SIXTEEN

The Grossman family now rented the space that used to be her father's workshop. All six had moved in a week ago, as more and more Jews relocated into the ghetto. Julia rushed downstairs and waved the Grossmanns well before stepping out the door.

Julia hurried onto Nalewki Street—late for work. The air was frosty, and a thin layer of snow covered the ground. Yet, even in her haste, she enjoyed the soft crunch under her feet as it drowned out the busy street noise. As she walked along, she felt a presence next to her. She turned and saw the familiar face of Adrian. He looked serious yet friendly.

"Julia, I need urgently to speak with you," he said as he gestured for her to follow him into a side street.

"Can't this wait? I'm already late."

"It's about your work. Trust me, you need to know this."

My work? She was intrigued and followed him down the quiet street until Adrian turned and said, "Your job is no longer safe—you must not go in today."

She dismissed his words with a chuckle. "I work at probably the safest place in the city, don't you think? There's no one but SS men and a few *Volksdeutsche* there."

He looked at her but said nothing.

"Okay, humor me, Adrian. Why shouldn't I go in? Is the resistance going to attack the place? Hardly seems likely with all of those Germans armed."

"It's not us. It's the Gestapo."

She let out a nervous laugh. "They're going to raid their own place? Come on, Adrian, I don't have time for this." She moved away, back toward the main street.

"No, they're raiding the place because they found out that Furmanski is helping the Jews, hiding some of them around the city."

She stopped in her tracks. "He's doing what?" she asked softly, and after a pause: "How do you know?"

He stepped closer. "Because he's part of our network."

Julia felt her knees weaken and took a deep breath of the cold morning air. "For how long?"

"Over a year now, since the Germans took over. You know that they're now rounding up or killing intellectuals and suspected resistance fighters?"

She stared at him.

"Well, he makes sure they're hidden all over Warsaw, and we arrange for them to be smuggled out of the city."

Julia's boss was such a perfect host to his German patrons. She sighed in disbelief.

"He's already gone, so don't worry about him. He left the city last night when we found out about the raid. They won't catch him."

Is Adrian telling the truth?

"I realize this puts you in a tough position," Adrian continued. "I know your family depends on you."

"It will be hard finding something else, especially when they close the ghetto in two weeks," Julia said.

"We may have a solution," Adrian said. "You could join us."

Julia let the words sink in.

"I hardly know you, and I don't even know if you're telling the truth now."

"How about this?" he said as he reached into his backpack, withdrawing a small blue scarf. "Think about it, 'cause we could really use you. We take care of our people and their families. All I'm asking is that you meet with one of our leaders and they'll tell you about the job. Sleep on it, and if you're interested—no strings—wear this scarf as you go out to get groceries tomorrow morning. You always go around seven, right?"

"You've been keeping an eye on me?"

He said nothing and held out the scarf. "We take things very seriously."

Julia hesitated but took the scarf, and Adrian said, "Tomorrow. I hope you consider it."

*

Even before Julia reached the café, it was clear Adrian was telling the truth. The café street was blocked off on both sides, and two army trucks were parked in front. Soldiers had kicked the door in, broken pieces of glass testament to their violence. A small crowd gathered, and Julia pushed her way into the safety of their numbers.

As she did, some of the soldiers came out, looking disappointed. Her heart leaped. *Maybe the others were warned as well.* If it hadn't been for Adrian, she would be in the back of one of those trucks.

She waited anxiously as nothing happened for a while. Then, to her dismay, she saw a familiar face escorted to one of the trucks. *Oh no, not Marco!* Julia felt her eyes sting, and she blinked hard to keep her composure.

The rest of the soldiers walked out of the café—evidently not finding other offenders—and boarded the trucks. Then, they revved the engines and cleared the street. The crowd quickly dispersed, and Julia found herself utterly lost—unsure what to do next.

*

The following day, Julia beat the morning queue at the bakery. She secured a rather fresh piece of dark bread—always a treat. As she stepped into the street, she pulled her blue scarf a little closer to her face, making sure to expose it properly.

She proceeded slowly but purposefully as she scanned the street ahead of her. *Perhaps I misunderstood Adrian?*

She felt a light tap on her shoulder. Startled, she dropped her grocery bag.

"Follow me, Julia," a woman said. She looked fit and no older than thirty.

Julia picked up her bag and hesitated for a moment. The woman smiled reassuringly and nodded at her scarf. "That color looks great on you."

Shaking off her doubt, she followed the woman, who took quick steps through several side streets. Even though Julia was very familiar with her neighborhood, she didn't know the small building the woman stopped at. Most of the buildings were large, a mix of shops on the ground floor and apartments on the upper floors. This building looked more like a garden shed. She then realized that was precisely what it was; the main building had been destroyed, and all that was left was this shed forged from leftover wood.

"Come inside," the woman said as she opened a rickety door.

It was cold and sparsely decorated inside. Other than a couple of chairs, there was nothing indicating anyone lived here. The woman gestured to one of the chairs, and they both sat down.

The woman caught her looking around and said, "I apologize for the simple surroundings. We move a lot, as you might imagine."

Julia nodded. "That's fine, as long as we're indoors, right?"

The woman smiled and undid her own scarf a little. "Now, Julia, I realize you're a little overwhelmed by what happened in the past few weeks."

She shifted in her chair. "Maybe a little."

Another reassuring look. "First things first, you can call me Aga. I work with our resistance, and I'm going to be very blunt with you; we want you to join us as a courier."

"A courier? Like a messenger?"

Aga shook her head. "It's not the same. We have plenty of messengers in the city. Even when they close the wall, we'll have plenty of children able to deliver messages both inside and outside the walls. No, what we need from you is more important. More dangerous, too."

Julia tried to keep a straight face and not show any emotion. *Just listen; let her do the talking.*

"You may not know much about us, but *we* know *you*. We know about that tank you blew up. We've kept our eyes on you ever since."

Julia felt herself blush.

"Anybody can become a messenger, but for someone to be a courier, they need bravery like yours and one other thing." She paused before pointing to her own face and blond hair. "You need to be able to blend into a crowd of Germans and look and act like them. They should never suspect you're the thing they hate most."

"I'm not sure I can do that," Julia said nervously.

"Nonsense," Aga said. "You've been serving drinks to Nazis, much to their delight, I've heard. You appear to be fearless—unshaken in the lion's den." She stopped talking and looked at Julia with her bright green eyes.

"Are you a courier yourself?" Julia asked.

"I am, I've been doing this for six months now. I was one of the first."

"How many are there?"

"We're a small group. No more than a dozen girls so far. Girls much like you."

"What would I do?"

The woman smiled as if Julia's question were a small victory. "I'm glad you asked."

Julia listened as Aga told her stories of her life over the past six months. She had traveled through Poland—and had even ventured into Germany twice—visiting resistance cells all over the country. She'd delivered messages and smuggled food and medicine from city to city—even smuggled weapons into Warsaw recently.

"How do you travel? Don't the Nazis suspect anything? Aren't you stopped in the streets?"

Aga shook her head. "That's the brilliance of it. If a man were to do this—travel on his own—he would be stopped the moment he stepped aboard a train. But young women don't draw attention. And the few times I've been stopped, I would tell them I'm visiting family in another city."

"So you're not using any false papers?"

Aga gave her a funny look. "Of course we do. But I have a very Polish name now, and they've never questioned me further. It's all about being confident and convincing."

They sat in silence for a moment, and Julia studied the little garden shed. She wondered if she would be able to do all the things Aga told her about. Nevertheless, she looked at the woman with a fresh perspective, with a new level of respect.

"I've attacked German tanks during the siege. I'm not sure I would be okay if I were stopped by a patrol, carrying something illegal." She held her breath; maybe Aga would tell her she wasn't fit to be a courier after all. Instead, the woman looked back with understanding in her eyes.

"Do you think I felt ready when I started doing this? Of course not. I wouldn't have gotten past a checkpoint when I started. They would've spotted me right away. But that doesn't matter. We know you've got the courage, the heart. But, perhaps most importantly, you're motivated. You've shown as much so far."

Julia averted her eyes; she felt bashful under the compliments. "I'm not all that great."

"But you are! And you can become a marvelous courier, a real asset to the resistance," Aga said, her eyes lighting up. "Trust me. I've trained all the girls so far, and I can spot a good one."

"Can I ask you something?" Julia was keen to change the subject away from herself.

"Anything."

"Why did you choose to do this? I mean, it sounds dangerous, and any day could be your last."

"It wasn't up to me," Aga answered without hesitation. "I knew I couldn't sit around and do nothing while the Nazis took over our country. I needed to do something, to fight back." She spread out her arms, opening up her body. "But look at me—I'm no fighter. I can't go fist to fist with any soldier. So I decided I needed to use my other qualities." She tapped the side of her head. "I joined the resistance as a messenger, and when I was asked to deliver a message to another city, I decided I could also bring back their message and more."

I feel the same way. "I'm also not making a difference."

"Of course, and that's why you're perfect." Aga's eyes focused on her, and Julia felt like she looked straight into her soul. "So, are you in?"

Julia hesitated only briefly. "When do I start?"

CHAPTER SEVENTEEN

Natan looked out onto the quiet street ahead. He was a few blocks from Kasia's home, close to the Royal Castle. Despite its bomb-damaged roof, the majestic red building looked as imperious as ever.

After completing his first mission, Natan was accepted into the Gray Ranks, and distributing the *Biuletyn Informacyjny* became a common task. He was adept at finding new spots in the city to leave them. He'd even placed them on the postboxes in hallways of large apartment buildings. He figured most good Poles wanted to know what was going on but might not have the courage to pick up the bulletin from a public place. Moreover, it came with a bit of extra risk—if people knew what he was doing, they could report him, and he would be caught one day. Nevertheless, Natan felt confident he picked suitable buildings.

Today, however, he had a very different mission, although it was also part of the propaganda war he waged as a Ranger—the most junior rank within the Gray Ranks. Natan carried a small bucket of white paint under his bulky winter coat. Whenever he was sure there were no German patrols nearby, he'd take out the bucket and paint the *kotwica*, the Polish emblem of resistance, which was like the *V* signs painted in the rest of occupied Europe. The kotwica was a combination of the letters *P* and *W*, with the *P* protruding from the central part of the *W*. The sign looked like an anchor, and Natan painted it wherever he could.

He'd almost finished another kotwica when he heard hurried footsteps farther down the street. Natan looked up and dropped his brush, standing so quickly that he knocked over his small can of paint.

"Halt! Bandit!"

He'd quickly gotten used to the phrase the Germans used for anyone in the resistance, and he bolted in the other direction. Fortunately, he hadn't lost any of his speed, even though there were no more games of football these days. He glanced over his shoulder and saw the two troopers still chasing him. *They're in much better shape than most of the others. I need to get off the streets!* He ran south, away from the city center—there would be fewer patrols and plenty of places to hide.

Natan dashed into a tiny alleyway he knew went nowhere. There was a wall about three meters high and he scaled it with ease. He'd taken this shortcut many times before, and he didn't think the soldiers chasing him would know where to find the handholds he'd discovered earlier. He jumped down on the other side and listened for the Germans trying to climb the wall. He heard them struggle, fail, and curse in German.

Natan smiled, confident they were not going to follow him. As he did, the face of one of them peered over the wall.

Shit—the other one must've given him a boost.

The German swung his legs over and now sat on top of the wall. "You're not getting away, bandit!" he shouted.

Natan didn't wait—he started running. He heard a familiar sound as the German cocked his gun. He almost froze from panic, but his survival mindset kicked in, and he found another gear as his lungs protested. *Keep going!*

When he was almost at the other end of the alley, a shot rang out, its loud echo bouncing off the walls in the narrow passage—the bullet burying itself into the wall to his left before he had a chance to duck. Natan forced himself out into the street. To his right, he heard the whistle of another bullet flying past his head before shattering a shop window. People screamed and dropped to the ground, hands covering their heads.

Natan kept going, expecting to hear another gunshot, as the German soldier would clear the alley soon. He crossed the street and stumbled through the remains of a shop building. He almost tripped over some loose wires, but he kept his balance as he made it to the other side. Still no gunfire, and he started to believe he had gotten away. *Don't look back—keep going.*

Exiting the ruins, he crossed a garden and dashed into another heavily damaged building. He navigated through its corridors and found what he was looking for in the far corner. He opened a concealed latch and climbed into the confined space underneath, quickly closing the latch.

As he stood in uncomfortable darkness, he knew there was no safer place. Even if the German soldier had seen him enter the shop, he would be overwhelmed by the options to search on the other side. All the buildings around Natan's hiding place were damaged. *They'll give up; it's not worth the risk.*

He waited for half an hour before climbing out of his cramped surroundings; he needed to report to his squad in as soon as he could. His commander had called an emergency meeting, and the chase meant he was now running late.

*

As soon as Natan saw his commander's face, he knew something was wrong. He'd rushed across town and barely made it in time. He sat down and noticed two vacant seats in their circle.

Mischa looked serious and started without preamble: "Two of our comrades were captured by the Gestapo this morning."

Natan swallowed hard; he'd been dangerously close to capture himself. It was easy to make a mistake—the Germans were everywhere.

"We have to assume they're being interrogated as we speak, if they are still alive," Mischa continued, a slight crack in his voice. "Even though they are both brave, we also know the Gestapo have a way of getting information even from the most hardened members of our organization."

Natan shuddered. He'd heard about the interrogation techniques used on those unfortunate enough to be captured. They would disappear into the basement of the infamous Pawiak Prison. It was one of the most important reasons to be extremely careful. It was often said that those shot in the street were better off than those hauled away in trucks, and Natan didn't intend to find out if that were true.

"This means we have to assume our cell is compromised." Mischa looked at the seven young men sitting around him. "And you'll all be reassigned."

Although Natan knew capture was always a possibility, he hadn't expected this to happen so soon. He was just getting used to his new role and the boys in his cell. Even though none of them knew each other's real name or background, he'd forged bonds with them. He was especially fond of Mischa, who had spent many hours sharing his experiences with them. He looked up to the man, and he hoped he could one day share his knowledge with new recruits.

Mischa interrupted his thoughts. "Lew, you're going to report to one of the assault groups." Like everybody in the resistance, Natan had picked his own nickname: it was Polish for lion.

The others looked at him in admiration, and Natan didn't know how to respond. *Assault? Already?*

Mischa smiled. "Don't act so surprised. I remember what you said when you joined. You still want to kill Nazis, don't you?" He didn't wait for an answer as he continued. "Go—Ludwik outside will tell you where to report."

Natan stepped outside as the others were given their instructions. None of them knew exactly where the others were going to ensure everyone knew as little as possible. It would serve them well if anyone were caught.

After receiving his instructions from Ludwik, he hung around until the others had left. Then, Natan walked back into the room where Mischa stood deep in thought—he looked a little startled when Natan spoke up.

"I appreciate being assigned to the assault group," he started. "But I'm not sure I'm ready yet. It's only been a month."

"Nonsense. You've already seen frontline duty during the invasion, haven't you?"

"Well, yes, but I was only carrying wounded soldiers. I've never fired a gun."

Mischa smiled. "Look, if I didn't think you were ready for this, I wouldn't have recommended you. I would've sent you back to propaganda work in another cell. But you've been bolder than anybody else—posting bulletins right under the noses of the Nazis. I don't think anybody has painted as many lampposts in Old Town as you have."

He was right. Natan had taken a particular liking to painting the phrase *Nur für Deutsche*—only for Germans—on the streetlights. Mischa had told him it terrified the younger, new German soldiers to see such a public threat after arriving in Warsaw. Natan wouldn't mind carrying it out now that he was going to join the assault section. He'd love to see the boots of an SS soldier dangling under the dim light of the streetlights for a change. There had been plenty of his countrymen hung up like that.

He turned back to Mischa. "You're right, I do want to fight them."

"And you'll do a great job. Now go, they're expecting you."

*

Natan went straight to the new meeting place. As he arrived, his pulse quickened, his hands clammy. The building was nondescript, like the other hideouts he'd been to in the past month. He stepped inside and immediately saw the setup was very different from what he was used to.

The hallway was eerily silent, and even as he listened for other sounds, the only thing he heard was his shoes softly clicking on the hardwood floor.

Out of nowhere, a man appeared from one of the doorways. He looked at Natan without surprise. "Lew?"

Natan nodded, and the man gestured for him to follow. Then, tentatively, they stepped into a dimly lit room, where seven others sat waiting. All in their early twenties; Natan was the youngest in the room.

The man who let him in closed the door and waved at an empty seat. Natan sat down—all eyes were on him. He fumbled with his hands, not knowing what to do with himself.

Breaking the silence, the man spoke. "Welcome to our squad, Lew. I'm Maciek, the leader of this cell. We're glad to have you."

Judging by the looks on the faces of the other men, Natan wasn't so sure. Most of them looked on with neutral expressions, but two looked openly hostile as they introduced themselves. It did nothing to calm his nerves.

They spent the rest of the afternoon going through assault strategies.

"What did you think of the first class?" Maciek asked. "Were you able to keep up a bit?"

Natan nodded. "I think so. It helps that I know most of the places you were talking about. Even some of the examples you used from during the siege." He studied Maciek's face and estimated he was at least ten years his senior.

Maciek's eyebrows shot up in surprise. "How so? Those aren't very well-known locations, or battles, for that matter."

"I was part of the defense," Natan said neutrally. Inside, he was hoping to impress his new leader.

It worked.

"Really? What did you do?" Maciek asked, leaning forward.

Natan told him about his job as a stretcher-bearer, and Maciek asked him if he'd also fought the German soldiers.

"I didn't. The army was still in the city back then, and they defended the walls. Or at least tried to. The Germans were much better equipped, as I'm sure you know."

"I was part of one of the battalions in charge of defending the Old Town," Maciek said, his eyes glistening in the dim light. "You're right—we had no chance."

"Yet nobody even thought about giving up. I've never seen that many wounded men in my life, but every time I got to one of the hospitals, if you can call them that, they were pleading with the nurses to let them return to their friends."

Maciek nodded but said nothing. Natan suddenly didn't feel like the rookie anymore. "Have the others in our cell seen battle before?"

"No," Maciek said softly. "They all volunteered after we surrendered. Most of my army friends were taken to POW camps. Some of us managed to hide and joined the resistance. Others left Warsaw. I don't know what they're doing now. I hope they joined up with the rest of the army or other resistance groups. We need them." His eyes were sad, but his face was set in hard lines as he turned back to Natan. "But that's all in the past. I'm glad to see you have some experience. We're going to need it. Mischa told me you have a particularly strong hatred for the enemy. Why is that?"

Natan knew he shouldn't share too many details, so he kept it vague. "I lost some people that were very close to me—in the bombings."

Maciek understood and didn't press any further. He looked ready to leave.

"Can I ask you one more thing?" Natan asked and continued when Maciek nodded. "When I joined today, some of the others didn't look too pleased."

"We've seen our fair share of recruits not making it. We've also lost people to the Nazis, and some of the boys are a little apprehensive about welcoming new faces."

"Anything I can do about that?"

Maciek smiled. "Show them what you can do. Remember what you did during the siege, and take that with you when we have missions. Don't worry, you'll have a chance to earn their respect soon enough." With that, he turned for the door. "Time to go—it's almost curfew."

CHAPTER EIGHTEEN

The young boys on the sidewalk couldn't be more than seven years old. They held out their hands in desperation, looking hopefully at every passerby with their hollow, pleading eyes as they tried to shield themselves from the cold with their ragged clothing. Julia's heart ached for them, and she knew she'd find more beggars at the next intersection.

The street was awash with people—running their errands on one of Warsaw's most prominent shopping streets. Julia had nothing to spare for those begging for scraps. Ever since the ghetto walls had closed two and a half months ago, her family's situation had deteriorated. Instead of one family subletting downstairs, they now had two. They had also taken in two young boys whose parents had been murdered by the Gestapo in their own apartment across the street. They couldn't pay rent, yet they were another two mouths to feed.

Not that there was much food coming in, either. When the gates to the ghetto were sealed, little time was wasted in limiting the rations for the relatively tiny but overcrowded ghetto of 400,000 souls. Within the first week, they had switched to a food rations system, meaning that Julia went to bed hungry and woke each morning starving.

She'd seen more people collapsing around her in the past month than ever before. The only reason her family was hanging on was her job with the resistance. They supplied her with extra rations, which they somehow smuggled into the ghetto. Julia was in training to become a courier, and she suspected she'd soon be involved in the smuggling as well. She'd spent a lot of time with Aga, who taught her how to blend in, be inconspicuous, and—most importantly—improve her German. But apart from all the training—which was very useful, she did not doubt this for a minute—Julia was itching to get started.

She turned off Nalewki, holding on to the small package her father had asked her to deliver to a customer of his. Julia failed to see the tall man blocking her path in the narrow street. She moved sideways, but he mirrored her, blocking her way. She frowned and took a step back. *What does he want?* The man was twice her size and looked at her menacingly as he took a step toward her.

Julia didn't hesitate and turned to run away—but found another man blocking that side as well. She was trapped. Before she could scream, they had pounced on her, one of them quickly pulling a burlap sack over her head while the other man lifted her from the ground. Julia flailed her arms and kicked with her legs, but it was no use. She couldn't see anything, and her assailants could easily dodge her attacks. She screamed in frustration, the sound muffled by the sack. They carried her farther down the alley before quickly opening and closing a creaking door.

She was set down on what felt like a wooden chair, the same strong arms still holding her in place. Within seconds, the other man grabbed her arms and forced them behind her back. She struggled, but the two men put their weight into their efforts, and she felt a strong piece of rope cutting into her wrists as they tied her arms behind the back of the chair.

Julia breathed hard, struggling for air in the burlap sack. She was close to panicking, but she forced herself to focus. *Who are these people?* Everything pointed to a Gestapo ambush. *Have they found out about my role? I haven't even started properly yet.* She stopped struggling and listened. It sounded like another person had joined her two captors.

"Who are you?" she asked shakily, in German. "What do you want from me?"

There was no response as her legs were tied up against the front legs of the chair.

She heard people shuffle and the scraping of a chair that was pulled up next to her. Julia heard the squeak of the wood as somebody sat down.

"Okay then, Julia." A man's voice. He was close to her, and the first thing she noticed was that he spoke Polish. "Why don't you tell me about your *Banditen* work? Where were you going? Were you meeting someone?"

She was surprised to hear there was no hint of an accent in his voice. If these people were part of the Gestapo, they had recruited Poles. She racked her brain—she didn't know of any of her countrymen working for the Gestapo. The Germans—sure, plenty of them had switched sides, but she thought the Gestapo was a closed organization, open only to Germans. *Better stay quiet.* She pursed her lips.

The man sighed. "You don't want to talk? That's okay, we have time. We've got plenty of supplies, and we can wait until you're ready. How are your arms? I'm sure you must be getting a little uncomfortable by now."

They had indeed gone numb, her fingers tingling. Her legs were starting to get restless but were held firmly in place as she struggled to reposition them. *Can't. Move.*

The man chuckled. "That's what I thought. Not very comfortable. It'll only get worse."

She bit her lip. *I'm not going to tell you anything.*

"But that's okay. I'll start, and you can jump in whenever you want," he continued, unperturbed by her silence. He struck a match and lit a cigarette. A few seconds later, the smoke hit her nostrils as he exhaled into her face. She coughed as the smoke filtered into the hood.

"We know you're a messenger for the resistance, and we know you're smuggling arms into the ghetto," the man said, methodically checking off her supposed crimes. "I'm sure you know this is illegal. You could be shot on the spot. In fact, we could leave you here in this room, and nobody would ever find you. Do you realize this?"

Julia swallowed hard. *How does he know about this?* Sweat started to form on the small of her back.

The man continued. "Aren't you going to deny this? You're very quiet for someone who is in a lot of trouble. You can stay quiet, but if you do, we're going to assume you're guilty. And then we'll take you somewhere else, where they can get the full story."

The sweat was also forming on her forehead, and she had trouble breathing. Another waft of smoke, and she burst into a coughing fit.

He waited for her to recover before speaking the words that chilled her to the bone: "Just so we're clear. I'm talking about Pawiak."

So they were Gestapo, after all.

"I don't work for the resistance!" She practically screamed through the hood. "Why are you doing this to me?"

The man laughed out loud. "So she does have a voice! Well, this is a start—now we're getting somewhere, Julia. Where were you going?"

Julia now had tears pouring down her face. At least the hood hid that, for now. "I was getting some groceries."

"Why were you carrying this, then?" Even though she couldn't see, she knew he was holding the package her father had given her.

"Those are nothing, just old shoes."

"You sure you weren't meeting someone? Don't lie to me, Julia."

Julia shook her head. "I'm not lying."

The man stood up, and through the bottom of her hood, she saw his shoes. They were well worn, which was surprising. Anyone in the Gestapo would have proper boots. He dropped his cigarette butt and crushed it on the floor.

He paced the room, and she focused on the sound of his footsteps. Then, she heard a swoosh as he opened the curtains, and she saw daylight filter into the room through her hood. Then, he spoke again.

"I don't believe you. I'm taking you to Pawiak."

Her heart dropped, as did her head. She knew it would be the end, and she considered telling him the truth. About to open her mouth, she hesitated. *What about my parents and Olek? And Aga, I can't betray her.*

Julia swallowed hard and steeled herself. If they were going to take her to Pawiak, that would be okay. She wouldn't tell them a word, either. Then images of all the horrible things she'd heard about the interrogation basement came into her mind, and she wasn't so sure. She shuddered—tears were now flowing freely. *I don't want to die.* The hood was wet, and she felt her shirt sticking to her back.

She hardly noticed when they untied the ropes around her ankles and wrists. She was lifted from the chair, and she struggled to stay upright as her knees felt weak.

Then, she was blinded by the bright light as the hood was removed. She closed her eyes and then opened them again—blinking as they adjusted to the light—and she gasped. *It can't be.*

Standing before her was a very familiar face.

It was Aga.

Julia looked at her in confusion. She turned around to see two men standing by, their eyes fixed on her.

"I . . . I don't understand," she stammered. Julia rubbed her wrists and felt the feeling return to her hands. Aga stepped closer.

"I'm sorry you had to go through that," she said as she embraced her. "But we always have to make sure our girls can withstand capture and interrogation."

Julia held on to Aga and felt a wave of relief wash over her. "So, this was a test?" she asked softly.

They broke the embrace as Aga nodded, and a smile appeared on her face. "And you passed it with flying colors. For a moment, I didn't think you were going to speak at all."

Then she heard the voice of the man who'd interrogated her. "And when you did, you gave me hardly anything. You didn't tell me anything I didn't already know. Remember, never mention anything personal—you have no relationships."

"They'll use that against you, for sure," Aga said. "But the most important thing is, you didn't crack. Not even when you were about to be shipped off to Pawiak. It takes a lot of courage not to lose it at that point."

The man nodded. "We've had girls break down and tell us everything about their training, even giving up the names of the people they worked with."

Julia sat down and felt her pulse returning to something resembling normal. Aga handed her a cup of water, which she gulped down.

Aga pulled up a chair across from her. "This means you're one of us now, Julia. You're a *kashariyot*—a courier."

Julia nodded, her mind still hazy. She heard the words, but they didn't really register. "So, what will I do next?"

"Your first mission is ready. You're going to help smuggle more food into the ghetto. We can't depend on the *Judenrat* to feed us, I think that much is obvious."

Julia felt her mind clear and nodded. The Judenrat was responsible for all supplies of food, water, and medicine in the ghetto. The Nazis had appointed them. Even though they did their best, they were no more than a puppet organization following German directives. And from the rations the Germans provided, it was clear they didn't have their best interests at heart.

"So, what will I do?"

"You're going to establish contact outside the ghetto and set up a smuggling route." Aga handed her a small pouch. "Here's new papers identifying you as a Polish worker in the ghetto. You'll work for a German company. This gives you free passage to and from the ghetto."

Julia took out the papers in amazement. The new passport identified her as Krystyna Janow. Her Arbeitskarte confirmed she worked as a secretary for Többens and Schultz—the largest factory in the ghetto producing German army uniforms. She knew quite a few people who worked there. There was one other piece of paper with an address scribbled onto it.

"That's the address for your contact. The people there are Polish, and they're sympathetic to our cause. They will be able to supply you with food. So make your way over as soon as possible."

As she put her new papers back into the small pouch and tucked it into her jacket, she looked at Aga, and it dawned on Julia. She was part of the resistance. She was finally going to make a real difference.

CHAPTER NINETEEN

On the other side of town, Natan casually walked down the street, returning from his Friday class on attack formations. It had been preparation for their first field training the next day. Natan was thrilled; it would be the first time he'd get to put into practice all the theory he'd learned in the past two and a half months.

They had planned to go earlier, but the weather had been dismal, and they'd postponed the training a few times. Temperatures had risen in the past week, and Maciek had decided tomorrow was going to be the day. They'd get onto a train into the countryside and meet up with other cells there.

Despite his casual demeanor, Natan kept a close eye on his surroundings. He was only a few streets from home, but he didn't want to chance getting stopped by a patrol today. He was carrying something that would have him shot on the spot—a Vis 9mm pistol. Even though he had no bullets, there was no reason for anyone to walk the streets of occupied Warsaw with one. He'd been asked to take it after class and keep it secure for the next day's training.

He'd been honored and had gladly accepted—he certainly didn't want to seem weak in front of his peers. But now that he was outside in broad daylight, it felt heavy in his pocket. Natan glanced at the faces of the people on the street; were they giving him second glances? *Stop imagining things; you're fine.*

As he closed the door to the apartment, he let out a deep sigh. He took off his coat, which was soaked in patches with sweat.

Kasia was in the kitchen and greeted him cheerfully, and he considered what to do with the gun. He could leave it in his pocket, but then it would be in the hallway, and he wouldn't be guarding it overnight. He decided he needed to take it to his room. Should he tell Kasia? He decided she needed to know and took it out of his pocket.

She took a step back. "Wow, where did you get that? And why is this in my home?" She put down her spatula and stared at the gun.

"Don't worry, it's not loaded," Natan said. "I'm keeping it for tomorrow's training."

Her expression didn't change. "That still doesn't explain why it's here."

"We can't exactly take one big bag with all our training supplies, you know?"

She lifted the lid of the pot on the stove and stirred. The sweet smell of paprika filled Natan's nostrils. "All right, all right," she said. "Well, it seems like you certainly got the riskiest item to carry around the city."

He sat down, and his stomach grumbled. He hoped dinner was almost ready. "The guys have been giving me a hard time about being the youngest of the group. They keep saying they're not sure I really did all those things during the German invasion."

She looked cross. "Well, that's nonsense. You were on the front lines!"

"I know, but I'm still a rookie. Tomorrow will be the first time I can show everybody what I can do. Carrying the gun to the training is important." Natan's voice had risen a bit; he was excited.

Kasia tasted the stew and nodded approvingly. She took the pot off the fire, ladled two generous servings into bowls, and served one to Natan. She sat down and blew in her bowl. "Well, I'm proud of you, Natan. And they'll see soon enough they were wrong to mock you."

He took a bite and burned his mouth. "It's fine—I'm still the new guy."

"Even after almost three months?"

He shrugged, blew on his spoon and took another bite, and savored the taste. Kasia was a fantastic cook, even with the limited supplies they had. "It's fine. How are you doing?"

She sat up. "Well, I have some exciting news as well. We're smuggling more shoes out of the factory to give to those poor people who have nothing."

Natan smiled as he took another bite of his stew. "That's great! How many pairs have you sent over the ghetto wall so far?"

"Almost a dozen, now. I'm cautious because I don't want the German overseer to suspect anything. But so far, they don't seem too bothered. I think your father would've approved, don't you?"

Natan felt a small knot in his stomach at the mention of his Papa. His parents were with him every day; when he walked the streets, he sometimes made a detour to the ruins where his home used to be. He would stand there for a few minutes, looking at the rubble, remembering his careless youth and their big plans for the future. He looked back up at Kasia, and her eyes showed she was reading his thoughts.

"Yes, he would've been proud of you, Kasia," Natan said, clearing his throat as his voice croaked at the final words. "He would probably tell you to smuggle out more shoes."

She smiled and reached across the table, taking his hand in hers. "And he would be so proud to see you today, as well. His son the resistance fighter."

They finished the rest of their dinner in silence.

*

Natan was surprised at the activity at the Warsaw Główna station. He never had an excuse to go there, and the last time he'd been on board a train was well before the war when his parents took him out to the countryside. It looked very different today. The city's central station had taken heavy damage during the fighting, and the Germans had only bothered to install a simple new roof. There was none of the grandeur he remembered from his previous visits.

He looked up at the giant board with departures and headed for his platform. The people around him all appeared to be in a hurry, and he mimicked their behavior, hoping to blend in.

He made his way to the platform without incident, the train waiting on the far side. The clock suggested he had a good five minutes to spare.

As he neared the train, his heart skipped a beat. A police officer appeared at the top of the stairs near the train. Sure enough, the man looked in Natan's direction and stared. *Oh great, he's spotted me.* Natan knew he had no choice but to continue heading toward the train. It would be highly suspicious for him to turn around now. The small backpack he carried suddenly felt very heavy. Apart from the pistol, he also brought a copy of *Combat*, a military textbook they would use during the training.

He tried to control his breathing and act normal. Despite this, he felt very conspicuous, and it was hardly a surprise when the policeman barred his way in the middle of the platform.

"Where are we going, young man?" he asked in Polish. Even though the Germans were in control of the city, there were still Polish police officers— mules for the Germans; Natan detested them. *Be polite, Natan—you're not doing anything illegal.*

"Hoping to get on this train, sir. I'm visiting my family in Siedlce this weekend." He kept his face open and spoke pleasantly.

The man gave him a stern look. "Let's see your ticket."

Natan produced the ticket, and the officer briefly inspected it. He saw the worried faces of some of his mates looking out through the window. He ignored them and focused on the policeman, who handed back the ticket.

"Identification? Are you allowed to go out of the city?"

Natan had his Arbeitskarte ready, as well as a forged document stating he was free to travel to his family in the countryside. *I hope it's good enough.* The officer took his time, and when a frown formed, Natan felt a flash of panic. *It's not good enough.*

"This factory, what do you do there?"

His pulse lowered a little as he answered evenly: "I help process the leather. My father used to own it, so I know how to cure the leather, and I help the new people."

The officer stared hard at him, and Natan thought he didn't believe him. He then handed back the papers, and Natan breathed a silent sigh of relief as he exhaled.

"What's in the backpack?"

Shit, of course, he'd ask about that. Farther down the platform, the locomotive hissed and let out a sharp whistle. The train would be leaving soon. Natan decided to take a chance.

"Just clothes, sir, would you like me to show you?" He crouched down and slowly opened the backpack. The gun was hidden at the bottom, as was the copy of *Combat*.

He started taking out the rolled-up clothing on top. The policeman looked on as he continued unpacking his backpack.

Another whistle of the train, and Natan looked up. *Come on, let me go.*

The policeman's interest was waning as Natan took out another shirt.

The officer waved his hand dismissively. "Okay, okay, it's fine. Get on your train before your family wonders why you didn't make it."

Natan quickly stuffed his clothes back into the backpack. "Thank you, sir."

The officer was already marching away on the platform, no doubt looking for another victim.

Closing the backpack, Natan dashed for the train as the conductor whistled for departure. As he jumped on board, the conductor closed the door behind him.

Entering the compartment—searching for a free seat—he spotted familiar faces scattered around the train. Finding an empty seat in the back, he sat down and let out a sigh, clutching his backpack. Perhaps this was a good start.

CHAPTER TWENTY

J ulia was up early after a restless night. It was the Sabbath, and she prayed with her family in their cramped living room. Their faith gave her some peace, and she was happy to appease her parents with this small act.

After prayer and a simple breakfast, she dressed in her best clothes and headed out. Her father had protested about her being out on the Sabbath before, but when she returned with the extra rations to keep them all from going hungry, he'd relented. He'd asked her if she was selling her body—he'd heard many girls had resorted to that kind of behavior. She'd been quick to convince him it was nothing like that, and that had been the end of the matter.

On her way to the western checkpoint, she walked the quiet streets. *Would the people on the other side of the wall still live an everyday life? Did the Germans ration their food as well? Did they know about what was going on inside the ghetto walls?* As she approached the checkpoint, she was dismayed to see not merely Polish policemen hovering around but also two Gestapo agents.

That was unexpected. Aga had told her to expect police at the checkpoint— some Jewish, on their side of the wall. She was used to them patrolling inside the ghetto, and as long as she gave them a wide berth, they'd leave her alone. However, the Gestapo was different, and it was odd for them to be checking papers of people leaving the ghetto. She considered turning back but thought better of it as she saw one of the Germans scanning the queue. They would probably come after her if she ducked away. So she stayed put, and the line slowly moved along.

As she waited, she eyed the people in front of her. They looked very much like her, although their clothes were much nicer. The man in front of her turned around and greeted her pleasantly, in German.

"What brings you to this side of the wall?"

It took her a few seconds to realize this polite man was addressing her, and she smiled before answering. "I'm heading home after a long night in the textile factory." She hoped her accent wouldn't give her away too much.

"Your German is quite good," he responded. "Do you work at Többens and Schultz?"

She hoped he didn't know anyone there as she nodded. "I work in the office. I take care of the paperwork."

He looked surprised. "Aren't you a bit too young for that?"

"Well, these are strange times, sir, and I'm quite good with numbers."

"I guess you're right," he said, his eyes drifting to the front of the queue. "This is taking so long; I wonder what the holdup is."

Julia nodded, hoping to avoid further conversation that might draw attention to her.

The man was called forward, and Julia was next in line. She felt apprehensive, but she also knew there was no way back now. One of the Gestapo agents was eying her, and she kept her face as neutral as possible. Yet, inside, her stomach was in knots. *Remember your training; deep breaths.*

As she went through her cover story in her head, something happened at the gate. The man she'd been talking to gestured wildly with his arms.

"But I am a German citizen! What do you mean my papers aren't in order? Recheck them. I told you, I'm here to inspect the quality of the—" He was cut off as one of the agents punched him in the stomach. He gasped for air as he doubled over.

"Shut up, old man," the Gestapo agent said. "We'll be the judge of your papers, and when we say they're not in order, that's the end of it. Don't think you can tell us what to do." He snapped his fingers, and two other young men in the same uniform appeared from nowhere. They took the man by the arms and dragged him to a nearby van. They opened the doors and unceremoniously threw him in the back. As he realized what was happening, he protested once more, his face red with indignation.

"You can't do this to me! I work for the Reich, and I'm a member of the party!"

A loud clang stifled his cries as the doors shut and the van sped away.

Julia felt her blood run cold. Suddenly, she wasn't so sure about her papers anymore. Then, as the van disappeared around the corner, she heard one of the men shout: *"Nächste, bitte."*

She stepped forward, mouthing a silent prayer. *Please let my papers be good enough.*

Her hands trembled as she reached for her papers. *Remember, your name is Krystyna.* The Gestapo agent who had interrogated the man quickly ran his eyes over her documents. He looked at her—checking her photograph—and appeared satisfied. After a brief pause, he handed her papers back and waved her forward.

Julia stood frozen for a moment, and he nudged her. "You're holding up the line."

She continued in a daze, bracing herself for him to change his mind and have her hauled away in a truck as well. He didn't, and she recovered to take in her surroundings. The first thing she noticed was the lack of starving people on the streets. There were fewer beggars here, no orphaned children with bloated bellies, and no corpses of those who hadn't woken up after a night in the cold. Instead, people rushed by as they went about their business. She walked past empty stores, and when she peeked into a bakery, there was only marginally more bread available than on her side. Nevertheless, death was not as present here.

Julia continued through the streets, a German patrol on every corner. She walked carefully, afraid to stand out. It took her a few more turns until she found herself in front of a surprisingly small apartment building. Most buildings in the city were at least three stories high, but this had only a ground floor where a shop used to be—the windows boarded up—and a door to the side. She knocked, and while she waited, she hoped she'd memorized the address correctly. She listened for sounds behind the door, and after a minute, she heard someone slowly coming down the stairs.

"Who is it?" a woman's voice said, only slightly muffled by what turned out to be a thin wooden door.

Julia remembered the passphrase: "Offering carrots for a winter's night." It sounded ridiculous, and Julia held her breath. She was relieved to hear a lock unbolted, and when the door opened, a young woman appeared. "Come in," she said as she pulled Julia inside.

The woman mounted the stairs without another word, and Julia followed her. At the top, she went through an open door and waited impatiently for Julia, who darted in quickly. The woman closed the door.

"So you're the new girl?" the woman snapped at her as she looked Julia up and down.

"I guess I'm at the right place. You know Aga, right?"

The woman looked up, and Julia noticed her eyes were soft. Julia was surprised, as her initial demeanor had been distant, hostile even.

"I'm sorry, I'm a little nervous," the woman said frankly and held out her hand. "I'm Renata, but everybody calls me Renia. I'm happy you made it—I'm sure it wasn't easy getting out of the ghetto."

Julia took her hand, baffled by the quick change in attitude. "That's okay. I know you're taking a big risk, letting me in."

Renia waved her to a chair and walked to the stove, where she took a small kettle and poured two mugs. "Coffee?" She shook her head and corrected herself. "Well, what passes for coffee these days. I'm afraid we haven't had the real thing for a while now. Still, it's hot, and it'll warm your bones."

Julia gratefully accepted the warm mug and almost burned her mouth as she took a sip. Renia smiled. "Careful, it's boiling."

Julia studied her host's face. She was probably only a few years older than her.

Renia took out a small bag, much like the one Julia used for her groceries, and from it, she took out a couple of carrots and four potatoes. She handed them to Julia. "You can take these back into the ghetto. I know it's not much, but I've only recently started saving food to take over the wall."

Julia put her mug on the small table and held the vegetables in her hands. It had been a long time since she'd seen this much food. In the ghetto, they sometimes had to make do with a single potato for the whole family. Only when someone smuggled in a bit of food, they might have some more. But Julia knew they were still in a much better position than most people living beyond the wall.

She wanted to take the food to the other side, but something held her back. She handed the food to Renia, who looked surprised.

"I have to see how hard it is to get back inside first. This is my first time out." She told her about the Gestapo agents, and Renia nodded, understanding.

"I'm sure they will check your bag when you go back. You might be lucky once, maybe twice, but eventually, they'll catch you."

"How quickly do you think you'll be able to find more supplies?"

"Well, there are lots of people in our network who want to help," Renia said. "I think we'll be able to collect at least three times this amount of food per day. Probably more when we're successful."

Julia was touched. "I didn't know what to expect from the people on this side. I'm sure you can't spare that much yourself." Her mind flashed back to the near-empty stores outside.

"They can't. But they realize we need to help our Jewish Varsovians. Not everybody has forgotten about you."

Julia felt her eyes sting and quickly blinked. She didn't want to come across as emotional. Even though it was great that she could get a steady food supply, it left her with a big challenge; how to get it over the wall. *Small quantities I can probably smuggle in under my clothes, but no more.* She knew too few people with passes who could come and go.

"I haven't even thanked you for helping us," Julia said as her focus switched back to the little room.

Renia looked at her from across the table, setting her mug down. "You don't have to. I think you're doing a much more dangerous job. The only thing I do is collect food. The hardest part is yours."

Julia finished her drink. Renia was right—it was up to her to come up with a way to get the food into the ghetto. She was suddenly restless and anxious to see how hard it was to get back in. She got up, and Renia did the same.

"I will be back soon, probably on Monday. I'll come up with something— we must find a way," Julia said.

They walked to the front door, and Renia looked at her with alert eyes. "Be careful. I'll be here when you're ready to take the food into the ghetto."

Outside, Julia considered taking the long way back to the ghetto. Life seemed somewhat normal here, and her meeting with Renia had lifted her spirits. *Perhaps there was hope?*

She headed for the checkpoint she'd crossed earlier, walking along the wall. At intermittent intervals, she noticed guards strolling along. They would spring into action whenever someone came too close, telling the offenders to keep their distance. Not that many people were trying this; it seemed they were aware of the rules on this side, as well. If they tried to get near the wall on the other side, the only warning people would receive was a burst of gunfire.

Julia shuddered and walked on. She turned the corner and got to a smaller street, the wall to her left. A group of children played a game of football with a makeshift ball made out of newspaper. It probably wouldn't last long, but they seemed happy for now. A little way down the street walked another patrol, but they seemed unconcerned by the children's proximity to the wall.

She slowed down and watched the patrol approach. When they passed the children, one of the men looked up, shrugged, and walked on. Julia was surprised. On her side of the wall, the game would've been interrupted long ago, and the children would be lucky to go home without any bruises from the Jewish police. A thought struck as she neared the checkpoint. She shook her head. *That's taking it too far.* She joined the queue, took out her papers, and clutched them carefully.

To her relief, there were no Gestapo agents this time. *They must've found whomever they were looking for,* she thought. Maybe it was even the man who'd been ahead of her that morning. The Polish police were searching a woman's bag in front of her, and Julia paid close attention, making sure not to be too obvious. She saw them turn the small purse upside down, its little contents now spread out on a small table. The woman remained calm, and it seemed this was standard practice.

Julia knew there was no way she would be able to smuggle in the amount of food Renia would supply her with. As the woman in front of her packed her belongings back into her purse, Julia looked back. The children had left, their tattered paper ball drifting in the wind. She would have to explore her idea. It might be the only way.

CHAPTER TWENTY-ONE

Julia crossed to the other side of the wall on a dreary Monday morning. This time, there was no Gestapo, and the Jewish police waved her through after a cursory glance at her papers.

Today, she'd decided on a risky but solid plan and was now on her way to an alley.

It was only four meters wide, the wall connecting the buildings on either side, creating a dead end. It fitted Julia's purpose perfectly, and she held her breath as she neared the wall. She knelt at the base and dug her fingers into the wet ground. Whatever pavement had been there before must have been destroyed during the bombings. She kept digging and reached a sandy layer surprisingly quickly. She smiled to herself; this spot would do very well.

*

It was dark when Julia returned to the same spot the following evening. She was relieved to see two silhouettes within the shadows as she neared the wall. They greeted her using the code phrase she'd agreed on with Aga. They didn't introduce themselves, and Julia pointed to a spot where the wall intersected with one of the buildings, blocking the moonlight and making it a slightly darker place.

"Let's start over there. Even though I don't think anybody will pay this alley much attention, let's stay out of sight."

The men nodded and started digging. They'd brought small shovels, which they'd concealed under their coats. Despite the cover of darkness, Julia felt nervous, and she couldn't help but glance toward the street. Finally, all appeared quiet, and she relaxed a little.

The men made good progress. One of them looked up, his face glistening with sweat, illuminated by the faint moonlight. "We're about a meter deep. Good enough?"

Julia peered down the small hole. *If you didn't know it was there, you'd miss it.* She nodded. "Let's dig underneath."

The smaller man crept down and started to dig in the direction of the ghetto. The other man took the pile of sand and clay and scattered it along the wall. *That's smart,* she thought. There would be no pile of dirt to betray their work.

They made good progress, and before long, she could see only the man's legs on their side. The larger man was about to scatter another load of soil when they were interrupted by the sound of an approaching car. Julia and the man froze before he realized his companion couldn't hear anything. He quickly reached down and made two sharp tugs on the man's pants, who immediately stopped digging.

The sound increased as the car approached the adjacent street. Julia and the other man dropped flat onto the cold ground. They were close to the side of the building, but there was nothing to hide behind. Julia felt her heart thump in her throat as the cones of the car's headlights further illuminated the street. The car came into view as it slowed to a stop a few meters past their alley. Julia held her breath. *What are they doing here after curfew?* She looked across to the man, who held a finger to his lips.

The engine died, car doors slammed, and voices spoke in hushed tones. Julia was unable to make out the language. Footsteps echoed in the quiet street, and Julia felt her heart skip a beat when figures appeared at the entry of their alley. She felt her throat constrict as she picked up a few of the words now—German without an accent.

They stood—talking in low tones—for what felt like an eternity. Julia held her breath. *Did they find out about this? Is this the end of my fledgling career as a resistance fighter?* The chill of the ground started to filter through her clothes, and her teeth began to chatter.

She considered her options. These men must be part of the Gestapo. No one else would be on the streets at this time, and certainly not in a car. She couldn't make out their faces, but they appeared to be wearing civilian clothing. An icy chill ran down her spine. *How can I explain why we're digging a tunnel in the middle of the night? I can't end up in Pawiak. Will I be interrogated—tortured?*

They stopped talking, and one of the men stepped out of view. She heard a click as he opened the trunk. A few seconds later, it slammed shut, and he came back into view. Julia's heart dropped. He handed machine guns to the others while he held a small pistol. They turned toward her, and Julia momentarily closed her eyes, waiting for the beam of light and shouts that would spring everybody into action. She didn't know what her companions would do, but she doubted they'd go without a fight.

As she opened her eyes, she saw the men at the alley entrance, standing near a door. The man with the pistol opened it, and the others rushed in. He remained outside, listening as they bounded up the stairs.

Julia looked at the man lying next to her. He shook his head. *Maybe the Germans aren't here for us after all.*

The Gestapo agent struck a match and lit a cigarette, entirely at ease as he leaned against the door.

It didn't take long for the others to return. It was a familiar sight as the men with machine guns escorted another group of men out of the building. Julia counted five as they cowered and stumbled out with their hands on their heads. She felt dread building in the pit of her stomach. They would never fit in the car; it hardly had enough space for the four Gestapo men.

They were taken to the middle of the street, two of the Gestapo men handling them while the others kept their guns fixed on them. Julia wanted to look away, but her eyes were drawn to the macabre spectacle. The men were told to get on their knees, some of them now pleading for their lives.

As the two Gestapo men stepped away, one of the men on the ground decided he wasn't going to wait. He got up and bolted down the street, and for a moment, it looked like the others were emboldened by his courage. They looked up, hesitated, and then the decision was taken out of their hands.

The crackling of the machine guns was deafening. It reverberated against the buildings, and Julia buried her head into the sandy ground as she covered her ears. Shots went on for a good five seconds until all was quiet again.

The Gestapo men spoke in normal voices now. Their leader checked the corpses spread out on the ground. He kicked each of them before lifting his pistol and letting off another shot to the head for good measure. It was unnecessary. There was no way any had survived the barrage unleashed seconds ago.

Satisfied with their work, the agents got back into the car and raced off down the street, paying no further attention to the bodies.

Julia stayed on the ground for a bit—no longer feeling the cold—until the larger man cleared his throat. He held out his hand.

"Time to finish our tunnel," he said impassively, although there was pain in his eyes as well.

She took his hand and nodded. "Their deaths won't be in vain."

*

Two nights later, Julia shivered as she held two kilos of potatoes, a bundle of carrots, and some hunks of dark bread. It would still be another three hours before the sun made its appearance on the horizon. She was alone this time, standing by the little tunnel.

She sat on the ground, her back against the building. As she did, she thought she heard something. Her hopes rose as she put her head down the tunnel entryway. It was faint but unmistakable; there was movement on the other side. She controlled the urge to offer any sound of encouragement, and she pulled her head back to the surface.

The next few seconds felt like an eternity. She held her breath, eyes fixed on the tunnel exit. For a minute, nothing happened. But then, almost out of nowhere, the head of a ten-year-old boy appeared from the darkness. His face was covered in dirt, but a cheeky smile lit up his face.

Julia felt a wave of relief pass over her, and she helped the little urchin up out of the tunnel. As she did, another face peered out as her second—even younger—smuggler made his appearance.

Without further delay, Julia handed them the bags of food. They took them gratefully, and before she knew it, she was alone again. As she exhaled—louder than she realized—she crouched down near the tunnel and indulged in a small smile. She had done it.

And this is only the beginning.

PART III

SOSNOWIEC,

300 KILOMETERS SOUTH

OF WARSAW,

26 JULY 1942

Chapter Twenty-Two

Julia stepped onto the platform, her white dress flapping in the gentle summer breeze. She took a deep breath and enjoyed the fresh country air. The ride had been over two hours—with plenty of delays—and she was happy to get off the train. The village of Sosnowiec was new to her.

The train pulled away as Julia made her way through the tiny station hall. Today's mission carried a lot of weight, and she set out to find her contact.

Even though she walked with confidence—her face betraying not a hint of nerves—she was on high alert as she scanned the people on the village square. She walked down the cobblestoned main street lined with small shops, surprised to see very little German presence here. *You're not in Warsaw, Julia, try to relax a little.*

Sosnowiec was no more than a large village—a suburb of the much larger Katowice—and within fifteen minutes, the clusters of houses started to thin out. She walked until she reached a large farmhouse with a small barn. Confirming she was at the right place—Number 24—she opened the little gate, which creaked loudly, prompting a dog to race around the corner. It wagged its tail and approached her cautiously. Julia stopped and held out her hand, which the dog sniffed and then decided all was okay before it trotted back to the house and flopped onto the porch.

A man in his early 40s opened the front door as she approached. He looked at her with squinting eyes. "Who are you?"

"I'm here to see Aniołek," Julia said without introducing herself.

The man shook his head. "No one by that name here, I'm afraid." He spoke dismissively, but he didn't close the door.

Julia walked on toward him.

"I have news from Warsaw," she said. "Aniołek will want to hear it."

The man studied her as the dog came down the porch steps and nuzzled up to Julia, and she stroked his head. The man seemed to relax as he further opened the door. "Come on in. Aniołek isn't here, but he should be back soon."

She followed him into the kitchen, where he sat down at the head of a large oak table. A wood-burning stove radiated unneeded heat, so Julia sat down as far as possible from it.

"So, let's start with your name," he said. "You obviously know where you had to go, so you know who I am."

She did. Aga had told her to find Józef, and even though he wasn't Jewish himself, he was sympathetic to their cause. Anyone who needed shelter was welcome to sleep in his barn. Because of the remote location, it had been an undiscovered refuge so far. If he were caught, he would be sent to one of the concentration camps, if not worse.

"I'm Krystyna," she said, using the name in her passport. It hadn't taken her long to get used to using it whenever she was on a mission. The only people who still called her Julia were her parents, Aga, and Aniołek—the man she had traveled all this way for.

Józef stood up and reached for two glasses. "Water?"

She nodded, and he handed her one. She gulped it down. He refilled her glass and sat down again. "Aniołek left for Katowice two days ago. He should be back tomorrow."

"Do you know what he was going to do there?"

Józef shook his head. "He doesn't tell me—I don't ask. He might not even be in Katowice, for all I know."

Julia knew what he meant. Even though Józef hadn't been discovered to harbor Jews, it only took one nosy neighbor to report him. *Better to keep him in the dark.*

"You look a little tired," Józef said, interrupting her thoughts. His large eyes looked inquisitive, and there was a slight grin on his face. "Maybe you'd like to rest while you wait for him? There's plenty of space in the barn."

Julia did feel tired. Apart from being thirsty, she was also hungry. Józef seemed to sense it and moved to the countertop. "But first, have some bread and cheese. It's not much, but it's the best I can do. The cheese is homemade, even."

Julia couldn't remember the last time she had eaten cheese.

*

Julia awoke in semidarkness, feeling rested. She lay on the small mattress Józef had shown her, hidden away behind all sorts of farming equipment. Although she didn't know what time it was, the first trickles of sunrise filtered through the cracks in the wooden walls. She figured it must be around four in the morning and wondered why she was awake so early.

Then she heard something. Her ears pricked up, and she heard it again. The sound of very faint footsteps—there was someone in the barn. *Józef never mentioned anyone else.* She reached for her coat, where she kept a small pocketknife.

She sat up and opened the knife. As the person came closer, she could hear their breathing. Julia clenched her fingers tighter around the handle.

The other person was very close, and Julia held her breath. Whoever it was, they knew exactly where to go, and she saw a large hand pull back the curtain and reveal her intruder.

Julia let out a small shriek and dropped her knife.

"Mordechai!" She jumped up and wrapped her arms around the man.

Julia had never been so relieved to see her friend, whose name was Mordechai Anielewicz, although he was better known by his nickname: Aniołek. They broke their embrace, and she picked up her knife. "Why did you think it was a good idea to sneak up to me in the darkness? I was ready to slash you."

"I don't think you would've done much damage with that," he said with a grin as he sat down on the mattress next to hers. He looked tired, but his eyes were as energetic as ever.

"I was back early, and when Józef told me you were here, I didn't want to wait." His face turned serious. "If they sent you all the way from Warsaw, you must have urgent news. The elders know I'll be back next month at the latest."

The elders—the Judenrat, the men put in charge of the ghetto by the Nazis—were tasked with carrying out the Germans' orders, but as Jews themselves, their loyalties lay firmly with their people.

"That's why I'm here. Unfortunately, Czerniaków killed himself a few days ago."

Mordechai looked alarmed. "He did what?" Adam Czerniaków had been the leader of the Judenrat since the ghetto was established.

"He took a pill. The Germans have started mass deportations from the ghetto," Julia continued, and she took a deep breath before saying more. "It started only a few days ago, but they are clearing out entire blocks. The SS shows up in the street and orders everyone living there—men, women, children, elderly—toward a place they call the *Umschlagplatz*. They've set up a square in the middle of the ghetto where they make all these people wait until a train takes them away."

"Do you know where they're taken?" Mordechai asked calmly. His face showed concern—but oddly, no surprise.

She shook her head. "They won't tell us anything other than that they're being relocated to work camps."

Mordechai stood up and paced the small space. His brow furrowed more deeply, and Julia studied him.

"I don't believe they're taking them to work camps at all," he said as he looked at her. "And I'm sure you have your thoughts as well—about what's going on."

There were ghettos in every large city in Poland, and while the Nazis did their best to conceal what was going on, Julia had seen and heard more than most.

"There's no point sending small children and the elderly to work camps," she said. "I've seen women with babies put on those transports. It doesn't make sense." Mordechai's eyes welled up, and he swallowed before continuing. "I don't know much more than you. There were rumors, but now that they've started these transports from Warsaw, it's enough to start taking them more seriously." His voice trailed off. "Especially if it was enough for Czerniaków to take his own life; he must've known more."

"What rumors?"

Mordechai paused as if he were considering not answering. Instead, he looked up and met her eyes. "I think our people are being sent to their deaths."

Julia was quiet for a few seconds, shuddering as she asked, "Will you come back to Warsaw with me? We must do something about this. You know the elders won't."

Mordechai sat down again and shook his head. "Even the elders can't hide behind their fear of reprisals anymore. If this carries on, there won't be anyone left to punish." His voice shook, a hint of anger filtering through. "I will come back to Warsaw, but let me wrap things up here first. I need to return to Katowice tomorrow, but then I'll take the next train back north. I should be there in a few days."

Julia thought about her family, in the ghetto with nowhere to go, while she spent most of her time outside the ghetto—outside the city, even—where she could probably avoid these trains. She felt her chest tighten. *What will happen to them?*

Mordechai interrupted her gloomy thoughts. "We should get some breakfast. It will be a long day for both of us. You'll take an early train back to Warsaw and set up a meeting with the elders for two days from now. There's no time to lose."

She managed a weak smile as Mordechai left. If there was one person she trusted to convince the elders to take action, it was Mordechai.

*

"Cowards, idiots," Mordechai fumed as they left the building.

Julia struggled to keep up as they stepped onto the deserted sidewalk. "Calm down, Aniołek—someone will hear us."

He marched on with great strides, heading toward his home in the ghetto. There would be no support for any form of resistance. *They're going to sit by as the Nazis empty the ghetto, hauling us to our deaths.*

They entered a building a few streets away and headed for one of four small flats. Mordechai's apartment was on the second floor, and he mounted the stairs two steps at a time. Julia knew the other occupants in the building didn't know who he was, and she felt quite safe here. They stepped into his apartment, and Julia closed the door. He stood by the window, deep in thought. She stood near the door and waited.

After a minute, he broke the silence. "What do you think we should do?" he asked, his gaze still on the street outside.

"What do you mean?"

He turned to her. "Do you agree with the council? Is my plan too risky? Shouldn't we fight back?"

"We can't do nothing," she started, carefully choosing her words. "But they're right about retributions. We've seen it in Warsaw, but also the other cities." A few months before, the Gestapo had set up makeshift gallows along the track running into Kraków's central station—bodies of resistance fighters hung there as a macabre warning to those entering the city.

Mordechai nodded. "Do you believe what they said about relocating people to work camps and factories?"

People were put in the backs of trucks—and now on trains—and no one ever heard from them again. *It doesn't add up.*

"No," she answered softly. "But I don't know where they are going, either."

Mordechai turned to her. "They're sent to their deaths—I don't know where to, though."

They were silent for a while. *He's right. There's no other explanation.*

"I have an idea," Mordechai said, sitting down at the small kitchen table, waving her to the other chair. "How many smuggling routes into the ghetto do we have these days?"

"Four. We're close to connecting to one of the main sewers that run under the wall from the east, near the Old Town. Once that's done, we won't have to use the smaller tunnels anymore. And we've started work on more tunnels connecting to the sewers around the city. We should have plenty of options within a week or two."

Mordechai's face lit up. "That would seriously reduce the risk of getting caught, right?"

"Absolutely. And we could smuggle much more, even in daylight."

"That's great news, Julka. Do you think we could use those routes for things other than food?"

She nodded. "I don't see why not."

Mordechai's face was serious, but his eyes twinkled with excitement. "If we find a way to get guns on the other side of the wall, would you help me smuggle them into the ghetto?"

Guns? She shifted in her seat, and he pressed on. "I know it's risky, and when we start fighting them, things may get worse before they get better. But think about your family as well. Don't you want someone to be fighting for them when the Nazis show up in their street?"

Julia swallowed hard. *This is why I joined the resistance.*

"Okay. Let's do it. But how do we get those weapons?"

Mordechai smiled. "I knew I could count on you. Let me talk to some people on the other side. I'll put you in touch with them, and then you can take care of the logistics."

"And when we get the guns, what will we do? People trust the Judenrat." *Even if they shouldn't.*

"Let me worry about that. There are plenty of people who will follow me."

Julia looked at the young man across from her. At only 23, he exuded the confidence of a seasoned general ready to lead his army. She'd follow him anywhere and felt a flurry of excitement bubbling up in her stomach. She was going to get those guns to him, no matter what.

CHAPTER TWENTY-THREE

Natan opened the front door to the apartment and almost bumped into Kasia, who was on her way out.

"Not at the factory today?" Natan asked.

"I was sent home. Sometimes the Germans want me to clear out of the offices in the afternoon. They say they want to check the inventory without me, but I think it's an excuse to get me out of the way."

Natan smiled. Kasia made it her mission to make sure the factory continued to run as smoothly as before. Even though they were producing for the Germans, she couldn't stand seeing the proud Borkowski factory churning out cheap-quality shoes. She insisted the people in the ghetto deserved the best quality and continued to smuggle out shoes for them. From what he'd heard, people were starving on the other side of the wall. They needed every little bit of comfort they could get; warm and dry feet helped.

"You know, if you've nothing better to do this afternoon, you may want to join me on my errand," she said as he was about to take off his shoes. It was a habit he'd picked up at Kasia's—no outside shoes in the apartment.

She never asked him to join her without reason, and his interest was piqued. "Where are you going?"

"Meeting with someone from the other side of the wall. They want to talk about raising the number of shoes we can supply."

"How would it make sense for me to be there?"

For some reason, his question annoyed her as she raised an eyebrow. "Your name is still on the door, you know. And officially, you still work there, as well. Besides, it might be good to see what's going on on the other side of the wall."

He agreed and stepped back into his shoes.

It was a short walk to a small tavern near the ghetto walls. Kasia had a bit of a spring in her step. *She's excited about this—she really cares about the people trapped over there.*

They stepped into the tavern, where only a handful of other patrons sat scattered around a few tables. It was midafternoon, and most people were either at work or had no money to go to taverns. Kasia picked a table in the corner and nodded to the barkeep. He promptly served them two mugs of weak ale. Natan took a sip, and even though it wasn't anywhere near the quality of the brews they'd enjoyed before the war, it was better than nothing. The malty taste relaxed him a little, and he turned to Kasia.

"So, who are we meeting?"

"I'm not sure. I've never met her before, but she comes highly recommended."

"How will we recognize her?"

"My contact told me she'd recognize me."

Natan shrugged and took another sip of his ale while his mind wandered back to earlier that day. He'd spent the entire morning working on assault plans with his cell. Things had changed recently, as Poland's scattered resistance cells had united into one organization: the *Armia Krajowa*—Home Army. It meant Natan's Gray Ranks were no longer isolated, as the Home Army was in direct contact with the exiled Polish government in the United Kingdom. Now it was recognized as the official Polish army—their efforts legitimized, even if the Germans still considered them bandits. He knew the risks he took every day; he'd seen what happened to captured comrades. They were often savagely tortured, sometimes dismembered, and left to bleed to death on the streets of Warsaw. The Germans did not consider prisoner-of-war rights applicable to the Home Army. Natan especially enjoyed missions in which they attacked members of the hated SS and Gestapo. He'd spent the morning planning another attack on the SS headquarters, and he was sure the leadership would give it their blessing.

"Ah, that must be her," Kasia said, interrupting his thoughts.

He looked up to see a blond woman walk in, about a year or two younger than him. She wore a simple black dress, and she scanned the tavern confidently before settling on their table. Her eyes met his, and Natan felt a slight flutter in his stomach. She walked over without hesitation and looked at Kasia after glancing at Natan.

"Are you waiting for Adam?" she asked Kasia.

Kasia nodded. "He seems to be late again today."

The young woman sat down, a hint of a smile on her face. "How do they come up with these passphrases?" She turned to Natan and said, "I thought I was meeting only a woman, so I was a little surprised to see two people sitting at the table. I was about to head out when I decided I could chance it anyway. Not too many other people fitting your description"—she nodded at Kasia—"in this place."

She spoke quickly but with a soft voice, and Natan was mesmerized. She leaned forward and lowered her voice a little as her eyes focused on Kasia. "We appreciate the steady supply coming into our side over the past year." The barkeeper placed a mug in front of her and left without another word. She ignored the drink and continued. "We're almost done finishing a new route, and we could take more shoes into the ghetto—do you think you can supply more?"

Kasia shifted in her chair and took another sip. "I've been very cautious, as it's only me doing this. I don't want to draw any attention."

"Is there anyone who might want to help—some of the other workers, perhaps?"

She's bright, quick. Certainly not wasting any time. He sat back and observed the women's conversation.

Kasia looked thoughtful before responding. "There's a lot of rotation in the factory." She shook her head. "I don't trust anyone there now."

The young woman across from her looked disappointed, but only for a moment. Her eyes lit up, and she said, "How hard would it be to get someone in?"

"You mean to get them a job?"

"Yes."

"New people are coming in all the time. I guess we could give it a shot," Kasia said with a shrug. "Do you have anyone in mind?"

"Not yet, but we have plenty of people on this side of the wall—Poles—who would be willing to help. Let me ask around."

She reached for her drink and took a small sip as her eyes scanned the room. There was something else on her mind. She put her glass down and looked across the table, briefly meeting Natan's eyes before her own shifted back to Kasia. "There's one more thing I wanted to ask."

Kasia remained silent, holding her gaze.

"Do you think you'd be able to supply us with slightly different merchandise?"

"What kind are you thinking about?" Kasia asked, sitting up a little straighter.

"We need to start thinking about defending ourselves properly," the young woman said, looking a little vulnerable for the first time. "Do you think the Home Army might be able to supply us with weapons?"

Kasia's face remained impassive, but Natan sensed her unease. He sat up a little straighter.

"I wouldn't know anything about weapons," she said. "I take care of my part in the factory." Her eyes briefly darted to Natan's, and he gave her an imperceptible nod.

"What's changed that you need weapons?" he asked. "I thought it was food and medicine you needed?"

The young woman looked at him, meeting his gaze with her bright blue eyes without flinching. "You haven't heard?"

"No." He'd heard the rumors, but he wanted to hear it from her.

She took a deep breath as if steeling herself. "The Germans have started clearing out the ghetto. Every day they show up in a different neighborhood, block the streets, and take everybody to a central location. There, these people are loaded up in cattle cars and taken away, a train departing every day."

So the rumors are true. "Do you know where they're taken? I mean, this also happens on our side of the wall."

Her eyes flashed in anger. "It's not the same," she said, her voice rising a little. "It's the occasional truck on this side, when they find people in the resistance. These are people that have made their choice to fight—they know the risks. On our side, it's entire streets. It doesn't matter if you're old, young, or anything in between. It doesn't matter if you can walk or need to be carried there by your family. Everybody goes on the train." She paused for a moment. "The only thing the Gestapo tells us is that these people are taken to work elsewhere in the Reich."

Natan was silent as she took another sip of her drink. He wondered what she'd been through so far. She was young, sure, but he also imagined the resistance in the ghetto wouldn't send just anybody with such a request. *Can I trust her?*

"I hear the Home Army also struggles to find weapons," he said noncommittally.

She looked at him without speaking, her blue eyes studying him curiously.

"But what if we ask around a bit for you?" he said. "I'm sure we can get in touch with some people, right?" He looked at Kasia, who nodded.

The woman sat up, a hint of a smile appearing on her face. "That's all I'm asking for now."

"If we get you the weapons, will you be able to get them in securely?"

She nodded before he finished speaking. "Absolutely."

She's so confident. "Why don't we meet again in three days? We should know more by then."

They stood up, and before she turned away, Natan said, "I'm Lew, by the way."

She looked at him—and he thought he spotted a sparkle in her eyes—and she answered, "I'm Krystyna."

*

Natan spotted Krystyna at the same table they'd shared three days earlier. As he joined her, he noticed she wore a different dress, one that looked almost new. She caught his gaze and smiled.

"These clothes are pretty nice, right? It's the best way not to be stopped by patrols. If I look like a respectable woman, the Germans are less likely to ask me anything. They assume I'm a well-to-do woman out on an errand." She looked completely at ease, her eyes full of anticipation as she leaned forward. "So, did you talk to your contacts in the Home Army?"

On his way over, Natan had dreaded this moment. He'd spoken to Maciek, who had made it clear they had too few weapons as it was, never mind supplying the people in the ghetto. Natan hadn't given up and had pushed to the point where Maciek had warned him—in no uncertain terms—to calm down.

"He said there aren't enough weapons to spare. I'm sorry, Krystyna."

She didn't look surprised as she sank into the back of the simple bench. On the contrary, she looked like she'd expected this.

"That's okay—at least you tried," she said. "I knew it was going to be a long shot. The Home Army hasn't exactly been helping much so far, even though we are trying to organize something of a resistance on our side."

Natan felt bad. "How so?"

"We mostly work with the resistance in the other cities and try to stay connected. Warn each other, sometimes send messages to other ghettos, and when possible, we smuggle food or medicine from one city to the other."

Natan couldn't contain his curiosity. "Is that what you do?"

She paused before answering and looked at him for a few seconds, sizing him up. "Yes. That's exactly what I do. It's why I wear the clothes I do. It's how I know how to blend in and not draw attention." She cast her eyes down. "It's why my name is Krystyna, and I'm a different person from the one I am when I'm at home. It's why I'm sitting with you in this café on the other side of the wall."

Natan was stunned. The young woman sitting across from him looked vulnerable, exposed. He didn't know what to say, and she continued.

"I do this because I believe the only way we can survive is by sticking together. And so far, that's worked. Do you have any idea what it's like to live in these ghettos, away from everyone else? We used to share our streets, our buildings, and our shops until the Nazis took over." She looked up, a faint spark of defiance glowing in her eyes. She didn't wait for his reply. "But we feel so alone. It's as if the rest of the country has decided to leave us. That's why there's a small group of people trying to keep us alive. And I'm proud to step on trains to wherever I'm needed. I've seen more of our country than I did before the war. Every time I leave my family, I'm not sure if they'll be there when I return. And now, with those trains taking my people to God knows where. I have trouble sleeping when I'm not near my parents and my brother."

She choked up, and Natan wanted to reach across the table to comfort her. He hardly knew this young woman, although every fiber of his being ached to help her.

Krystyna sniffled and recovered, clearing her throat. "Look, I really want to fight back. I realize our chances aren't good. The Nazis have unlimited firepower, but I can't stand around and see my people shipped off without a fight. Do you know what I mean?"

More than you know. "Maybe there's another way to get you those guns."

"How so?" She looked surprised.

Unconvinced, even. I need to tell her. I can trust her.

"I didn't tell you the whole story earlier."

She sat back up, looking apprehensive.

"When I said I would ask my contact in the Home Army, I asked my commander."

Krystyna's expression changed again, her eyebrows rising a little. "So you're—"

"I joined the resistance almost two years ago before it was the Home Army, and I was still a teenager." He spoke fast as Krystyna looked at him. "I know a lot of people, people who care about this country and its people—all our people. And they have connections and ways to get things."

Her lips curled into something of a smile. "And you think they will help you now?"

Natan waited a moment before he answered. He didn't want to raise her hopes too much, but he desperately wanted to encourage her. "I don't think it'll be easy, but it's worth trying." He met her eyes. "Is your route into the ghetto still secure?"

"A new route through the sewers will be done this week. It will be the safest passage, so we can use it."

"Good. There's no time to lose. Shall we meet back here in a week?"

She nodded and—to Natan's surprise—reached across the table for his hand, gently squeezing it. "It would mean the world to us, Lew." Then she got up and left without another word.

As he looked at the door closing behind her, his hand felt a little warmer.

CHAPTER TWENTY-FOUR

Julia cleared the checkpoint into the ghetto and carefully placed her papers back inside her jacket. An hour before, she'd felt a little giddy when she saw Lew at their table at the café. She wasn't sure if she'd felt that way because of the hope of good news, or if it was something else . . . even just Lew himself. The Home Army man had made an impression on her from the first time they met. His intense gaze and way with words had set him apart from most other men. He exuded an air of confidence mixed with a sadness she couldn't quite place.

Oh, come on, Julia, stop acting like a schoolgirl.

Lew had good news, and she was on her way to tell Mordechai, who she knew had a meeting with some of the elders. She approached the building, wondering if the meeting was over yet, and spied Mordechai coming out. From his face, it looked like it had not gone well.

"Let's walk," he grumbled as he paced ahead. "I need some fresh air."

"That bad?" Julia struggled to keep up with him. He was a tall man, and she had to take three steps to his every two.

"There's not reasoning with them. Everything I suggest, they shoot down. They still don't think the deportations are a problem." He looked frustrated and kicked at a piece of stone that bounced down the uneven pavement. "How did your meeting with your Home Army contact go?"

She scanned the area around them, and when she was sure they were alone, she answered in a low voice. "He's found a way to get us light weapons."

Mordechai stopped in his tracks and turned to her. "What kind? Pistols? Machine guns?"

"As far I as understood, they would be machine guns." Lew had told her they produced weapons from spare parts smuggled out of the German weapons factories, which they then assembled themselves. Mordechai listened and didn't so much as flinch when she mentioned the price, which she thought was exorbitant. He walked on, although at a slower pace now, looking thoughtful. Julia silently kept by his side—she knew better than to disturb him while he considered the options. They crossed the street into a slightly more crowded thoroughfare. There were beggars everywhere. Even though the ghetto was being emptied, there were still too few places for everyone to have a roof over their head. Evacuated buildings were off-limits to the remaining dwellers, which didn't help. Some people had defied the order and moved into those buildings, only to be dragged out and shot in the street. After that, few people took the chance.

"Do you think we can trust him? The Home Army has never been enthusiastic about helping us."

Julia had considered the same after her first meeting with Lew. She had gone back and forth between suspicion and trust. What if they simply took their money? There would be nothing they could do about it, no one to turn to. But after their second meeting—when she'd told him about what she did and the plight of her people—he appeared genuinely concerned. Even though his commanders had told him they were not going to help, he had gone out and found a way.

"Yes, we can trust him. I trust him, Aniołek," she said, using the nickname she hardly ever used when it was the two of them.

He looked at her hard for a few seconds. She held his gaze, making an effort not to flinch. Slowly, he nodded. "Okay. That's enough for me."

She exhaled in relief. Even though she was confident about the mission, nothing would happen if Mordechai had any doubts.

"How many guns can we afford?" she asked.

"Money isn't our biggest problem—it's about the quality. We have plenty of support inside and outside the ghetto. What we need to establish first is whether we can trust these people producing the guns."

Julia understood. "So, what would you like me to do? Start with one?"

"Yes, and I want you to smuggle it into the ghetto yourself. This is too valuable to be done by the children."

Julia swallowed hard. "That's fine. I can use the new route."

He looked at her. "Is it secure enough? We haven't used it before, have we?"

"We haven't, for the diggers would've broken through the last wall today. I need to check tomorrow."

"Do you trust the people on both sides?"

"Yes," she answered without hesitation.

"Then that's how we'll do it. I need until tomorrow to get the money, so you can tell your contact we're ready to move."

She looked at Mordechai closely as they walked on and neared Nalewki Street. He looked tired, with dark circles around his eyes from the strain of running the resistance in the ghetto without any support.

"What about the elders?" she asked.

He looked up, a spark of defiance in his eyes now. "What about them? To hell with them—we don't need 'em. We need weapons, not their approval. They don't need to know."

They reached the crossing with Nalewki Street, where Mordechai stopped and put his hand on her shoulder. "Julka, when we have these weapons, we finally have a way to fight back. It will make the biggest difference yet in our struggle. Get it done, whatever it takes."

She nodded, and he stepped onto Nalewki Street, disappearing into the modest stream of people. She turned the other direction and made her way home. She needed to see her family before she undertook her biggest mission yet.

*

Natan stepped into the street first, searching for a sign that they were in the right place. Krystyna followed a few paces behind and looked at him inquisitively.

"Are we lost?" she asked, her eyes scanning the street.

Natan's eyes shot between the derelict buildings on the intersection. "No, it should be here. The street we exited should cross with Traktorzystki Street," he said with more confidence than he felt. He walked on and looked up at one of the buildings. "Yes, this is the right street," he said as the sign confirmed this was Number 5 Traktorzystki.

"It's at Number 50, right?" she asked as they passed a group of older men sitting in the shade, engrossed in a six-man chess game.

Natan nodded nervously. Krystyna had come back the very next day, and he'd been surprised to hear they had the money for the guns. Natan's contacts had agreed to Krystyna's request—they assured him that the quality of the firearms would leave no doubt to their craftsmanship.

"It's right up there," Krystyna said, pointing at a gray apartment building farther down. She increased her pace in anticipation, and Natan took bigger steps to keep up with her.

The main gate was open, and they stepped inside a small courtyard. A few men sat smoking hand-rolled cigarettes inside, glancing up only momentarily before returning to their card game. Garbage cans filled the walkway on either sides, and Natan wrinkled his nose.

"Second floor, right?" Krystyna said as she went straight for the first staircase.

Natan nodded and clutched the small duffel bag he was carrying tightly, keeping his eyes on the men in the courtyard. Krystyna was already halfway up the first flight and turned back, looking impatient.

They climbed the stairs, and as they turned to reach the second floor, their path was blocked by a group of four boys. They couldn't be much older than 15, and they looked threatening. Two of them sat hunched on the stairs while the others leaned against the wall and railing. Natan felt the hairs on the back of his neck stand up. *Something's not quite right.* Krystyna stopped and waited for him to catch up.

One of the standing boys spoke. "I've never seen you before—what are you doing in here?"

Natan made an effort to respond calmly. "What's it to you? We're meeting some friends."

"Friends? You look too fancy to have friends here." The boy looked at Krystyna—she was dressed well enough to look out of place. The men in the courtyard wore rags, like these boys.

"What's in there?" the boy asked, slowly getting up, his eyes focused on Natan's duffel bag.

Krystyna glanced at Natan, a flash of panic in her eyes. He wasn't going to let a bunch of urchins intimidate them and took a step forward. "None of your business. Get out of the way—we're already late." He spoke with more authority than he felt.

The boys made no effort to move. They huddled closer, making it impossible for Natan to move past them. As Natan took another step up, he saw the boy leaning against the railing reach into his pocket. A second later, he heard the distinct click of a knife opening. His heart dropped as the boy flipped the knife and casually held it by the side of his body.

The other boy followed Natan's gaze and flashed a crooked smile. "How about you show us what's in the bag?"

I should've brought a weapon, after all. Now, with the four of them and one wielding a knife, the odds were firmly stacked against him.

"Come on, boys—we're just carrying some books." He reached into the duffel bag and grabbed one, one he knew didn't have any money in it. Instead, the decoys were on top. He held it out in front of him, careful to keep it out of the boys' reach.

They looked on, their expressions varying from disappointment to suspicion.

"Give us the bag," the leader said as he and the boy with the knife slowly but menacingly walked down the steps. "Or maybe the pretty girl has something for us?"

Krystyna flinched, and Natan felt anger rising up. Krystyna looked at him, her eyes focused and calm. *Does she know how to fight? I'm not going to hand over that money.* He put the duffel bag down on the floor in front of him and clenched his fists.

The boys seemed to take this as a cue to retrieve the bag, and two of them approached Natan while the others hovered menacingly at the top of the stairs. *A little closer now.*

The leader was now on the same level as Natan and Krystyna, reaching for the duffel bag on the floor. He seemed confident—cocky even—as his friend stood a few steps behind him, casually flipping the knife between his fingers. As the leader grabbed the bag, Natan swung his leg back and kicked the boy in the chest with all the strength he could muster. The boy dropped the bag as he struggled for air. The other boys stood frozen, and the one with the knife hesitated for a moment as his knife locked back into a closed position.

It was all the pause Natan needed as he launched himself at him and wrestled him down on the stairs. They slid down a little, and Natan gripped the wrist of the hand holding the knife. He squeezed with all his might, and the knife clattered to the floor. Krystyna appeared next to him and quickly grabbed it. The other boys at the top of the stairs had recovered from their initial surprise, and Natan could see them bounding down. So blinded by rage, Natan continued to wrestle with the boy on the ground and landed two punches in his face.

"Lew, take this!" Krystyna shouted as she held out the knife. He momentarily let go of the boy to take the blade when the young leader of the group appeared next to her, snatching the knife from her hand. Krystyna dug her fingernails into his face.

The boy lost his balance and fell down a few steps, still holding the knife. He howled in pain and anger as he wiped his now bloody face on the sleeve of his shirt. Natan heard voices in the staircase, and he knew there would be more people here soon. *We need to get out of here.* The other two boys reached him and attacked him as one. Natan lost his balance and they were on him in a flash, pummeling him with their fists.

Through the barrage, he heard a voice call out from a distance. "Enough of this nonsense! Get off him!"

Suddenly, the punches stopped, and he looked up to see the boys standing at a distance, looking up. Krystyna faced the same direction, and Natan looked up, too. At the top of the stairs stood a man who looked both confused and angry.

"Are you Lew?"

Natan nodded and struggled to say "Yes."

"You better come up, then."

Krystyna helped him up, and the boys let them pass, the man's glare having changed their entire attitude. When they reached the second floor, the man led them to the first door, and as they entered, he waved them to a heavy antique wooden table that seemed oddly out of place in the simple apartment. Krystyna sat next to Natan as the man disappeared for a few seconds before returning with three glasses of water.

"Are you feeling a little better?" he asked as he set the glasses in front of them.

Natan drained the glass in one go as Krystyna took a big sip of her own. "I'm all right." He rubbed the back of his head, finding the spot where it throbbed. He could feel a bump forming.

He sat down as well, looking into Natan's eyes with concern. "Well, your vision seems pretty clear. Your eyes looked a little glassy in the stairway."

"Who were those kids, anyway?" Natan asked, keen to take the conversation away from himself. *I'm fine.*

"Just some thugs, like everywhere in this neighborhood." He waved dismissively. "You met them in the wrong place at the wrong time, I guess. They're generally harmless."

"So, do you have the gun?" Natan asked, keen to take control of the conversation.

The man got up and walked to a large wooden crate in the corner of the room. He fumbled with the lock until it clicked, opening the heavy lid with an effort. Natan got up—his head still a little cloudy—as the man took out an object wrapped in a dark sheet. He carefully closed the lid and unrolled the sheet on the table. When he finished, they looked at an MP 40 submachine gun—the weapon of choice for most of the German army.

Natan glanced at Krystyna and saw her eyes widen with fascination.

"This is unbelievable," she said. "But this doesn't make sense. The Germans don't produce this model in Poland, do they?" She picked up and cradled the gun.

The man looked impressed. "You're right. We only work on the Vis pistols in the factory in Radom. We got lucky." Krystyna inspected the gun, and he continued. "As you may know, the Home Army still carries out sorties in the countryside. We caught a German patrol off guard as they were driving through one of the towns near Radom. The two soldiers didn't even put up a fight when we surrounded them outside the village. We didn't believe our luck when we saw they were carrying not just their own weapons, but a case of additional MP 40s and plenty of ammunition."

"I thought the Home Army didn't want to supply guns to us?" Krystyna asked.

He smiled and nodded. "Officially, we're not involved. Let's say the brass doesn't need to know about everything we do."

He stepped over to the chest and took out a small bag filled with 9mm rounds. He placed it on the table and slid it over to Krystyna.

"Do you know how to handle this?" he asked as he started counting out the bullets, placing them on the table.

Krystyna looked up and shook her head. "Not really. I mean, I've seen them before, but I've never actually fired one. But that's not a problem—there will be plenty of people in the ghetto who have. And if they haven't, they'll find out how. What about you, Lew?"

She handed the gun to Natan, and he inspected it, unclipping the ammo magazine and checking the bolt. It gave the satisfying cocking sound he expected. "We have a few of these in our cell. I know how it works, but I've never had the pleasure of shooting one. It's quite bulky, so it's not the best weapon to use for our more stealthy missions. It would be great for any kind of ambush in the streets of the ghetto, though, especially if you're in a building shooting down."

"So you know how to disassemble it?" Krystyna asked as he put it back on the table.

"Oh, for sure. That's easy," Natan answered. "This is an impressive gun, not in the least because anyone can quickly take it apart and fix whatever is causing an issue. It's the perfect weapon to have on the battlefield."

Natan was excited for Krystyna—this was a tremendous boost for her people. He wouldn't mind having a few more of these for the Home Army, but he was here to help her. He looked at the other man, who seemed just as pleased to help, as he showed Krystyna some more of the inner workings of the gun. She paid close attention as he showed her how to load the magazine. Natan wondered how many more guns they could smuggle to the other side. Even if they were lower caliber Vis handguns, that would be better than nothing.

"How about I show you how to take it apart and put it back together?" Natan said to Krystyna. "We won't be able to walk the streets with a fully assembled gun."

She looked grateful, and he took the MP 40 apart in under three minutes. Her eyes never left his hands, and she asked plenty of questions. Then, with all the pieces of the gun now neatly organized on the table, he put it back together. He did this twice more before handing it to her.

"Do you want to try?"

She confidently started disassembling the gun. Natan was pleased to see she was meticulous in keeping all the parts organized. It was the only way to put the gun back together quickly. Natan had found out the hard way when he simply scattered the pieces on the table the first time he tried this in the Gray Ranks training. It had taken him at least three times longer than did the more structured approach.

Krystyna was a quick student, and she managed to put the gun back together within ten minutes.

"Again," Natan said.

The second time, it only took her five minutes.

Krystyna put the gun down and said, "I think I've got the hang of this. Shall we go?"

They took the gun apart, and Krystyna put most of the pieces in the duffel bag, hidden under a thin layer of books. She stuffed the barrel under her shirt to avoid it protruding from the bag later.

They paid the man and shook hands as they stood in the doorway. "Godspeed. You're a brave young woman, and I'm honored to help you. Reach out to Lew when you're satisfied and need more guns. I can't promise more of the MP 40s, but we've got a good setup for the pistols."

"Thanks for everything so far. I'm sure I'll be back soon."

The older man stood at the top of the staircase to make sure the kids wouldn't harass them on the way down. It was unnecessary—the stairs were deserted.

Natan and Krystyna stepped into the quiet street, and she turned to him with a triumphant smile.

"This is a big victory," she said, her eyes glistening a little. "Thank you so much, Lew."

He waved his hand dismissively. "If it weren't for you setting up the smuggling route, this would be useless. Get it across the wall, Krystyna. And tell me when you need more weapons. I'll be here, waiting for you."

She surprised him as she leaned in and gave him a gentle hug. He felt her arms around the small of his back and gently put his hands around her frail shoulders. It lasted only for a few seconds, and then she was off, confidently walking down the street. He waited until she was out of sight before he went in the other direction. As he did, he felt like he was floating on air.

Chapter Twenty-Five

A few hours later, Julia stepped into the wet street on the other side of the wall. She took a deep breath and inhaled the fresh, humid air, suppressing a smile as she walked down the street. She had met Mordechai and handed him the MP 40. He'd been elated to receive the machine gun and impressed to see her so proficient in assembling it for him.

He had then surprised her by repeating the disassembly and assembly process almost as quickly as Lew.

After she left Lew on the other side, she'd kept a low profile as she made her way to a small apartment building almost adjacent to the wall. There, she was let in by an older woman who had been relieved to see her. The door to the small basement was hidden in plain sight, and she'd descended to find the entry to their newest tunnel hidden only by a stack of firewood. Julia was quite pleased with the setup—it would pass most inspections, as the pile sat innocently in the corner of the basement.

They'd dug a small tunnel to one of the main sewer pipes, and it had been only her second time down. It had taken her a bit longer than expected as she struggled to find her way solely on touch. Any form of illumination could give her away, and there were strict rules about always keeping the passages quiet and dark.

On the other side of the wall, she used a short tunnel into an abandoned building. There, she climbed a ladder to emerge back above ground. She'd barely contained her excitement when she walked out into the street and had to stop herself from running. She was delighted to have completed such a critical mission. Most importantly, she had set it up from start to finish. And now Mordechai had given her the green light to continue, to reach out to Lew for more guns. As she turned into Nalewki Street, she looked forward to seeing her parents.

She stepped up her pace and reached the house minutes later. She unlocked the door and found the Grossmanns to be out, their quarters dark. Julia mounted the stairs and opened the door to the apartment, expecting to find her mother preparing dinner—she'd brought some extra rations for dessert. As she stepped in, she was met by silence. She peeked into the small bedroom; two beds were unmade. Her own bedsheets were neatly tucked in. Julia frowned as she returned to the living room. There were some clean dishes in the drying rack, and Julia ran her fingers over the dry plates.

She sat down at the small kitchen table and checked the small clock on the cabinet—it was almost five. There was no reason for her mother not to be home on the Sabbath. There should be candles lining the room—ready to be lit—as they prepared to say their blessings before dinner. *Where is she?*

She stood up and looked out the window. *Wait, where are all the candles?* Even though the sun was still up high in the sky, she expected to see the flicker of candlelight in their neighbor's windows. Instead, they were dark. Down below, no passersby used their street as a shortcut.

Julia felt an unmistakable feeling of dread building up in her stomach.

She dashed to the bedroom, took a deep breath, and opened the only closet in the room. Then she sat for a minute, staring at the empty space. *It can't be.*

Julia stood up, rubbing her eyes as they began to sting. She opened the front door and rushed down the stairs, through the empty apartment. In the street, she ran to the neighboring apartment building. It towered over their little home at four stories high. The main door was open, and she entered the dark hallway, flicking on the lights. She stood in the silence, then strained her ears as she softly walked by the doors of the small apartments—more eerie silence.

Reaching the end of the hallway, she knocked on some of the doors. Julia felt the knot in her stomach tighten as she waited, desperately hoping one would open and one of her neighbors would dispel her fears. Each door remained shut, and she mounted the stairs, repeating the process on the second floor.

When her knocks remained unanswered there as well, Julia leaned to the wall and slouched to the floor in the hallway. The hall lights went dark as the timer ran out. She didn't bother turning them back on but sat in the darkness. Tears now rolled down her cheeks, and she pulled her knees up to her chest. She dropped her head and put her hands in her hair.

The Nazis had come for her family and everybody else on the street. Julia tried to swallow the lump in her throat as she wiped her cheeks. Her parents would have been marched to the Umschlagplatz, where a train was waiting.

Julia stared into the darkness of the hallway, only a sliver of light coming from the staircase.

She tried to get up, but her knees protested, and she slumped back on the floor, drained of energy. She closed her eyes as a terrible realization dawned.

Julia had no one left—she was now completely and utterly alone.

CHAPTER TWENTY-SIX

Julia wrapped her coat a little tighter against the January wind as she left the Miła Street headquarters of the Żydowska Organizacja Bojowa—they called it the ŻOB or Jewish Combat Organization. Mordechai's words still rang in her ears: "Ask if the Home Army are willing to up their weapons supply into the ghetto—we need more."

It had been almost six months since she had smuggled that first gun, the MP 40, into the ghetto. Since then, Lew somehow kept finding guns everywhere, so she'd continued the runs. Mordechai's new, more partisan organization had about 40 guns spread around the ghetto.

She hurried through the streets as she made her way to the eastern checkpoint, avoiding the tunnels. German patrols had intensified on the other side of the ghetto walls, and she needed to be extra careful.

As she passed the empty houses and small apartment buildings, her mind returned to the previous months. Despite more than a hundred thousand ghetto inhabitants dying from disease and starvation in the first year, the Germans decided their plans for the Warsaw Jews weren't advancing quickly enough. They stepped up their efforts, deporting over six thousand people a day from the ghetto. Mordechai had continued to urge the council elders to fight the deportations, but they wouldn't listen until it was too late. As he'd suspected, the trains had not been bound for labor and relocation camps but for a place called Treblinka, not far away from Warsaw. The stories that had come back from people who had come close enough to inspect the camp had chilled Julia's blood.

Upon arrival, the doors of the cattle cars were opened, and SS men stood barking at the terrified people to leave their suitcases and any other possessions on the ramp. The next stop was an undressing area, and then on to their deaths in the most horrifying place of all. Julia shuddered as she pictured the gas chambers. At first, she hadn't believed it could be true. But as more reports came back, Julia had no choice but to accept that this was the fate of the people on the trains. Every morning when she woke up, she thought of her parents, of her brother. How terrifying their last few hours on earth must have been. How they must've clung on to each other as the doors to the gas chambers closed, leaving them in darkness. The desperation they must've felt when they realized the air they breathed no longer brought life.

The ghetto was emptied at a steady pace for two months as two daily trains departed the Umschlagplatz. Then, the deportations suddenly stopped. Over a quarter million people had been sent to their deaths at Treblinka, but now, the 30,000 remaining Jews were allowed to stay. That had initially puzzled Julia, but then it became clear that the German factories and workshops needed to continue to operate. The Germans required their slave labor force.

Mordechai was confident they would return to finish the job, and he had started setting up an armed resistance within the walls—ordering the construction of makeshift bunkers and barricades. Julia passed one of the most extensive fortifications on Muranowski Square and was heartened to see more than a dozen men hard at work. They carried all sorts of debris—from large pieces of concrete to wooden beams—as they fortified buildings and barricades across the square. Mordechai was determined they wouldn't go without a fight when the Germans returned.

It took her a few more minutes to arrive at the deserted checkpoint, manned by the Jewish police. They appeared uninterested as they glanced at her papers to let her through. Her position at Többens and Schultz meant she could still come and go as she pleased.

As she crossed the street, her heart beat a little faster. Despite all the horrors, she'd found a bit of light in the darkness. She opened the door to the café that had become their regular meeting place. Lew was sitting in a corner, absorbed in a book.

He looked up and smiled as she sat, and he put the book down and looked at her with twinkling eyes. "The news is that some of the engineers working on the machine guns are close to finalizing the designs." She let him speak a little longer as she took off her coat, enjoying his enthusiasm. He'd mentioned a while ago that the Home Army was designing its own gun.

"So that means they might start testing the gun as soon as next month."

Julia smiled. "We can use all the guns you can produce."

"Well, it would take a little longer for them to go into production, as we'd still need to set up workshops, but it's very encouraging! Can you imagine— we won't be dependent on taking guns from the Germans or finding those weapons caches all over the country."

He'd told her about the dangerous work of searching for and retrieving the hidden crates buried all over Poland. When the Polish army had surrendered— over three years ago now—they had had the clarity of mind to bury as many of their weapons and as much ammo as possible. Many of the former soldiers were now part of the Home Army, and they would undertake dangerous missions to retrieve these crates. The Germans knew about the caches as well, and if they were caught during these missions, it usually meant a one-way trip to one of the Gestapo dungeons.

"Before those guns are ready, do you think you can help us out with some more of the pistols from the existing workshops?"

Lew nodded. "I think so. We have a steady stream of weapons coming in, and more and more people within the Home Army are sympathetic to what's going on on your side of the wall."

"Ammo, too?"

"I'll do my best, but it should be okay."

She opened her mouth to say something when the door to the café burst open. She jerked her head to look—always worried it might be the Gestapo. Instead, it was a familiar face, and she calmed herself as he approached their table.

"Fredi, what's up?" Lew asked, shaking the other man's hand. Julia knew Fredi from the times the young man had helped carry weapons and ammo in her smuggling runs. She suspected he was part of Lew's cell, but she didn't know for certain and had never asked.

Fredi's eyes were alert, a little nervous even. He scanned the room before speaking softly.

"I thought I'd find you here," he said, focusing on Julia. "I'm afraid I have some urgent news."

Julia sat up, suddenly feeling the familiar dread washing over her. She raised an eyebrow. *Come on, out with it.*

He took a deep breath, his eyes focusing on the table before looking back up. "I was just at headquarters, and we have strong intel that the Germans are preparing something big."

Julia's heart dropped. *This can only mean one thing.*

"The SS is preparing to come into the ghetto again soon."

They were quiet as Fredi's words sank in. Julia looked at Lew; the twinkle in his eyes had faded. Fredi seemed almost apologetic as he fumbled with a napkin on the table.

"You're sure it's the SS?"

Fredi nodded. "As sure as we can be with what we heard. Whatever's going on, there's a lot of movement near the larger SS locations. Our scouts also report more movement around the checkpoints."

Julia was nauseated. "They're going to resume the deportations . . ."

Lew spoke up quickly. "We don't know that for sure. They might have different reasons for coming in." He sounded unconvincing.

"We always knew they were going to come back," Julia said. "They were never going to leave us be." People were clinging on to whatever scraps of life they still had, with food rations far below what they required. The only reason people were still alive was the organized resistance and the continued food smuggling. Famished children took their chances scaling the walls for half a loaf of bread every day.

"What are you going to do?" Fredi asked, interrupting her thoughts.

She looked up, not sure how to answer. *What are they going to do if I run now? I'd throw away everything I've been fighting for.*

"I'm going to go back to the other side and warn Aniołek," she said as she stood up. "Whatever the Germans send our way, we're going to defend ourselves."

Lew looked at her with admiration as he stood up. "And we will help you in any way we can."

Julia looked at the tall, slender man and felt a wave of affection wash over her. Without thinking, she stepped closer and wrapped her arms around him, hugging him hard. His hands moved on her back, and Julia leaned into Lew's embrace. *Maybe everything will be all right.*

"Whatever guns you can get us, sooner would be better than later," she said, stepping out of the embrace.

Lew was all business again as well. "Meet me here in two days; I'll speak to my commander."

"Sure." Julia quietly pressed her hand on Fredi's shoulder in thanks and then turned and left the café, controlling the urge to look back.

*

Natan waited in a small room. He knew he'd been well on time—he'd checked the small clock in the hallway before entering. What's keeping Maciek?

Pacing the room, he considered his approach. He wanted to help Krystyna and make more of a difference. When he'd left the café the day prior, he'd reached out to his usual connections for more guns. The response had been disappointing, with all but one saying they were sorry, but they had been instructed not to sell any more guns to anyone outside the Home Army. That left his commander—Maciek was sympathetic to the Jewish plight but had always toed the Home Army party line.

The door opened, and Maciek hurried in. He looked tired, dark rings lining his eyes.

"What was so urgent you needed to see me right away?" he asked. "I'm not used to summonses from you." Irritation was evident in his voice as he sank into one of the chairs.

"I'm sorry, but this is important." Natan would not waste any time. "I'm sure you're aware the Germans are preparing to move into the ghetto any day now?"

Maciek sighed and rolled his eyes. "Not this again, Lew. I told you we can't spare any more guns."

"I know, I know. I wanted to ask if you knew anything more about it?"

His commander looked up at him, squinting. He looked thoughtful before answering. "There's been significant movement in the SS divisions, enough to suggest they're going to round up more of the people in the ghetto, yes. We have some sources working within the police force confirming this. What's it to you?"

So it's true. Maciek was typically well informed and quite willing to share intelligence with his cell.

"Well, I know we can't pledge any additional weapons to the people there," Natan started, and Maciek nodded. "But they've been preparing for this inside the ghetto walls, building barricades and—"

Maciek raised his hand, silencing Natan. "Come on, Lew, let's not play games. I know you've been helping the ŻOB for a while now. Whatever happens unofficially, that's your business. But as your commander, I can't pledge anything extra unless the command approves it." He stood up and offered a small smile. "Ask me what it is you want, Lew."

"I want to fight with them when the SS moves in. I don't want to stand by and do nothing. We need to help them."

Maciek looked at him, and for a moment, Natan thought his commander would acquiesce. But then Maciek shook his head. "Absolutely not."

Natan felt deflated as Maciek continued. "I can look the other way when you're not directly involved. Hell, I'm proud of what you're doing, even if I can't say so officially. But I can't have my people fighting when the government in London is telling us to back off. I'm sorry, Lew—it's not going to happen."

"But aren't the Jews in there as Polish as we are?" Natan tried. His disappointment was starting to make way for anger, and his ears prickled.

Maciek suddenly looked cross. "Lew, enough. You're not going to join the fighting. That's an order."

Natan opened his mouth, but Maciek was already at the door, turning around. "And one more thing. Don't think of summoning me on such short notice ever again."

With that, he stepped out and closed the door with a loud thud, leaving Natan alone with his thoughts.

Natan stood for a moment, not sure what to do. He was furious, and he had only barely managed not to storm after his commander. *How can he be so indifferent?*

He moved to the door, grabbed the handle, and paused. Krystyna's face flashed before him. Could he simply let her fight her own battle while he waited on the other side? It would be easy for him to find a weapon, maybe even a machine gun. *I can make a real difference.*

But that would be ignoring a direct order from his commander. He opened the door and stepped into the hallway. This was one of the smaller hideouts for the Home Army, and it was pretty quiet. As he descended the narrow stairs, he saw the familiar face of Fredi near the front door. He caught up with him, and they left the house together.

It was a sunny but freezing January afternoon, and puffs of vapor came from his mouth as Natan spoke. "Do you think I should help Krystyna when the Germans move in?"

Fredi chuckled. "I was wondering when you'd come up with that."

"What do you mean?"

"You seem quite fond of her."

Natan stopped as Fredi walked on a few paces before turning back. "I admire what she's doing," Natan said. "I don't know a lot of women—or men, for that matter—who take risks as she does." He caught himself. "I'm not sure I would call that being fond of someone."

Fredi smiled. "I know what I saw yesterday, and whenever you speak about her. Admit it, Lew—you like the girl. And I can't blame you."

Natan caught up with him and considered his friend's words. Perhaps he did like Krystyna for a bit more than just her bravery. "It doesn't matter now," he said dismissively. "Right now, they need our help."

The smile hadn't entirely disappeared from Fredi's face. "So, what do you suggest? Did you get some extra guns?"

"Not really," Natan said as they walked on, readjusting his cap to shield his eyes from the sun. "But I still think we can help them."

"Okay, I'll bite. How?"

"I'm thinking of going in through the smuggling route."

Now it was Fredi's turn to stop. "You're crazy. Did you talk to Maciek about that?"

Natan nodded. "He's not keen."

"I bet he's not! It's the worst plan I've ever heard. The Germans are moving in with a large force. You know what happens when they set their minds to something, right? And what do you think will happen if they catch you? You'd be lucky to be put on a train with them—'cause if they find out you're not a Jew but a member of the Home Army, they'll send you off to a Gestapo torture chamber." He gave a low whistle.

"They'd never find out." *I'd die before that happens.*

Fredi shook his head in disbelief. "Don't do it, Lew. You'll be on your own. You don't know how well those Jews have trained. They'll probably be overrun; how many weapons do they actually have over there? Stay on this side, help them smuggle weapons across the wall, and wait for an opportunity on our side. You know we are here for you, right? You can't go rogue like this."

Natan wanted to argue, but he looked at his friend. *Maybe Maciek and Fredi are right.*

As he said goodbye to Fredi, Natan turned in the direction of Old Town. He wasn't going to break his promise to Krystyna.

CHAPTER TWENTY-SEVEN

It was still dark when Julia awoke. It took her a few seconds to realize she was in the ŻOB headquarters with Mordechai crouching down beside her.

"It's starting—let's go," he said as more people around her were roused from their sleeping spots.

Julia was now wide awake and got up, fully dressed—she hadn't bothered even to remove her coat and shoes for sleep—and she quickly followed the other people. As she descended the stairs, the basement was open, and several younger boys were carefully carrying small guns and bombs upstairs from their weapons cache. Mordechai was already in the largest room, a living room converted into their briefing area.

Julia was the only woman among the seven fighters, some of the most experienced and loyal fighters of the ŻOB. They had been handpicked by Mordechai for today.

All eyes were on Mordechai, and other than the shuffling of feet by the boys carrying weapons into the room, no one spoke as they waited for him. The boys neatly placed the guns on tables near the walls and hurried out as Mordechai addressed the group.

"It appears the warning we received from our Home Army contacts was correct," he said as he looked into the room, his eyes fixing on Julia a little longer than on the others. "The SS has entered the ghetto through the southeast checkpoint. From what we've heard, they have already started emptying some of the buildings there. A train has also been seen moving into the Umschlagplatz."

Julia swallowed hard and looked at the faces of the men around her. There was a mix of fear and determination in their eyes.

"We knew they were going to come back, but they don't know that we're waiting for them," Mordechai continued, raising his voice. "They think they can come in here and simply take us away like sheep to the slaughter. You're here this morning as leaders of your small communities."

He was silent for a moment as the tension in the room increased, and Julia realized she was holding her breath. She exhaled when Mordechai continued.

"But today, we fight back. Let there be no mistake about it. We will be outnumbered and outgunned, and only a few of us can claim any fighting experience." The men around Julia shuffled on their feet—most of them had fought in the Polish army during the first German siege. "But we have the element of surprise, and we have one thing they don't: We're fighting for the lives of our children, our families, and our people. We're fighting for survival."

Mordechai moved to the table and picked up an MP 40, perhaps the first gun Julia had smuggled into the ghetto. He slung it over his shoulder and looked at the men.

"There's no more hiding our weapons. Let's show those Nazi pigs we will not go quietly!" His voice now boomed through the room—his jaws clenched, his eyes burning. The tension in the room was palpable as the men moved toward the table to pick up their weapons.

"Go to your stations and follow the plan," Mordechai said when they were all ready to go. "May God be with you!"

The men let out a mighty roar and filed out of the room. Julia remained in her place and looked to Mordechai.

"Let's go," he said. "I want to know if there really is a train at the Umschlagplatz."

Outside, Julia was surprised to see a different group of men waiting for them. Mordechai nodded at them, and they quickly headed down the street. It was quiet here, as people were still asleep and unaware of what was happening on the other side of the ghetto. The Umschlagplatz was only a few streets from their headquarters on Miła Street, and the walk took less than two minutes. The cold, bright white lights illuminating the area left no doubt the transport was back in operation. As if on cue, the distinct sigh of a steam engine coursed through the air. Voices on the other side of the wall spoke in the harsh tones of the language Julia had grown to detest: Germans preparing a transport.

"Quick, follow me," Mordechai said in a hushed tone as they moved away from the Umschlagplatz. They ran back through Miła Street toward the southeast checkpoint.

Silence was replaced by voices in the distance, quiet at first but soon echoing around the mostly empty buildings. Panicked cries cut through the morning air, and Julia clutched her pistol a little closer to her chest. The SS were bursting through front doors.

Instead of going straight to the source of the sounds, Mordechai led the group in a wide arc and entered the courtyard of a ruined office building. The other side of the building faced Zamenhofa Street, where the Germans were rounding up the people.

After crossing the courtyard, they found shelter in one of the rooms of the building. Mordechai turned to the group. "We're going to stop that deportation," he whispered, barely loud enough to hear. Julia strained her ears as her heart skipped a beat. *Stop the deportation?*

Mordechai explained his plan, and they all nodded. It was bold and straightforward. "If you have doubts, speak now. If you're not up for it, walk away now. Once you follow me out there, though, there's no turning back."

No one spoke, their faces set in grim determination.

"Very well, let's go."

The other side of the street was brightly lit. The SS had brought *Kübelwagens*, the cars' headlights lighting up Zamenhofa Street. The scene in front of them was familiar, but it still shocked Julia. There were at least 200 people crowded on the street. Families with young children and the elderly stood lined up outside their homes. *Just like Papa, Mama, and Olek.*

All around them, SS soldiers manhandled people for no reason, kicking out at random for unknown infractions of the rules. A young man protested when what appeared to be his wife was pushed to the ground. He was pulled away from the group, his face contorted with a mix of fear and anger as he lashed out at one of the SS men. Two others approached him and kicked him in the back and then the groin as he doubled over on the pavement. One of them then took out a pistol and calmly shot the man twice in the back of the head. As he lay motionless on the ground, the woman he'd stood up for shrieked from the column of people.

One of the SS men then shouted, silencing her immediately. She turned her head away and continued to sob quietly as another woman next to her tried to console her.

Farther down the column, more shots sounded. People tried to resist being taken to wherever it was they were going, and the SS had made short work of their protests. The column was now almost silent.

Mordechai snuck away from the building, toward the column of people, as soldiers were distracted by something going on. He reached the group of people at the front and took his place on the side. He looked back, indicating for the others to follow his lead.

One by one, the young men around Julia did the same, and before long, they were all in the group of condemned. Julia steeled herself, took a deep breath, and quickly checked the magazine of her pistol. It was fully loaded, and without another thought, she dashed from her hiding place toward the front part of the column.

Her heart was pounding. Within seconds, she'd crossed the short distance and now joined the people in the group.

She was just in time as a whistle shrieked, followed by a command in German.

"Los geht's!" Let's go!

The column started moving down the street toward the Umschlagplatz.

Julia kept a close eye on Mordechai, only a few rows ahead. She scanned the area and saw SS men calmly walking on either side of the column. They looked at ease, chatting with each other as they walked in pairs. They had little to fear from these people, lifted from their beds and out onto the streets in little more than ragged clothes.

They reached the corner of Zamenhofa and Niska Street, and Julia's throat constricted a little. She swallowed, but her throat was dry, and she had to suppress a cough. She kept her eyes on the back of Mordechai's head, making sure not to lose sight of him.

When the whole procession had rounded the corner, she saw a slight movement of his head. It was easy to miss, but it was enough for Julia. She drew her pistol and took a few steps to the side of the column. As she did so, she saw Mordechai step out of the group in front of her, and she took the final steps herself as well.

Suddenly, she was no longer part of the group of people as they moved past her. Time appeared to slow down as she saw Mordechai in front of her, slinging his MP 40 from under his jacket as he aimed it at the SS soldiers at the front. Their careless demeanor changed as the horror of the situation dawned on them. Small bursts of fire erupting from the MP 40's barrel accompanied the unmistakable roar of automatic gunfire. The SS soldiers—surprised and caught off guard—didn't stand a chance as a hail of bullets ripped through them.

Behind Julia, the sound of more modest gunfire drew her attention as she turned and saw the other fighters aiming at the SS men nearest them.

The people in the column responded in different ways. Some shrieked in panic and confusion while most ducked to the ground. Those closest to the resistance fighters grabbed their chance and fled into nearby buildings as the orderly column changed into an unorganized swarm.

With most people either running or on the ground, a new problem presented itself. The SS soldiers guarding the other side of the column had seen what had happened and had more time to respond. Some found cover in the buildings or behind debris and were now in an excellent position to return fire.

Julia heard more guns clattering into action on the other side and threw herself to the ground. She turned her head toward the source and saw a retreating SS soldier. He was on his own and blindly firing into the crowd. He was within reach of Julia, but he hadn't spotted her yet. She raised her compact Vis 9mm and squeezed the trigger. The gun recoiled in her hands, and she steadied herself for another shot. The soldier was still standing and had heard the shot. He turned toward her, their eyes locking for a moment. Julia quickly squeezed the trigger twice more, praying as she did so. She heard the rattle of the machine gun and closed her eyes as she waited for the bullets to hit.

The sound stopped, and she opened her eyes. The soldier lay on the pavement, his gun next to him. She had no time to celebrate her victory as there was more automatic gunfire from the back of the procession, followed by cries of anguish.

More soldiers had come to the source of the sound, and they had quickly taken out some of her fellow fighters, who now lay motionless on the ground.

"Everybody down, now!" they shouted. The few people that continued to run were swiftly shot.

Julia looked to where Mordechai had been. Her heart dropped; he was unaware of the approaching soldiers. He turned to his left, and the muzzle of his MP 40 shot more fire down an alley. Then, it stopped abruptly, and she saw the surprise on his face. The gun had jammed.

A soldier approached Mordechai from his blind side as he struggled to unblock his weapon. The soldier raised his gun but moved closer to get a better shot.

Julia didn't hesitate—and lifted her gun. With only a few bullets left, she gauged that the soldier was within range. She aimed and fired twice, getting up and moving toward the soldier and Mordechai as she did. The soldier looked in her direction, and she cursed. She'd missed. Only three bullets left as her heartbeat pounded in her head. The soldier looked surprised and, for a second, didn't respond. Mordechai had also heard the shots and turned toward the soldier—now only a few meters away from him. The soldier aimed at Julia, and Mordechai took two big steps toward him and then launched himself at the man.

The soldier tried to aim his gun at Mordechai instead, but he was too late. They tumbled to the ground, the gun sliding away from them.

Julia kept running toward them, expecting a bullet in her back at any moment. Despite her fears, she didn't look back. To her horror, she saw the soldier was a much better fighter than Mordechai. It didn't take long for the soldier to gain the upper hand, and he was now on top of Mordechai, pinning him down. Mordechai struggled, but the German was too strong.

Julia was about ten meters away when she saw a flash. The soldier had drawn a knife and was aiming for Mordechai's throat. In a massive effort, her lungs protesting at every step, she sprinted closer, then stopped and took aim from a few meters away, as the German moved his arm down for the kill.

Julia closed one eye and aimed for the soldier's chest. Two loud bangs erupted in the morning sky, drowning out all other sounds around her. She heard a loud thud as she ran on, ready to fire her last bullet.

To her relief, she found the German soldier slumped beside Mordechai.

Mordechai looked up with big eyes, his shirt covered in blood.

"Are you okay?" Julia asked, alarmed by the blood he was wiping off his face.

He patted his chest. "Not my blood," he said as he quickly got up.

Before they could say anything else, there was more gunfire behind them. The SS reinforcements were now indiscriminately shooting at anyone that moved.

Julia's eyes went back to the dead soldier. The bullet had taken half the man's face, and she stood frozen in place. The sound around her faded as she looked at the man in horror. *I did this. I killed a man. But I had to. It was him or Mordechai.*

"Julka!"

She turned to see Mordechai looking at her with urgency. Her ears popped, and the sound of gunfire and screaming people came rushing back. "We have to go, now!" Mordechai screamed.

She took one more look at the dead soldier before Mordechai pulled her away, dragging her to take cover in an old grocery store. As they did so, the gunfire behind them increased as the SS soldiers turned their guns on the helpless people in the street.

They escaped through the back door of the grocery and returned to their headquarters a few minutes later. The area north of Zamenhofa had been relatively quiet, with the Germans focusing all their attention on the sortie Julia and Mordechai had escaped.

Mordechai didn't waste any time as he barked orders at the group of messengers waiting around.

"Tell all the outposts to attack anything or anyone wearing a German uniform."

The young boys and girls rushed out of the building, anxious to spread the word.

Julia looked at the young leader of the resistance and handed him a towel. "Here, clean yourself up a little, Aniołek," she said.

He did so without protest and seemed lost for a moment. Then, as if struck by lightning, he looked at Julia with clear eyes. "You must go to Muranowski and tell the men what happened."

She nodded but didn't move. "What are you going to do?"

"I'm going to stay here for now and coordinate our defense. They will come back with more men soon enough. They won't accept their defeat so easily."

"We lost a lot of good people there, Mordechai. We barely made it out ourselves."

He nodded sadly. "I know. But we can't let their deaths be in vain. Go now."

She sighed softly and headed for the door.

"Julka."

She turned at the doorpost.

"Thank you . . . for saving my life back there."

She said nothing, the look between them enough.

"And be careful out there. I can't lose you."

CHAPTER TWENTY-EIGHT

O nly a few hundred meters away but separated by the ghetto wall, Natan looked out a narrow window. When he'd heard reports of the SS moving into the ghetto, he'd taken his pistol—he was now senior enough in the Gray Ranks to carry his own—and a few homemade Molotov cocktails for good measure. He'd slipped out of the apartment while the first rays of sunshine made their way across the horizon. It hadn't taken him long to realize the Germans were entering the ghetto through several checkpoints, and he avoided the crowded southeastern gate.

Instead, he'd found a small house near a spot where the wall turned a corner on the north-eastern side. He knew this house was abandoned—like the adjacent houses—as they'd been heavily damaged during the initial fighting. It suited his purpose just fine, and he'd settled in.

Several columns of SS soldiers on their way to the ghetto had already passed, heavily armed—most of them carrying MP 40s and Mauser submachine guns—and he wouldn't stand a chance in a firefight.

Instead, Natan had decided to wait for the pairs of guards patrolling the ghetto perimeter. Plenty of people would try to escape once news of the SS's arrival spread on the other side. He was determined to make sure at least some people would succeed. He'd take out as many guards as he could.

He looked up and down the street. There was gunfire coming from the other side of the wall, but this side of the street was empty. Maciek would be furious if he found out Natan had gone rogue.

Natan peered out a little, craning his neck, and saw two men walking in the shadow of the wall. It was hard to make out their uniforms in the semidarkness, but there was no mistaking the rifles slung over their shoulders. The faint orange glow of a cigarette lit up as the men approached his position.

A wave of adrenaline shot through Natan's veins. He quickly looked to the other side of the street—still deserted. The men were in no rush, and Natan estimated it would take them some thirty seconds to reach his spot. He took out his pistol and checked the magazine—eight bullets. The distance between his second-story window and the wall was only four—maybe five—meters, and it would be an easy shot for him, especially if they kept their current pace. He'd have the advantage of his elevated position, but more importantly, the element of surprise.

Natan was pleased to see they had their heads down, occasionally looking up at the wall but never in the other direction. He crouched down on his knees and raised his pistol, using the window frame for extra support. He aimed it at the spot where he expected the men to pass and focused his eyes slightly to the left.

The sound of voices increased, and then the figures entered his peripheral vision. He breathed in and held his breath as the first man entered his sights. Without hesitation, Natan pulled three shots, aiming for the man's chest. The Vis 9mm responded immediately, the sound reverberating against the walls of his small hideout.

The man sank to the ground, and before his partner could respond, Natan had moved the barrel of his gun a little to the left and released another three shots. The man didn't stand a chance as the bullets tore through his chest and neck. One of the bullets hit the wall as it exited through the other side of the man's throat.

The first man lay motionless on the pavement, but the second guard hadn't been quite as fortunate. He lay gurgling in the quiet street, choking on his own blood. Natan considered applying a coup de grace and aimed his pistol at the man's head but then thought better of it. *How many innocent people had these men left to die as they tried to escape the ghetto?*

The man started coughing as Natan put his pistol away. It took a few more seconds before a guttural choking sound ended in silence. Natan got up, ready to move to the next hideout a little farther down the wall.

As he moved toward the back of the room, he suddenly heard the unmistakable sound of boots on the pavement outside. They were close, and he stepped back to the window, carefully peeking out. An entire column of SS soldiers marched—no, they were running—down the street. To his horror, they were headed straight in his direction, and they would reach the corpses of their compatriots within seconds.

Natan stood frozen in the little room, clutching his pistol. There were two bullets left in the magazine, and he had a few extra stuffed in his pockets. The approaching column of soldiers slowed down outside, voices filtering through.

He opened the magazine of his Vis 9mm and carefully refilled it. He then listened to the voices below, staying low and out of sight.

"They're still warm," one of the voices said. "Whoever did this is still close."

"We should search for the Banditen responsible," a high-pitched voice said.

There were murmurs of assent, and Natan estimated there were at least a dozen men below his window. He wouldn't stand a chance if they found him. Even if he held off a number of them, his pistol was no match for the automatic weapons they would indeed be carrying.

"We need to assist in the ghetto—need to get to the gate down the road," a new voice said with authority.

Natan's hopes rose—maybe they wouldn't search for him after all. He held his breath.

This time, there were plenty of grunts below. This new voice didn't have the support of the group.

"I say we quickly search the area here and then go to the Jew zone."

It was the same high-pitched voice receiving plenty of support. Natan's heart sank as the soldiers below agreed to search for him. He knew they would find him if he stayed here, but he didn't know where to go. If he moved, they would surely hear him. He pulled his little duffel bag closer as the soldiers below argued about the best way to split up.

"What if there's an ambush? What if we're outnumbered?"

"Nonsense, we'll find them. They must be in one of the houses here."

Natan reached for one of the bottles in his bag and unscrewed the cap, the smell of lighter fluid penetrating his nostrils. He carefully stuffed a rag into its neck. This was his only chance, and he took a deep breath as he quickly peeked down from the window—the soldiers were still there.

He lit a match—the sound as it caught fire sounding like a roar—and held it to the rag. Its flame slowly grew, and Natan quickly turned the bottle upside down, making sure the bottom of the rag was now soaked in lighter fluid. He waited as the flame slowly crept down the rag. It seemed to take forever, but when he was sure it was lit correctly, he got up and threw the bottle out of the window, aiming it at the middle of the group.

He was out the door before he heard the swoosh behind him. It took only a second for agonized screams to pierce the air as he practically jumped down the stairs. His Molotov cocktail had found its mark.

He clutched his pistol, his finger on the trigger, reached the ground floor, and raced through a ruined living room—the bombardments had knocked down most walls. The heat of the bomb's fire in front of the house and the smoke filtering in stopped Natan from firing a few shots into the smoking inferno. There was no need to draw more attention to his position, revealing him to whomever might have survived outside. The cries died down, and the roar of the fire was the only sound.

As he opened the back door, the cold morning air streamed in, and he took a deep breath. He quickly wiped a few beads from his forehead before venturing out to the quiet alleyway behind the house.

With his heart pounding, he set out, keeping his pistol firmly clasped in his hands. When no German soldiers appeared, he quickly sprinted away.

He made for the main road at the end of the alley, where he could cross into a maze of abandoned buildings and sewer passages. He sprinted past the houses, anxious to get as far away as possible. Almost at the end of the alley, he was hit hard on his shoulder and tumbled onto the ground.

He landed on the ground, and the pistol slipped out of his grasp. He checked himself but felt no blood. Then, surprised, he looked to where the impact had come from.

Only two meters away lay another young man, rubbing his head, his eyes unfocused. He started to get up, and Natan saw the skull on his collar. His blood ran cold. *What is someone from the Death's Head unit doing in the city?* He'd heard about the *SS-Totenkopfverbände* division before, but they operated only in the concentration camps as far as he knew. The men in these divisions acted without mercy, and would kill babies if they were told to.

The other man's eyes were starting to clear, and he looked around. Their eyes met, and Natan saw the man's look of surprise. For a second or two, neither of them moved, sizing each other up. The German then spotted Natan's pistol—still out of reach—and his expression changed.

"You're the bandit!" he uttered in the high-pitched voice Natan had heard earlier. The man grimaced as he tried to get up and slumped back onto the ground.

That was the opening Natan needed. He turned on his side—ignoring the searing pain in his shoulder—and reached for his Vis 9mm. He used his other arm to steady himself while aiming toward the German.

The SS soldier had also reached for his sidearm, and Natan saw the flash of a Mauser pistol. It took all the strength Natan had to aim his gun—using his injured arm—at the center of the German's body. When he squeezed the trigger, he yelped as the force of the recoil shot through his arm, the pain bringing tears to his eyes as the pistol flew out of his hands, and he lost all strength in his arm—the pain of his shoulder immobilizing him. As he lay in the cold alley, nursing his shoulder, he waited for the shot that would end it all.

But the German made no sound. Natan used his good arm to sit up, wincing in pain as he did. The German sat against a wall on the other side of the alley, staring at Natan. His hand was still wrapped around the Mauser resting on his lap, but something was off. The man's eyes were hollow—he was dead.

Natan got up, the pain in his shoulder now a constant throbbing, and moved closer to the German. He was amazed to find a small hole in the man's uniform, below the skull insignia on his chest. A dark stain was forming around it; Natan had made the shot of his life. The bullet had struck the man in the heart, killing him instantly.

Natan took the Mauser from the man's death grip and pocketed it. He was about to turn away when he thought to reach down and unclip the skull insignia from the collar. Natan studied it; it was much lighter than he'd expected, the weight of its symbolism weighing heavier than the mere few grams in his hand. Then, he placed it in his inside pocket and limped away, anxious to leave the dead Nazi in a forgotten Warsaw alley.

CHAPTER TWENTY-NINE

It had been four days of constant fighting, and Julia was exhausted. She had spent her time moving across barricades, fighting the Germans wherever she could. Their enemies were well equipped, all of them carrying automatic weapons and a seemingly infinite amount of ammunition. Whenever they thought they'd pushed the SS men back, a new squad would show up.

The Jewish fighters didn't have the luxury of reinforcements. Instead, they took whatever break they could when there was a lull in the fighting. The gunfire never ended.

In their latest hideout, there were men, women, and even children hiding among them now. People had flocked to the barricades for protection among the fighters. Whenever she had a bit of space, she invited people to hide in their fortified buildings.

They were fighting a lost battle. There were too few armed fighters to stop the deportations, and the SS had been smart enough to keep them occupied and pinned down while they hauled people to the Umschlagplatz using other streets. Despite this, Julia and the rest of the fighters still had their small victories. Their intimate knowledge of the little streets, alleyways, and booby-trapped buildings gave them a slight advantage whenever the Germans were foolish enough to engage them off the larger thoroughfares.

In the distance gunfire droned on, but it was mercifully quiet in her street. However, Germans could be around the corner, preparing for their next attack. She crawled to the front of their barricade, nothing more than a haphazard pile of stones, sand, and debris. It blocked one of the main passages through the ghetto, and fighters were hiding in the windows to the side of the street. The street was relatively narrow, so it was hard for the Germans to reach them.

One of the boys in her squad, Tanek, kept watch, peeking over and around the barricade every few minutes. It was a dangerous job, for there had been reports of German snipers.

Tanek turned around as Julia approached. "All clear the last time I looked."

"Good—let's hope it stays that way. We could all do with a little rest." She sat on a big stone next to him. "It's been a while since any of the messengers came by here. I wonder what's going on on the other side."

The boy nodded. "It seems like everything's pretty much the same everywhere. Last I heard, they were clearing the streets around Gęsia."

That wasn't surprising, either. The Germans would want to make sure access to their trains was secured.

Tanek stood up and looked at her inquisitively. "Did you hear that?"

Julia listened carefully. There were voices at the other end of the street. She didn't have to listen hard to hear the familiar harsh German tones.

Tanek carefully peeked over the barricade and then quickly fell back down to the ground. "At least fifty soldiers!"

"Any heavy armor? Tank?" Julia asked.

He shook his head. "Only soldiers. But it's a bit odd—they're just standing there, almost out in the open."

Julia couldn't contain her curiosity and peeked around the barricade, making sure to use a different spot than Tanek had used. The SS soldiers stood on the other end of the street, at least 200 meters away. Those in the front held their machine guns ready, but they were not in formation. *Why aren't they preparing to attack?*

She considered her options as she lowered herself back to the safety of the barricade. The Germans were out of range for most of their weapons—their fighters carried pistols, a single MP 40 in one of the buildings to her right. It didn't make sense to waste any ammunition when the enemy was so far away. Their pipe bombs and Molotov cocktails worked well only from close range.

So what are they doing there?

She checked the men in the windows above her. They, too, had spotted the soldiers, but held their fire. *Smart.*

Tanek glanced over the top again. "It looks like they're leaving," he said, a hint of surprise in his voice.

Julia took another peek, and sure enough, the soldiers were moving away.

As the voices of the retreating soldiers trailed off, Julia noticed another change. The drone of gunfire she'd become so used to as a background noise had disappeared.

Tanek looked equally surprised. "What happened to the gunfire?"

"Maybe a cease-fire?" Julia said, hardly believing it herself. *They won't negotiate with us, surely.* She shook her head. "I don't know. Let's wait for a bit, but keep an eye on the road. Could be a trap."

Julia decided to check on the people behind the barricade. Many of the fighters had used the recent lull in fighting to take a rest, and she found most of them inside. It was an odd sight—a half dozen ragged men sleeping on the uneven, rocky, and dusty floor of a bombed-out building. She chuckled—if she could rest her head anywhere, she'd probably fall asleep within seconds as well.

There was some commotion outside, and she went out to see the familiar face of Zofia, one of the messengers. Even though the girl was only 13 years old, she was one of the bravest girls Julia knew. She'd run between the different bunkers and fighting spots to relay the latest news from headquarters. She didn't carry a weapon and had been shot at many times in the past four days.

"I'm so happy to see you. What's going on?" Julia said as the girl came straight to her.

Zofia was smiling. "The Germans are leaving the ghetto! They started leaving about two hours ago, first in the south and then, after they cleared the Umschlagplatz, the north side as well. You need to come back to Miła Street as soon as possible."

Julia was surprised and relieved at the same time. *Have we beaten the Germans?* She could hardly believe it. There were still plenty of people in the ghetto, but it looked like they had won for now.

"What about Mordechai?" she asked Zofia.

The girl shook her head. "I haven't seen him for a few days now. Last time I heard he was fighting near the Többens and Schultz factory."

Julia nodded. "I'll be right there."

Zofia was already on her way to deliver her message to the fighters a few streets down.

Julia took a deep breath and looked at the barricade. They had made it, and with only a few casualties along the way.

*

As Julia made the short trek to Miła Street, she was horrified by what she saw. The streets were littered with corpses, most of them men in front of the buildings. They had resisted their deportation, and the Germans had shown no mercy. Sometimes she came across a line of corpses—bullet holes in the walls silent witnesses of organized executions.

Even more striking than the evident signs of death was the eerie silence in most of the streets. The sound of gunfire had camouflaged the clearing of the houses, and the people that lived here only days ago had now gone to a place synonymous with death—Treblinka.

Julia shuddered as she picked up her pace and kept her eyes on the ground in front of her. How many people had perished in the last days? How many had they saved from the death trains? She hoped Mordechai had answers. *If he's still alive.*

As she turned onto Gęsia Street, she saw the wall separating them from the rest of Warsaw.

She entered Miła Street and headed for Number 29. She was relieved to find the building intact—the Germans hadn't found out that this was their headquarters.

Inside the small hallway was alive with activity. She nodded at a few familiar faces—messengers and fighters alike—as she turned into the main briefing room. The last time she'd been here was only four days ago when they'd found out the SS were marching into the ghetto. There were only two others in the room, and they greeted her with haggard looks. She sat down in one of the chairs and closed her eyes, suddenly exhausted as she relived the nightmare of the past few days.

The SS had come at them hard, and the first two days had been challenging. Mordechai had asked her to support wherever the Germans hit them hardest, and it meant she and her small squad had been fighting all over the ghetto. She hoped Mordechai would be here soon. She hoped her friend was still alive.

"Julia?"

She opened her eyes and was happy to see Zofia's face.

"Were you asleep?"

She sat up a little straighter. "Of course not—I was only resting my eyes for a second." Julia saw that more seats had filled around her. *Where did they come from?* Maybe she *had* dozed off.

"I thought you'd like to know Mordechai will be here shortly," Zofia said. "He's keen to see you."

She felt a wave of relief at the news and thanked Zofia, who hurried out of the room. As she exited, a familiar figure appeared in the doorway. Mordechai. The bags under his eyes had further darkened, and he looked even thinner than usual. *He's not eaten or slept in the past days, either.*

Despite his haggard appearance, his step was confident as he made his way to the front of the room. He scanned the faces of the people present, and a weak smile appeared when he met Julia's eyes.

"So happy to see you all here," he started. Mordechai never wasted time, and everybody turned to him. Julia looked around and only now realized she recognized very few of the faces. *We've lost a lot of people.*

"I'm sure you're all exhausted, and you deserve some rest after this. The good news is that we've beaten the scum out of the ghetto. We surprised them with our resilience, and everybody should be very proud." Mordechai paused for a moment, looking each of them in the eye. "But as you know, this will only be temporary. We've lost many of our brothers and sisters. Some of them died valiantly in battle, defending their loved ones. Others were, despite our efforts, shipped off on the trains."

Mordechai's eyes were sad, and he took a moment before he continued. It was clear he was struggling. When he spoke up again, his voice trembled. "But this has only shown what we can accomplish if we fight back. When we're prepared."

Some of the men were nodding now. Julia balled her fists.

"And when they return—and make no mistake, they will—we will be even better prepared. Our countrymen on the other side of the wall can no longer turn their eyes away from what's happening here. They, too, have seen what we're capable of."

Without assistance from the Home Army, they would not survive another attack.

"For now, I want all of you to rest. Miła 29 will be heavily guarded in case the Germans return. Find yourself some food and a place to sleep upstairs, and we will reconvene tomorrow morning. You deserve it."

He waved his hand, and the men stood up, grateful for the chance to find a place to rest for the first time in four days.

"Julka, before you go, a word?" Mordechai waved her over. The others filed out, and Julia was happy to have some time alone with him. "How are you?" he asked.

She shrugged her shoulders. "Tired, mostly. Grateful I'm still alive. You?"

He smiled. "About the same. It's still hard to believe what we've done, though. Of course, I hoped we would hold out for as long as possible, but I never dreamed they would retreat."

"We lost a lot of people, though," Julia said, the images of the streets earlier still fresh in her memory.

Mordechai looked at her with those sad eyes again and nodded. "I know. But remember, we've also saved a lot of people. And we can hold our heads high—we've fought back."

"And will continue to do so," Julia said.

"You're pretty special, Julka. Sometimes it's hard to believe you're only 18."

She blushed. "The leader of the resistance is only 24 himself, you know."

"Fair enough," he said, a tired smile now back on his face. "I need you to do something after you've had a chance to sleep."

Julia knew what he was going to ask. "You want me to go see Lew."

"Yes, I need you to ask him if the Home Army commanders have changed their minds at all—if we might have a shot at working together from opposite sides of the wall. I'm afraid we're going to need more weapons and explosives to survive a second assault. The Nazis won't let a group of ragtag Jews in a ghetto stop them. We need help."

"I'll head out right away."

Mordechai held up his hand. "No, you're going to get some rest first. You'll go first thing tomorrow morning. Go upstairs and sleep."

But I want to see Lew.

Taking in her frown, he added, "This is not a discussion."

"First thing tomorrow morning," Julia repeated as she left the room. She struggled to climb the stairs as the last bit of adrenaline left her bloodstream, and fatigue hit. She found an unoccupied mattress and lay down, pulling a musky woolen blanket over her body. She was out within seconds.

CHAPTER THIRTY

Natan hurried home through the cold but mercifully dry streets. He'd at first been worried when he received a summons from Maciek to report to the Home Army headquarters that morning. He was sure they'd found out about his rogue mission near the wall, and he was fully prepared to accept whatever punishment they considered appropriate. *It was worth it.*

But when he arrived, he'd found an amiable Maciek waiting for him. Instead of giving him a dressing down, his commander informed him of some new developments. The government in London had been shocked to hear about the recent atrocities carried out in the ghetto. The Home Army would intensify their support to the Jewish resistance. Maciek told him this meant they would look into joint acts of resistance on both sides of the wall, but most importantly, more weapons would be shared with Jewish resistance. His commander had asked him to reach out to his contacts.

Natan had been stunned and delighted, and he couldn't wait to tell Krystyna. Before Natan left, Maciek had told him he'd heard about multiple attacks on Germans on their side of the wall. Without asking if he had been involved, he let Natan know he was proud of the men who'd made those efforts.

Arriving in the cobblestoned streets of Warsaw's Old Town, Natan headed straight for Kasia.

When he arrived at her apartment, he mounted the stairs two at a time and opened the door. He took off his shoes and tossed his coat over the rack, and stepped into the kitchen. Kasia stood near the stove and looked at him with an expression he couldn't place.

"Is there anyone else with you?" she asked.

"No, what's wrong?" he asked, raising an eyebrow.

Kasia ignored him as she opened the main door and looked out into the hallway. She turned back, satisfied, and said, "Follow me."

She opened the door to her bedroom and motioned for him to come in. He hesitantly took a step forward.

"What's this all about, Kasia?" It was nothing like her to be so mysterious.

"Just come in, Lew."

He frowned, surprised to hear her use his nickname at home. He stepped into the dark bedroom—the curtains were drawn. Kasia flicked the light switch, and Natan gasped.

On Kasia's bed sat Krystyna.

Natan blinked hard as she got up, grinning at him. "I thought you might be surprised," she said.

On impulse, he stepped toward her and opened his arms. There was only a slight hesitation before Krystyna entered his embrace. Her breath made the little hairs on his neck stand up.

"I think I'll leave you two for a bit," Kasia said. "I'm sure you have plenty to catch up on." She closed the door, and after a few more moments, Krystyna broke their embrace.

"I'm so happy to see you're alive," Natan said, and Krystyna sat down on the bed again while he leaned against the dresser next to the bed. "How did you find this place?"

Krystyna smiled. "Kasia. She told me if I was ever in trouble on this side of the wall, I should come here."

Natan nodded, but he wasn't surprised. *Kasia never mentioned any of this. She simply knows what's right.* "Is it true what I've heard, that many people were shipped off?"

She nodded, a veil of agony passing over her face. "They came in the morning, like you said. We were ready, but there were too many of them." She told him about the past days, including the attack on the SS column on the first morning.

Natan was impressed. "I'm sure many of the people in that group managed to escape, right?"

She nodded. "I suppose so. We lost a lot of good men, though—only Mordechai and I survived in the end."

"But you fought back." Natan was adamant. "If you hadn't been there, they would all have been put on that first train to Treblinka."

Krystyna looked back at him with a distant expression, as if she were somewhere else. Natan decided to tell her about his ambush. She listened attentively, her eyes never leaving his.

"And apparently, I wasn't the only one fighting that way," he said, smiling.

Krystyna looked puzzled. "I thought you were the only one who wanted to fight with us?"

"I did, too, but apparently, there were more of us who couldn't just sit back and watch."

"Well, it's nice to know some people care, but it didn't help us much, I'm afraid." She looked a little uncomfortable as she averted her eyes. When she met his eyes again, she looked serious, her brow furrowed. "That's why I'm here. I need to ask you something."

Natan sat down next to her and held up his hand. "Wait, I wasn't done yet. There's something I haven't told you yet."

"What's that?" She looked up, the furrows in her brow deepening, a bit of confusion in her eyes.

He told her about his meeting earlier, and her eyes lit up as he told her about the Home Army's support. "That's fantastic news, Lew! I can't wait to tell Mordechai!" She stood and threw her arms around his shoulders.

"I wasn't sure how I was going to find you, and then you show up here as soon as I get home," he said, laughing now. "A bit of luck, after all!"

"I can't tell you how much this means to us. We felt so abandoned."

Natan winced, and she quickly recovered. "I'm sorry, I didn't mean you. But Mordechai has tried to get the support of the Home Army for so long, and they always ignored him. But now, things will be different, especially if we plan our attacks together."

He nodded and fumbled with his hands.

"What are you thinking, Lew?"

There's only one way to find out if she trusts me. "I think it might be time to tell you something nobody but Kasia knows."

She sat up, her eyes alert.

"I'm sure you've been wondering about something since the first time we met," he said, extending his hand. "I know I have. I'm Natan."

Krystyna didn't immediately respond, leaving his hand in the air for a second or two. Then she smiled, and her eyes sparkled as she reached out and took his hand, her touch soft and warm.

"Julia," she said. "My name is Julia."

CHAPTER THIRTY-ONE

Much to everyone's surprise, the Germans had not returned after their previous attempt to clear the ghetto. Mordechai was in charge of all resistance efforts in the ghetto. News of his heroics had spread among the ghetto population, and more people had flocked to the cause. That, along with the support from the Home Army, had strengthened their belief they could withstand a new German attack. More fighting posts had been installed, most of them no more than some fortifications in the ruins—positions set up in windows where fighters could attack from elevated positions. Most of these posts were equipped with no more than a collection of homemade Molotov cocktails and wouldn't survive a proper siege. Nevertheless, it gave the people in the nearby buildings a chance to fight back—a sense of purpose.

Julia stood alone in familiar surroundings. Few people knew about the significance of this location, and yet she always felt a little apprehensive when she removed the rubble. She listened closely, and when she was satisfied she was alone, she quickly cleared the stones and sand to uncover a wooden plank on the floor. It would be another area of debris in an abandoned, derelict building to the casual observer. She took a deep breath before she removed the plank. Even though she had done this many times, the putrid smell coming from the opening still hit her hard as she breathed in again. An uncomfortable feeling started in the back of her throat, and she made sure to take short, quick breaths. The nausea passed.

Now somewhat accustomed to the smell, she stepped down into the dark tunnel, using the simple ladder they'd constructed. When she was almost entirely below the floor, she reached out and pulled the wooden plank back into its position, instantly shrouding herself in darkness.

By touch, she found her way down, the soft rustle of soil at her feet confirming she'd reached the bottom. She crouched on her hands and knees—the passage was narrow—and crawled farther down the tunnel, hardly noticing the increasing sewer smell.

She was at ease in the darkness. The sound of flowing water—or in this case, water and sewage—surged as she climbed down into the main sewer.

Julia stretched her back—a little sore from the crawl—and proceeded along the stream. Thankfully the water level was low. She had to take another turn, which she knew by heart, and then she passed underneath where—above ground—the wall was, and moved outside the ghetto.

Julia saw a glimmer of daylight filter through the top of the sewer ahead. She was glad to see, a little further down the sewer, a familiar figure waiting for her. *Natan.*

She hadn't seen him for over a week. *I've missed you,* she thought, though the words did not come to her lips.

Natan was carrying a large bag. She gasped when he pulled out an MP18 submachine gun and handed it to her. She felt goosebumps forming on her arms as she ran her fingers over the cold metal.

"How did you get one of these? Didn't your commanders want to hold on to this for themselves?" she asked, keeping her voice low. *So this is why he wanted to see me in person.*

"We ambushed a column of SS soldiers last week," Natan said in the same hushed tones, his teeth gleaming as he stepped into the light and showed his grin. "They all carried MP 40s, and two of them had these MP18s. Command thought you could use one or two of these on the other side."

Julia was impressed. "It mustn't have been easy to ambush a SS group armed with these."

"It was well planned," Natan said.

"Were you part of the ambush?"

"Unfortunately, I had to sit this one out. But I've seen my share of fighting in the last few months."

Natan always had valuable intelligence on what was happening on the other side, which Julia would share with Mordechai, but she was especially interested herself in hearing about Natan's missions. Mordechai insisted she focus all her time on the smuggling routes into the ghetto. She'd set up half a dozen new routes, smuggling everything from food and medicine to weapons and explosives. Even though her network had expanded, she made a point of doing several runs herself to set the example.

She put the gun back into the bag, which Natan then handed to her. "There are two pistols in there, as well as ammo for most of the guns you have. Careful, it's pretty heavy."

Julia pretended she hadn't noticed and quickly slung the bag over her shoulder. It was indeed heavy, but she didn't mind; she would carry this to the end of the tunnel, where the others would be waiting to take its contents to the different hideouts in the ghetto.

"There is something else I need to tell you," Natan said, and she felt him take her hand. "Some of our brothers in the Blue Police have heard some disturbing news."

The Blue Police were instructed to find the smuggling routes, and execute any smugglers they picked up. Thankfully, plenty of the men on the force had strong ties to the Home Army, and they made sure to inform the army of any danger. One of Julia's routes had been compromised when someone had betrayed them. But because someone on the inside tipped them off in time, she lost no cargo or—more importantly—smugglers.

"What is it?" Julia asked. Natan's face was in the darkness, but she'd picked up a slight quiver in his voice.

She heard him swallow hard before saying, "The Germans are coming back to the ghetto."

Julia's heart went cold, and she involuntarily squeezed Natan's hand. "When?"

"It could be any day now. But Julia, it's not going to be the same as last time. From what I'm told, they're bringing heavy weapons. There's talk of tanks."

Julia was quiet before responding. Her throat felt dry, and she swallowed a big lump. "We're as ready as can be."

He took a step closer, his handsome face further illuminated. "I've been thinking—maybe you could fight from the other side of the wall? I worry about you, Julia."

She took a step back, releasing his hand. "What? How can you even suggest this? I can't abandon my people!"

Natan shook his head and took another small step toward her. "I know. I didn't mean it like that . . . I just—"

Julia interrupted him. "Then how did you mean it? What else could you mean?" She felt her cheeks flush in anger, but she didn't care. *How does he not understand?*

He gripped her hand, his eyes meeting hers with a desperate gaze. She didn't pull back this time. "I don't want to lose you, Julia. And I'm afraid. Afraid that, despite everything we're doing, it won't be enough. If the rumors about tanks are true, well . . . that fills me with terror."

Julia felt tears well up in her eyes and pulled him close. "I can look after myself. There's no need to worry. I think this side is as dangerous as ours." She had trouble believing her own words. "And how would it look if I left all those people who are counting on me—when the fighting starts? I can't do that, Natan, I really can't."

They held each other's hands in silence for a moment before Natan nodded. "Okay. But promise me you'll be careful. Don't go running into the front lines; they need your brains there." He gave her a sad smile. "Mordechai's all right, but he's nothing without you."

Julia smiled through her tears and wrapped her arms around him in the darkness. "I know you'll be fighting for me on the other side."

"Not just me—the whole Home Army in Warsaw will be ready as soon as they attack."

"Then I have no doubt we'll give those Nazis one hell of a fight together," she said, this time believing it. "And when it's all over, I'll come and find you."

Without another thought, she moved her head toward him and found his lips with hers. As she closed her eyes, she savored his warmth as it radiated through her body. *I don't want this to stop.*

When they broke their embrace—their eyes now closer than ever before— Natan chuckled. "Now there's something worth fighting for."

*

Julia wasted no time in warning Mordechai when she returned to the ghetto the same afternoon. He was composed, with barely a reaction—as if he'd expected this. He'd sent messengers to assemble his most trusted fighters.

The others had rushed to the headquarters, and Mordechai had pulled out a somewhat crude map of the ghetto. It was scattered with dots indicating the different fortifications—ranging from simple barricades in the street to heavily fortified buildings with machine guns pointing down from the windows.

Julia had been sent to Wołyńska Street, and she'd spent the night dozing, falling in and out of sleep. It was now almost six in the morning, and the streets were still dark. She stood up behind the ten-foot fortification and stretched her legs and aching back. Even though she was well prepared for the cold night— she had worn plenty of layers—sleeping on the hard ground had been anything but comfortable.

She looked at the men around her, still asleep but for the sentries, one on either side of the bunker. She nodded at one of them and asked, "Any movement?"

The man shook his head. "It's been quiet, and no messengers, either."

Julia walked along the barrier of stones and rubble. She'd spent a lot of time fortifying this position and knew every little nook and cranny. The Germans would have a tough time breaking through the barrier with guns alone. They'd need to get close enough to lob their grenades over the partition, but they would never make it that far. She looked to one of the windows a little farther up the street, where the muzzle of a machine gun pointed out. *Good luck trying to get past that beast.*

She took a sip of water from her canteen before carefully screwing the top back on. Water was scarce, and she didn't know how long it would be until she could refill her bottle. One of the sentries whistled at her, and she turned her head in his direction. As she did, she caught a beam of light from the street on the German side.

All her senses switched on: the sound of muted voices and shuffling boots was suddenly clearly audible. *They're back.*

She moved to the center of the barricade, the men rushing toward their positions as sentries whistled sharply, the noise cutting through the silence of predawn. Julia looked up at the windows on either side of the street and saw quick flashes of light confirming the fighters had heard the battle call. The area behind the barricade that had been quiet only moments ago was now a hive of activity. Men collected their weapons, ranging from short-range pistols to submachine guns. Other carried crates of crude pipe bombs they'd assembled themselves. Julia prayed they would work.

After a few minutes, the men settled and waited in silence. Only a soft rustle of wind blew through the street as all eyes were focused on the other side. The muted voices had changed to murmurs. She swallowed hard.

There was movement as shadows stepped into the bright beam ahead. Before long, the enemy made its terrifying appearance—rows and rows of well-armed, well-rested, and trained soldiers turned the corner in organized military fashion.

One of the men turned to Julia. "This isn't the *Wehrmacht*—the regular army—is it?"

"No," Julia said, her voice an octave higher than usual. "That's the *Waffen-SS*." She shivered as the soldiers lined up, their arrogance visible even from a distance. Then, as the last of them turned the corner, they stood still, as if waiting for a signal.

She wasn't sure what the Germans were waiting for, but she knew they needed to move closer before they could unleash the fury of their *Schmeisser* machine gun to do its damage from above.

The standoff lasted for a few minutes until there was movement behind the SS soldiers. Julia squinted to see what was happening, and was dismayed to see a haphazard-looking group of 30 move forward. They did their best to look confident, but they lacked both the composure and the crisp uniforms of the SS soldiers they passed. Their oversized uniforms of different shades of gray and black made them look every bit the hated outcasts they were. These were men of the Jewish police, carrying out the Germans' orders within the walls.

Julia spat on the ground. "If they come close enough, we treat them like we do the Germans," she hissed at the men around her. There were grunts of approval.

As soon as the Jewish policemen reached the front of the column, a shout was heard. They spread out to the sides of the street and started moving toward Julia's barricade. She gripped her gun a little tighter. *So it begins.*

The men walked slowly, and Julia had to control herself so as not to fire too early. The trap was set. She felt a presence next to her—Zofia, the messenger.

"Mordechai wants to know if you're ready," she said before her eyes focused on the policemen approaching. "I guess you are."

Julia nodded. "Tell him the plan is in motion. We'll take them out as soon as they come in range."

Zofia nodded and sprinted off a few streets down to Miła Street, where Mordechai and the other commanders oversaw the entire defense.

Julia turned back to the street, where the policemen had halted their approach 200 meters from their position. She frowned. *What are they waiting for?*

She got her answer almost immediately, as a roar that almost shook the ground came from the column of SS soldiers. They started moving forward at a high pace, practically running toward the barricade now. The policemen held their ground in the middle of the street—armed with nothing more than batons.

The SS soldiers passed the policemen. *Just a little closer,* Julia thought, praying the men in the windows above would stick to the plan.

The soldiers were now only 50 meters away from her. She could make out their faces. They were young, and a few sported devious smiles as they aimed their submachine guns in her direction, anxious to fire at anything that moved. The tension around her was palpable, the men clutching their weapons tightly.

The first row of soldiers was now so close she could almost look into their eyes. They couldn't be more than 20 meters away. She looked up at the window to her left and saw a flash.

Less than a second later, she heard the whoosh she was waiting for, followed by the first cries—another whoosh, then a deafening explosion that seemed to be right next to her.

Almost instantly, the rattling of a machine gun started from above. Julia exhaled in relief. That was their Schmeisser. She heard the impact of the bullets on the street and peered over the barricade. Another whoosh scorched her eyebrows, but what she saw lifted her heart.

The street had turned into an inferno; Molotov cocktails rained down from the windows, their fiery contents further fueling the already raging flames on the street. Bullets ripped through the smoke, finding their targets and tearing through flesh and bone. Explosions shook the ground as their homemade grenades were tossed into the column of SS soldiers.

Julia raised her gun, ready to shoot anyone making it through the flames, but it was unnecessary. The German soldiers howled in pain as the fire and bullets tore through their uniforms and forced them to the ground. They rolled in the streets, desperate to extinguish the deadly flames. Some of the charred bodies no longer moved, and those still alive tried to flee back to the relative safety of the other end of the street. Few of them escaped the hail of bullets raining down from above.

It ended almost as quickly as it had started. The explosions stopped, the fires died down, and, finally, the rattle of the machine gun ceased. As the smoke slowly cleared, the carnage in front of the barricade became visible. Julia gasped. The street was littered with burned soldiers. A few still twitched, every movement followed by a pitiful moan. On the far side, a few surviving soldiers hurried around the corner. The street was quiet again, but for the soft crackle of the smoldering fires.

A shot rang through the air, and then another. A bone-chilling shriek followed, and Julia's eyes shot toward its source. One of the German soldiers twitched violently on the ground as he tried to reach for his leg. Blood gushed from his left calf, and another bullet split one of the cobblestones next to his face. The men in the windows were taking shots at the injured soldier.

The terrified soldier tried to crawl away, but his injured leg had immobilized him. The shots continued until one of them found its mark, and the man's skull was split in two. It was quiet for a few seconds until the first cheer from one of the buildings prompted all the men at the barricade to erupt in a victorious roar.

Julia let out an animal roar. *The plan had worked! The SS have retreated!* She looked at the men around her, relief clear on their faces, hands lifted to the sky as they embraced each other.

Julia smiled and looked for Zofia. Surely she would be back from the headquarters by now. She wanted Mordechai to know about their victory as soon as possible. But the girl was nowhere to be seen.

As the men settled down and went in search of something to drink inside the building, Julia heard a low rumble of a car engine in the distance. She perked up her ears and turned her head toward the far side of the barricade.

The sun was making its way up into the sky, and the first rays of light hit Wołyńska Street, making it easy to spot the terror that rolled around the corner to where the retreating German soldiers had been only fifteen minutes before. There was no mistaking the protruding turret in the middle of the vehicle. *A Panzer tank!*

Julia was gripped by panic; her worst nightmare had come true. Around her, the men were too busy celebrating their victory to notice the terrible danger. Julia forced herself to focus—they had discussed this possibility, but she never really thought it would happen. She hoped the men in the buildings remembered what they needed to do. Even more so, she hoped they hadn't wasted all their ammunition in the previous ambush.

She had to get everybody's attention as quickly as possible. Without another thought, she yelled, "Tank!"

The murmurs died down instantly as they turned—first toward her, with surprise and disbelief in their eyes. And then—as she pointed down the street—their expressions changed to pure terror.

The Panzer continued rolling down the street, its turret pointing menacingly at their barrier. They were well within range, and if the operator decided to shoot, their barricade could be demolished by one well-aimed shot. She steadfastly remained behind the barrier, the men following her lead.

As the tank slowly rolled toward them, another vehicle turned the corner. This was an armored car, also equipped with a turret. It lined up behind the tank, and—much to Julia's horror—another column of soldiers appeared behind it. They made sure to keep the two vehicles between them and the barricade. *Smart. They have learned from what happened only minutes ago.*

The two vehicles slowly passed an old yellow-brownish building, its glass windows blown out. The soldiers were still keeping their distance.

Then, seemingly out of nowhere, an explosion so fierce it shook the ground made Julia duck far under the barricade. There was another minor explosion, and she checked her surroundings. The barricade was still intact, and she quickly looked in the direction of the tank.

The large tank at the front was engulfed in flames but still mobile. It was turning away from them, its deadly turret now pointing in the opposite direction. The smaller armored car was in the same condition, angry flames melting its tires and rendering it immobile. The soldiers had retreated a little, but it appeared none of them was injured in the attack.

The largest vehicle was burning, and Julia wondered how the men inside were still alive. She cursed when it reached the end of the street and turned the corner. The other vehicle remained in the middle of the road.

There was a moment when nothing happened, both sides unsure what to do. But then, the SS soldiers appeared to realize they were still better equipped and trained than the ghetto defenders. They had simply approached this barricade the wrong way. Orders were shouted across the lines, and then the men—Julia estimated there were at least two hundred of them—fanned out across the street.

Before she realized what was happening, the men on the opposite end of the street started firing at the barricade. Most of the bullets were stopped by the debris, but some of them found their way through.

"Everybody down!" someone shouted as bullets whizzed overhead.

Then, a massive explosion from above. The soldiers were firing antitank missiles into the buildings facing the street. As the gunfire ceased, the column was rapidly approaching. She looked to where she knew their machine gun was placed and was dismayed to see the facade of the building had been torn away by the earlier explosion.

The approaching German soldiers lobbed hand grenades into all the nearby buildings. *I hope they all got out in time.*

Their situation became hopeless, with 200 heavily armed soldiers bearing down on the barricade and no support from above. They didn't stand a chance against the advancing Germans. *We have to go!*

"Abandon positions! Pull back! Pull back!" Julia screamed, surprising herself.

The other men looked at her, their eyes registering surprise. But before Julia had time to repeat herself, more German machine guns erupted into action. It was all the motivation her people needed as they ran from the barricade. Julia ran as fast as she could, the guns still rattling behind her.

CHAPTER THIRTY-TWO

Only a few blocks east, Natan sat crouched on the other side of the wall. His friend Borys sat alongside him, untangling a small bunch of fuses.

"I'm going to murder the person who prepared this bomb," Borys said, cursing softly. "Don't they realize they need to keep the fuses nice and organized? This is a mess."

Natan looked up and saw their fellow cell member Tomasz a little farther down the street. He raised his thumb—all clear. Despite this assurance, Natan still felt his heart in his throat. Their city had turned into a war zone overnight, the rattle of automatic gunfire a constant drone on the other side of the wall.

When the assault had started, he'd rushed to the agreed rendezvous point, where Borys and Tomasz were waiting. They had to sneak through the streets of Old Town, ducking into ruins of buildings as they avoided the columns of German soldiers making their way to the different entrances. There would be no questions asked if they were spotted—there was absolutely no reason for them to be on the streets. The pistols they carried would be insufficient against the carbines and machine guns the soldiers had.

Natan had been anxious to reach their hiding place on Freta Street. The old school building was directly opposite the ghetto wall; they'd hidden explosives there a few days prior. As they sneaked in through the back door, he hoped nobody had found them.

They'd hidden the explosives behind an old cabinet, and Borys and Natan moved it aside. Much to his relief, the small bag was still there, hidden under a thin layer of sand. They'd retrieved it, then exited the building through the front door after making sure there were no patrols on Freta Street.

"Okay, I think I've got it," Borys said, holding up the thin fuse he'd untangled from the rest. It wasn't longer than maybe a few feet, and Natan realized they would have to move quickly once it was lit.

"Is it a slow burner?" he asked, reaching for the small bag with the rest of the bomb.

Borys shook his head. "I doubt it, and I can't tell from looking at it." That confirmed what Natan suspected. "I think we'll have about 30 seconds to get the hell away from here."

Natan took out five pipes and a short length of tape. He handed it all to Borys, who carefully wrapped the pipes together. He unscrewed the top of the middle pipe, and a pleasant, musky smell wafted out. He knew the bombs were assembled by taking the TNT from grenades and from shells that hadn't exploded on impact. It was a dangerous job salvaging the material, as these explosives were highly volatile.

Borys inserted one end of the fuse into the bomb and screwed the cap back on, the fuse now protruding from one side. He looked up at Natan and said, "I think it's ready."

"Will it be strong enough to blow up the wall?"

"Oh yeah, for sure. Five of these will easily blast through—we'll get an opening at least two meters wide."

An explosion on the other side of the wall rocked the ground, and Natan's mind went to Julia. *I hope they had enough time to prepare.*

"Okay, let's do it," he said as he returned to the task at hand. "Light the fuse."

As he spoke the words, he heard Tomasz whistle. He turned to his friend and didn't immediately see him. He did, however, spot the column of German soldiers approaching. He made out the figure of Tomasz pressed against the wall, clutching his pistol.

Borys had followed his gaze and quickly lit a match. The flicker of the fire seemed much brighter than usual, and Natan nervously glanced at the approaching column. They marched on without giving them any special notice. Borys cursed as the match died before he could light the fuse.

"Hurry up," Natan whispered as the sound of boots increased. *Too many of them.*

Borys struck another match—this time closer to the fuse—the soft crackle of the sparks flying off the lit fuse sounding like music to Natan's ears. Borys was already on his feet. "We have to go now!" he said, pulling Natan up from the ground.

They were both up and running away from the wall, heading for the school building. This attracted the attention of the soldiers in the front of the column, who stopped and drew their weapons.

"Halt!" Natan heard behind him, followed by the familiar "Banditen! Banditen!"

The building was still ten meters away when the first shots crackled through the empty street, the sound reverberating between the buildings and the wall. Natan braced himself while he pushed on, expecting to feel the impact of a bullet any time now. Then he heard a familiar sound through the bursts of submachine-gun fire—it was the more modest sound of a Vis 9mm.

Surprised screams came from the column. His heart skipped a beat; Tomasz was firing his pistol at the soldiers from close range. Even though he had only eight bullets loaded, he made them count as he stepped closer to the column of 50 heavily armed SS soldiers.

Natan momentarily stopped in awe to see the surprised soldiers turn their attention away from him and Borys as two Germans dropped to the street. Tomasz, however, didn't stop firing. Another soldier went to the ground as Tomasz displayed excellent marksmanship.

Natan hardly heard Borys as his friend tugged at his jacket. "Move, Lew! Keep going!"

But Natan's eyes were fixed on Tomasz taking on an entire column. As Tomasz fired his final bullet—finding its mark in the chest of one of the soldiers—the heartbreaking click of the empty magazine was audible even over the other sounds.

"Now!" Borys yelled at Natan, dragging him the last few meters to the school building. Numerous MP 40s exploded into life outside as they crashed inside—none of the bullets impacting anywhere near them.

They ran to the back of the school, the sound of gunfire fading behind them. When they reached the back door, Borys turned around, and Natan nearly ran over him.

"They butchered him!" Borys declared, his eyes shooting fire.

"He's a bloody hero," Natan said, leaning over with his hands on his knees, catching his breath, his heart pounding in his chest. "If he hadn't done that, they would've surely gotten all of us."

Borys nodded vigorously. "I can't believe he did that. Did you see how many he got?"

"At least four."

Borys's eyes focused, and he held up his hand. Natan looked at him. "What?"

"It's all silent out there. That's not right."

Natan realized what Borys meant. The bomb. It should have detonated by now. "Do you think it failed?"

"It must have. It's been more than a minute."

"Do you think they somehow stopped it?"

Borys shook his head resolutely. "No way. Would you walk toward a live bomb? The fuse must've failed."

"So Tomasz died for nothing," Natan said, a feeling of gloom washing over him. Then the reality of their situation returned. He turned his ears to the other side of the building. "We should get out of here. They must've seen us enter the school."

"I don't hear anything, but you're right."

Natan stepped toward the door but then stopped. "What about Tomasz? We can't just leave his body there."

"We'll come back for him."

"But what if the Germans—" Natan didn't finish his sentence, the thought too dreadful.

"They've got bigger things to worry about," Borys said. "They've got a fight on their hands on the other side of the wall. Besides, we can't go back now. If someone spots us carrying a body through the streets, we might be in more trouble. Never mind if Germans are loitering around."

Natan was torn, but he knew Borys was right—there was nothing he could do for his friend anymore.

"We need to think about getting away from here ourselves first, Lew." Borys carefully opened the door, turning his head to check for any sign of an ambush. Satisfied the coast was clear, he opened the door farther and stepped into the alley behind the school.

Natan followed his lead, expecting German soldiers to spring up out of nowhere. But nothing happened as they ran down the alley. Natan's heart grew heavier with each step. They'd lost one of the best fighters in the Gray Ranks, and they had left his body in the street. He'd never abandoned someone before, and he vowed this was the first and last time. As they ran back into the Old Town, the sun broke clear of the buildings, the rays doing nothing to warm the chill in Natan's heart. He'd find a way to avenge Tomasz's death.

CHAPTER THIRTY-THREE

Julia faced Mordechai with disbelief as they studied the ghetto map together. "We've lost almost all our positions?"

Mordechai sighed heavily. "They came in too strong, Julka. Yours wasn't the only place they attacked with tanks. Once they realized we had blocked the streets, they brought the heavy guns. Our barricades aren't built to withstand bazookas and tanks."

"What are we going to do?"

For the first time since she'd met Mordechai, he looked at a loss. The defense of the ghetto had started with several victories. Despite abandoning her barricade, they had taken out many German soldiers, as well as the armored car. It had been the same across the ghetto; the Germans had not expected the resistance to be this well prepared. The bombs raining down from the windows had surprised the invaders, and for a very short while, it looked like they might withdraw, as they had a few months earlier.

Those hopes were quickly dashed when fresh soldiers poured into the ghetto, more cautious this time. It was only the fourth day of fighting, but messengers were reporting fighters running out of ammo or—worse—that positions had been abandoned or littered with corpses of ŻOB fighters. *We're fighting a losing battle.*

A young boy knocked on the door. "I'm sorry to interrupt, but I was told to find you immediately."

Mordechai looked at him impatiently. "What is it?"

"Well," the boy started but hesitated when he noted Mordechai's look.

"Go on; it must be important," Julia said.

The boy found his nerve. "They're burning the buildings around Smocza."

Julia wasn't sure she had heard him correctly. "What do you mean, burning the buildings? How?"

"There are soldiers with flamethrowers," the boy said, his voice shaking. His eyes shot between them.

"You saw this with your own eyes?" Mordechai said, his tone urgent.

The boy nodded. "It's right next to the factory."

"But those blocks aren't empty." Mordechai looked aghast as it dawned on him. "They're burning people out of the buildings."

"Only when people are quick enough to get out," the boy said softly. "The fires spread so quickly that some of the people on the top floors can't get out anymore. I saw it myself."

They were quiet for a moment, and Julia was horrified to think of what was going on only a few streets away. Mordechai spoke first. "Thank you, you can go." The boy hurried out.

"I need to go over there," Mordechai said, and he moved toward the door.

Julia caught up with him and grabbed his arm. "Absolutely not." She spoke with more confidence than she felt, and the resistance leader looked back at her with surprise. "It's too dangerous, Mordechai. You need to stay here and plan our next moves. We've lost too many good men and women in the past few days—some very experienced people. We can't lose you now."

Mordechai shook his head. "That's exactly why I have to go. I need to fight; I need to lead from the front!" He tried to pull away from her, but Julia tightened her grip and pulled him back.

"No, Mordechai. What do you think will happen when you're shot? Who's going to lead us? We can't do this without you. I can't do this without you." She paused for a moment and saw the hesitation in his eyes. Her friend was torn.

Julia pressed on. "Let me go instead. I know the way—I can sneak through."

Some of the usual fire returned to his eyes, and she felt him tense. "I can't ask this of you, Julka. You've only just returned. Have you slept more than two hours at a stretch in the past four days?"

"Have *you*?" she countered. He was right; after she had to abandon the position at Wołyńska, she found shelter with a family who had opened their door to her as she ran from the oncoming soldiers. She had stayed with them overnight, but she hadn't slept. Instead, she kept her eyes on the front door, expecting soldiers to break through at any minute. When morning came, she'd been delayed by heavy fighting. She'd joined the men and women as they struggled against the German onslaught, and she'd fought for two full days and nights. When they finally had to give up this position, too, there had been a lull in the fighting, and she'd caught up with Mordechai on Miła Street.

He opened his mouth but then closed it again, and sat down. He looked thoughtful and said, "Okay. But I want you back here within the hour. No fighting this time, Julka. I want you to scout what's going on at Smocza and tell me if what the messenger said is true."

Julia nodded. She had no doubt the messenger told the truth; she only hoped it was an isolated incident. "I'll be back before you know it."

*

She was careful to stay away from the main thoroughfares. Even though she would reach Smocza Street a lot faster going that way, she also knew most of the fighting was in those streets. She decided to stay close to the wall on the east side of the ghetto. Most of the buildings were empty; the people living here had been the first on the trains to Treblinka.

Instead of taking Nalewki Street, she ducked into a building she knew would open up into a courtyard. From there, she could enter the ruins of the small houses facing Ganse Street. She listened closely before crossing quickly. She made it to the other side and entered a tall apartment building. As she picked her way through the rubble, she heard nearby gunfire from the east. *Those must be the fighters holed up in the brush factory.* Mordechai had told her they were holding their position, having already fought off two Germans attacks.

She was now on Nowolipki Street, one of the main streets in the ghetto that ran from east to west. There was no way to avoid this particular route. She smelled the fire before seeing smoke rising in the west, beyond the Többens and Schultz factory. Even after so much destruction, she was not prepared for what she saw on the horizon. The dark plumes blocked out the sunlight, and Julia shuddered as a chill ran down her spine. Although all her senses were telling her to get away, she knew she had to see what was happening.

The street was deserted, the crunch of the glass under her feet testament to the earlier mayhem. She stayed close to the shops, ready to duck into one of the buildings if she encountered any Germans. She needn't have worried; there was no one left here. She had to divert to the middle of the street as one of the houses had collapsed, blocking her passage. It looked like the Germans had used grenades to destroy the pharmacy. She sighed; the Nazis made sure nothing of value remained.

Julia felt relieved to get off Nowolipki again and to duck into Karmelicka Street, which ran adjacent to the factory grounds. Surely the German soldiers would leave the factory alone—it was run by German business owners, after all. But here the smell of smoke and fire intensified, and it was obvious why— the flames spewed from the top windows of the higher apartment buildings only a block away.

The boy hadn't exaggerated. She ran down the street toward the flames but caught herself before she reached Smocza. The heat of the fires scorched her face. She hugged the wall and peeked around the corner. What she saw there made her blood run cold.

Fires raged from the bottom floors of the buildings on Smocza and Nowolipie Street. The angry flames had consumed the simple wooden houses built between the brick apartment blocks. Most of the windows of these sturdier buildings had shattered, and the street was littered with glass. Farther down the street, German soldiers sauntered—confident and alert as they scanned their surroundings—the barrels of their guns pointed out in front of them. They were alone in the streets.

A loud whoosh inside one of the buildings caught her attention, the sound followed by a bright orange explosion. Within seconds, the building was enveloped in dark smoke and angry flames. She then saw the source of the fire—confirming what the messenger had told her earlier—a soldier carrying a long protruding barrel with a small fire at its tip stepped out of the building. The fuel reservoir was on his back, and the man with the flamethrower shouted something at the soldiers. They laughed as he moved on to the next building.

Julia looked on in horror—there was no doubt anymore. The Germans were burning down the ghetto.

She was enraged. For a moment, she considered pulling out her pistol and firing it at the soldiers. But as she scanned the area, she saw there were small squads of these flame-throwing soldiers all around. She might be able to take out one—maybe two—before the men with the automatic weapons would end her resistance. And what good would that do? She felt helpless—powerless—as the soldiers continued their murderous task with relish.

Julia turned away, anxious to report her horrible findings to Mordechai, when she heard nearby gunfire. Instinctively, she turned to the source of the sound. Two soldiers stood in the middle of the street, their guns pointed upward. Julia followed their gaze, and her stomach turned.

A man stood in the window of the top floor of one of the buildings. He looked out, and despite the distance, Julia could see the panic in his stance. He ducked as the soldiers fired another salvo in his direction, their bullets missing their target as they harmlessly impacted the thick walls of the building.

The soldiers stopped firing and mocked the man, who looked out again. The flames rapidly made their way up the building as they billowed out of the window below him. Julia suspected the Germans had set the stairs on fire. *He has nowhere to go.* The soldiers were smoking out anyone still hiding there.

The man disappeared inside for a moment, and Julia's hopes rose. *Maybe he's found a way out after all.* But then an explosion came from within the building, and seconds later, a huge blast of fire tore through the windows, lighting up the street. The soldiers who had been shooting were cheered by their colleagues further up the street, who turned toward the gruesome spectacle, too.

Julia dropped her head as the flames died as quickly as they'd appeared. The fire must've reached the main gas pipes of the building. She was about to turn away when she heard more hooting. When she looked up, she was dismayed to see the man now standing in the window opening. His clothes were on fire, and he seemed to hesitate only for a moment before he launched himself out of the fourth-story window.

Julia looked away but heard the loud thud as he hit the ground. Her world went quiet for a moment—but for the roar of the flames. Then the silence was pierced by more whooping of the soldiers in the street. She didn't bother to turn back to see them inspecting the body. She suddenly felt exhausted and turned back into the relative safety of Karmelicka Street. She slumped to the ground, her back leaning against the wall of the factory. Hot tears rolled down her cheeks as frustration built and overtook the last of her energy. She sat in quiet desperation until the chill from the ground seeped through her pants to bring her back to her senses.

She stood up and wiped her face with the back of her sleeve. *I can still fight.* She took her pistol and checked the magazine. There was no need to be stealthy anymore. If she encountered a German patrol, she would be ready for them. Carefully clutching her gun, she ran down the street, back to where she came from.

She returned to find Mordechai poring over a map of the ghetto. Most of their positions had now been marked red—lost. They held on to only a few places, mainly on the eastern side of the ghetto.

"They're sending in more and more armored cars and tanks," he said, his expression serious. "And from what you've told me, they no longer seem intent on simply emptying the ghetto."

"No, they're razing the buildings from the west. Everything's on fire." Then Julia added, "People who resist are shot in the street." On her way back, she'd stumbled onto a patrol of half a dozen soldiers. She hid in an alley, and they hadn't spotted her. She'd soon seen why they were there, as a man emerged from a building across the street. He hadn't seen the Germans, and she had felt powerless to warn him. When they spotted him, they had turned the barrels of their Mausers in his direction and fired.

Julia had told Mordechai about the flamethrowers, and he had listened with despair. She'd never seen him this downhearted before, and she worried about him.

"We need to concentrate our defense here." Mordechai pointed at the map.

"Muranowski Square?" Julia was surprised. That was very close to their headquarters.

He looked at her with clear eyes. "Yes, we need to stop them from getting to the Umschlagplatz. If we're not fighting to keep people away from the trains, what are we really doing? We can't be everywhere at the same time—that much has become clear."

Julia looked at the map. They still held the only other position at the brush factory, a few streets south of their headquarters. But, even that wasn't certain, as it had been more than an hour since they had received their last report.

"All our remaining weapons and ammo are here," Mordechai said, pointing down to the cellar below them. "And the barricades we've set up around Muranowski are the strongest we have. If we can keep supplying with weapons and ammo from here, we should be able to hold out long enough."

"Long enough for what?"

He looked at her for a moment before responding. "For the Home Army to send their reinforcements. Until the Germans realize they can't take all of us—and they give up."

Julia looked at him. Despite the desperation of their situation, he managed to cling to a small bit of hope. The best they could hope for was sabotage missions as the Germans rolled into the ghetto.

"Okay," she finally said. "I'll go down to Muranowski and prepare."

"No."

She raised an eyebrow in surprise.

"I have another task for you."

What can be more important than fighting at Muranowski?

"It's likely we won't hold our position, even if everybody fights at Muranowski," Mordechai started, his eyes tired but with a spark of fire. "And we need to prepare for this as much as we can. When we fall, the ghetto falls. We are the last line of defense. And you know why we're doing this, right?"

"To protect our people," Julia said softly.

"To save our people," Mordechai corrected. "And that's why I need you to return to your smuggling route."

She was dumbstruck. "I'm not sure I can smuggle more weapons into the ghetto, and I doubt we have enough—"

Mordechai raised his hand as he interrupted her. "You're not smuggling anything into the ghetto. You're going in the other direction."

CHAPTER THIRTY-FOUR

Julia urged the smallest of the bunch forward. "Come on—just two more corners to turn, and we're there."

Despite the darkness, she could see the child's weary, frightened expression. The boy was only six, and one of the older children helped him as they struggled through the slushy, tepid water.

Julia had taken the five children down into the sewer for what would be the last mission of this kind. Mordechai had insisted she focus all her energy on taking them to safety on the other side of the wall, where the Home Army had readily agreed to find shelter for them. Julia had been overjoyed to see Natan volunteer to secure the other side of the tunnel.

She'd left the ghetto with mixed feelings that morning. The German army's efforts intensified as soon as they realized the ŻOB was making a final stand at Muranowski Square, and they were pouring even more men and tanks into the ghetto. At the same time, they continued to raze the unprotected parts of the ghetto, and fires raged everywhere through the place Julia had called home.

She felt as if she were abandoning the fight, but Mordechai had made clear that she needed to get out to survive, and he promised to join her once their position became untenable. The evacuation of their fighters had begun in the morning, using the tunnel leading to the sewers near Muranowski. Once outside the ghetto walls, the fighters fled into the nearby Michalin Forest. Julia would join them there as soon as she had the opportunity. *There is nothing left for me back there.*

But first, she needed to focus on her present situation. The children followed her in the darkness, holding hands so as not to lose each other. They turned the final corner, and Julia stopped dead in her tracks. There was light pouring down from above—the manhole cover was open. *Natan wouldn't open the manhole cover like that. Unless something's wrong?*

She turned to the children and put her finger to her lips. "Shhh," she said. "We need to be very quiet now. Everybody stay very still."

The children remained quiet, sensing the urgency of her words.

Julia had switched her routes many times this week. She wanted to make sure no one caught a glimpse of the children. This final route ended in a small alley—she'd used it many times in the past year. It was perfect—the entrance to the sewer was at the end of the alley, so anyone looking to ambush them could be easily spotted. Natan would have opened the manhole cover only a little bit—allowing a modest sliver of light to come in—so that she knew it was him.

A chill ran down her spine. *Who is waiting up there?*

*

Natan had spotted them as soon as he took position in one of the buildings across the street from the alley. There was only one explanation for the three SS men hovering there—someone had ratted them out. He felt his blood boil as he thought of the scum who'd trade their souls for a few Reichsmarks in reward.

He checked his watch. Julia would be here in a few minutes—there was no time to lose. The men were about 50 meters away, and he noticed they'd completely removed the manhole cover. That was good. Hopefully, Julia would see something was off—he hoped she noticed the manhole cover was completely removed. Maybe she would go back, and the soldiers would be left disappointed.

He pondered this for a moment and felt a twinge of doubt creep in. What if Julia was so busy with the children that she didn't notice? It was a gloomy day, and perhaps she wouldn't see? *Damn it—too many unknowns. I can't wait around here.*

It would be impossible to sneak up on the men. That was precisely why they'd picked this spot to come up from the sewer—Natan had the perfect overview of what was going on. But now, it worked against him.

His heart skipped a beat as the soldiers all turned their heads to the manhole. One of them held up his hand, and the others nodded. He reached for his belt, and Natan broke into a cold sweat as the man held up a grenade. The others followed, and they crouched down.

That must be Julia. A knot tightened in his stomach. *If they can hear her, she's already made the turn.*

He reached for his gun and was suddenly relieved he'd decided to take the bulkier automatic weapon instead of his trusted Vis pistol. He had 24 rounds available in this Mauser machine gun.

Natan got up and—without another thought—climbed through the window of his hiding place. He quickly glanced up and down the street—there was no one else about. He tried to steady his shaking hands as he jogged toward the soldiers who were still hunched around the manhole, their eyes down.

He kept his eyes on the Germans as he headed straight for them. He aimed the barrel to the center of the group, hoping his aim would be true. As he kept moving forward, he saw the soldier holding the grenade pull on something on the handle. *Activated!* The man held it and said something to his comrades as if he were counting down. The others reached for their belts as well, and as one of them turned, his eyes met Natan's.

The soldier yelled in surprise as the other two turned to Natan. There was disbelief in their eyes as they saw the haggard Pole running toward them with one of their own weapons.

Natan didn't hesitate—he pulled the trigger, and the forceful recoil of the gun surprised him as the muzzle momentarily had a life of its own. Natan quickly recovered, strengthened his grip, and adjusted his aim. He didn't stop moving as he sprayed bullets at the soldiers without restraint. Then, the gun clicked—the magazine was empty.

His bullets had found their mark—soldiers lay motionless on the ground next to the manhole. Their leader still held the grenade, somehow clutching onto it, his hand near the manhole. Natan wasn't sure if he was still alive, and he hesitated. Then, the man's body convulsed, and let go of the grenade. The little stick rolled away toward the open manhole and rested right on the edge. Natan dashed toward the danger and—in a last desperate effort—launched himself toward it. As he did, he saw he was too late.

*

As soon as Julia heard the gunfire, she swiftly turned the children around. In their panicked attempt to get away, the children at the front had fallen into the filthy water. They cried as their heads went under, and Julia struggled to get them back on their feet. They howled, and their panic spread to the others.

"Take my hand!" Julia said, desperately trying to remain calm. *What's going on up there?*

The oldest child—a slight boy of 12—took the hands of two of the children, and Julia calmed the other two and led them back around the corner, where they could hide, and she motioned to them to wait.

"Don't make a sound—we need to be very quiet now."

"What's happening?" the older boy whispered, his eyes wide.

Julia reached out and took his hand. "I don't know, but I'm going to find out as soon as the shooting stops," she said. "I need you to be brave and look after the rest, okay? I'll be away for only a minute. Don't go anywhere."

He nodded before letting go of her hand.

What a brave boy. It was all quiet now, but for the sound of the sewer water gurgling past them. Julia strained her ears—she expected the sound of boots coming down into the sewer any second now. *They've found out about our route.*

As she crept toward the corner, she was careful to take small steps, hugging the wall. She peeked around the corner and saw only the bright light streaming in from the open manhole—there was no one else there. Julia took a deep breath and steeled herself. She was about to turn the corner when she heard a small splash ahead. She stopped, not sure she'd heard it correctly or whether her mind was playing tricks on her in the darkness.

Julia reached for the wall for some extra support and put one foot around the corner. As she did, there was a sudden flash brighter than daylight in the tunnel ahead, and she jerked back, eyes closed, as a deafening explosion roared through the sewer, its force knocking her off her feet. Her world went silent for a few seconds as her head went underwater. When she came back up—coughing and gagging on the revolting sewage—her head was spinning, and her ears ringing, drowning out all other noise. Her left shoulder felt like it was on fire, but she ignored the pain. She had to get to the children.

It took all her self-control not to panic as she braced for another explosion. Instead, she struggled backward, fighting the current of the water now silently rushing past her against its usual flow.

She heard them before she saw them. As her hearing slowly returned, she heard crying in the distance. *It doesn't make sense—they are just around the corner.* Then her ears popped, and suddenly, their cries came through clearly.

"I'm coming!" she shouted, no longer caring who might be listening above ground. The children were too important.

She reached them where she'd left them, in a high spot where the flow couldn't reach them—they hadn't moved. All five sat there, the youngest crying quietly, all shivering as they pressed against the wall.

"What was that?" asked the oldest.

"I don't know," Julia lied, laying a reassuring hand on one girl's head. Her shoulder protested and she winced. "An explosion. Is anybody hurt? Are you okay?"

None of the children had suffered any injuries, and Julia slumped down next to them, relief washing over her. They all huddled together, a little girl crawling onto Julia's wet lap.

"What are we going to do now?" asked the oldest, glad to carry on with his deputy duties.

They didn't have a lot of options. They couldn't go back—the ghetto was burning, the resistance fleeing. The entrance to the tunnel back in the ghetto might have already collapsed under razing fury of the SS. And if they'd found the tunnel, they would have blown up the entrance. *We have to press on.* But she couldn't take the children to the manhole without knowing who was waiting for them. *Perhaps they won't come down at all. It's easy to get lost in the sewers, and they don't know their way around down here.*

"We're going to stay here for a little while longer," she said. "Just to be safe."

She was relieved the boy didn't challenge her—she wasn't sure she could handle that right now.

They sat in the darkness, and Julia stroked the hair of the girl on her lap. *What does her future look like?* The little one shivered, and Julia pulled her closer. They sat in silence for a few minutes, and then the oldest boy tapped her shoulder. "Look."

Julia looked up and felt her heart skip a beat. There, on the wall ahead of them, danced a beam of light from the tunnel around the corner. She put her finger to her lips and shushed them. Soft, cautious footsteps echoed in the distance, and Julia held her breath as the beam grew brighter. *Please don't turn in our direction. Keep moving.* She pulled the girl's head closer to her chest.

A single figure appeared, silhouetted by the flashlight beam. *Just one?* The beam swooped left to right. If they came into her passage, she would no longer be able to hide.

To her horror, the light shone in their direction. She held her breath and felt the children around her do the same.

As the light grew closer, she suddenly heard the footsteps stop. The beam shone the other way. It appeared that whoever was there wasn't sure where to go.

"Julia?" came the quiet voice.

Julia felt weak with relief and lost all her composure. Then fear returned, and she started shaking. Could it really be? Or was her tired mind playing cruel tricks on her?

"Julia? Are you here?" A little louder now.

There was no doubt anymore.

Natan..

PART IV

WARSAW,

31 JULY 1944

CHAPTER THIRTY-FIVE

I t was still early, but the sun was already making a quick ascent in the clear sky above when Julia and Natan left Kasia's building, where Julia now lived with them. Julia took a deep breath of summer air. "Looks like it'll be a beautiful day. Too bad I'll be spending most of it in the darkness."

Natan nodded as they strolled down the street as if taking a pleasant walk. "It won't be much different for me."

She raised her eyebrows. "I thought there would be plenty of preparations going on?"

"Sure, but that also means a lot of planning and listening to briefings," he answered, looking unenthusiastic. "Until we get the go-ahead to start the attack, we're lying low."

They turned east and watched the street traffic increasing until they reached the now-familiar ruins of the ghetto. The wall still stood in most places, a scar running through the city center. Beyond the wall, there was nothing left. The buildings had all been razed to the ground. Not content with burning the buildings to ruins, the Nazis had used explosives to destroy whatever portions of the buildings were still standing. It was an ever-present reminder of the evil they were capable of.

Natan appeared to sense what she was thinking. "Come, let's take a different route today." He took her hand and gently pulled her away from the wall.

She shook her head. "No, it's okay. It's not going to change anything. Besides, I think it's good to know what we're fighting for." *This was my home, my family, and my friends. They took everything from me.*

"You miss him, don't you?"

Mordechai. "There's not a day I don't think of him." *Or my parents. Olek. I can never forget.*

Natan didn't immediately say anything, but they continued on their usual route.

"Mordechai was a true hero. I'm sorry it took our command so long to recognize his efforts," Natan said. "If it weren't for him, there would've been no resistance within the walls, and I'm not sure you would even be walking beside me today." The sad smile was more like a grimace.

Julia felt her eyes sting a little, and she blinked hard. "I know. If only he'd joined the other fighters when it was clear they couldn't fight off the Germans in the end."

"He didn't want to leave anyone behind," Natan said softly.

Natan had had to help her climb out of the sewer; her fall after the explosion had dislocated her shoulder. They'd taken the children to their hiding places and gotten medical help to get her shoulder back in joint. Natan had then insisted she stay with him and Kasia.

She'd stayed quiet in their place for the first week as the fighting died down on the other side of the wall. Most fighters had retreated through the other tunnels, and she'd clung on to the hope that Mordechai was one of them.

It had been idle hope. As they cleared every bit of the ghetto, the Germans found the ŻOB headquarters on Miła Street, where 300 people hid in the heavily fortified basement. The soldiers had used gas to force them out, but only a few surrendered. The others were suffocated or ingested cyanide pills before they could be captured. Mordechai had stayed with these people, making his final stand. *He never intended to flee the ghetto,* Julia marveled to herself over and over.

"Come, let's sit down," Natan said as he gestured toward a bench. "We still have some time to enjoy the sunshine."

They sat down, and Julia turned her face to the rays, savoring the warmth. She closed her eyes and took Natan's hands in hers, gently resting them in her lap. "How much longer until the Home Army is ready?"

He inhaled sharply. "Could be any day now. Radio Warsaw has been broadcasting news of the American and British victories in the west for days now."

"And the Russians in the east."

"The government thinks we need to hold out a little longer," Natan said, pausing for a moment. "But General Bór thinks we should weaken the German positions in Poland."

"He wants to fight?"

"He thinks the British and the Soviets will help us once they see us attacking the Germans. It's the encouragement they need to launch a full attack on the Nazis in Poland as well," Natan said.

Julia felt excitement building in her stomach. "And can he do that? I mean, doesn't he need approval from the government in London?"

"Technically, he's the commander in charge in Poland. If he decides to mount an operation, that's his call." Natan looked uncomfortable.

"And will he?"

"I think so; there's talk of our battalion reporting to Wola soon."

Julia's enthusiasm was dampened a little. The Wola district was on the city's western outskirts and would likely be close to the battle lines. Natan would be in the thick of any German advances and counter-attacks. Even though the experienced Colonel Radosław commanded Natan's Zośka battalion, the odds would be against them.

"You seem worried," she said.

He pulled his hands from hers and rested them on his thighs. "I'm not so sure we're strong enough to take on the Germans, even if they appear weakened. Our intelligence is shaky at best. We think they're struggling on the battlefields around us, but we don't know for sure. And I don't trust the Soviets. They were fighting alongside the Germans only four years ago. We were there, Julcia—don't you remember?"

She did. And she understood why Natan doubted the Soviets. Stalin might have turned against Hitler, but that didn't automatically mean he would come to Poland's rescue.

"I don't know how long we'd be able to hold out against them," Natan said. "We've seen what they can do when they're determined."

She glanced across the street, a gap in the wall showing the charred remains of her former home. *Indeed we have.*

They sat in silence for a few minutes, prolonging their moment in the sun together. Then, finally, Julia turned to Natan, who sat with his eyes closed. She studied his handsome face, the hint of a beard making him look more mature than his 22 years. Meeting him had been the only brightness in her life these past years, and she adored him. *He's the reason I'm still alive.*

She leaned over and kissed him, briefly surprising him, but he quickly recovered and wrapped his strong arms around her. She savored his touch, his smell, before hesitantly breaking the kiss.

"I think I should go—so-called important work is waiting," she said, frustration evident in her voice.

They both stood up, and Natan said, "I know you want to be more involved, but what you're doing *is* important, too."

"I know, I know," she said, unconvinced. "I just don't look forward to spending the whole day in a basement pouring lighter oil into bottles."

Natan pulled her back toward him, holding her tight as he looked into her eyes. "Get through the day, and I'll be waiting for you when you get home tonight."

"I can't wait," she said as she gave him a quick kiss and broke free of his embrace. They went in different directions, but with the same purpose—to prepare for the moment they would fight back. *And for this, I cannot wait, either.*

*

Natan reported to his battalion at six a.m. the following day for a briefing that confirmed what he'd suspected—General Bór had ordered an attack on the German positions in the city. They were told to prepare for what Bór had labeled W-Hour. All battalions of the Home Army in Warsaw would attack at the same time that afternoon. They would overwhelm the German positions and take back the strategic positions in the city.

Natan's Zośka battalion was assigned to the Wola district, where they split up, and he found himself near the Jewish cemetery across from the St. Kinga School, which had been converted into a German stronghold. Natan was to keep an eye on any activity there. Whatever happened, they needed to lie low until W-Hour—there were to be no attacks before five p.m.

Natan and another 20 men were hidden in an abandoned building across from the cemetery, and they'd successfully kept a low profile throughout the day. It was now close to four, and Natan was anxious to get started. His shoulders were tense, and he rubbed them for some relief.

"Feeling nervous?" asked Toni, next to him. They'd spent the last six months on missions together, and Natan considered him a good friend and trusted him with his life. Toni had also fought in the defense of Warsaw and was one of the many former army men in the Zośka battalion.

"Maybe a little," Natan said as he checked the magazine of his Sten machine gun for the tenth time that afternoon and patted it at his hip, then pulled out his pistol. "We're really doing this, aren't we?"

Toni nodded. "I hear you. It wouldn't be healthy if we weren't at least a little nervous. I can't remember ever feeling completely ready for a battle. But the plan is good, and the Germans don't know we're coming." He looked upbeat, and Natan felt a little more at ease. Despite that, he remembered how Julia's people had felt confident when they started their uprising in the ghetto. Mordechai, too, had thought they were ready. But they had held out for less than three weeks. He swallowed hard and tried to focus on the task at hand.

"How many do you think are in the school?" he asked.

Toni shrugged. "I'm not familiar with this area. Didn't Radosław say it should only be a small unit?"

"For a place where they're supposed to be storing weapons, I'd expect more than a small unit, don't you think?"

"Good point. I guess we'll find out soon enough. What time is it?" Toni looked out at the cemetery, no doubt keeping an eye on the position of the other fighters.

"Half past four."

"Okay, well, better get everybody in position."

Natan nodded. The other members of the battalion would attack the school from the other sides. They planned to pin the Germans in the school, giving them no option other than surrender.

As Natan and Toni motioned for the others to get ready, there was a burst of automatic gunfire nearby. Natan turned his head toward the source of the sound, only a few blocks away.

"They're too early," Toni said, cursing. "Trigger-happy idiots."

"We don't know what happened—someone may have been found out."

"Nonsense—somebody didn't stick to the plan. Too many inexperienced youngsters with guns too eager to start killing Germans." Toni looked angry as he signaled to the rest of the men to stay put.

"What should we do?" Natan asked.

Toni was resolute. "We stick to the plan, we wait. Listen to the gunfire—it sounds like it's centered around the Tobacco Monopoly building."

Natan strained his ears. Toni was right—and the gunfire was dying down. Still, not knowing what was happening so close by gnawed at Natan's mind. "What do you think is going on?"

As Toni opened his mouth to respond, the gunfire intensified, coming from the other direction, closer to the school.

"Shit," Toni growled. "They're too early!"

More gunfire echoed through the nearby streets, and Natan could see the men around them getting restless. He looked to the school, where nothing appeared to be happening. That was odd—he'd expected the soldiers to show some interest in what was going on around them.

He almost missed the footsteps behind him. But by instinct, he turned, clutching his pistol, and was relieved to see it was a young boy sporting the red-and-white Home Army armband. He looked flushed.

"Orders from Commander Radosław are to attack immediately," he said, panting as he crouched next to them.

"Do you know what's going on over there?" Toni pointed in the direction of the Tobacco Monopoly building.

The boy nodded. "The commander intercepted a bus—with rifles, ammo, and explosives—down the street. Took down some Germans, too."

Toni looked surprised. "Well, well, well. Seems like we may have some luck after all. Let's get the men going, Natan. Time to take the school." He turned back to the messenger. "Tell the commander we're starting our assault."

"Yes, sir." The boy disappeared, and Natan admired his bravery. He couldn't be more than 14 and would be sprinting across the front lines without regard for his safety.

"Ready?" Toni asked with a keen look at him.

Natan nodded. "Ready." He tucked away his pistol and readied his machine gun.

The men carefully exited the building, crossed the street, and approached the low cemetery wall that gave them some cover from the school. Natan looked to his left and nodded to the men carrying explosives. Each held in their hands or had stuffed into their waistbands incendiary Molotovs as well as several pipe bombs. *I hope they can get close enough.*

He looked at Toni, still close to him. "Everybody's in position."

"We'll wait for them to launch the attack." He pointed to the left of the school building, where—as if on cue—four men carrying a heavy machine gun emerged from the bushes. They sprinted across the street, and Natan held his breath. If these men were struck down, their best weapon would be lost. They made it to the other side without incident and installed the gun on the fence surrounding the school.

Seconds later, the muzzle of their machine gun lit up, its distinctive sound echoing through the street.

"Now!" Toni shouted, and the men in the cemetery scaled the wall, jumped down into the street, and ran toward the other side.

Natan kept his eyes on the school windows and thought he saw someone.

The roar of the machine gun increased. He lifted his weapon and aimed but then realized he was still too far away.

To his left and right, the other members of the Zośka battalion emerged from their hiding places. There were now more than sixty men and women storming the school, most of them armed with little more than weapons taken from their kitchens, and they were careful to stay close to the fighters with guns. Nevertheless, they charged forward with fury.

Natan's group reached the fence surrounding the school. He aimed his machine gun at the nearest window as they carefully approached. Natan felt his heart in his throat and pressed the butt of his gun farther into his shoulder. It did little to control his shaking hands.

The rattling of the other machine gun stopped, and was replaced by an eerie quietness. The men and women of Zośka looked at each other, surprise and indecision on their faces. Why weren't the Germans fighting back?

Then, excited shouts were heard on the other side of the building. "They're escaping from the back! They're running away!"

Toni and Natan exchanged a look, and recognition flashed in the experienced soldier's eyes.

"They're heading for the Gęsiówka camp," Toni said.

Gęsiówka was a small concentration camp the Germans had set up in the former ghetto area near Old Town. From what they knew, they still kept almost 400 Jewish slave laborers. The camp was well fortified, but the fleeing soldiers still had a significant distance to cover to reach its safety.

Without hesitation, Natan got up and ran toward the school entrance. Peeking inside, he saw what looked to be the last of the German soldiers exiting through the back door. Toni crashed through the door and into the hallway. "Come on! We can still catch them!"

They quickly reached the other side, and Natan lifted his gun, his finger on the trigger. The fleeing Germans were already under fire on the other side of the school. They were indeed heading toward Gęsiówka, two guard towers looming up in the distance. Natan could see the guards on alert, their machine guns aimed in their direction.

Despite this, they were still out of range, and the German soldiers were in no-man's-land. A number were struck by bullets from the Zośka battalion, resulting in loud cheers from those without weapons.

Natan sprinted through the small garden, anxious to catch up with some of the fleeing soldiers. He'd kept his Sten raised and pointed in their direction. The Germans no longer looked back as they ran for their lives. They knew they needed to cover only another 100 meters to get to the safety of the camp.

When Natan was confident he was close enough, he aimed his Sten and pulled the trigger. The strong recoil of the gun forced his aim to the left, and he was disappointed when none of the soldiers fell.

He was about to push forward when a strong hand grabbed his arm. He spun around, looking into the determined face of Toni.

"Stop, Lew! Stop! You're getting too close!" he shouted at him over the sound of gunfire all around them.

Natan shook his head. "I can still get them—I know I can!" He tried to wrestle away from Toni, who now held his arm with his other hand.

"Look ahead, Lew!"

As Toni's words died down, there was no mistaking a new sound on the battlefield. The heavy machine guns mounted on the guard towers started spewing fire as the German soldiers approached the camp's walls. Some enthusiastic Home Army fighters had chased them and ventured too close, and they were now within range of the German machine guns.

The few seconds the men needed to realize their mistake proved fatal. Within moments, those in the front were struck down, bullets tearing through their bodies. Those behind them quickly turned around, but the hail of bullets caught some.

Natan looked on in horror and stood frozen. Toni shook him and pulled him back toward the school. "Come on, Lew! We need to fall back, we have the school!"

The sound of the machine gun was overpowering, and Natan hardly responded to Toni's words. A hard slap in his face brought him back to reality. His cheek burned as he turned to Toni.

"Now, Lew! NOW!"

Slightly dazed, Natan nodded as he followed his friend away from the gunfire. They reached the school and hurried inside, where they found the rest of their battalion. Natan and Toni walked down the hallway, the classrooms now filled with men and women in various states. Natan was encouraged to see the positions around the windows secured by their fighters, their guns pointing outward as they peered for danger.

A man motioned to them. "Have a look at this, Toni, Lew."

They entered a small classroom to find rifles, a machine gun, and plenty of ammunition on one of the tables. "We found this stashed here," the man said, pointing at a large cabinet in the front of the classroom. "They must've forgotten about these when they made their retreat."

Toni looked pleased. "We'll take anything they don't need anymore. This is great." He picked up the machine gun, an MG 15. "Why don't you take this and mount it facing Gęsiówka, in case they get any ideas of coming back."

The man picked up the gun and hurried out of the room.

Natan and Toni continued their inspection, and when they were satisfied all positions were adequately covered, they returned to the back room. They looked out of the window facing the camp, where everything had quieted down.

"We should search for survivors when darkness falls, right?" Natan asked, scanning the area between them and the camp, littered with the bodies of their fallen comrades. From a distance, he couldn't make out whether any of them were moving.

Toni shook his head. "We still have hours of daylight left. Besides, do you see those over there?" He pointed to the guard towers where the machine guns were installed, each with a set of searchlights. "I'm sure they'll turn those in our direction. It would be suicide to go out there. And I bet they're already getting snipers ready."

Natan was quiet as he considered Toni's words. His friend appeared to sense his discomfort and put his hand on his shoulder. "There's nothing we can do for them. The chances of any of them still being alive are very slim, anyway.

They were too close, and you saw the impact of the bullets, right?"

Natan nodded silently; he wasn't sure he'd ever forget.

There was some commotion in the hallway, and Toni stood up and headed to the door.

"Over here, boy!" he shouted to the same messenger they'd seen a couple hours before.

"Orders from the commander are to keep this position until further orders," the boy said. "The rear is secured, so you don't have to worry about that. Focus on whatever is happening near the camp." The boy spoke with the confidence of an experienced fighter, and Natan remembered he probably was, despite his age. He'd probably joined the Gray Ranks at the start of the war, and he had now climbed up to be one of Colonel Radosław's field messengers.

The boy left, and Toni turned to Natan. "You want to take a short nap? I'll keep an eye out for Germans." Natan wanted to protest, but Toni held up his hand. "Don't worry, I'll wake you if anything interesting happens. But for now, I think the Germans are also licking their wounds in there."

Natan decided it wasn't a bad idea; he didn't know when he would be able to rest next. He moved to the back of the room and curled up against the wall. He was asleep within seconds.

CHAPTER THIRTY-SIX

Natan—much to his surprise—got a good night's sleep. Nothing much happened in their area during the night, with only a few of their men taking potshots at what they assumed were Germans around the gates of the camp.

The next day was mostly spent keeping an eye on the perimeter around the school and waiting for news from the messengers coming in every few hours. They learned the fighting was heavy all around, with most casualties on their side. Despite this, they had the Germans abandoning several positions, as the Zośka battalion had done with the school.

Whenever they weren't on sentry duty, the men spent their time playing cards and telling stories of previous battles. It was getting dark, and Natan was playing a game of skat when Toni rushed into the room, his eyes conveying urgency.

"Lew, time to go—things are happening near Karolkowa!"

Natan tossed his cards, grabbed his Sten gun, and followed Toni, who was already halfway down the hallway. Natan caught up with him and asked, "Problems?"

Toni didn't look back and kept walking as he answered: "Reports of Germans tanks in the street. It's only two blocks down, so Radosław wants us to investigate and take them out if we can."

"How? We don't have any antitank weapons."

Toni shook his head as he opened the door and the warm summer-evening air gusted in. "No, but we've got two guys with a PIAT heading over."

Natan hoped they made it in time; if tanks were rolling through the streets, they would need the antitank gun to stop them. Unfortunately, the PIATs were scarce; the British had airdropped the weapons in the past months, but many of them had overshot their destination and ended up in German hands.

Four other men caught up with them, carrying grenades and Molotov cocktails. These weapons were not as effective as the PIATs, but they could use any kind of explosive they could get their hands on.

"How many tanks?" Natan asked.

"Three."

Natan swallowed hard; even if they managed to get off a perfect shot with the PIAT, they needed a lot of luck to pull this off.

They turned into Okopowa Street and entered the tallest apartment building, taking the stairs two at a time until they reached the fifth floor, and hurried toward the street-facing window.

They were just in time to see the two Panther tanks turning into the street. The third tank followed at a distance. These were the most common tanks used by the German army and formidable on the battlefield, though less so in the restricted spaces of the city.

The tanks slowly advanced down the street, and Toni instructed the men with the grenades to take positions near the windows. He spoke as the tanks came within striking distance: "We only have one shot here, guys. I want us to drop those bombs on the first tank as it passes that window"—he pointed at the first window on that end of the room. "Once we've taken it out, they won't be able to roll forward, and then we try to take out the second tank. Make sure you wait for the second tank to be level with that last window." The men crept closer to the windows, their foreheads glistening with sweat in the heat. They only had a Molotov and a grenade each. They would have to be highly accurate—there would be no second chance.

"I guess the boys with the PIAT didn't make it," Toni said softly to Natan. "I want you to provide some covering fire after they've dropped the first bombs. Try to disorient those Nazis in there, okay?"

As Natan nodded and clutched his gun, he could now hear the tank's engine close by, the debris crunching underneath its tracks as it crawled along the street below them.

"Now!" Toni shouted, and the men at the front dropped their grenades and Molotov cocktails down toward the tank. Natan held his breath as nothing appeared to happen for a second. Then, as Natan aimed the muzzle of his Sten down, a scorching heat shot up, the whoosh confirming the Molotovs had landed. The billowing smoke made it impossible to see if they had hit their target, and Natan waited to pull the trigger.

Then, only a few seconds later, four explosions rocked the street below. Natan heard metal scraping the ground and knew the grenades had hit their mark. As the smoke cleared, he saw the first tank had stopped moving and was engulfed in flames. He didn't hesitate—he fired a few short salvos in the direction of the second tank.

Toni cursed between his salvos, and Natan stopped. "What's wrong?" he asked.

"The second tank is backing up and out of reach!"

The tank was reversing quickly, and two soldiers crawled out of the first tank and ran toward the second. Natan aimed his Sten, but Toni stopped him.

"We don't want to give away our position," he said.

Natan put his gun down, but as he did, the tank's barrel began slowly turning toward them. "It's too late—they've already spotted us!" He pointed to where the soldiers had taken cover behind the second tank.

There was fear in Toni's eyes. It would be a matter of seconds before the tank would be in a position to fire at their building. When it did, it could easily blow out two floors. Toni hesitated for only a moment before he shouted, "Everybody out! Now!"

Natan was first to reach the stairs. He practically jumped down the steps as he braced for the sound of the shell hitting their building. Halfway between the first and second floors, a massive explosion rocked the staircase under his feet. He had just managed to grab onto the railing when Toni and the other men caught up with him. They reached the ground floor within seconds. There, they approached the street side, knowing the tanks were to their right. Peering around the corner, Natan saw the first tank was still on fire. Behind it, the second tank now stood awash with flames as well, its barrel limply pointing downward. The third tank retreated around the corner toward the Pfeiffer factory, the crew of the second tank rushing to catch up with it.

As they move into the street, Natan looked at Toni in disbelief. "What happened?"

Before Toni could answer, they heard shouts and whoops from across the street. They looked up to see two men waving at them. On the windowsill was the unmistakable shape of a PIAT antitank weapon.

A huge smile appeared on Toni's face. "Well, I'll be damned. They did make it in time after all."

They waited for the fire to die down before inspecting the damage to the tanks. Unsurprisingly, the first tank was completely destroyed. The Molotov cocktails and grenades had done their damage, blowing out all the machinery to operate the tank, including some of the wheels that operated the caterpillar track.

The second tank, however, was in much better shape. The PIAT missile had struck the front, rendering the cannon useless. The rest of the tank appeared to be in good working condition.

"They probably decided to flee after they saw what happened to their mates in the first tank," the man carrying the PIAT said. "I think we can fix this and use it ourselves."

Natan could hardly believe their luck. "You can fix this?"

"Not me, no," the man said. "But we have some army mechanics in our ranks. I'm sure they could fix this barrel up nicely."

"Let's get those boys over here, shall we?" Toni said. "The sooner we can get this back into action, the better." He turned to Natan. "Let's head back to the school and get some reinforcements to guard the tank. I'm sure the Germans won't be too happy about losing it."

When they reached the school, a messenger was waiting for them, looking impatient.

"Glad to see you, son," Toni said. "We have some good news for Colonel Radosław." He then told the boy about what had happened up the street. The boy listened attentively, not interrupting Toni before he spoke up himself. "Well, that's the second tank we've captured tonight, then."

"Second tank?" Toni's eyebrows shot up.

"That third tank was intercepted at the Pfeiffer factory. The crew surrendered. They were carrying what appeared to be most of the shells as well."

Toni started laughing. "That's fantastic! So we now have two tanks at our disposal?"

The boy smiled. "I'm going to let the colonel know about this. I'm sure he'll know what to do with them." He stepped toward the door but then turned back. "Do *you* have anyone who can operate these?"

Natan frowned and looked at Toni, who got visibly taller and straighter as he said, "We have plenty of people here who can drive a tank. Tell Colonel Radosław we're ready to operate them both." The boy looked skeptical, and Toni added, "We've got more than 100 Polish army men here—we'll make it work."

As the boy disappeared, Natan asked the still-smiling Toni, "Do we really?"

Toni's smile broke into a wide grin. "Not yet, but let's go ask our people here. We need to get those tanks up and running!"

*

The following day, Natan and Toni walked the short distance back from the salvaged tank to the school. The Germans had made no efforts to recapture the tank, and the Home Army had further fortified the area around Okopowa Street.

"I still can't quite believe the mechanics fixed the tank almost overnight," Natan said as he kicked a pebble down the street. "Do you think we need to hide it somewhere?"

Toni shook his head. "As far as the Germans know, it's no longer usable. It might be best to keep it in the street if any of their scouts come to check the position. I think they would become suspicious if the tank were moved."

Good point. Toni has plenty of battle experience.

"So, what do you think happens next?" Natan asked as they entered the school. It was good to have had a few hours' sleep after the harrowing and energizing events of the day before.

"I don't know. From what we've heard, the field hospitals are overcrowded. It might be going well here, but who knows how long we're able to hold out? I think we should press our advantage with these tanks."

In the hallway, a man hurriedly approached them. He looked flushed and spoke quickly. "Follow me, please; the colonel is here for you."

Natan was surprised. "Radosław is here?"

The man nodded and guided them to one of the classrooms. Inside stood their commanding officer. They both snapped to attention.

Radosław raised his hands. "No need for that. At ease."

Natan barely relaxed as he faced the imposing man. He'd never met him before, but for Radosław to come to them, it must be important.

"I'll get right to it. I'm impressed by what you did last night. This is a huge victory for us." He paused for a moment as he looked into their eyes. Natan noticed he was haggard, but his eyes burned fiercely. "I believe you've found men capable of operating the tank in Okopowa?"

Toni nodded. "The crew is ready, sir."

"Perfect—we'll need them right away." Radosław looked pleased.

Natan glanced at Toni, who looked excited, but also puzzled. The big man cleared his throat. "What are we going to do, sir?"

Radosław motioned at a small map of Warsaw on the desk in front of him. It had red dots drawn all over the inner city.

"We've taken the positions in red, and this is the school we're in right now," Radosław said, tapping his finger on the map. "And here are our headquarters in the Old Town. The problem is that we've lost control of our supply route from headquarters to Stawki, meaning it's almost impossible to communicate and supply our western positions."

Natan followed the route with his eyes. Their position was right in between Old Town and the districts west of Wola. He double-checked the map and only saw one option to regain a direct route to the west. "We need to take Gęsiówka," he said softly.

Radosław looked up, surprised and impressed. "Exactly. It was always the plan to liberate the camp, but we would be slaughtered if we were to attack it with our light guns. But now that we have two tanks at our disposal, we stand a chance. We can take out their heavy machine guns." Radosław now turned to the window, pointing at the guard towers looming over the walls. "We take the camp, and we open up some routes running through the old ghetto."

"When do we attack, Colonel?" Toni asked.

"Now," Radosław answered.

It took them less than an hour to prepare. The Zośka battalion fanned out into the ruins of the buildings around the school. Natan had made his way forward and was in a structure only 50 meters away from the walls of the camp. He led a small squad tasked with taking out any guards or soldiers on the wall once the fighting started. A similar team was positioned on the opposite side of the street leading to the gate.

Colonel Radosław had stayed behind in the school, overseeing the attack on the well-fortified camp. Natan could see the helmets of the SS men guarding the small, sandbagged outpost and noted an additional machine gun at the gate. Two guards were peering out from each of the towers.

Natan bit his lip—Radosław had laid out his plan to the rest of the squad leaders, and there had been only one question: What if the Germans took out their tank? The colonel had taken their concerns seriously but explained the Germans had no reason to suspect they'd have a tank. All their defenses were geared toward taking out regular fighters. He was confident they could take the camp with minimal casualties.

"Everybody ready?" whispered Natan to the men behind him, receiving several thumbs-up. He looked toward the school, waiting for the signal to start. There was no sign of the tank yet, but Natan knew it was lined up in Okopowa

Street, behind the school and hidden from the guard towers.

Even though he knew their assault was imminent, the rattling of the machine gun still jolted him. They had moved the captured MG 15 to a building closer to the camp's entrance. They were now firing at the guard towers, and Natan saw the guards ducking for cover. More gunfire erupted, and it took the crew in the nest at the gate a moment to react.

When they did, the thunder of their MG 42 bounced between the buildings. Natan ducked as the bullets impacted the nearby walls. The rattle of the gun drowned out all other sounds as he signaled for his men to keep their heads down. When the sound suddenly stopped, he forced himself to look up through the window. The guards in the towers must have recovered their courage and scrambled to get back into position. Across the street, the Polish patriots were attacking the other guard tower. The guards in the tower closest to Natan had their backs to him and his men and were focused on the squad attacking from the other side. *We can take them out!*

"Quickly!" he whisper-shouted to his men. "We're going to take out the guards!"

One of the men looked unsure. "What if the machine gunners see us? We'll be sitting ducks!"

"We'll have those guards taken out before they get a chance to spot us!" Natan said as he crawled through the open window. *We have to move quickly!*

The man followed hesitantly, unlike the others who quickly followed Natan. Once out in the open, they crawled toward the guard tower. The guards were still oblivious.

Natan looked at the machine gun nest, where the gunners were reloading. *This is our chance.*

"Now!" Natan shouted at the men behind him as he got up and pointed his gun at the men in the guard tower, now only five meters away. It was an easy shot, and as he pulled the trigger, the guns of his comrades exploded into life around him. Bullets tore through the bottom of the guard tower, and within seconds it was over. The guards hadn't stood a chance.

Natan felt a rush like never before and stood in a daze for a moment. But his men were horrified, and it took him a second to register why.

Their attack had attracted the attention of the MG 42 gunners, who had finished reloading their gun and were turning it toward Natan and his men. He didn't hesitate. "Run! Back to the building!"

He ran for his life. *Please let me survive this—I want to see Julia again.*

Despite the constant gunfire from all directions, he could hear the gunners click the gun into place behind him. The building was only a few meters away. Without hesitation, he dived headfirst through the open window and rolled on, the others doing the same. They barely made it in time, as a hail of bullets struck and cement exploded around them. While the others had their hands on their heads as debris rained down on them, he looked around and saw they were missing one of the men. *Where's Konrad?*

He counted the seconds and prayed. *Come on—what's taking the tank so long?*

He'd reached a half minute of counting when it happened—an explosion overpowering even the sound of the MG 42 rocked the street. Large chunks of concrete crumbled from the walls and ceiling around Natan, and for a moment, he thought the building might collapse. But as the last bits of dust filtered down into his hair, he realized the sounds from outside had changed. Something was missing between the short bursts of automatic gunfire that sounded almost hesitant—the MG 42 had gone quiet.

Natan felt hope rising in his chest as he carefully peered outside, in the direction of the German machine gun nest. He blinked hard, not sure if his eyes were deceiving him. There was a pile of stones and mangled metal where the machine gun and the gate to Gęsiówka had been. The walls on both sides of the gate had collapsed, the guard towers were abandoned.

"Look, Lew." One of his men had risen to his feet next to him and pointed at the school. There, in the middle of the street, stood the Panther tank, its turret still smoking. Behind it, the doors to the school opened, and the fighters who had waited in reserve streamed out. Some took over behind the tank as it rolled toward the camp.

Across the street, the other fighters emerged from the buildings, their guns pointing at the camp entrance, not entirely sure what was going on.

"Let's go," Natan said as he climbed out of the window. He found the body of Konrad, who hadn't made it to cover in time. *I'm sorry.* But they must move on—Konrad would have wanted that, too.

Returning his gaze to the camp, Natan saw movement through the dust-filled air. He froze and held up his hand to stop his men. He crouched and aimed his gun at the entrance. The tank was still more than a hundred meters out, and men came out of their positions everywhere. *Is it a trap?*

A figure appeared, and then another. As they emerged from the haze, Natan lowered his weapon. These weren't German soldiers. The people stumbling their way through the rubble looked frail. They were the Jewish inmates of Gęsiówka.

"The Germans have fled! They've left us!"

CHAPTER THIRTY-SEVEN

Julia went against the stream of people—primarily women, children, and the elderly. Instead of heading east with them, into what they hoped was safety, she was heading west to the Wola district. She'd heard about the Zośka battalion's capture of the Gęsiówka camp, and she could no longer sit by, pouring Molotovs in the workshop. She wanted to make herself useful in the Gęsiówka camp, and if Natan were still there, he'd be able to get her in, for sure.

As she approached a barricade, a young man in a ragged army uniform and a Home Army armband halted her. "Where are you going?"

"Gęsiówka," Julia responded confidently.

The man was momentarily taken aback before shaking his head. "Do you have permission?"

Julia considered lying to make her way through but decided against it. "I didn't know I needed it," she answered evenly as she tried to pass him.

He stepped sideways, blocking her path. Julia caught a glimpse of a young woman carrying a baby wrapped in a dirty blanket, the woman overjoyed to reach the barricade and get to the eastern side.

"No civilians beyond this point," the man said, a little more firmly this time. "Don't you know the Germans are burning down Wola?"

She shook her head. "But I need to find the Zośka battalion—I can help in the camp."

"Sorry, you're not going through here," he said, and he waved her back.

Julia turned around. It was going to be impossible to sneak by the guard, whose eyes she felt boring into her back as she walked away. *It's not fair!* Farther up the street, she spotted a group of men wearing Home Army armbands turning a street corner, heading west. *Maybe they're going to Wola?*

She caught up with them as the two dozen men—most of them young—casually marched toward another barricade. She caught the eye of one of them and smiled. "Say, where are you going?" she asked as he smiled back at her.

"Wola. Lots of fighting there—we're reinforcing the positions."

Julia felt a tingle of excitement. "Which positions?"

He shrugged. "Don't know yet—wherever we're needed, I guess." He took out a packet of cigarettes and lit one, not bothering to offer Julia one.

"Can I come with you? I need to go to Gęsiówka."

The man took a long draw and then blew out the smoke with a satisfying smack of the lips. "What do you need to do there?"

"They need extra help in the kitchens, so I volunteered. But I'd feel a lot safer if I can tag along with you on the way over."

"Sure, fine with me."

Julia controlled her excitement and stepped in line with the men. Some nodded but most ignored her as they marched past the checkpoint. The guard didn't even notice her; he was too busy talking to the people coming into Old Town as they swarmed him for information. *Those poor people don't even know where they're supposed to go.*

They left the checkpoint behind, and as they diverted from the main streets, the traffic thinned. Soon, it was only the Home Army squad. Then, suddenly, the man leading the group held up his hand.

"Spread out, and stay close to the sides of the street. We don't know if there might be Germans hiding here." He looked at Julia and frowned, but he didn't say anything. She stayed close to the man she'd spoken to earlier; he carried a machine gun, and that made her feel a little safer.

The group was silent as they stalked through the streets. Julia felt the tension rise at the sound of gunfire in the distance. She scanned residential buildings around her. *Have the Germans ventured this far into Wola yet?*

As they approached a corner, the man in the front raised his hand. They all stopped, and Julia perked up her ears. There were voices around the corner. She listened more carefully—they were speaking German.

The man in the front peeked around the corner, then hurriedly pulled his head back. Even though Julia was a reasonable distance away, she could see the fear in his eyes. A few of the other men did the same, and the murmurs quickly spread to the rest of the group.

"There's at least 50 SS in the street ahead," one of the men said. "They're resting but blocking our way."

The man in the front looked unsure of what to do next. The other men crowded around him—they were pushing him to make a decision. Some of them felt they should engage the Germans, but others weren't so sure. Julia thought it was a terrible idea to attack—not even half of them carried automatic weapons, in stark contrast to the Germans ahead.

"We're not going to attack," the leader said, and she breathed a sigh of relief.

"But what are we going to do, then?" someone asked. "We need to get past them, and there's only one way they can go when they start moving again."

"We'll need to take a detour," the leader said. "We won't stand a chance."

The other man was unconvinced. "Who says we won't run into more German troops? If they're already here, there must be more!"

Julia thought they both had good points, but she knew it would be suicide to attack the well-trained troops. She scanned the street behind them—perhaps they could hide in one of the houses? Or . . .

"Why don't we go below ground?" she suggested.

The men turned to look at her, and she felt her cheeks flush a little. She'd blurted out what she was thinking, and now she had their attention. Determined to prove herself, she pushed on. "We can go into the sewers and make our way to whatever rendezvous we need farther own." She pointed at a manhole cover behind them.

"Who are you?" the leader asked. He was small, but his gaze was intense. The other men kept quiet as he approached her. "You're not one of us."

Before Julia could answer, the young man next to her spoke up: "She needs to help out in the camp. I told her she could come with us."

The man ignored him and now stood uncomfortably close to Julia. "Have you been down in the sewers before?"

"Yes." Not in the Wola area, but that's not what he asked.

"And you could find your way down there?"

"Of course," Julia said. "Do you have any lights on you?"

The man looked unconvinced as he looked her up and down. Finally, he said, "A couple."

There was movement up ahead. "They're heading our way! The soldiers are moving!"

The man looked back and cursed. He turned back to Julia. "Lead the way."

A couple of the men lifted the manhole cover she'd pointed out, and Julia was relieved to hear no water rushing by below. She could see the bottom of the narrow tunnel—it was only three meters below ground.

"Quick, jump down and move to the left," she said to the first man. The rest rushed toward her, and they soon crowded around, impatiently waiting their turns. "Keep moving down to make space. And be quiet!"

Julia looked to the corner of the street, where the first soldiers would appear at any moment now. She heard their voices increase and urged the men on. Eager to get underground, it took less than a minute for most of them to disappear. She followed them down the small ladder , a fighter pulling the manhole cover shut, instantly shrouding them in darkness.

"No lights, and stay quiet," she whispered to the man next to her, and he quickly relayed the message.

As they sat in the darkness, she listened to the sound of the soldiers passing overhead. She held her breath as they approached the manhole cover. Then, when she was sure the soldiers were far enough down the street, she started moving to the front of their column.

"Can somebody hand me a flashlight?" she whispered, a little louder this time.

The sudden brightness blinded her, and she shielded her eyes, then took the light and moved to the front. She knew they had to go in that direction, and even though she didn't know where she was going, she was keen to keep her bearings. It was easy to get lost in the tunnels.

She guided the men through the tunnels, often stopping to check for any sounds of patrols above them. Whenever they neared any ladders, she would slow down and kill the light. Finally, after five minutes, she heard the sound of rushing water—a larger drain must be near. She followed the sound and was relieved when their smaller tunnel opened up into the main drain running in the same direction. They continued for another 100 meters, where she stopped near a ladder. Daylight streamed in through a grill at the top.

"This is it—we should be well into Wola now," she said.

"How do you know you're in the right spot?" the leader asked as he looked up.

Julia swallowed. "I don't."

"What?" He looked at her with exasperation. "Why did you bring us here, then?"

"We don't know how far the Germans have advanced, but we should be only a few blocks farther down. We have plenty of barricades in Wola, right? The camp should be up here."

"If you're so sure, why don't you go first?" another man said.

Julia glared at him but saw the other men were nodding their heads. She caught a few of their looks—they were scared. "Okay, sure," she said with more confidence than she felt, and she climbed up the ladder.

She reached the top and listened carefully. She had no idea what was waiting for her up there, but there was no way back now. She heard nothing, and she took a deep breath as she gently pushed the grill up. She braced herself—if there were any Germans, this was it for the quarry in the sewer.

She lifted her head a little and looked down the street. It was quiet, but a strong smell of smoke penetrated her nostrils, although there were no fires she could see in any direction. When no shouts in German halted her, she removed the grill completely. *It's all a bit too quiet here. Where are they?*

That's when she noticed the corpses. Two dozen bodies were piled haphazardly near the entrance of a nearby house. Julia gasped as she met the lifeless eyes of a girl no older than eight staring at her from across the street. She almost lost her balance and quickly grabbed on to the railing of the sewer ladder.

"All clear?" The voice from below sounded distant. Julia felt faint.

She scanned the rest of the street. The corpses were everywhere. Some people had tried to flee while others had put up a fight, evident from their torn clothing, bloody hands, and bullet-ridden bodies. People had chosen to stay with their loved ones until the end—bodies lay intertwined in front of their houses.

Julia climbed out into the street, still struggling to believe her eyes. The other men appeared from the sewer, their leader now standing next to her.

"So it really is as bad as they said back in HQ," he said softly.

Julia turned her head sharply. "You knew about this?"

"We heard reports, but would you have believed it if you hadn't seen it with your own eyes?"

"Nothing surprises me anymore." Julia was suddenly keen to get away from the street and the death all around. She realized she didn't know where she was. "How do I get to Gęsiówka?"

The man pointed down the street. "It's a few blocks down. That's probably the best place for us to find out where they need us, as well."

When the last man emerged from the sewers, they set out together through the quiet streets, more bodies evidence of the SS's advance through the district. The smell of fire and death was everywhere.

Julia walked near the front, keen to get to the camp and Natan. Things could change so quickly. From everything she'd heard, the Germans had abandoned the camp entirely, and it had become an essential position for the Home Army.

"Stop!" The sharp voice of the group's leader pierced the silence. "Barricade ahead."

One of the men said, "It's one of ours, but something isn't right."

Julia frowned. *What's wrong?*

The leader crouched down and peeked around the corner. He turned back and said, "It's not our men."

"What?" Julia said out loud. "How is that possible? We're on the right side of the battle lines, right?"

The man nodded. "But when you look at their uniforms, you can see the panther stripes."

"What does that mean?"

The man looked worried. "There's only one unit in the German army that wears those, and that's the SS. It's a bit odd, though—I wouldn't expect them to be wearing them for fighting in the streets."

"Did they see us?" someone asked.

"I'm not sure. I would've expected them to fire at us if they had."

"So, what do we do?"

The man looked undecided. Were they going in the wrong direction?

As they stood there, they heard voices call out from behind the barricade. *Oh no. They've spotted us.*

The leader made a decision. "Everybody fall back, back to where we came from," he said, panic in his voice.

Julia followed him, but then the voices called out again, a little louder. Something didn't seem right, and she strained to listen. She held up her hand. "Do you hear that?"

The man next to her stopped and listened as well. His eyes went wide. "That's Polish."

More men stopped, and their leader—already halfway up the street—turned around. "What are you waiting for?" But then, he heard it, too. "They're telling us to come back? Did I hear that right?"

The wind carried the voices from behind the barricade, and it was clear now. "Come over here. We're the Home Army!"

"It must be a trap!" one of the men shouted. There was murmured assent.

"What if they're not?" Julia said. *What if we're running away from the very place we're supposed to get to?*

The leader of the group found his resolve and turned back to the street corner. More voices joined in, and they became louder, more urgent. "Come back—we need your help!"

He sounds Varsovian, even. She joined the leader at the front and couldn't contain her curiosity as she quickly stuck her head around the corner. She gasped as four men—wearing the same SS uniforms—now stood about 20 meters before the barricade. She was alarmed at first but then saw they had their weapons pointed at the ground. Then, she smiled as another couple of men climbed over the barricade. She turned back to the men behind her.

"It's okay," she said with a smile. "They're with us."

"How can you be so sure?" the leader asked.

"Have a look yourself," Julia said, waving her arm. "And look at what they're wearing on their arms."

Now that the men were beyond the barricade, their distinctive red and white armbands were visible.

*

"I'm sorry, but there's no way you can go to Gęsiówka." The small, stout man crossed his arms and shook his head. "The Germans have taken over everything between here and the camp. Wola is burning, and there are too many of them in the streets. We've tried to break through, but it's useless."

The men wearing the SS uniforms had indeed been Home Army fighters. They had stumbled onto a cache of the clothes and had taken them for themselves.

"So there's no way to get to Gęsiówka?"

"Not unless you think you can sneak through the German lines and patrols. I wouldn't recommend it, though. We haven't seen a messenger from that side for over a day now. The last we heard, the SS were razing the area, murdering anyone in their way." He looked pained, his eyes sad. "As I said, we tried to stop it, but they have brought in heavy machinery, and all their soldiers are armed with machine guns. We can't fight them out in the open."

"So you stay behind this barricade?"

He nodded. "We've been told to stop them from breaking through farther east. We need to stop them from breaking through to the Old Town."

"If I may make a suggestion," the man said, uncrossing his arms. Julia raised an eyebrow but said nothing. "Why don't you stay with us for now? We can use all the help we can get here."

Julia looked around the area. *Maybe I can get to the camp later—I won't get any closer than this.* Men were hauling rocks of all sizes, placing them a few meters ahead of the barricade. "They're creating a tank trap, aren't they?"

"Indeed they are." The man looked impressed. "How did you know?"

"I've had my fair bit of experience with those, as well." As she walked toward the group, she scanned the new tank barricade—the rocks were positioned too neatly, making it easy for any German soldiers to break through. She rolled up her sleeves and grabbed a small bucket she found next to the pile of debris. She started filling it with small, sharp stones. Julia knew a few tricks these men didn't.

CHAPTER THIRTY-EIGHT

Natan walked down the main street of the camp. Even though it was a relatively small area—Gęsiówka took up one block—it felt bigger. That had a lot to do with the number of people housed here. When they'd liberated the camp almost a week before, they'd found nearly 400 Jewish prisoners. The famished men and women had told them the Germans had fled into the ruins of the old ghetto and had left behind everything they couldn't carry. Natan's Zośka battalion had found a fully functioning and stocked kitchen with supplies that would last them weeks. The Jewish prisoners joined their battalion, a number of them resuming their duties in the kitchen, but most eager to assist the Home Army.

Part of the Zośka battalion had been instructed to secure Gęsiówka, safeguarding the communications and supply lines between the Wola district and Old Town. Natan had initially been pleased to stay put—the camp's high walls provided a sense of security not found in the regular barricades in town.

After a few days, things started changing, and Natan became restless. People from all over the district heard about the liberation and the captured food supplies. Natan understood they were desperate, and he didn't begrudge them any of the food, but their commander had enforced strict rations to ensure they kept enough supplies for the fighters. The people coming in brought reports of what was going on around them. News of entire streets being murdered by rampant SS squads made Natan's blood boil. In response, Colonel Radosław had sent out frequent sorties, and Natan had been in one of the first.

What he'd seen in the streets of Wola had been worse than anything the people fleeing from the area had told him about. German flamethrower squads had made their rounds, burning everything in their way. The streets were on fire, angry flames spreading between buildings. A constant blue haze hung in the air, making it difficult to spot German ambushes. They'd been shot at from the few buildings that weren't burning, but they were unable to return any fire as they simply couldn't see who was firing at them.

And the bodies were everywhere: men, women, and children—the SS kill squads did not discriminate. The SS had forced citizens from Wola to follow the murdering SS and burn the bodies in the street. The stench of these fires also made it down to Gęsiówka whenever the wind blew in their direction.

"Lew!" a voice called out, shaking Natan from his thoughts. He looked up and saw Toni with a young boy in tow, making his way toward him. "We've got a problem."

Natan raised an eyebrow. There were always problems. "What's wrong?"

"We're running out of water," Toni said matter-of-factly.

"How's that possible?" Because of the camp's importance to the Germans, they'd kept everything running, including the connections to the waterworks.

"Germans have started destroying the last remaining waterworks in the city. Ours has been hit as well," Toni said. "It's a good thing we have another connection on the other side, but we don't know how long that will last. The pressure is already dropping, so it's probably only a matter of time before that one gives out as well."

"Makes sense," Natan said. *If they can't have the camp, they'll simply make it useless.*

They'd restored the position at the main entrance as best they could, creating a solid barricade and installing their machine guns. There was also the Panther tank, which was now placed within the camp's walls. The Germans knew this and hadn't made any attempts to recapture the camp. Yet.

"So, what are we going to do?" Natan asked. If they ran out of water, they would have to fall back into Old Town, and they'd lose their strategic position.

Toni smiled wryly. "*We* aren't going to do anything." He nodded at the boy next to him, who'd been quiet so far. "He has a message for you."

"The colonel wants an update on the camp situation," the boy said, his voice deeper than Natan had expected. "He requests you to come to the HQ in Old Town to report on what we can do."

"Just me?" Natan said, glancing at Toni, who stood by passively.

The boy nodded. "He specifically requested you. He said you've been here from the start, and he wants to hear from you directly."

Natan was surprised. It wasn't common for a fighter like himself to be summoned for such reports. Perhaps Radosław had an ulterior motive?

He nodded. "I'll make my way over right now—let me get my gun."

"Whenever you're ready, but please hurry. The colonel said it was urgent." He turned away.

"You're not joining me?" Natan asked.

"I need to deliver another message over there," the boy said, pointing, and then left.

Toni let out a low whistle. "Heading into Wola on his own. Must be some message."

Natan walked toward his barracks. Toni followed him as they entered the cramped building.

"While you're there," Toni said, "can you ask about reinforcements? I thought they were supposed to arrive days ago."

Natan nodded. "Of course." He grabbed his Vis, then changed his mind and took his MP 40 instead. He grabbed a spare magazine and stuffed it in his pocket before rushing outside. Toni followed him to the gate.

"Get back here as soon as you can, Lew. I have a feeling the Germans might decide to attack our camp any time now."

Natan looked his friend in the eye. "Don't worry; I'll be back before you know it." With that, he nodded at the two guards at the gate, stepped through, and walked into the street. As he left the walls of Gęsiówka behind, he clutched his gun a little tighter.

He crossed into the cobblestone streets of Old Town without incident. The streets were mostly deserted, but a few desperate people rushed by on solitary quests, probably for food or water. There was little evidence of the fighting here—the only area in the city the Germans hadn't managed to break into yet.

On the way over, he'd decided he wanted to check in on Kasia and, hopefully, Julia. It was a very slight detour to the apartment in Old Town, and he could spend a few minutes making sure they were okay. He hadn't been home for over a week.

He stopped in front of the building and was relieved to see everything looking normal. He opened the front door and quickly climbed the stairs. As he reached the door to the apartment, he felt a quick flutter in his stomach. *I hope she's here.*

Natan opened the door, careful not to make too much noise—nor too little—and startle the women. Kasia jumped out of her chair with shining eyes and hugged him as he walked into the kitchen.

"Natan! I was so worried about you! Where have you been all this time?"

He wrapped his arms around her and was surprised to feel her shaking. She was usually so composed, but her cheeks were wet as she turned to face him.

"It's a long story and one I'm afraid I don't have time to tell now," he said as he walked into the small living room. "Where's Julia?"

"She's not with you?"

The words felt like a punch to his gut, and he flinched. "Why would she be with me?"

"I think you'd better sit down." The smile on Kasia's face faded as it made way for concern. Natan sat down—now worried—and Kasia took a deep breath before she continued: "She went to look for you a few days ago, after news filtered through about your liberation of Gęsiówka. She said she had to find you."

"And you let her?" he interrupted, his voice sharp.

Kasia raised an eyebrow. "You know what she's like when she's got her mind set on something, Natan. Besides, I don't tell her—or you, for that matter—what she can or can't do."

He dropped his eyes. "Sorry," he said as he started pacing the room. *Where did she go? She should've been able to take the same route I did, right? Maybe she doesn't know about it.*

Kasia handed him a glass of water. "So you didn't see her at all?"

He shook his head. "She obviously didn't make it to the camp. There's no way I would've missed her there. She would've asked around; everybody knows me there." He downed the glass in one gulp.

Kasia refilled his glass and looked out of the kitchen window. She turned back to Natan, her eyes focusing on his. "I know you're worried, and I am, too, but we both know Julia can handle herself. She's been in tighter situations."

He started pacing the room.

"Natan!" Kasia raised her voice. "You can't do this to yourself. Julia's fine. She's probably helping people as we speak; you know what she's like. She'll show up."

"Maybe you're right," Natan started. He couldn't hide his worry. "And you haven't seen what I've seen."

She looked at him sternly. "Then you know there could be a perfectly good reason why Julia decided to help out on her way over to you, right? She can't walk away from people in need. She wouldn't even leave the ghetto when it was burning on all sides."

He nodded, and he felt a strange feeling of pride. "She wouldn't leave those children."

"Exactly. She'll find you, I'm sure of it."

Natan stood for a moment, still considering where Julia could be. He then realized it was no use. If she somehow managed to get into Wola, there would've been hundreds of places where she felt she needed to help. He could only hope she'd avoided the murderous SS squads. He balled his fists at the thought—she wouldn't just have avoided them, she probably would've taken a shot at them.

"Okay," he said, facing Kasia. "I need to go. But I want you to promise me one thing."

She looked back at him mockingly. "You're going to tell me what to do now?"

"I'm serious, Kasia," he said, pretending not to notice the rebuke. "Stay here, stay in Old Town. It's the safest place in the city."

"I know. I'm not going anywhere. I should be telling you to be careful, but you don't listen to me, now do you?"

He opened his mouth to argue, but Kasia drew him in for a hug. "I'm still going to tell you, Natan. You're the only family I have left. Be careful."

"I will," he said as they stood like that for a good ten seconds. When they broke the embrace, he turned for the door without looking back. As he hurried down the stairs, he felt a tear rolling down his cheek. Kasia would be fine— she'd always been. As he stepped into the street, he vowed he'd find Julia as soon as he'd delivered his report.

*

It was late afternoon when Natan exited the headquarters. Radosław hadn't kept him waiting—he'd been ushered into a briefing room as soon as he arrived. The colonel had been very interested in his update, and Natan had spent a good half hour answering questions around the situation in the camp. He mentioned the water shortage and the increased number of people coming to the camp for food. In the end, Radosław decided they should hold on to Gęsiówka for as long as they could. They needed to keep the lines between Wola and the Old Town in place, no matter what, and Natan had been promised more reinforcements. As Natan headed out of the briefing room, Radosław warned him the Germans had broken through their southeastern lines and were pushing toward the Old Town. Natan would have to be careful as he made his way back, as the SS had deployed smaller squads throughout the city.

He hurried along, impatient to get back to Gęsiówka. Maybe Julia had arrived by now, and if she hadn't, he would look for a way to find out where she was.

He then heard the voices, distant at first, but as he walked on, there was no mistaking the hum of many voices in the air. As he approached Podwale

Street, the main thoroughfare, it sounded like some sort of street party. Natan couldn't remember the last time he'd heard so many people so close to each other, and he hurried around the corner. *What's going on?*

The scene that greeted him was astonishing—a massive, frenzied crowd marching down the street. *At least 300 of them!* They were shouting, singing, and some danced on top of a slow-moving vehicle. Children waved Polish flags, the largest flying prominently from a makeshift flagpole mounted onto the vehicle. Natan tried to make out what it was, but he didn't recognize it. *A tractor?*

The vehicle was still a good 200 meters away, and Natan approached a young man marching by. "What's this?"

The man looked at him with an odd, feverish expression. "It's a German tank! They abandoned it near the barricade a few blocks down."

"What do you mean, abandoned it?"

"They realized they couldn't get past the barricade, and then the driver got out and ran away, leaving it there. And now it's ours!" The man looked impatient, and he moved on, shouting at his friends to wait for him.

Natan looked at the people in the street. He saw a few people wearing Home Army armbands, but most of the people were civilians—women and children crowding around, smiles on their faces as they all tried to get a better view of the war bounty that rolled down the street. Natan needed to get back to the camp. *There are too many people here anyway—I'll hear about it later.*

He considered his detour. It would lead him along the edge of the Old Town and would take a bit longer, but he remembered Radosław's warning about the German breakthrough in the southeast. They could be lurking outside the Old Town borders.

The vehicle had moved only a few meters in the time he was there, and now it appeared to be stuck. Some people were moving debris out of the way, while others pushed without much success. *It'll take a while to get it to HQ at this pace.*

Natan chuckled and turned in the other direction, keen to get away from the large crowd. *They would make an excellent target for an air attack if the Germans knew they were here.*

As the thought went through his head, he stopped dead in his tracks. *It can't be.*

He spun his head around, and as he did, a mighty explosion threw him to the ground after a flash brighter than he'd ever seen blinded him. His world went black.

CHAPTER THIRTY-NINE

Julia approached the gates of Gęsiówka with trepidation even though she now wore the white-and-red armband of the Home Army. She looked up at the guard tower and was surprised to see a female face peering back. The woman was around her age, anxiety in her eyes.

As she neared, the woman leaned over the simple wooden railing of her tower. "What do you need?" she asked, her voice high-pitched but not unfriendly. "We're not expecting any reinforcements, certainly not from Wola."

Julia realized she made an odd sight—a solo fighter coming from the Wola district. "Please let me in—I'm looking for someone." She pointed at her armband.

"Do you have news from Wola?"

She shook her head. "I can only tell you there's no one left there but a few people hiding. Please, let me in."

The woman seemed to hesitate but then disappeared. A moment later, the gate was opened by a man. "Quick, get inside."

Julia entered the camp, where Home Army fighters were going about their business, along with people carrying supplies. At the far end of the camp, there was a smoking chimney.

"That's the kitchen," the man said as he closed the gate. "You look tired—but perhaps you're also in need of a hot meal?"

Julia looked at him in disbelief. "You have hot food here?" She hadn't had a warm meal since she'd left to find Natan, which was now more than ten days ago.

The man nodded. "The Germans left quite an operation behind when we took the camp. They had plenty of Jewish inmates working for them. They've joined us, now."

Julia was stunned and didn't immediately respond. The thought of a proper meal seemed too alien to be true.

"Where did you come from, anyway?" the man asked. "We don't get a lot of people coming back from Wola."

Julia's mind went back to the previous week. After she'd joined the men at the barricade, they had worked day and night to secure their position. No attack came in the first two days, and they'd fortified themselves to a point where Julia was sure the Germans couldn't break through. It was on her second night there when things changed dramatically.

People of all ages poured toward their barricade, fleeing Wola. Julia heard stories of the SS burning down entire buildings, but not before locking the doors so people couldn't get out. Escapees told stories of whole streets being blocked off as the SS systematically emptied buildings and lined people up in the street and shot them. Mothers were forced to watch as their children were murdered before they fell to the same fate.

The news had enraged the fighters at her barricade, and they'd decided to fight back. Julia joined one of the nightly attacks from the shadows.

As the SS cleared block after block in Wola, the fires followed as the corpses were burned in the streets. A thick layer of black smoke hung over the city for days on end, making it difficult to breathe.

"Never mind," the man said, taking her back to the present. "Why don't you go over there and get yourself something to eat. There will be plenty of time to report on wherever you came from."

Julia nodded absentmindedly and walked into the camp. Even though she would love to eat, she had no intention of going to the kitchen. Before she could even consider food, she needed to know he was okay. She stopped a man carrying a sack of potatoes. "Say," she asked, "where can I find the men of the Zośka?"

He pointed to a building down the narrow throughway. "They bunk over there, although most of them will be out."

She thanked him and headed straight for the building. As she entered, she ran into a bulky man who looked surprised to see her.

"You're not one of us, are you?"

Julia shook her head and decided not to waste any time. "I'm looking for Lew. I was told I could find him here."

The man's eyes narrowed as he looked her up and down. "Who's asking?"

"These are the Zośka battalion's barracks, right?" Julia asked, ignoring his question.

He nodded. "Sure, but who are you?"

Julia felt frustration bubbling up over all the questions. *Aren't we supposed to be on the same side?* She sighed and opened her mouth to give the man a piece of her mind when she heard a familiar voice from the back. "What's going on here, Wacek?"

Toni.

She pushed past Wacek—who was too surprised to react in time—and rushed toward Toni. "You can't believe how happy I am to see you!" she exclaimed.

Toni smiled as he recognized her and drew her in for a big hug. "Krystyna! I was wondering when you'd show up."

They broke their embrace, and she looked at Toni. Rugged as always, but his eyes showed something new—exhaustion.

"Where can I find Lew?"

A shadow passed over his face, and he averted his eyes for a moment out of the window. He then returned his gaze to her. "He left for HQ three days ago. We were having problems with the water supply. He was supposed to report there and return the same day. We haven't seen him since."

"Three days ago?" Julia did a quick calculation and gasped. "But that was when . . ."

He nodded. "When the bomb went off on Podwale—"

"—right where the headquarters are," Julia said softly. *Had he been near the explosion?* She'd heard that it had knocked down nearly a whole block. She looked back at Toni, who stood silently, his eyes sad. The unasked question hung between them, and Julia broke the silence—she had to know. "Is Lew dead?"

Toni didn't immediately answer as he walked to the window and stood there for a moment. Then, he said in a voice that was almost a whisper, "I don't know. There were more than 300 people in the area, and many didn't make it. A messenger came in a few hours after the explosion, but he had little news. The whole block was destroyed, and the people near the bomb, well . . ." His voice broke, and he took a moment to find his composure. "They said there was nothing left of them."

Julia looked at the big man who'd seemed so imposing only a few minutes earlier. He now appeared to be a man defeated, one who also cared deeply about Natan.

She took a deep breath. "We don't know if Lew was in the area. Maybe he'd already left and got caught up somewhere else?"

Toni nodded without conviction as he continued blankly staring out of the window.

Julia stood next to him and took his hand, which felt soft and clammy. "I can't give up on Lew being alive. Until someone tells me for sure he's dead, I have to believe he's somewhere."

Toni's eyes drifted to their joined hands, then up to her face. "So, what are you going to do?"

"There's only one place I can go," she said with conviction. "Old Town."

Toni nodded. "Before you do, let me show you the safest way. The Germans have pushed forward in the past few days; plenty lie between us and where you're going."

She nodded. "I'd appreciate that."

"And one more thing, Krystyna. You're going to come with me and have something to eat first. You look famished."

*

Julia left Gęsiówka through the back gate an hour later. Toni had given the directions that would get her as close to the Old Town as possible. He'd warned that the Germans had surrounded the main entry points and were relentlessly shelling the city center. They'd also posted snipers around the perimeter, and her Home Army armband would make her an obvious target. Despite that, he'd urged her to hang on to it for when she ran into their people. In the end, she decided to hide it in her jacket pocket, prepared to show it as soon as she caught up with other fighters.

She hurried through the streets, careful to avoid the main thoroughfares. It was a significant detour, but she couldn't risk running into any Germans. Even without her armband, a young woman alone on the streets was asking for trouble. She instinctively ducked every time she heard the rumble of the German artillery. The sound increased with every step closer to the Old Town. In Wola, the artillery had been background noise, far away from her position. Here, it shook the ground beneath her feet.

She found occasional shortcuts where entire buildings had been reduced to rubble. She doubted anyone still lived in this part of the city, but she remained careful and checked the armband in her pocket more than once. As she emerged from a courtyard, she noticed the kotwica symbol on the building opposite. It was simply a "P" with an "A" anchored underneath to the untrained eye, but Julia knew exactly what it meant. She looked up and down the street before crossing. She found another smaller version next to a door. She quickly opened it and found rickety stairs leading down into the dark basement.

Reaching the bottom, she saw a flicker of light to her left. As she got closer, she heard soft voices, which instantly died down as they heard her approach.

"It's okay—I'm Home Army," she said in her Warsaw accent. There was no response. She stayed close to the wall and pulled her armband from her pocket, then stepped into the light, her outstretched hand holding her armband. She hoped no one was too trigger-happy as she walked into a small room lit by a single candle. The faces staring back at her looked terrified. Two young children with their mother, presumably, and a woman who appeared to be in her sixties—it was hard to tell.

"Can I pass through to the Old Town here?" Julia asked them in a soft voice.

The mother picked up the candle and pointed at a space behind them. "The walls of the cellars of the other buildings are all smashed up. Keeping going that way until you can't go any farther. You can then climb up, and you'll be near Miodowa Street."

She thanked them and continued down the dark passageway, finding her way by touch when no light leaked through the ceiling. She trod carefully and soon found the exit.

Climbing up a surprisingly sturdy set of stairs, she opened the door and was temporarily blinded by the bright daylight. As her eyes adjusted, she looked around and found herself in a small room with an open window. Outside she spied the Royal Castle ahead, confirming she was now in the Old Town. The sound of nearby gunfire heightened her senses, and she carefully stepped into the street, her eyes quickly scanning in all directions. The street appeared safe, and she headed in the direction of Podwale—still on the wrong side of the battle lines.

She found her people only a few blocks down Kilinskiego Street. It was here where the destruction of the explosion became visible, near the junction with Podwale Street. The barricade had been repaired—although it didn't look quite as imposing as it probably had been before—and it was adequately staffed, guns pointing in her direction.

Julia was surprised she'd not run into any Germans but decided it probably had to do with them staying out of the way of their own artillery shells.

She felt nervous as she neared the barricade, even though her armband was clearly visible. She hoped whoever looked at her from behind the barrier didn't mistake her for a German soldier. She chuckled at the thought as she considered her appearance. No German soldier would wear these rags. Besides, there were no women in the SS squads attacking the city.

She slowly walked on and noticed a few heads appearing in the windows above her. She raised her hands, pointing at the armband, and shouted:

"I'm Home Army. I come from Gęsiówka!"

A voice quickly responded. "Keep moving, daughter of Poland! Hurry!"

She sprinted the final 50 meters and took the hand of one of the men who'd climbed on top of the barricade. He helped her over, and another couple of strong hands lifted her down. All eyes were on her.

"I'm sorry, I'm not sure I heard you right," one of the men who'd helped her down said. "Did you say Gęsiówka?"

Julia nodded as murmurs spread along the barricade. "They're still holding out there? And how did you make it here? The Old Town is surrounded."

She quickly recapped her journey of the last . . . hour? *Couple of hours? How long did it really take me?* The men listened breathlessly, and when she finished, it was quiet.

Julia then asked, "This is where the bomb went off, right?"

The man who'd helped her down, who introduced himself as Juri, crossed himself as he nodded. "Many of our people perished here." He pointed to the corner of the street, to a large crater. "That's where it happened. We built the barricade using whatever was left of that building. The streets were soaked with blood." A shadow passed his face as he struggled to continue.

Julia looked down and noticed the cobblestones were indeed a shade darker than usual. She gave Juri a moment before speaking. "I can't imagine what it was like here after that. I'm here because I'm looking for someone." She paused, and he looked up, his eyes inviting her to continue. "His name is Lew, and I believe he was nearby when the bomb went off." She described Natan, and the man listened without interrupting.

"Many men fit that description, I'm afraid," he said, almost apologetically. "I can't say that I've met him."

Julia nodded and looked at the other men standing nearby. They shook their heads. She suddenly felt weary, but she forced herself not to lose hope. "Where were the survivors taken?"

Juri looked at her with compassion. "They were taken to a field hospital a few streets down. They keep moving it, though, as the German bastards keep bombing our hospitals."

Julia shuddered. *Pigs. Is there nothing they won't do?* "Thank you, I'll go check over there, then."

"I hope you find him, but don't get your hopes up too much," Juri said, his eyes glistening. "I lost all my brothers in the blast. I hope you have more luck."

She nodded and left without another word. She felt her eyes sting as she walked away, the man's raw pain stabbing at her heart. She prayed, not for the first time, that Natan hadn't been anywhere near the explosion.

*

She hurried down Podwale Street, anxious to leave the destruction behind. The area showed the evidence of the recent shellings that rained down on the Old Town, as entire buildings had disappeared—the ground still smoldering. The street was quiet, and she looked for the distinctive red cross markings of the hospital. Julia started to worry as she walked for a good five minutes without finding the hospital. Didn't Juri say it was just down the street? She began to doubt herself and thought about turning back when she saw a woman crossing the road ahead.

The woman wore something resembling a nurse's uniform, and Julia called out, startling her. She stopped, and Julia quickly caught up with her. "Sorry about startling you, but do you know where the hospital is?"

The woman eyed her suspiciously at first until she noticed Julia's armband. "Of course, I'm on my way over."

"Do you take care of the survivors of the bomb?" Julia said.

The nurse nodded. "We're overflowing, but yes, most of them are over there." They walked toward a large residential building down the street. She caught Julia's surprised look at the doorway. "We're no longer marking the hospitals. The Stukas bombed the last two. I managed to get out only because I was working in the basement. The attack killed over 50 people instantly, and another ten died later because of their burns." She stated this matter-of-factly, but her eyes conveyed concern.

"How many people do you have here?" Julia asked as they entered a crowded hallway. People lined one side of the hall, most of them with minor injuries. A man wearing a stethoscope sat crouched down, attending to a young woman carrying a toddler.

"I'd say there's always around 200 people here, but they come and go," the nurse said. She suddenly looked impatient and keen to get rid of Julia. "Is there anyone you're looking for in particular?"

She gave her Natan's description and added he was a Home Army fighter.

"All the fighters are in the basement. If he survived, he'll be down there." She pointed at an open door at the end of the hallway and hurried off.

Julia descended into the basement, heart pounding in her chest. Halfway down the stairs, the stench of sweat, blood, feces, vomit, and urine hit her nostrils. She grabbed the handrail as she gagged, fighting down a strong wave of nausea. When it passed, she focused on breathing through her mouth, the thick air enveloping her more with every step down. She reached the bottom and was dismayed to find a dimly lit room packed with men—and a few women. At least fifty people were crammed into a space fit for maybe half of that, at best. They lay side by side, some sharing the makeshift mattresses as they coughed and wheezed.

Julia fought the urge to hurry back up the stairs, telling herself she had to know if Natan was among these poor creatures. She slowly walked down the narrow walkway in the middle of the room and forced herself to look at the faces. Some were more dead than alive, their eyes closed, their chests heaving up and down as they struggled to breathe. A young boy—he couldn't be much older than 16—whimpered softly as he held his bandaged hands out in front of him. She looked away and continued farther into the basement, where patients must have been for longer, for the condition of these men was worse—they were missing limbs or had their heads entirely wrapped in bandages. She neared the end of the room, the light getting fainter, but a new smell entering her nostrils as she accidentally forgot to breathe through her mouth.

She coughed and almost doubled over as she recognized the smell. It had lingered everywhere she'd gone in the past few weeks. It was the smell of decay, the scent of imminent death. She concentrated hard to make out the faces of the people on this side of the room.

They lay with eyes closed, their faces deathly pale. She blinked hard and turned back toward the stairs, a feeling of despair rising from the pit of her stomach—Natan wasn't here. *Have I lost him?*

As she did, she noticed something move in the darkness. A figure in the corner, behind the living dead. She stepped closer, stepping over another patient to see better.

She bent down and saw a man, tightly wrapped under the blankets, but she thought she could make out enough of his contours to give her a glimmer of hope. Julia carefully reached for his face, aware of the bandages, and gently touched the fabric.

As she did, the man's eyes opened. He let out a gasp, the whites of his eyes contrasting sharply with the darkness of everything around him. He looked as if he were suddenly awakened from a dream. Julia quickly withdrew her hands from his bandages and held them up in the air apologetically.

Then the expression in his eyes changed as they focused on her with recognition. His body relaxed, and he mumbled something inaudible. She moved closer, and as she did, saw a flash of the brown eyes she knew so well. She felt her knees buckle as she heard his strained whisper.

"Julcia . . . is that really you?"

CHAPTER FORTY

Natan lay in his corner in the basement, his eyes focused on the stairs. He'd spent almost two weeks in the hospital, and he couldn't wait to leave. He didn't remember much of the first week, only that he'd drifted in and out of consciousness, waking up only when a nurse came to bring him something to eat or drink or to numb the throbbing pain in his head. His mind had been hazy, and when Julia appeared to hover over him, he didn't believe it was really her. Only when she returned the next day and the next, he realized he wasn't dreaming.

She'd brought food superior to what the nurses fed him, and his condition improved dramatically. Even though he shared some of the food with the men around him, it did little good—they were strangers almost every day. They were brought in from nearby positions—fighters like himself struggling against the ongoing German onslaught. Few lasted longer than a night in the basement.

Most of the men were unconscious, and only a few recovered enough to speak—but Natan gathered enough information to tell things were not going well, and the number of men in the basement continued to swell. If that wasn't bad enough, the constant impact of the artillery shells hitting nearby buildings—with dust and sand falling from the basement's roof—kept him awake day and night. Natan couldn't remember when he'd last had a proper sleep in his week of consciousness. He'd pestered the nurses about releasing him, but they'd been adamant: he was in no position to go back to the fighting.

He rubbed the bandages around his head as he tried to focus on the *Biuletyn Informacyjny* in front of him. He could make out the words in the headline, but the letters of the article kept moving. Frustrated, he tossed the pamphlet to the side. He looked to the stairs again and was disappointed when there was no movement yet. *What's taking her so long?*

After regaining consciousness, he'd found out he was one of the very few survivors of the bomb attack with the so-called tractor. It had been a small, armored vehicle the Germans called a Borgward. It was specifically designed to carry a high volume of concealed explosives missed by the men who'd captured the vehicle.

Natan sat up against the wall and shook his head in the semidarkness. What fools they'd been, taking the Trojan horse right past the barrier. A jolt of pain shot through his head, and he flinched, closing his eyes. It passed after a few seconds, and he'd gotten used to it by now. He opened his eyes, rubbed his temples, and was pleased to see a familiar figure making her way down the stairs.

Julia met his eyes and deftly navigated herself through the crowded basement. She sat down next to him and gave him a quick peck on the cheek. "How are you feeling today?" she asked as she handed him a piece of bread from the small basket she carried.

He took a bite of the stale bread. "Ready to go." He chewed furiously. "Did you tell the nurses upstairs?"

She nodded but averted her eyes.

"What?" he said, swallowing the first bite before ripping off another piece.

"They said they don't think you should leave—they say your concussion is too severe."

"Nonsense," Natan said, his mouth full. "I'm sure there are men in worse conditions out there fighting."

"They're worried you'll make it worse," she said as she spotted the *Biuletyn Informacyjny* next to him. "Did you read this?"

"Yes," he lied. "Soviets are making their way over, and the Germans are being pushed back in the west by the Americans. Sounds like it's a matter of time. I want to play my part. I'm going crazy down here."

Julia looked at him, her eyes showing concern but also understanding. She nodded as she took his hand. "If you really feel you're ready, then let's go. I'll be with you, you know that."

"Let's go," he said as he pushed himself up from the cot. His head spun, but he clenched his teeth as he grabbed on to the wall.

Julia jumped to her feet and took his other hand. "Are you sure?"

Before he could answer, another voice boomed behind her. "Where do you think you're going?"

It was Martha, the nurse in charge of the basement. *Not her, not now.*

"I'm leaving," Natan said as he took a few steps toward Martha, still holding on to Julia.

She blocked his way to the stairs. "You need to rest, Lew. Your concussion isn't anywhere near healed." Martha crossed her arms, and Natan decided arguing with her probably wasn't going to help much. He held up his hands as he said, "Okay, you're right. But I can't stay down here any longer. People are dying, and there's a new person next to me every day."

Martha moved closer to him and shushed him. "No need to make it worse," she said as her eyes darted around the room.

He brushed the comment off and said, "What if I promise I'll head straight home with her?" He pointed at Julia, who nodded. "And stay in bed for another week?"

She looked at him suspiciously. "How do I know you won't head straight back to your battalion? I know your kind."

He smiled and pointed at his bandages. "You think they're going to let me fight like this? They'll be worried I might shoot our own people." Martha's face showed indecision, and he pressed on. "Besides, she won't let me go unless she's sure I'm back to my old self—right, Krystyna?"

Julia gave him an almost imperceptible frown but nodded as she looked at Martha. "Of course."

"Look, you can even come and check on me—I'll give you the address," Natan offered, knowing full well she wouldn't have time—or interest—to do so.

Martha gave him and Julia a hard stare but then raised her hands in surrender. "Fine, if you think you're better off at home, be my guest." She stepped to the side and made another dramatic gesture toward the stairs. "But nowhere near the fighting for at least another week, Lew!"

"Of course!" He hurried past her before she had a chance to change her mind. Julia helped him up the stairs, and as he looked back, he saw Martha was already moving another patient to what had been his spot for two weeks.

The bright light blinded Natan as they stepped outside. He hadn't been out of the basement for two weeks, and his eyes protested fiercely.

Julia put a hand on his shoulder. "Take your time; there's no rush. It *is* a very sunny day," she said.

As his vision cleared, Natan blinked hard as he looked around. "Aren't we supposed to be on Podwale?"

"We are." Julia pointed up the street. "The Royal Castle is up there."

He scanned the street from the castle back to where they stood. He hardly recognized the Podwale Street from when he had passed through two weeks before—there was nothing left of the prominent thoroughfare lined with tightly packed buildings. Instead, he looked at a crater-ridden landscape, much like the Jewish ghetto. *Now I know what it must've been like for her.*

Julia followed his gaze. "They've been shelling the Old Town for weeks. I'm sure you've heard, even in the basement."

Natan was in a daze but nodded. "Sure, but I didn't expect this."

"They've also sent in the Stukas with firebombs," Julia said, pointing at a dark plume of smoke rising in the distance. "Wherever they suspect people are hiding, hospitals especially, they'll send the Stukas."

"It's a miracle I'm alive, then," Natan said, suddenly anxious to get some distance from the building. "Is the whole Old Town like this?"

Julia nodded. "Pretty much, although there are areas where it's not so bad."

"Kasia?" He felt a wave of panic.

Julia quickly held up her hands. "She's okay, and she doesn't want to leave."

Natan shook his head, feeling restless. "She has to get out of here—it's just a matter of time until they hit her building."

"Why don't we go see her? Let's see how you handle a walk."

He turned to her, annoyed. "Don't tell me you agree with that nurse down there now? You agreed I needed to get out of there."

"Of course not, but you've been down there for two weeks. Come." She gently took his hand, ignoring his outburst.

It took them longer than expected to make the trek through the Old Town. There were obstacles at every corner. Bricks from collapsed buildings blocked their way, which meant they had to take many detours. Natan begrudgingly accepted that his two weeks in the hospital had impacted his fitness, as they had to make a few stops along the way.

"It's the climbing through the rubble, mostly," he said as they sat down. "Give me a minute to catch my breath." In reality, his head was spinning, and he was having trouble focusing. Julia was there to guide him and patiently sat beside him as he caught his breath.

They continued for another fifteen minutes until they reached Kasia's building. Natan struggled up the stairs and was relieved when Julia opened the door to their apartment. "Kasia's expecting me," she said with a faint smile.

Kasia rushed toward them and hugged him hard before stepping back to inspect. Her eyes betrayed her worries, and Natan was sure he looked even worse than he felt. Nevertheless, he tried to keep a brave face and said, "It's great to be home."

"You'd better sit down," Kasia said as she guided him toward a chair at the kitchen table. She quickly placed a steaming bowl of broth in front of him. "It's only potato and a little bit of carrot, but it's better than nothing."

"Nothing is what I got in the hospital," he said as he picked up a spoon to take a big bite. He felt the warmth of the broth spread through his body and sighed contently. "This is the best food I've tasted for two weeks—it's delicious."

Kasia and Julia both smiled, but he caught the concern in their eyes as they watched him eat. When he finished, he pushed the bowl aside and looked at Kasia.

"Julia and I think you should get out of Old Town," he said.

Kasia raised an eyebrow and crossed her arms. "Do you, now?" Her mocking tone did nothing to hide what she thought of his suggestion. "And where will you go?"

"We'll rejoin the battalion, of course. That's why I left the hospital."

Kasia turned to Julia. "And you're allowing this?"

Julia looked uncomfortable as she drummed her fingers on the table. "We think you should get out of the city. There's a way to get out, you know. I've heard the Germans are offering amnesty to civilians."

Kasia let out a sarcastic laugh. "I'd rather take my chances here than count on their mercy!" She sat down next to Natan. "I'm afraid you're in no position to tell me what I can or can't do." She gently touched the bandages around his head. "You're in no state to fight yourself, don't you know?"

He felt uncomfortable and looked to Julia for support. She shrugged. *I'm on my own.* "It looks worse than it is," he said. "I can help out around the barricades, for sure."

"Look, Natan. I've survived almost five years of the Germans throwing everything they have at us. I think I can hold out a little longer. The last thing I'll do is surrender," she said, now stroking his bandages softly. "But I'll leave the city on one condition."

Natan's ears perked up, and he turned to her. "What's that?"

"I'll leave if the both of you do so, too."

"There's no way I'll abandon the city or my brothers!" Natan said indignantly. "They need all the men they can get. You haven't seen the situation in the hospital, Kasia! People are dying every day." She looked at him in silence, nodding as he continued. "We need to hold out only a little longer. The Americans and Russians are closing in from both sides. There's nowhere for them to go!"

"I guess we're all staying then," Kasia said. "Where would I go? This is my home, like it is yours. I'd rather die here, fighting or otherwise." She stood up, took his bowl, and placed it in the sink. Exuding an air of calm, she filled the kettle with water and put it on the stove. She then turned back to Natan and

Julia. "I understand you want to fight, and I know I can't stop you. Neither of you. But you must also respect my decision."

Natan looked at her, the woman who hadn't hesitated to take him in after that fateful day almost five years ago. "Okay," he said, and he slowly got up. "But Julia and I will have to go. I can't stay around while the rest fight."

"So you're going back to the battalion today?" Kasia asked as she poured the steaming hot water into three large mugs. She reached for a small tin and scooped generous portions of substitute coffee in the mugs. "You're not taking some more rest?"

The sweet scent of the brew filled the room as Natan shook his head. "I've had enough rest. It's time to do something."

Kasia set the mugs in front of them and sat down opposite him. "Then I can only wish you Godspeed and pray you'll come back sooner rather than later." She took her mug and held it up. "I know what you two are like when you've set your mind on something."

Natan clinked his mug to hers and Julia's. He held it close to his lips, savoring the warmth against his face. He looked at Kasia and Julia and counted himself fortunate to have two people who cared for him so much.

"This will be over before you know it," he said as he took a sip. "We'll push the Germans back into the Vistula."

*

It didn't take long for Natan and Julia to find his old battalion. As they made their way west toward Gęsiówka, they quickly hit a barricade. They were told only a small group had stayed behind in the camp. Natan's battalion had been deployed across checkpoints in the Old Town. One of the men knew Toni, and he'd pointed them in the right direction. Much to Natan's relief, he'd found his friend almost immediately, and Toni had told them Colonel Radosław had ordered the entire squadron back to defend the Old Town. The Germans had overrun most positions in the rest of the city as they advanced with heavy artillery, tanks, and continued air support. Natan was shocked by the news; from what he'd heard in the hospital, he thought the Germans were on the ropes. Toni ensured him this was hardly the case—wherever the Americans and Russians were, they were taking their time getting to Warsaw. He'd sent Natan and Julia to report to one of the command posts a few streets down—he didn't know where they'd be needed most, but they could certainly use their help.

They entered the building into a crowded hallway. It wasn't unusual for command posts to be busy, but as they navigated past the people hanging around, Natan was shocked to find even more people sleeping on the floors in the adjacent rooms. He looked at Julia, who seemed just as surprised.

"Are you sure we're in the right place? This feels more like a hospital," Julia said, reading his mind.

"They all look like fighters, though, and they don't appear injured," Natan said as he noticed a few familiar faces. The men and women all looked exhausted.

Natan stopped a young man carrying a large stack of folders. "Where can I find the commanders?"

The man pointed to the stairs. "Second floor, can't miss 'em," he said before moving on.

They reached the second floor, where it was noticeably quieter. A man exited one of the rooms and looked at them enquiringly. "Help you with something?"

"We want to report for duty," Natan said. "I've come out of the hospital, and I'd like to rejoin my battalion."

"Which one would that be?" the man said impatiently.

"Zośka," Natan replied.

The man looked taken aback as his demeanor changed. "You'll need to speak to Major Jan, then, but he's not to be disturbed right now. Why don't you wait downstairs, and I'll come and find you when he's ready." He waved dismissively at the stairs behind them.

Natan glared at the man and opened his mouth but felt Julia tug at his sleeve. "Let's do that, Lew. I'm sure the major will be ready for us soon enough."

He followed Julia down the stairs and, as he did, felt slightly queasy. Natan grabbed the handrail to steady himself and catch his breath.

Julia turned around, her eyes showing concern. "Perhaps it's not such a bad idea to take a break. Come, let's go in here."

He followed her as she entered one of the rooms on the first floor. People sat around playing cards, talking quietly, while others had retreated to their own corners. Natan and Julia found a spot next to the door.

"Why don't you sleep for a bit," she said. "I'll keep an eye out for the major. You heard what Toni said; they need all the men they can get. But they'll need you at your best."

Natan nodded, exhaustion overwhelming him. It had been a long day since he'd left the hospital. He placed his head on Julia's shoulder and was asleep within seconds.

CHAPTER FORTY-ONE

Julia hurriedly crossed the street after the sound of a nearby explosion died down and entered the building as another explosion nearly pushed her inside. She carried a small basket with gauze—or what passed for it. The hallway was even more crowded than a week ago when she'd arrived there with Natan. People now lined both walls, and she had to step over outstretched legs as she headed for the back room.

Another young woman stood waiting for her, looking cross while she tapped her foot. "Took you long enough!" She snatched the basket and headed off without another word. Julia glared back before someone else called out: "Krystyna, a hand, please?"

She turned to see Ewa waving at her from a doorway, and she quickly headed over. Ewa ran the hospital's ground floor and genuinely cared and took her time, unlike some of the other nurses.

"We need to move him upstairs," Ewa said, pointing at a middle-aged man with a pale face. "He can't get up by himself." They lifted the man to his feet, supporting him under his arms. They took small, deliberate steps as they slowly guided him up the stairs into an already crowded room.

"Thanks," Ewa said as they walked back into the hallway. "It's funny how you can never find someone to help when you need them, right?"

They descended the stairs, and Julia scanned the hallway. "A lot more people in today."

"It's only getting worse, but from what I've heard, it's not much better at the other hospitals," Ewa said, her eyes already on a young fighter being carried in. "Put him in a bed over there," she said, pointing at a door farther down the hallway.

A voice came from behind Julia. "Krystyna?" She turned and was surprised to see one of the secretaries from upstairs—where the military command had their offices. He jerked his head toward the ceiling. "They need you upstairs."

She followed the man, wondering what it could be, feeling a shiver run down her spine. *Has something happened to Natan?* He'd returned to his battalion the same day they arrived at the command post. He'd been back two days ago, but only to give a short report on what was going on in his unit—the news hadn't been encouraging. They were being pushed back into the Old Town.

As they reached the second floor, Julia was escorted through a doorway, within which a man she'd never met before waved her to a chair and dismissed the secretary, who softly closed the door.

She sat down and, before the man could say anything, asked, "Is this about Lew?" She couldn't help herself.

The man looked surprised for a moment before shaking his head. "No, I wouldn't summon you for that." Despite his dismissive tone, his face was more forgiving. Julia found herself leaning in a bit closer. "You're Krystyna."

"Yes."

"You can call me Jakub," he said, sitting up a little straighter. "You've worked in the hospital for a while now, right?" Julia nodded, and he continued. "Then you know how bad our situation is. To be honest, we can't defend the Old Town any longer, and we're getting ready to evacuate as many of our people as possible."

Julia frowned. "Evacuate them where?" *And how?*

Jakub looked thoughtful, carefully considering the following words. "There's only one place we can go from here, and that's downtown."

She thought about the streets outside. It seemed impossible to simply pack up all the wounded and take them through the rubble. "But the Germans have us surrounded."

He nodded. "I've been told you're familiar with the sewers?"

Realization dawned on Julia, and she shifted in her seat. "Well, yes. But mostly those running between the Old Town and the ghetto."

Jakub stood up and leaned on the table, his eyes focusing on Julia. "But you know what it's like down there; you've done this before. You know how to keep your bearings, right?"

She swallowed hard as she considered his question. She wanted to say yes, to help out in any way she could. But she also had her doubts—she thought back to the last time she was down in the sewers, escorting that group of Home Army men into Wola. She looked at Jakub, a hint of desperation in his eyes.

"Krystyna, you won't be alone down there. We have people helping out, but most of the fighters we're evacuating have never been down there. We don't know how they'll respond, especially when they're wounded and scared. We need people like you.

"Okay," she said, slowly nodding. "I'll do it."

His eyes lit up as he moved away from the table. "We'll start the evacuations tonight when darkness falls. You should try to get some rest before that. It'll be a long night." He sat down, and Julia felt like she was being dismissed. Then, as she opened the door, a thought popped into her head, and she turned back.

"What about the people downstairs? Those that can't walk? They won't be able to get down into the sewers."

Jakub was scribbling on a notepad and looked up. He put his pencil down and said, "I'm afraid we can evacuate only fighters. Or men who can be patched up sufficiently."

"We're going to leave them behind?"

"We have no choice," he said. "We'll mark the building as a hospital."

Julia knew that wasn't going to help much, but bit her tongue. "What about the other people in the Old Town?"

"They will need to look after themselves," he said, impatience in his voice. "We'll regroup and attack the Germans from downtown. It's all about keeping the resistance alive. And we can only do that with able fighters." He picked up his pencil and returned to his writing.

It was a death sentence for those left behind. The SS wouldn't discriminate between fighters and civilians—they were all Banditen to the Germans. *Especially the people in the Old Town who'd helped the Home Army.*

She glared down at Jakub, who continued to scribble away, now oblivious to her presence. Julia opened her mouth but then thought better of it. It wouldn't make any difference—a commander of the Home Army wasn't going to listen to her objections, valid as they were. But she could do something else. She ran down the stairs and was out of the building before anyone could stop her. *I have to warn Kasia.*

*

Julia was dismayed by what she saw as she rushed through the destroyed streets. Every other building was reduced to rubble, bomb craters marking every corner. The few people she ran into walked around in a daze, searching for any kind of shelter, their clothes torn, their eyes glazed over from hunger and thirst. Julia tried to send a few of them toward Podwale Street, but her words barely registered as they looked back at her with hollow eyes.

She pushed on, getting more worried about Kasia by the minute. Had the bombs also found her home? Would she find the woman who'd become like a mother to her buried in a grave of mangled wire, bricks, and dust? She shook the thought from her mind—Kasia would've found a way out once she'd seen how bad it had become. Doubt gnawed at her as she climbed over a pile of debris in the middle of the street. As she climbed down, careful to avoid the splintered pieces of wood at the bottom, she heard a sound that stopped her heart. She froze as she looked up and ahead, hoping the rumble of the engine was farther away than she thought. It wasn't—she threw herself on the ground.

A small plane appeared a few seconds later, and Julia prayed the pilot wouldn't notice her. She looked up, and, in that brief moment, her eyes met the pilot's as the Stuka roared past her. It gained height, and Julia thought she might be safe as it climbed and turned away. Then, it took a sharp turn, back in her direction—it was coming for her.

Her eyes darted around as she frantically searched for cover. Staying in the middle of the street wasn't an option, and she started running. Behind her, the terrifying howl of the Stuka's sirens pierced her ears—it was in a steep nosedive and preparing to drop his deadly cargo.

Then, as the sound of the sirens became so loud she thought it might pop her eardrums, she saw a ditch on the side of the street. It looked deep enough to provide cover from whatever the Stuka was dropping. She dashed and jumped down without another thought.

Ignoring the sharp pain in her ankle as she landed, she heard a distinct click in the air—the Stuka had released its bomb. She put her hands over her head and buried her face in the cold mud as the plane roared past overhead. The siren stopped abruptly as the engine changed into a different gear—the plane was climbing again.

Julia braced herself and waited for everything to end. There were no flashes of her life passing before her eyes, just sheer terror as time slowed down. She saw Natan's face, serene and smiling. She buried her face farther into the mud. *I don't want to die.*

She felt the impact of the bomb before she heard it. The ground shook, a loud swoosh and a burst of heat. *Am I on fire?* She tried to breathe, but no air came through her constricted throat. She turned her face and gasped for air. Julia fought her rising panic and opened her eyes. She was still in the ditch. She looked at her hands, she felt her hair—everything was still there. There was no blood.

She looked up to see the Stuka disappear out of sight and cautiously stood as she took in a large gulp of air. In her hazy state, she suddenly heard voices, then she shook herself back to reality, and the voices came through at full volume. She turned her head, and that's when she saw the flames.

She hadn't noticed it before—she'd been too occupied with herself—but now she saw the top floor of a three-story building farther down the street was ablaze. Flames, along with the thick, pitch-black smoke caused only by incendiary bombs, billowed out of the windows. On the ground level, people rushed out, their panicked cries filling the previously quiet street. The Stuka had bombed the building.

Julia clambered out of the ditch, ignoring her ankle, and headed straight for them. She climbed over the first pile of debris and skipped over a small bomb crater when a familiar sound made her stop in her tracks. The howl was unmistakable, and as she turned, she could almost feel the Stuka graze her hair as it roared past overhead.

This time there was no time to find cover. The siren stopped, and Julia threw herself to the surface of the street, covering her head with her arms. She prayed she was far enough away. A smaller explosion jolted her, and the heat rushed toward her a second later. This time, it was more intense as the smell of burned hair—hers—filled her nostrils.

When the heat wave passed, the first thing Julia noticed was the silence. There were no more cries, and the street had gone deathly quiet. She opened her eyes and reluctantly turned them toward the building, still some 50 meters away. She blinked hard—it couldn't be. The second bomb had blown away the top two floors. They had simply vanished into thin air. She looked for the people who'd stood in the street earlier, confused about where they'd gone.

As she staggered to her feet and approached the building, she saw them. She felt her stomach turn, and she gagged as her body convulsed, throwing her to her knees as she vomited. As she caught her breath, she forced herself to look at the charred remains of the people strewn in front of the burning building. Some of their clothes were still smoldering as little fires fed on the oxygen returning to the air.

She listened carefully, suddenly feeling very vulnerable in the middle of the street. Perhaps another Stuka was on its way? Then she thought she heard voices inside, but the ground floor was a blazing inferno. *Surely nobody could still be alive?*

The voices sounded again. There were still people trapped inside the building! She looked for something—anything—she could grab to clear the rubble in front of the building. She saw nothing but stones.

The voices became more desperate, and Julia felt flushed as she scoured the area.

Then, a loud creaking sound came from the building. It was as if the building itself sighed under the heat of the fire. People screamed in terror, their voices drowned out by the roar of the flames, and Julia looked on in horror as the ceiling of the only remaining floor, along with the pillars that supported it on the sides, collapsed. A cloud of dust erupted into the sky.

Julia strained her ears, praying to hear something, anything. But she was met only with silence, the only sound the crackling of the flames sucking the last bit of oxygen from underneath the rubble.

CHAPTER FORTY-TWO

Natan was getting impatient. He leaned against the wall of the Bank of Poland building, or what was left of it. Little more than the skeleton of the building remained, but at least it gave some feeling of cover. That, and the darkness of the night.

He looked to the man next to him, who'd been obsessively checking his small pocket watch throughout the evening. "Is it almost time?"

The man nodded. "It's almost 2:30. Are you ready?"

Natan had been ready since 11, now almost four hours ago. He couldn't wait to break through the German lines and get out of the Old Town. When it was announced they were to regroup in the downtown area, he'd been elated. The constant shelling of the past week had taken its toll, both mentally and physically. He'd seen the number in his battalion dwindle every day, as heavy shells from the German artillery reduced buildings—and the men within them—to dust. He counted his lucky stars every morning when there was a short lull in the shelling. Perhaps the Germans needed to sleep, too.

The initial plan had been for all the Home Army battalions in the Old Town to attack from different positions at 11 the previous evening. Natan's Zośka battalion had been ready, and they'd been stopped at the last minute when a messenger told them to delay the attack. It wasn't until an hour ago that they got the all clear to attack in the middle of the night. Meanwhile, it seemed like the Germans were expecting something, as the shelling had intensified in the last few hours.

Toni was on the other side of the building, and Natan caught a glimpse of his friend, who gave him a thumbs-up, and Natan did the same. He was glad the big man had survived all their ordeals. Experienced fighters like Toni were getting scarcer every day, and they needed them to keep the younger fighters in check. Natan looked at some of the fresh faces around him. They didn't lack enthusiasm—all were keen to fight—but they lacked experience. *Compared to those boys, I'm an experienced fighter myself.*

Suddenly, a sharp whistle pierced the silence—two shrill shrieks in quick succession—the sign to attack. Natan slung the strap of his MP 40 over his shoulder, feeling the weight of the gun in his hands.

"Let's go!" he shouted. The young men didn't need any encouragement as they followed him. *Probably as anxious as I am to get moving.*

They fanned out and left the dark Bank of Poland building behind. On this chilly late-August night, the sky was clear as they moved toward their first waypoint at Bankowy Square. Natan stayed low as he stalked forward, his eyes darting left and right, the dark figures of his battalion keeping formation. That would give them a fighting chance.

It wasn't long until they approached the square, and this is where they needed to be cautious. They had little intelligence about the Germans' positions but assumed they'd fortified themselves in the surrounding buildings.

Another quick whistle and they fanned out further. The dark square was illuminated only by a weak crescent moon. He tried to focus on the buildings, straining his eyes to make out evidence of a German ambush. He proceeded slowly, feeling very alone. The others were undoubtedly trying to find their positions in the buildings around the square.

He reached the square and stayed close to the wall of one of the buildings—careful to keep out of the moonlight, fearful it would give away his position. There was an open window to his right, and as he climbed through, the clatter of heavy machine-gun fire erupted on the far side of the square. The Germans had fortified themselves well.

Natan landed in a dark room and stayed low, the memory of the damage done by machine-gun fire at Gęsiówka still fresh in his mind. Keeping very still, he listened for any sounds in the building. There were none—he was alone. Natan peeked through the window facing the square, which had erupted into a frenzy. Across the square, the Germans fired at anything that moved.

Natan could see traces of the other fighters who had found their positions. Some were in buildings, others hid behind pieces of debris scattered around the square.

They needed to cross to the other side to get to the battle lines downtown. Someone would need to take out the German machine gun. They soon reached a deadlock. The machine gun stopped, and it was quiet in the square for a moment.

Then, out of nowhere, a soft whooshing sound broke the silence. An instant later, Natan saw something flying through the air. It hit the building on the other side of the square in a bright, white explosion. Someone had fired an antitank rocket at the machine gunners. Natan found himself smiling—it was unorthodox but brilliant.

Another rocket soared across the square. And another. The first one impacted harmlessly above the machine gun, but the second found its mark— the explosion amplified by millions of sparks as the machine gun ammunition flared up. Another whistle and men poured forward on Natan's right. At the front, Major Jan led the charge.

As the other fighters understood what was happening, cover fire erupted from all sides of the square. Natan took his MP 40 and fired controlled bursts at the building where the Germans were holed up.

There was no reply as Jan's men closed in on the building. Natan and the other men held their fire. Finally, the men reached the building, and as Jan led his troops inside, there was a massive explosion. Natan looked on in horror as the building collapsed onto itself, and the men who'd entered.

The Germans had booby-trapped the building. Those fortunate enough to still be outside quickly sprinted away. Natan waited for more gunfire, but it soon became clear the Germans had abandoned the position.

He climbed through the window and stepped onto the square, where others appeared around him. Soon, they all crossed the square and regrouped in front of the building.

There was confusion about what to do next as some of the men tried to dig into the debris of the building. Others simply stood by, stunned.

"It's no use." Natan turned to the source of the deep voice speaking at volume. "Our brothers died for Poland, and they are the reason we've taken the square. We need to move on and reach the battle lines."

Natan looked closer and recognized Jerzy, possibly the most experienced fighter in their battalion. He'd been part of the planning of this attack with Jan. They must've discussed what would happen if Jan fell.

"Follow me," Jerzy said. "We need to keep moving."

There were murmurs as they moved out, heading farther south along Senatorska Street. As the men passed the ruins of the building, many crossed themselves.

They reached another German position on Senatorska Street. This time, however, it wasn't a single machine-gun post. The Germans had fortified several buildings on the corner, around a large church. The Zośka battalion found itself ranged against a far superior force, and with the first rays of daylight appearing on the horizon, Jerzy made a decision.

"There should've been reinforcements from there," he pointed at a side street off Senatorska. It ran parallel with the church, and Natan immediately saw why they needed those reinforcements. The Germans would thus be flanked, forcing them to defend two sides. As it was, they could simply wait for Natan's battalion to commit men forward. Thankfully, Jerzy was more intelligent than that.

"We'll retreat to the Blue Palace and regroup there," Jerzy said. Sighs of relief greeted him—the fighting had taken its toll on the men. "We'll wait for the cover of the night before we try again." It would give them a chance to get some rest, perhaps.

They made the short walk to the ruins of the Blue Palace. Beautifully manicured gardens typically surrounded the baroque building. Now, the men slushed through mud and the occasional patch of grass as they approached the entrance. All but a few windows had been blown out, and only the building's south facade still had its distinctive green copper roof. Nevertheless, the men wanted to find spots inside.

Jerzy assigned sentries on the perimeter, although the chances of the Germans abandoning their positions to attack them here were slim—the Germans held the high ground.

Natan sat down on the floor near one of the broken windows. The sun was making its way up, and he was keen to get a bit of sunlight. The night had exhausted him, and he failed to suppress a large yawn.

"Glad to see you're still alive, my friend," said a familiar voice behind him. He was relieved to see Toni approach and lumber down beside him with a contented sigh, placing his machine gun on the floor. "That was quite the night, huh?"

Natan nodded. "I can't believe the Germans blew up that building. I didn't even think we'd try to storm it."

"I think they only did that at the very last minute," Toni said. "They must have had some extra dynamite and simply set it off, hoping for the best. They got lucky."

"How do you think the others are faring? I heard Jerzy say he'd expected the other battalions would be in the area as well?"

"They should've been here by now." Toni looked concerned. "And I doubt they'll be able to do much in daylight, either."

A heavy explosion thundered nearby, and small pieces of rock and a lot of dust came down from the walls.

"Must've been somewhere down the road," Toni said matter-of-factly. "Say, Lew, do you believe we have the Germans on the run?"

"Not at all," Natan said. "If anything, it looks like they're only more determined to hold on to Warsaw, whatever the cost. I think the Americans or Russians could be on our doorstep, and yet the Germans would continue to aim their artillery on the city."

"That's what I think as well. The shelling of the city—it doesn't make much sense from a military point of view," Toni said. "It's almost as if Hitler is trying to show us he'll destroy the city before giving us anything."

Natan nodded. "Well, I don't know how the other cities are doing, but I think it's fair to say we haven't taken this occupation lying down."

Toni gave a sad smile. "That's right. Whatever happens next, we've certainly fought for our country."

They were quiet for a while, and then Toni spoke up. "But let's imagine we survive all of this. What are you going to do?"

"That's easy." Natan only needed a few seconds to answer. "I'm going to marry Krystyna."

Toni smiled and reached into his jacket pocket. He retrieved a small flask and unscrewed the top. "I've been saving this for a special occasion. Now, even though we're in a ruined palace, surrounded by Germans and will probably die pretty soon . . ." He paused to let his macabre humor land. "I say your motivation to stay alive is worth celebrating, no matter how this ends." He took a quick swig of the bottle before handing it to Natan.

Natan looked at his friend and smiled, lifting the flask. "We're not going to die out here," he said before taking a sip of his own. The liquid burned as it made its way down his throat. He was going to stay alive to see Julia again.

*

By nightfall, they were ready to attack again. The men had spent the day sleeping and playing cards, and most were getting restless. Even though they'd brought some rations, they were keen to find something warm to eat.

A messenger earlier that evening had confirmed the arrival of the expected reinforcements on their flank. They would attack the German position at the church, while Zośka would get through the German defenses at the nearby Saski Gardens. They were told the defenses were weaker there, and they should be able to overwhelm the Germans.

Jerzy had kept the plan simple. They would spread out as they left the Blue Palace and attack the gardens from three different directions. He'd discussed the approach with the experienced fighters, and Toni had been given command of one of the squads.

"He knows what he's doing," Toni said softly as they made their way to their position. About 50 men and women followed them, keeping a safe distance from each other as they stalked toward the east side of the Saski Gardens. "It's a solid plan—the only thing I'm worried about is the German strength we got the tipoff about."

Natan had the same doubts—the information could be outdated. The Germans often adjusted their positions at the last minute. They also had the numbers to allow them to react quickly when they suspected they needed more men. "We can only go with what we've got," he said.

The Saski Gardens were across the street, and Toni held up a fist. Everybody stopped, and it went quiet along the lines. They were to wait until the other squads were in position, and then they would make the first move.

The wait was excruciating and Natan counted the seconds. He knew they were to attack fifteen minutes after leaving the Blue Palace. Toni wore a wristwatch, and Natan kept his eyes on his friend.

Toni finally raised his hand and signaled for the fighters to move forward. They got up as one and crossed the street to the low wall surrounding the gardens. They lined up, and when they were all in position, Toni whistled sharply.

They went over the wall and were met with—nothing. Natan had expected German resistance, but there was no response to them scaling the wall. They walked on, confused looks all around.

Then, one of the men to his left let out a shout and fired a few shots. Natan followed the sound and saw returning fire from the corner on the other side of the garden. He threw himself to the ground and looked for cover. There was none, and more gunfire erupted around him. Toni was crawling toward the German position, reaching for a grenade. The foxhole was a good 30 meters away, and Toni would have to get closer to have a chance.

Natan quickly followed his friend, the muzzle of his gun pointed out ahead of him, ready to fire. To his right, he heard yelps. The Germans were picking off the other fighters, but they hadn't yet noticed Toni and Natan.

They made steady progress, and they were now only ten meters from the foxhole, where five German helmets poked out. They were all turned away from them, and Toni looked back. Natan nodded, understanding what his friend needed, and gripped his MP 40 a little tighter, the sights firmly trained on the helmets.

Toni ripped the pin from the grenade and quickly got up. He took a few steps closer to the German position and gently rolled the grenade down the slight incline. One of the Germans spotted him but not the grenade. The man turned his gun toward Toni, who was already flat on the ground again, crawling in the opposite direction.

Natan pulled the trigger, and the MP 40 reacted instantly, and Natan was elated to see the German's gunfire spew harmlessly into the sky as he fell back.

The others responded as their comrade fell, but it was too late. The grenade had rolled into the foxhole, and they had no chance to respond. It exploded with a bright flash, the bodies of the men thrown out as the grenade did maximal damage in the confined space.

Natan held his breath and kept the muzzle of his gun firmly pointed at the foxhole as he waited for any movements. Toni crawled closer and looked inside. It was quiet for a few seconds, and then they heard him call out, "We got the bastards!"

Natan exhaled in relief.

*

After taking the Saski Gardens, they met up with the other battalion that had attacked the Germans from the flanks near the church on Senatorska Street. It had been a hard fight, but they'd driven them back, and together, the battalions moved farther south, downtown.

They crossed the Warsaw Stock Exchange ruins without any further incidents and encountered only limited resistance as they moved down Królewska Street. The Germans had withdrawn as the two battalions pushed on, and they finally reached the Home Army positions on the edge of downtown.

Natan had never been so relieved to leave the Old Town area behind. The fighters at Zielna Street cheered as the Zośka battalion marched past, the men slapping their backs as if they had secured a great victory. Natan understood why the men here were so relieved; they, too, were under siege and could use any help they could get. These men and women had probably escaped the Old Town in the same way they had.

As Jerzy dismissed them for the day, they spread out to find something to eat. They were warned there was little food here but were told to report to the hospitals. There would be meager rations for the fighters. Natan was hungry and desperate to eat, but he had a more important matter to attend to first. He approached one of the men at the barricades.

"Did you come from the Old Town as well?"

The man nodded. "Yeah, yesterday. We went through the sewers from near Podwale."

"What was the situation there like?" He hadn't seen Podwale—nor Julia—in over a week.

"Not good. The Stukas were targeting hospitals."

Natan felt a shiver run down his spine. "Just the ones at Podwale, or everywhere?"

The man shook his head. "Everywhere, man. But they took one big one out yesterday—it was close to Podwale."

"You know which one?" Natan felt panic gripping at his throat. Had they bombed Julia's hospital?

"Sorry, no. I was told when we were making our way over here in the sewers. I had other things to worry about."

Natan felt numb but recovered to ask, "Where did they take all the people?"

The man looked confused. "We're all spread out over the positions to defend downtown."

"No, the civilians. Where were they taken?"

"Oh," the man said, casting his eyes to the ground. "They were left behind."

Natan felt like he'd been punched in the gut. "Left behind? But that means we left them to die."

"I know. I'm sorry. Orders from the top." He looked uncomfortable, his eyes showing a mix of shame and regret. "I have to get back to my position. Best of luck to you." He shuffled off, leaving Natan in the street.

Natan looked around as his vision blurred. *What had happened to Julia? And Kasia?* He forced himself to focus and caught sight of Jerzy at the barricade, so he headed over to his new commander.

"I'd like permission to return to the Old Town," he said curtly.

Jerzy looked at him with utter surprise. "What? Are you out of your mind? Did you forget how we got here?"

Natan felt anger rise in him. "We left the civilians behind. Did you know that?"

Understanding appeared on his commander's face. "I see. Do you have family back there?"

Thrown off by the question, Natan didn't immediately answer. Technically, Kasia and Julia weren't family, but they were everything he had. "Yes. And I can't abandon them."

Jerzy was silent for a moment. "I'm sorry, Lew. You can't go back there. The orders are clear. We are to defend from downtown now. And I can't lose a single fighter."

Natan was furious. "But they'll be killed by the Germans."

"This is no discussion. You're staying," he said, now losing his patience. "And if I hear about you crossing our battle lines toward the Old Town, you'll be tried for desertion. Is that clear?" He put extra emphasis on the last words, his stare bearing into Natan's eyes.

Natan was about to speak when he heard a firm voice behind him. "Come on, Lew. You need to eat something." Toni motioned for him to follow.

Natan glared at Jerzy, who held his stare for a moment longer before turning back to the men at the barricade.

He allowed Toni to guide him toward a building where they put a steaming bowl of watery soup in front of him. He tried to take a bite but couldn't hold the spoon steady as his hand shook uncontrollably. He tried again, but his whole body was shaking now. *I have to find her.*

CHAPTER FORTY-THREE

Julia was relieved to leave the crowded building in the downtown area. She'd finished her final run through the sewers, and it had been different from the days before. Midway through the route—which she now knew by heart—there had been sounds in the tunnel ahead. At first, she thought it might've been other people making their way out of Old Town. Even though officially only Home Army fighters were allowed to use the tunnels, plenty of civilians tried their luck down there. She shivered as the image of the bloated corpse of the old man she nearly tripped over returned to her mind; once separated from the group, it was easy to get lost in the darkness.

They had carefully approached the sound, and as it got louder, she'd realized these weren't civilians—the voices coming from above were German. German soldiers were waiting near one of the manhole covers—it was the first time she'd heard them.

Thankfully, none of the fighters had panicked, and they'd backed down the tunnel and found a different exit. Whenever she emerged from the sewers, she always asked for news about the Zośka battalion before making her way back. There had been no news until yesterday, when she was told most of the company had made it downtown. Her initial hope was tempered when another fighter told her they suffered heavy casualties along the way.

The nurses at the small hospital at Jasna Street couldn't help her, but one of them had mentioned the Zośka battalion was stationed around Zielna Street, only a few blocks to the northwest. Julia hurried through the streets. It was odd to see plenty of people out and about here, after the abandoned Old Town. Even though there were mostly Home Army fighters—clearly identifiable by their armbands—she spotted plenty of civilians. They carried supplies between the outposts and barricades. Both men and women hauled large sacks of food—mostly potatoes, although she saw some vegetables poking out of the bags as well—or wooden crates no doubt containing weapons and ammunition. Other people ran through the streets carrying anything that could prevent the fires from raging through the area whenever a shell hit. Because the waterworks were practically destroyed throughout the city, the old wells in city courtyards were again put back into operation. When there was no water available, sand and stones were used to kill the fires. Since abandoning the Old Town, they'd lost access to the Vistula riverside.

It warmed Julia's heart to see the resilience of her fellow Varsovians. Try as they might, and despite the enormous arsenal at their disposal, the Germans still hadn't thwarted the Polish fight.

She reached Zielna Street, nothing more than a side street from Królewska, an avenue running along the Saski Gardens. She understood why they'd chosen Zielna as the location for their barricade—it was directly opposite the Saski Gardens, which in turn marked the battle lines between the Old Town and downtown. She confidently approached the barrier, an older fighter eying her with suspicion as she did.

"Are you Zośka?" she asked without preamble.

The man waved his arm at the barricade. "We all are." He spotted her armband, and his demeanor changed. "Anything we can do for you?"

"I came from the Old Town, and I heard you're all stationed here," she started. "I'm looking for someone—Lew. He's supposed to be in your battalion." She knew Zośka contained more than 500 men and women, but she couldn't think of a better way to find him.

"Can't say I know anyone by that name. But I only joined a few days ago, before we evacuated the Old Town." He turned toward the barricade and shouted: "Anyone know a man called Lew?"

None of them did. Her disappointment must've shown, for the man said, "Look, most of us are quite new, and we were all spread out during the attacks. Even though we lost a lot of men, it doesn't mean this Lew was one of them." He pointed to a row of buildings down the street. "Why don't you check over there? That's our little command post out here. If anyone knows about him, they will."

Julia thanked him and headed in the other direction. She forced herself to stay positive; this was just an initial setback. Natan could be anywhere. They might even have reassigned him to a different battalion.

At the first building, a small group sat smoking cigarettes in the sun. She passed them on her way in but then turned back as one of them looked familiar. The man also recognized her as he craned his neck. "Krystyna?"

It was Toni, and Julia felt a wave of relief wash over her—if he was still alive, there was a good chance Natan was, too. "You can't believe how good it is to see a familiar face," she said as she walked over to him.

"You must be looking for Lew." It wasn't a question, and she tried to read his face as he spoke the words. His face was severe, and she felt a stab of panic.

"Is he here?" she asked, her voice a little shaky now.

Toni stepped away from the group and motioned her to follow him inside. It was surprisingly neat, untouched by the war. Toni walked into a bright room with large windows, where two dozen men sat around playing cards, one or two even reading a book. There was no mistaking the familiar shape of the man in the corner, with his back to them—the man she loved. Her hands started shaking as Toni shouted over the murmurs: "Lew, we've got a visitor for you!"

He turned around and dropped his cards the moment their eyes met. He dashed across the room, and Julia felt his strong arms around her only moments later. As they kissed, a roar of applause broke out around them.

*

That evening, they sat on the steps in front of the command post. Although it was early September, it was still warm, even though the sun was setting behind the buildings. They held hands as they watched the activity in the street. They'd told each other about what had happened in the past week, and Julia was still recovering from Natan's experiences on the battlefield.

"It could've easily been you in that building on Bankowy Square," she said, squeezing his hand.

Natan kept his gaze straight ahead. "It's odd how that works, don't you think? Five years ago, I was concerned about when my next football game was going to be. Then, I never even thought about firing a gun. Now, I feel almost numb about the past few days. I realize we've lost a lot of good men, but I can't think beyond tomorrow."

They sat in silence as Julia considered his words. *He's right, of course.*

"What do you think will happen next? There's not much of the city left. I don't believe the Americans are going to be here anytime soon, no matter what's being said."

He nodded. "Me neither. And if they are coming, I doubt there will be enough of us left here for them to save. When we abandoned the Old Town, we lost a lot of good positions. It will be much harder to defend ourselves here."

The Old Town had the Vistula River to the east, making it difficult for the Germans to attack freely. Downtown was surrounded by other districts. "We can only try to hold out for as long as possible," she said softly. "And the Russians?"

"What about them?" Natan scoffed. "Last time they were here, they were fighting alongside the Germans. And it's not exactly like they've been good to us in the past. I don't trust them for a minute."

His words hung in the air before Julia said, "So, we're on our own."

"We've been on our own since the start. But they haven't beaten us, despite trying for almost five years. And even now, after they've thrown everything they have at us, we're still standing." He spoke passionately, fire in his eyes.

Her eyes watered, and she felt her heart swell. As long as they drew breath, they had a chance. And with that, they fought. They were all in this together. It didn't matter if you were a fighter, a civilian, or a Jew: you were a Varsovian, a Pole. And they would fight until the bitter end.

Something was happening inside the building behind them, and they turned to see a man running through the hallway, shouting as he passed the rooms. It was hard to hear, and they stepped inside. The man ran up the stairs, but the rooms were buzzing, with people talking excitedly.

"What's going on?" Natan asked as they entered the first room.

The young man beamed as he breathlessly spoke: "The Germans proposed a cease-fire! They're starting peace talks!"

Julia was stunned. "What? Are you sure?"

Another man joined them. "We've won! Bór is starting negotiations with the Germans!"

All around them, people hugged and slapped each other's backs as there were smiles all around. Someone came in carrying a bottle of vodka, and they all cheered boisterously. Julia wanted to join in, but an uncomfortable, familiar feeling gnawed in the back of her mind. She glanced at Natan, his eyes darting around the room, his face lined with the same doubts.

Something's not quite right.

*

The following week, there were talks of peace between the German and Polish commands. More than 20,000 civilians left the city unharmed, and in an unexpected show of mercy from the Germans, they promised prisoner-of-war status to any fighters willing to surrender. It caused quite the stir, but few were keen to take them up on the promise.

Natan and Julia both stayed put as the fighting died down somewhat. Natan spent most of his days around the command post and fortifying the nearby barricades. Julia helped out in various hospitals in the neighborhood. Even though the number of patients had decreased dramatically over the past ten days, there were still plenty of people in need. The Germans had stopped shelling the city, the battle reaching a stalemate. Apart from a few skirmishes, things appeared to settle down amid the peace talks.

That all changed on September 11, only four days after the negotiations had started. When Toni showed up, Natan and Julia were sitting outside in the afternoon sunshine, enjoying a short break from their duties. But, from the look on his face, something was wrong.

"Lew, better get ready to pack up soon. We need to report to Jerzy in an hour."

"Did they say why?"

Toni nodded. "There's a rumor going round that the Russians are making progress on the other side of the river."

Natan looked at Julia, who looked as surprised as he was. "They're finally making a push for it? How reliable is this information?" Natan still had his doubts about the Russians' desire to help them out. They'd been content to hold the bridges south of Warsaw without getting involved in the city. "If they really wanted to help us, they would've attacked the German artillery positions on the east bank months ago."

"I agree, but if we're summoned back to Jerzy, something must be happening. Get ready." He looked to Julia. "You, too. I have a feeling you might be needed soon, as well." He crossed the street, where more men of the battalion stood around idly.

"Do you think it's true?" Julia asked, her bright eyes showing concern.

Natan held up his hands. "The talk around peace was getting promising, but if the Russians are involved, it will change things. I heard the Germans are pushing for unconditional surrender."

"And you don't think Bór will go for that?"

"No, not unless there is absolutely no other way. I think if there's even the remote chance of the Russians joining us from the east, Bór will fight."

They sat in silence as the mood in the street changed. Men looked concerned and hurried inside to collect their few belongings. Everything suddenly felt different.

Natan stood up. "I guess I'd better get my things as well."

"Be careful, Natan," Julia said as she hugged him. "I'll be here waiting for you."

Natan held on to her for a few seconds, savoring the warmth of her body. They then let go, and he hurried inside. He found the other men gearing up, finding their weapons, and checking their guns. Nobody spoke a word, but they all knew; they were heading back into battle.

CHAPTER FORTY-FOUR

It was oddly quiet on the square in front of the Warsaw Polytechnic. Natan shifted, careful not to wake Julia, who had nodded off on his shoulder. The night had been cold, and even though they had a roof over their heads, the wind had free rein in the building—the windows had long been blasted out. The Polytechnic had been in the middle of recent skirmishes between the Parasol battalion and the Germans. Natan closed his eyes, keen to take advantage of the current lull in fighting.

Peace talks had indeed collapsed—a combination of unreasonable German demands and promising news of the Soviet advance causing General Bór to withdraw. Natan's Zośka battalion was sent back into battle. For more than three weeks, they were deployed all over the city, stretching from downtown to areas farther south, assisting reinforcements arriving from across the Vistula River in the east. It wasn't until a few days earlier that Natan's ever-shrinking battalion was assigned to the district of Mokotów, south of downtown. On his way there, Julia caught up with him and had insisted on joining him—she'd obtained a Sten gun herself, and he'd acquiesced. By then, the rapidly dwindling Home Army numbers meant that anyone willing to fight—especially those with weapons—were quickly welcomed into the ranks.

In Mokotów, the German forces had overpowered the shrinking resistance.

Julia and Natan—like many other fighters—had lost touch with their battalion, finding themselves wandering the streets on their own. They'd come across the Polytechnic on their way back downtown, where parts of the Parasol battalion had made their stand. There were less than thirty of them, and they knew it was only a matter of time before the Germans called in reinforcements, but they were staying put for now—there was nowhere to go.

Julia stirred. "How long was I out for?" she asked, her voice groggy.

"Maybe half an hour."

She sat up, looking confused. "It's still quiet. Has nothing happened since I fell asleep?"

Natan shook his head while Julia looked at the men sleeping on the ground around them.

"That's odd—I would've expected them to make a move by now. We've been stuck here for more than a day." She reached into a small bag beside them, broke off a piece of bread, and put it in her mouth.

"Nobody's moved. There's no point. They're waiting us out." *Nowhere for us to go with those machine guns pointed in all directions.*

Julia swallowed her bread and reached for another piece. "How long do you think we can hold out?" she asked.

He frowned. "We have supplies for a few more days, but I'm not sure they're going to wait that long. They could send in a Stuka any time they want."

"I didn't just mean us," she said. "I mean the city. The Home Army."

Natan thought briefly before answering. "I don't know. I'd like to believe the other battalions are doing better, but we're running out of supplies. Food, bullets, we have little left." He looked at his MP 40. He kept it in pristine condition, but he was on his last bullets. "The Soviets on the riverbanks haven't moved for weeks."

"They seem happy to wait things out." They were silent for a moment before Julia added, "It's over, isn't it?"

"It's not over as long as we're together. We're still here, so we have a chance." He patted his gun and hoped he sounded more confident than he felt.

"But we don't, not really! Surely the general must see this as well. Look at us.

Most of these men don't even have working guns or bullets. We're waiting for the Germans to pick us off. And I'm sure it's as bad across the city." Julia's voice was rising, drawing the attention of some of the other men. "We can't hold out much longer."

He took the hands of the strong woman he cared for more than anyone else—and he felt his heart ache. *Has our situation really become this hopeless?* He didn't want to believe it.

"This is not how it's supposed to end, Natan," Julia said softly. "I want more time with you. There's so much we still have to do together."

He felt his eyes sting. "I know."

There was movement on the other side of the room as men shuffled around some of the windows. "Something's happening on the square!"

Where's the machine-gun fire?

They looked out of the window, and Natan struggled to process the scene in front of him. On the German side, from between the machine guns, emerged a small group of men wearing Wehrmacht officer uniforms. Natan sucked in a deep breath through his teeth.

"Am I seeing this right?" Julia asked, her voice breaking.

The officer leading the procession held a white flag.

"I can't believe it," Natan mumbled.

"Look!" Julia pointed to the side entrance of the Polytechnic, where a door opened. Three Home Army men walked out, holding a stick with a white rag attached to it. Behind them, two men in noncombat clothing followed.

The groups met in the middle of the square, and everybody held their breath. Without another word, they made for the far side of the square together.

*

It had been hours since the two groups had left. Since then, all had been quiet on the square in front of the Polytechnic. The German soldiers still pointed machine guns across the square—but something was different.

Natan took a swig of water and handed his canteen to Julia. "They seem pretty confident"—he pointed to a group of fighters in the corner of the room. They had opened a celebratory bottle of vodka earlier—convinced the fighting was over—and had become louder with every shot downed. Some had now fallen asleep, while two still sat curled up against the wall, emptying the bottle.

"Can't blame them," Julia said, a thin smile on her face. "It's not every day you see Germans waving a white flag."

"Even so, there's no way they will give up the city. They have us on our knees."

Julia shook her head. "I don't think so, either. But the Germans aren't looking forward to another month of fighting, either. We've lost a lot of good people, but it hasn't come easy to them. Imagine how they must feel, stalking through all those narrow streets and ruined buildings, not knowing where the next attack will come from."

Natan nodded. Considering their limited supplies—and almost nonexistent support from the outside world—they had put up quite the fight. He was proud of his compatriots. Varsovians had stuck together, both Home Army soldiers and civilians playing their part in their fight against the Nazis. But despite their courage, Natan also knew the determined Germans ultimately outmatched them. He looked to Julia. "Perhaps they're trying another round of peace talks?"

"It's the best we can hope for. But what will happen to us? We're still bandits to them, after all."

As she spoke the words, there were rapid footsteps in the stairway. Natan grabbed his MP 40 and held it at the ready. Running was never a good sign.

He needn't have worried, as a young girl wearing a Home Army armband came in, panting and red-faced. *A messenger.* She paused for a moment, catching her breath, and then she smiled as she spoke in a surprisingly loud voice: "General Bór has agreed a cease-fire with the Germans! It's over! You're all to prepare for our surrender to the Germans."

Surrender? And we're supposed to be happy about that? Natan looked at Julia, the same doubts on her face.

In the corner, the men who'd been drinking all day stirred. "Did you say surrender?" one of them asked in a slurred voice. "They'll shoot us as soon as we come out of the building."

There were murmurs of assent, and Natan returned his eyes to the girl. She was still smiling, looking confident.

"They will treat us as prisoners of war," she said. "As long as we hand in our weapons, they will treat us like soldiers."

Natan was stunned. "Soldiers? Prisoners of war?" he mumbled. "That's quite the change."

Julia still looked shocked as she turned to him. "General Bór must have made some big concessions to get the Germans to accept us as soldiers."

The messenger disappeared and bounded up the stairs, where more fighters were stationed. As she did, the people in the room all processed the news in different ways. Some were ecstatic, slapping each other's backs in celebration, while others sat silently, not quite sure what to make of it.

Natan and Julia got up and looked out of the window. The change in atmosphere was tangible.

"Do you hear that?" Natan said as he took Julia's hand.

"What?"

"There's no gunfire."

Have we really survived the war?

Outside, there was more movement around the square as word of the cease-fire spread. Voices broke the silence as messengers shared the news in the streets. In a building across from them, a man draped a Polish flag from an open window. One by one, more flags appeared, ragged as most were. Faces appeared in the windows—reluctantly at first, but they joined in the celebrations when there were no German commands or shots.

A voice boomed through the room. "Everybody upstairs. Commander has an announcement!"

*

Fifteen minutes later, they filed out of the room with the rest of the fighters. The mood was almost celebratory; gone were the hushed whispers they'd become accustomed to. Instead, they talked animatedly, sharing their hopes for the future as they counted the wages that had been handed to them. It had been less than they'd been promised before the fighting, but nobody complained— by now, being alive was enough.

Natan felt Julia squeeze his hand. She looked worried. "Are you ready to celebrate with them? Ready to hand in your weapon?"

The commander had shared details of the Home Army's agreement with the Germans. They were to hand in their weapons in less than two hours, prove their Home Army status, and await further orders.

"They say the Wehrmacht will take us into custody," Natan said. "Perhaps they'll keep their word."

Julia shook her head ferociously. "But what if they don't? It wouldn't be the first time. And what if they hand us over to the SS? There's no telling where they'll take us. They've always considered us subhuman, bandits, scum. They had no problems stringing up whoever they thought was part of the resistance. And now they'll treat us as soldiers? As equals?" She bristled as she spat out the words, her eyes glistening.

Natan wanted to argue, but he bit his tongue. *She's right. She saw what they did to her people.* "It's not about the Wehrmacht, is it?" he said softly as he guided her to an empty room down the hallway.

She shook her head, her face now wet with tears. She struggled to speak the words: "For those people back there, this is the end of the war. For me, it only brings more uncertainty."

Natan pulled her toward him, and she buried her face in his chest. He'd never seen her so vulnerable, but he'd never felt closer to her, either. They were both orphans, having lost everything to the same enemy. He took a deep breath before he said, "You're afraid of what might happen when they find out who you are."

She stopped shaking and looked up at him, her eyes still misty, but with the fiery expression he'd come to know—and love—so well. "When they find out I'm a Jew." She took a step back and wiped her eyes with her sleeve.

"But how will they ever know? The commander said we would only have to hand in our armband to prove we're part of the Home Army. Then, you can say you lost your other papers."

"It won't do. There could easily be someone who rats me out. There are still too many Volksdeutsche around." She shook her head resolutely. "I can't take that chance, not now that we've come so far."

He knew Julia was right—people had betrayed their Jewish countrymen for the slightest of rewards. *But what can we do?*

"What if we don't surrender?" Julia said, surprising him.

He frowned. "That's not up to us. Bór has surrendered the city."

"I know, I know." She looked impatient as she continued. "But do you think the Germans will be as interested in the rest of the people as they are in the fighters? Don't you think it's at least a little suspicious they're making us this offer? Prisoner of war camps?"

Natan considered her words, finding it hard to believe what she was suggesting. "You're saying we don't join the others?"

She just looked at him.

"Let's talk to the commander," he said, already heading back to the briefing room.

The unit commander stood near the window of the room, his eyes on the square. Natan cleared his throat. "Sir?"

The man turned, his eyes unfocused for a second before recovering. "Yes? Are you about ready to go?" He pointed out of the window, where two dozen Wehrmacht soldiers stood waiting. They smoked cigarettes and looked relaxed as they hovered around the square, only a few meters from the main entrance of the Polytechnic.

"That's what we wanted to discuss, sir, if you don't mind," Natan said. He felt nervous, like he was doing something wrong.

The man raised an eyebrow but didn't speak, and Julia spoke up.

"We don't want to surrender."

The words hung in the air, the commander's gaze calmly fixed on her. Natan held his breath. *Is this some form of desertion?*

After what felt like minutes had passed, the commander stepped closer to them and spoke in a low voice. "You're going against the orders of General Bór?"

Natan swallowed hard and stayed quiet as Julia responded. "No, sir." She took a deep breath. "But we don't want to surrender to the Germans as soldiers. We don't trust them."

The commander stepped even closer, and he was so close he now towered over Julia. "Still, you must have an excellent reason for coming to me."

Julia craned her neck, meeting his gaze. "I do, sir. They killed my family." And after a pause: "I'm Jewish."

The tension in the room rose a few notches as they held each other's gaze—the petite, scruffy girl in fighter garb facing down a Home Army commander almost twice her size.

After a few seconds, the expression on his face changed. A thin smile appeared, and all tension left the room. "You do not lack motivation, young lady," he said. "I guess it's fair to say you're not done with the Germans yet?"

Julia looked surprised. "Done, sir?"

"What if I tell you there's another way to leave the city and not surrender, but it gives you absolutely no guarantees. It might even be more dangerous than what those men out there are currently doing?"

Julia looked overwhelmed, and Natan spoke up: "If it means we don't have to register with those men out there, we're listening." He looked at Julia, who nodded as she took his hand.

The commander nodded. "Then let me tell you what you're going to do. And please, listen carefully—there's not much time."

Natan felt Julia's grip on his hand tighten as the commander laid out his plan.

CHAPTER FORTY-FIVE

Julia focused on putting one foot before another, keeping her eyes on the ground. Natan walked beside her; his mere presence in the crowd of refugees trotting along calmed her. They left Warsaw about three hours ago.

It had been four days since the surrender. Julia and Natan left the Polytechnic through the back door, leaving their weapons behind. The commander had told them to hold on to their armbands, just in case. Through the ruins of the city, they'd passed comrades on their way to surrender, many carrying their weapons. Fatigued faces looked bewildered or hopeful, but all of them showed some form of relief. Julia wanted to reach Kasia's home as soon as she could.

Somehow, the building had survived the onslaught of the past month. They'd found Kasia there, and their emotions had finally gotten the better of them as the three embraced and wept. When they recovered, Julia and Natan had told Kasia about their plan to leave the city. She understood but said she wouldn't join them. Instead, she would report to the racecourse later that evening, where tents had been set up for people waiting for trains bound for Prushkov. The Red Cross had set up camp there, and Kasia had volunteered to help. Julia thought it was characteristic that she considered other people's needs before her own, even now.

"Do you think Kasia made it?" she asked Natan, speaking softly.

He looked up, his face her beacon in the sea of people around them. Those in the column were haggard, with torn clothes and tired faces, all looking much the same as they trudged after those ahead of them. There were hundreds—no, thousands—of people in the procession led by bored German soldiers. Despite the guards, Julia had seen plenty of people wander off. *The guards aren't very attentive. And why would they care?*

"I hope so. She was determined enough, for sure," Natan said. "I hope there was space on the train."

"Do you regret not going with her?" For a few seconds, Julia had considered joining Kasia, but she'd quickly dismissed the thought. The Home Army commander had given them a mission—a purpose—and she was determined to fulfill it.

Natan shook his head. "I don't think we would've been allowed on the train. Besides, this is more important."

Her heart beat a little faster, and she felt a surge of affection. He could have chosen to surrender with the rest of the fighters but had chosen the more perilous path with her. Their future was unknown beyond the transit camp they marched toward.

The Home Army soldiers had been the first to leave the city, and they had made an impressive sight as they marched four abreast through the streets, their heads held high.

Her thoughts were interrupted by a conversation beside the column. Two Wehrmacht soldiers were talking in clear voices, oblivious to anyone overhearing them. *They probably think we don't understand them.*

"Some of these creatures aren't going to make it to the transit camp," the taller of them said. He wasn't much older than Natan, and spoke in a deep voice.

The smaller man chuckled. "Well, they won't be our problem much longer. I can't wait for them to be on the trains. I hear most of them will be sent to help in the war effort."

"Well, not all of them. Some can hardly stand up by themselves. They're useless."

"I'm sure the SS will have a solution for them," the smaller soldier said with a grimace.

A shiver went down Julia's spine. *The SS?*

She looked across to Natan, who looked alarmed.

"I think we need to make our move soon," he said.

*

They marched for another hour before the German soldiers shouted that they would have a half-hour break. Some people fanned out into the barren fields surrounding the road, while others sat down where they stood. They were simply too tired to move any farther.

"Come, let's go over there," Natan said, pointing toward a patch of grass. Julia saw why he'd picked that spot. It was close to a small forest.

There were plenty of other people nearby, and Natan spoke in a hushed voice as they sat down in the grass. "We've been walking for over four hours now. This is probably the last stop before the transit camp."

Julia nodded. "They said it would be a day's walk, but they haven't been generous with the stops. We need to go."

"Why don't we go for the forest?" Natan said. "We can hide there." He held his head still, eyes scanning the surroundings. The guards sat alongside the road, smoking cigarettes and drinking from their canteens. They appeared relaxed and inattentive.

"Okay, let's do it," she said, her eyes on a break in the small forest. "There are people in there, trying to get some privacy while they do their business." Then she spotted the guards near the woods, and Natan said what she was thinking.

"If the guards ask, we just say we need some privacy as well." He looked a little nervous, but Julia couldn't think of a better idea, either. "I'll go first," he said. "Follow me when I'm almost there."

"Be careful," she warned, but Natan was already up, taking purposeful strides toward the trees. Julia's eyes darted between him and the closest guard. He was looking in the other direction as Natan closed in.

Come on, Natan, keep going.

When he was almost at the tree line, Julia got up and moved in the same direction. She felt light-headed and wiped her sweaty palms on her shirt. She kept her eyes on Natan and ignored the people around her. *Nobody's paying you any attention—you're going into the forest for a quick pee.*

The soldier had found someone at fault and berated the young man animatedly while Natan crossed the tree line and made his way into the forest. It wouldn't be long until he'd be out of sight. *He's going to make it!*

Julia was now only 20 meters from the trees when the soldier turned back in her direction. As he did, his eyes focused on Natan, almost invisible under cover of the trees. Julia froze as the soldier jogged in Natan's direction.

"Halt! Where are you going? You're too far; get back!" The soldier's shouts confirmed Julia's fears.

She heard Natan respond but couldn't quite make out the words. The soldier tensed before unholstering his pistol. *Oh no.*

The soldier looked back, hesitated, but then saw there were no other guards nearby. He looked undecided, and for a second, she hoped he might not chase Natan on his own. To her horror, the soldier ran into the forest, his pistol raised as he shouted for Natan to return.

Julia's mind raced as she considered her options. She looked around. Apart from a few people who'd stood near the soldier, nobody had taken any notice. The guards at the roadside still had their backs to them and were oblivious to what had happened. The people near the forest drifted away, anxious to avoid whatever trouble was coming. *It's now or never, Julia.*

She took large steps toward the trees, not daring to look back, praying none of the other guards took any interest in her. As she reached the first trees, she squinted into the dim forest. *I've lost him!*

In the distance, she heard the soldier's voice—angry and aggressive now. There was no response from Natan, but Julia ran in the direction of the sound, no longer caring if anyone saw her disappear into the forest. Then, a shot rang out, stopping Julia in her tracks. Another shot, and Julia felt her throat constrict. She stood in the cold, dark forest—now eerily quiet, but for the sound of her heart pounding in her ears.

*

The shot still rang in his ears as Natan hit the cold, muddy ground. There was a sharp, burning pain in his shoulder, and he stayed low, clenching his teeth while trying to control his breath. He reached for his shoulder—there was a bit of blood from grazing a sharp branch, but the bullet had missed its mark. *I got lucky.*

He listened for any sounds, but there were none—all was quiet. That was odd. He'd expected the crunch of the fall leaves on the forest floor as the soldier approached. *Is he waiting me out?* He felt exposed on the ground, with only some bushes obscuring the soldier's view of him. He was an easy target once the man found him. *I need to find somewhere to hide.*

There were plenty of pine trees around, but they wouldn't do. Then he saw the single oak tree about ten meters away. It had lost its leaves, but its thick trunk would provide ample cover. The tree was slightly downhill, and Natan considered his chances. He could roll down, and the soldier would have to be very fast—and accurate—to hit him before he made it. But maybe the soldier was still far enough away. *I have to try.*

The decision was made for him when he heard a stick snap nearby. The soldier was stalking closer. *I have to do it.*

He took a deep breath, gritted his teeth, and pushed himself to his feet. He kept low—hunched over as best he could—and made for the tree. There was a voice behind him, but the words didn't register. He could almost touch the tree when another shot rang out. He braced himself, but the bullet went harmlessly wide. Natan reached the tree as another bullet pierced the its trunk, sending splinters flying. He ducked behind the tree, crouching down, burying his back into the trunk and panting hard. He used his shirt sleeve to wipe the sweat from his forehead.

He was safe for now, but he could hear the soldier still approaching. The man was armed, and he had little to fear from Natan. *What am I going to do?*

"Come out now—you know it's over," he heard the soldier say in German. "I'll take you back to the group, and you can get that wound treated in the camp."

Natan snorted in contempt. *Does he think I'm an idiot?*

The man continued talking as he came closer. Natan kept quiet, but he was calculating his options. *What will he do when he reaches me? He'll kill me, for sure. I'm not going to let him take me like that, though. He'll have to come get me.*

The soldier had gone quiet, but Natan could still hear him approach—he couldn't be farther than a few meters from him now. With an effort, Natan pushed himself to his feet and clenched his fists. *While I'm still alive, I fight.*

He held his breath and waited until he heard the soldier's breathing on the other side of the tree. *I need to surprise him; it's my only chance.*

He took a deep breath, took a step away from the tree, and quickly swung himself around the trunk. There, as he lunged forward, he came face to face with the soldier. The man was surprised and dropped his pistol as Natan was on him in a flash. He panted as he tried to break through the man's defenses, but quickly realized he'd underestimated his opponent. He felt himself tire as he stopped punching and tried to shift his weight onto the man's chest. The soldier saw through his tactic with devastating effect as he caught Natan off guard with a mighty blow to the ribs.

It felt like a jackhammer hitting his lungs as the wind was knocked from him. He wheezed, and his vision went black for a second as he struggled to stay conscious. Natan gasped for breath, but his lungs didn't respond.

It was all the soldier needed as he broke from Natan's grip, shoving him off him. Natan saw it happening but all strength was sapped and he crashed into the earthy forest floor. The shock of what was happening kicked in, and he felt a rush of adrenaline as he sucked in a deep breath. His lungs burned, and the pain in his ribs was excruciating, but he managed to raise his arms as the man jumped on top of him.

The force of the man's blows was enhanced by the speed with which they rained down on him—the jabs connected with his stomach, face, and already shattered ribs. Natan tasted blood in the back of his throat and smelled its coppery scent as it made its way through his nostrils.

The punches stopped, and for a second, he thought it was over. Then he felt strong hands close around his throat and saw eyes with cold, calculated determination staring back. The man put his knees on Natan's limp arms, leaving him helpless. Then he felt the pressure on his throat, and he knew this was the end.

He thought of Julia. If this were how it ended, the last thing he'd see in this lifetime would be her face. As the life was slowly drained from him by German hands, he hoped she'd escaped, even if he didn't. *Maybe I distracted him enough for her to make her way out unseen. That's worth dying for.*

His vision blurred, and the only thing he felt was strong hands squeezing tighter around his throat. As drifted from consciousness, he saw Julia's face appear behind the German. Faint light coming through the treetops above her gave her the halo of an angel, and he smiled, ready to surrender to the impending darkness.

*

Julia brought her arm down with all her might. She aimed for the middle of the back of the man's head, and as the stone impacted his skull, she heard a sickening crunch. Nothing happened at first, and it felt like they were frozen in time, the German leaning over Natan as Julia still gripped the stone.

She brought it down again. And again. Possessed by rage, she didn't stop until her hands were covered in blood, the soldier's lifeless body slumped on the ground, his face barely recognizable.

Julia sank to the ground, shaking and sobbing, as she released the stone. She looked to Natan—dark, angry red marks around his throat, his eyes closed, an odd smile on his face—and feared the worst. *I'm too late.*

She shook him. "Natan. Wake up. Wake up!"

He didn't respond, and she shook him more forcefully, pounding his chest. "No, no, no! You can't be dead!" Tears streamed down her face as she sobbed uncontrollably.

There were voices in the distance, but she didn't care. *I'd rather die here with him than live alone.*

As she finished her thought, Natan's chest heaved. His eyes opened, and he coughed as he desperately struggled for air. Julia helped him up, and he looked at her with wide eyes, catching his breath. "You weren't an angel," he said as he saw the dead soldier next to him.

Julia now laughed through her tears. Her shoulders sagged with relief as she looked at the love of her life returning from death. "Are you okay?"

"I am now," he said softly. "I thought that was it." He pulled her toward him, and she felt his heartbeat as they embraced on the forest floor. She felt her own heart beating wildly, the adrenaline of the kill still racing through her veins. *Is this real? Is he really here?*

"You saved my life." She heard his voice, the words, but they barely registered.

He sat up, took her chin, and lifted her head, his eyes demanding her attention. He looked calm, serene even. She relaxed a little, but then the voices in the distance broke their moment. He looked alarmed as they both came to reality.

"We have to get out of here, now," he said, taking control.

The fog in her head cleared as she took Natan's hand and stood up. "Yes, let's go."

Natan reached down and pocketed the soldier's pistol. Julia took one last look at the German. In all these years, she'd never killed a man with her bare hands in cold blood. There was no anger, no guilt or remorse. It was simply revenge.

The voices in the distance were getting louder—soon, they'd be in range.

EPILOGUE

THE ENGLISH CHANNEL,

AUGUST 1947

Julia looked out onto the water, holding on to the railing as the ferry pulled away from land. On the docks below, a small group of people looked on as the ship's horn blared and the engines roared. The vessel started picking up speed, and Julia watched as Boulogne-sur-Mer slowly disappeared in the dense morning fog.

She took a deep breath of the fresh sea air, its salty smell so foreign to her when she boarded the ferry a few hours earlier. Now, as she looked down at the gentle waves of the English Channel, it smelled like freedom.

"Enjoying the breeze?" She turned to see the smiling face of Natan as he handed her a paper cup of coffee. She took a sip and savored the taste—she'd learned to appreciate the little things, and this was undoubtedly one of her favorites.

"You missed when Europe disappeared beyond the fog," she said as he snuggled up behind her, his arms around her waist. "I think I like the sea, Natan. It's so quiet, so peaceful."

They stood there for a moment, following the cawing seagulls as they circled the ship looking for scraps. Julia thought about how much her life had changed in the past few months.

After their escape in the forest, they'd joined the Home Army's Gorjec cell, where they continued to fight the Germans until the country was liberated by Stalin's Red Army in January 1945. Not trusting the so-called liberators, they fled south to Hungary, where they watched in horror as the Soviets tried their Home Army compatriots on charges of supporting Hitler's fascism. Natan's brothers from the Zośka battalion were imprisoned, with some of them sent to the gulags farther east. Going home had not been an option.

Natan interrupted her thoughts. "What are you thinking about? You look a bit glum."

She shook her head. "Do you think Kasia is okay? I can't believe she didn't join us."

"You know what she's like," Natan said with a faint smile. "She still believes everything will turn out fine once things settle down."

"But there was nothing left for her," Julia said, feeling a pang of guilt. Kasia had made it to the Red Cross camp and spent the remainder of the war there. When she wanted to return to Warsaw, she'd found the city had been razed to the ground by Hitler's forces. She'd decided to return to her birth city of Łódź, determined to rebuild her life there.

After the Germans surrendered to the Allies, there was a faint hope Poland would return to independence. The Soviets even called an election, but it was all show. The government put in charge by Stalin was nothing more than a Soviet puppet. The Polish government-in-exile had been pushed aside.

From London, however, exiled Poles were called to register, as the Home Army fighters were recognized as part of the Allied forces. Natan and Julia did so and, after an anxious few months, received their invitations to relocate to the United Kingdom.

"She'll find her way," Natan said as he finished his coffee. "She always does. And maybe she'll change her mind later."

The seagulls disappeared, screeching as they gave up their hunt to return to the French mainland. Julia turned her thoughts to the future. "What do you think England will be like?"

Natan's eyes sparkled as he moved next to her, leaning over the railing a little. "It will be an adventure. From what I've heard, everybody gets a job and a small house. In the worst case, we're put in a tent first, as they look where to place us. But Julcia, it's a new start. They need us, and they're asking us to help rebuild their country."

She nodded, a flurry of excitement tingling in her stomach.

"And they offer us something we won't get back home in Poland," he said, his face now serious, although his eyes were still beaming. "Freedom. We can be anything we want."

Julia smiled. He'd said this many times on the train. The British had been very forthcoming with information; they would be welcomed to the country, but they were expected to help rebuild it. Julia knew she would have to start at the bottom, but that was all right with her—she was used to fighting for her place. But she also hadn't given up on her dreams.

Natan read her mind. "You're going to be a lawyer, Julcia, I know it. As soon as we dock, we're going to register for schooling!"

A metallic voice boomed over the ship's loudspeaker, announcing breakfast was served in the restaurant. Natan took her hand, gently pulling her away from the railing. "How about we go see if they serve French or British cuisine?"

As the setting sun painted the horizon blood-red, she couldn't help but feel optimistic. For the first time in her life, things were looking up, and nobody was going to take her hope away.

Author's Notes

Thank you so much for reading *Warsaw Fury*. The story started forming as I was finishing my first book, *Beyond the Tracks*. The Home Army plays a smaller yet significant role in the earlier book. As I read more about the Polish resistance, I was stunned by how little I'd heard about the second-largest resistance network in Nazi-occupied Europe.

As the first country to fall to Nazi occupation—and with its central position and the largest Jewish population in Europe—Poland was destined to play a prominent role in Hitler's Final Solution. While many books, movies, and museums focus on the atrocious extermination camps—and these are stories that need to be told—I wanted to show the heroic efforts of the Varsovians as they battled the occupying forces throughout the war. While Julia and Natan are fictional characters, I'd like to highlight several real people and events they encountered in the story.

Mordechai Anielewicz really led the ŻOB at 21 years of age. His ambush on the SS, while they resumed deportations in January 1943, was vital as it gave the skeptical Home Army confidence in his ability to lead a Jewish resistance. That allowed him to prepare for the ill-fated Warsaw Ghetto Uprising, holding out for nearly four weeks. The German command had expected to empty the ghetto in three days. However, Mordechai never abandoned his people, choosing to die in the ghetto while encouraging his fighters to escape when it became apparent they were fighting a lost cause. While his body was never recovered, it is believed he died when the Germans attacked the ŻOB headquarters at 18 Miła Street on May 8, 1943. Today, a monument in honor of the ghetto heroes is erected on the site, with Mordechai Anielewicz prominently positioned, holding a hand grenade.

Within the ghetto walls, the smuggling of all sorts of wares—food, most importantly—was essential to survival. Rations for Jews were as low as 177 calories per day, compared to 2,613 calories for Germans. I based Julia's role as courier on the *kashariyots*—young Jewish women smuggling weapons, ammunition, and illegal documents between Jewish ghettos in Eastern Europe. While her story of digging the tunnel and facilitating the arms smuggling between Natan's contacts and the ŻOB is fictional, I believe this would be precisely the type of work these brave women would have been involved in. Warsaw's vast network of tunnels connecting basements and sewers played an invaluable role in the success of the resistance.

Writing a story set in 1930s–40s Warsaw requires attention to the position of Jewish Poles—I could not sidestep the matter. The book must do justice to the significance of growing antisemitism in Polish society at the time. The historical debate finds evidence on both sides—from Home Army fighters executing Jews hiding in the forests to Catholic Poles risking their own lives to provide refuge to their Jewish countrymen. I've attempted to offer a balanced representation of these different attitudes in the interactions of Julia and her family.

When I first read about the Warsaw Uprising, I was stunned by the modest attention it receives in our contemporary history books, as well as in popular culture. The valiant struggle of the Varsovian population as they made their ill-advised last stand against the Nazi occupiers deserves more attention outside Poland. People of all ages resisted—including the young messengers and scouts of the Gray Ranks—despite the Nazis' increasingly brutal efforts to suppress them. The stories left me amazed, shaken, and humbled. The Wola Massacre, the capture of the German Panzer tanks by the Zośka battalion, the liberation of the Gęsiówka camp, and the German Trojan horse attack near the Home Army's HQ all happened. I've spent hours reading Polish eyewitness accounts to construct the final part of this story. I've also had to cut scenes; the book would have been almost twice as long had I included everything. Despite this, I feel I've done the men, women, and children of Warsaw justice in my representation of their heroic struggles.

I wish I could have given this story a happier ending—where the Varsovians beat the Nazis back into the Vistula as the Allied forces arrive—but the truth was that Hitler ordered complete destruction of the city after General Bór surrendered.

And finally, we come back to Julia and Natan. Fictional as they are, I'd like to believe there were plenty of Julias and Natans who survived the war and built better lives for themselves, both inside and outside postwar Soviet-controlled Poland.

If you enjoyed reading the story, please consider leaving a review. As an independently published author, I rely on word of mouth to generate interest in my work. If you'd like to reach out, I'd love to hear from you. You can find my contact details on michaelreit.com. I read and reply to every single message.

All my very best,

Michael

'BEYOND THE TRACKS': AN EXCERPT

By way of a thank you for reading *Warsaw Fury* I'm thrilled to be able to share with you the first two chapters of my other book, *Beyond The Tracks*.

With thanks,

Michael

PART I

BERLIN, GERMANY

NOVEMBER 1938

CHAPTER ONE

The blood-red swastika banners dominated Berlin. Draped across storefronts, houses, or taking over entire buildings, they demanded attention. Oranienburger Straße was as busy as ever this frosty afternoon, and Jacob Kagan deftly maneuvered through the stream of people on their way to the U-Bahn. He approached the New Synagogue, its gold-domed roof a proud symbol of defiance amidst the sea of Nazi symbolism.

Jacob nodded at one of the men standing guard in front of the building. "Everything okay today, Hans?"

"No trouble," Hans replied, shaking Jacob's hand, "if you don't count the Hitler Youth over there. But we can handle them." *Just like you always handled us in class*, Jacob thought wryly. He felt sorry for Hans, who had recently lost his job having taught at the same school for almost ten years until the new government decided Jewish teachers were no longer welcome. Now he spent most of his time keeping away trouble from the largest synagogue in the city.

Across the street, five teenagers in dark green uniforms handed out flyers. A common sight these days, they were generally harmless unless drink was involved – which often ended in pub brawls.

Jacob shook his head. "I'm sure they'll get bored soon enough and move on."

"I'm not so sure." Hans scratched his beard and puffed vapor into the air. "They've been here all day." One of the youngsters, who must be no older than twelve, stopped an elderly lady walking past. His face was flushed, and he gesticulated wildly. She responded calmly, took one of his flyers, and gently pushed the boy out of the way.

"They give everybody a flyer," Hans said, while Jacob frowned. "Everybody but us."

"I'm sure you fellows are not the most popular people on this street," Jacob said as he gestured to the other members of the synagogue standing watch.

"I've never cared about being popular, Jacob. Most people hurry by, their gazes firmly on the pavement in front of them—occasionally, the odd man will give us a dirty look," Hans said with a shrug and a wry smile. "It's business as usual. Speaking of which, how's the pharmacy doing?"

"Business is surprisingly good!" Jacob answered. "I've been out delivering all day. People will always need medicine, even if they won't be seen in our store anymore."

"Some of the lucky ones," Hans said. "Glad to hear it—your father has always been good to the community."

"Papa does his best navigating the restrictions. Some of our suppliers are wary, so we need to be creative." He looked up at the clock across the street. "I'll see you later, Hans. I have a few more packages to deliver before dark."

Jacob merged into the growing stream of people heading south toward Kreuzberg – all the while his fists were clenched.

It was dark by the time Jacob made his last delivery to a long-term customer, Herr Müller. He had been especially happy with Jacob for delivering his medication and saving him a trip to the pharmacy. Jacob turned from Spittelmarkt back onto the main thoroughfare of Leipziger Strasse—the street was alive with activity. Streetcars occupied the middle, their bells clanging to shoo careless pedestrians out of the way, while commuters paused to shop before making their way home.

Jacob hurried through the street and turned a few corners. He was late for his meeting with Ethan, his lifelong best friend. It didn't take him long to open the door to the Augustiner, a tavern just a few streets from his home.

He looked around for Ethan as the door closed behind him. The Augustiner was one of the few places in Berlin where Jews were still welcome, and as a result, it was packed every night. Tonight the warm, smoky air enveloped Jacob like a comfortable blanket.

Jacob spotted Ethan at a small table in the corner. Jacob pushed his way through the packed room, and Ethan stood up to hug him. Jacob was usually the tallest person in the room, except when Ethan was around.

"You're a bit late—nothing like you," Ethan said, flashing a broad smile.

Jacob took off his coat with a grin. "Are you trying to grow a beard?"

Ethan proudly scratched at his two-day stubble. "I think I'll look very respectable in a few weeks."

"Not until you take care of that mess on top of your head," Jacob said. Ethan's hair was especially wild today.

"These curls? Never!"

A waitress set down two large mugs of beer, catching Ethan's eye, the pair smiled at one another before she headed back to the bar.

They lifted their mugs, took their first sips, and set them down at the table. Ethan looked around the tavern – taking in a group of middle-aged men who were laughing loudly.

Ethan's face turned serious. "Do you remember when we would go out on Saturday nights, and walk into any bar we liked?"

Jacob nodded. "Nowadays, this is as good as it gets."

"I miss those days, Jaco."

Jacob looked around and thought nothing of the elderly couple at the table next to them, sharing a plate of pickled sausage and a small carafe of red wine in silence.

"What will be next?" Jacob asked. "Changes are taking place all around the city. Did you hear about that young boy who was attacked by the Brownshirts last week? They beat him almost to death in front of a crowd. Nobody did anything."

Ethan nodded. "And people losing their jobs. How long has it been since your mother left the school?"

"She hasn't set foot in there for over five years now. She used to go to school happy every day, and now she just sits at home."

They were silent for a moment.

Ethan stood and picked up their empty mugs. "I think we should have another one. There's not much we can do about it all tonight."

Jacob watched his best friend navigate his way to the small bar. Ethan was right—there was nothing they could do. The Augustiner was one of the few places where people could pretend everything was still normal.

Ethan returned with two foaming pints he placed on the table. "Right, Jaco. Here's to not speaking about politics, Nazis, or other shitty things for the rest of the evening." He raised his mug.

Jacob clinked Ethan's mug and took a sip of his own. Ethan met Jacob on the first day of school when they were just six years old. An older boy pushed Jacob in the playground, and Ethan had come to his rescue. Ethan suffered a black eye in the scuffle, but the boys had been inseparable from that day onward. Now both twenty-one, they were as close as ever.

"Oh, great." Ethan's expression darkened. "Not these guys."

Four men walked into the bar, wearing the characteristic brown shirts of the *Sturmabteilung*. One of the men pushed aside customers at the bar, causing an elderly gentleman to lose his balance, though someone caught him just in time.

The other people at the bar quickly made way for the heavily-built men. Jacob shook his head and looked down at his beer. "That's the first time I've seen Brownshirts in the Augustiner!" He took another sip to suppress the anger building up inside.

"You think we can take them?" Ethan asked with a twinkle in his eye.

Jacob set his mug down. "Are you kidding? There's four of them."

"So? I'm sick of these guys showing up everywhere and acting like they can get away with anything."

Ethan never walked away from a fight, but he was pushing it now. Jacob turned back to the bar and sized the men up. They were clearly drunk; perhaps this wasn't their first stop tonight. It was an open secret that the Brownshirts served as Hitler's personal riot squad, bringing violence and destruction wherever they went, although they were not officially recognized by the government.

The Brownshirts brought their beers into the main room, where most of the people kept their eyes on the group, anxious to see what they'd do next. All the tables in the Augustiner were taken, someone would need to make way.

The largest one spoke up: "Any Jews in here?"

A hush fell over the room as people averted their eyes and focused on their drinks.

Jacob looked at Ethan, whose face had further darkened. Jacob felt his anger bubbling over and heard himself say, "Right here."

The men turned toward their table. One of them cocked his head. "How about you get up, then?"

The other men laughed, and they took a few steps in Jacob and Ethan's direction as the people around them held their breath.

Ethan was the first to react. "We're okay here, but perhaps you want to knock another old man off his legs?" he nodded toward the bar.

The larger man scowled. "What did you say?" He stepped closer to Ethan, who stood up from his chair. Jacob did the same.

"You heard me. Nobody wants you here. Everybody was having a grand time until you stank the place up." Ethan gestured across the room, where the stunned patrons were looking back at him.

The largest of the Brownshirts was taken aback for a few seconds, then quickly regained his posture and lunged at Ethan with surprising speed.

Ethan side-stepped and easily dodged the blow. He landed a punch to the side of the man's head, and he went down like a sack of potatoes.

This only enraged the others.

The smallest of the three turned to Jacob, who managed to avert the man's first attack but didn't expect the off-hand blow that connected with his shoulder as he crouched down.

Bring it on—I can dodge your slow punches all night.

The attacker was panting and snarling. "Hit back, you *kike*," he slurred.

Then came the moment Jacob was waiting for. His opponent stumbled into one of the tables and lost his balance. Jacob's fist connected firmly with the man's face before a satisfying crack followed. The man grabbed his face while he crashed down onto the table, glasses shattering around him as he slumped to the floor.

Jacob turned to see Ethan holding his own against the two other men— waiting for the perfect time to strike.

Suddenly, the tavern door burst open, and more Brownshirts piled into the Augustiner, pushing their way through the thick crowd. Jacob counted at least five.

"Ethan!" he shouted, pointing at the door. "Time to go!"

His friend gave him a quick nod. The two Brownshirts still blocked Ethan's path out of the corner, so he took a step toward them and feinted an attack. Both men took the bait and swung wildly. Ethan ducked, and two quick stabs to the ribs doubled the men over. He kneed one in the face and the other in the groin, leaving them in pain, twisting on the floor.

Ethan skipped over them and joined Jacob. "Okay, now what?"

Jacob looked to the door and saw to his surprise that the new Brownshirts hadn't gotten much closer. The people in the Augustiner had blocked their path, forming a human wall.

"Quickly, over here!" One of the barkeeps waved from the side of the bar.

Jacob and Ethan hurried toward the man, deftly avoiding the overturned tables. The barkeeper lifted the bar and indicated the door behind it. Just as they passed, the elderly gentleman who had been almost toppled earlier placed a weak hand on Jacob's shoulder.

"If only more people stood up to them, we wouldn't be in this mess," he said.

Jacob smiled as he hurried through the door Ethan had left open behind the bar. The cold evening air hit his face as he stepped outside. Ethan was already halfway down the deserted alley, and Jacob rushed after him.

CHAPTER TWO

It had been a while since Jacob and Ethan had been in a fight. Fortunately, the previous night's damage was restricted to a few bruises, and Jacob wondered how their opponents had spent their day. It felt good to put some of the Brownshirts in their place and get away with it.

Jacob opened the door to the pharmacy as he returned from the last delivery, his father busy at the counter, helping a regular customer pick up her prescription.

"Jacob! What took you so long?" The handful of customers in Kagan & Sons Medicine turned to look at Hermann Kagan—a small, stout man. "You only needed to cross Kreuzberg! It's been more than an hour!"

Jacob gave the customers a reassuring smile and went behind the counter to hug his father.

"I'm here now, safe and well," he said, grinning as Hermann tried to wrestle free from his grasp.

"Wonderful. Now let me go!" Hermann protested as Jacob released him. He was no match for his much taller and stronger son, and it was an odd sight—the pharmacist and his son jousting behind the counter. An elderly lady at the counter smiled knowingly.

Jacob casually tossed his bag behind the counter. "Any more deliveries?"

"No, we're done," Hermann said as he handed a small bag of medicine to the elderly lady. A modest bell clanged as the door closed on her way out.

Jacob watched as his father rang up orders for the last customers. Hermann had taken over the pharmacy twenty years ago from his father, who had built it from the ground up, and the business soon thrived. Then Hermann had worked hard to grow it into one of the largest pharmacies in the city.

"Jacob, can you help carry these to the back?" His father pointed to some boxes next to the door.

Jacob took them to the empty storeroom behind the counter—getting a steady stream of medication to the pharmacy was tough.

They stepped outside, and Hermann locked the door. It was already dark, and a chill hung in the air. Their neighbor, Herr Wagner, closed the door to his law office as well.

"Did you hear about vom Rath?" Wagner looked concerned.

Jacob tensed. "Is he still in the hospital?"

Ernst vom Rath, a diplomat, was shot inside the German embassy in Paris a few days ago. A young German-Jewish man named Herschel Grynszpan was arrested on the spot and admitted to the shooting. According to the newspapers, his original target was the ambassador, but he had not been present. Vom Rath had been in critical condition since, and the story dominated the German news.

Wagner shook his head. "He passed away a few hours ago. Goebbels was just on the radio." He checked the lock on his door. "He's calling it a Jewish attack on Germany."

Jacob looked at his father. Hermann's face was ashen in the glow of a street-lamp.

"Goebbels said the Jews should feel the anger of the people," Wagner continued. "I'm sorry, Hermann—I don't know what that means."

The words were a punch in the gut to Jacob.

"Hitler was looking for an excuse," Hermann said, his bottom lip quivering, "and the Grynszpan boy has given him the perfect excuse."

Wagner nodded. "They're talking about bringing him back to Germany to make an example of him, whatever that means."

Jacob had a good idea what it meant. His father looked like he'd aged ten years in the past few seconds. "Let's go home," Jacob said. "There's no sense in staying in the cold."

Wagner nodded and walked solemnly off in the opposite direction. Jacob and his father set off along the cobblestoned street, all the shop windows now dark. They passed the *Berliner Gasthaus*, one of the few places where light shone from behind the windows. A few tables were occupied, the people enjoying simple suppers of sausage and bread.

"I'm worried about Goebbels," Jacob said, breaking the silence. "Do you think this means they'll make us close the pharmacy?"

Hermann shook his head. "I don't know. There's no telling what they'll do. We've been lucky to stay open so far, I guess."

"We'll just have to wait and see what happens the next few days," Hermann continued. "There's not much we can do about it."

They walked home in silence, each lost in their own thoughts.

Jacob's mother always made sure there was a hearty meal waiting for her men at the end of the day. Elsa Kagan cleared the empty plates from the table, and Jacob followed to help her wash the dishes in the small kitchen.

The Kagans lived in a modest house that had been in the family for generations, and while they could certainly afford to move to a larger home, they preferred to stay in Kreuzberg. Elsa always said the house had the sort of character which couldn't be bought. Jacob agreed; there were so many memories here that he couldn't imagine living anywhere else.

"Just hand me those, Mama."

Jacob rinsed the plates before plunging them into the scalding water. His mother joined him at the sink and started drying the dishes while Hermann sat down with a newspaper and switched on the radio. Goebbels' voice boomed from the speakers.

"I hope they keep him there," Elsa said. "Who knows what will happen if he's handed over to the Nazis. I doubt there will be a trial at all."

Goebbels was calling for reprisals after the assassination of Ernst vom Rath and added that the German government demanded the extradition of Herschel Grynzspan from France.

"He'd probably receive a one-way trip to an SS basement," Jacob said. Rumors about the makeshift prison under the SS headquarters circulated Berlin, those unfortunate enough to earn an unsolicited invitation were never heard of again.

"It's such a shame. The boy must've been so desperate to do what he did," Elsa said, placing the dry plates in a cupboard.

Jacob drained the water and dried his hands with a small towel. "This gives the Nazis more incentive to blame all of us, even though we had nothing to do with it."

He put the towel down and yawned. "I'm going to go upstairs and study a bit."

Hermann smiled. "I should have the exam for you next week."

Jacob stopped. "Herr Lughart at the university came through?"

"He did. He's smuggling the latest exam out for you."

Jacob saw his mother smile. Even though he wouldn't be able to formally take the exam, this was as good as it got these days.

"I'll be ready, although this first book is quite tough," Jacob said as he bound up the stairs with a spring in his step. He closed the door to his room. He wasn't just going to be ready; he planned to ace the exam.

Jacob awoke in the middle of the night. It was dark, and it felt like he'd slept for only a few minutes. His eyes needed a few seconds to adjust to the darkness. He squinted at his watch on the bedside table—one in the morning.

He switched on the night light and got out of bed. Rubbing the sleep from his eyes, he felt his senses switch on. He heard angry voices outside and smelled smoke. He quickly dressed and opened his bedroom door. His father stood in his nightclothes in the hallway, a surprised look on his face.

"What's going on, Jaco? Is there some kind of protest outside?"

"I don't know, but I smell smoke."

Jacob raced down the stairs and looked out into the street. A dozen or so people stood outside, the small bakery across the street was ablaze. Angry bursts of fire shot from the bakery window, smoke billowing from all sides of the building.

Hermann appeared next to Jacob. "Oh no! Midas must've had an accident. Let's help him put out the fire." He went for the door before Jacob stopped him.

"Wait," Jacob said, a hand on his father's arm. "Look at the people around the bakery."

Their neighbor was frantically pleading with the growing crowd to help him fight the fire. The people didn't move as the baker rushed between his burning bakery and a well, carrying a small bucket. It was useless; the fire had engulfed the shop.

"It doesn't look like an accident," Jacob said.

One of the men said something to Midas, prompting a chorus of laughter from the others. Midas looked distraught and ceased his attempts to put out the fire. The crowd stood by idly as the flames consumed the building.

"We can't just stand here and do nothing," Hermann said, opening the door to the street. Jacob followed him, and they rushed toward their neighbor.

A few paces down the street, a jewelry store had its front window smashed, and several looters were running away, dropping necklaces as they went.

On the other side of the road, two men doused the front of a small butcher shop in gasoline while another man held a blazing torch. The men stepped away from the shop window, throwing the now-empty jerry can on the ground. The man with the torch casually lobbed it at the window, and the fire roared to life with a loud whoosh—the butchers was engulfed in flames within seconds.

Jacob looked around, their peaceful street transformed into a war zone.

What's wrong with these people?

"They're targeting Jewish businesses!" Hermann said, fear rising in his voice.

Papa is right, but what about—"I'll check on the pharmacy," Jacob said, rushing back to their home to grab the keys from just inside the door. "You stay here with Mama and don't go anywhere. Lock the doors!"

His father nodded and disappeared back inside the house.

Jacob ran down the street, reaching the intersection with the larger Gitschiner Straße. The mayhem was even worse here, with half the buildings on fire. A large man took a loose stone from the street and launched it at a shop window. The window exploded into a thousand pieces. Further down the street, a group of firemen stood working a large hose. Jacob was relieved; maybe they could salvage some of the damage?

As he got closer, he overheard who he assumed was the owner of the store, pleading with the firemen.

"But my building is burning down. Please help me!"

"I'm sorry, we can't," one of the firemen said. "We're only here to make sure it doesn't spread."

The plumes of smoke increased, obscuring the view of the surrounding buildings as pieces of stone crumbled down haphazardly.

Jacob ran on for another five minutes, almost to where their pharmacy was located. He braced himself as he thought of the mess he'd find there. *If a crowd were looting the pharmacy, there wouldn't be anything I can do about it.*

As he turned the corner, he was relieved to find the pharmacy untouched. The street was relatively quiet, and there were no fires, but there were plenty of people outside their homes. A young girl not much older than seven looked up at Jacob with big, frightened eyes. She wore but a nightgown, and her mother kept her close. A man stood next to them, holding a shovel, scanning the street with an air of defiance.

Jacob reached the pharmacy, where Herr Wagner stood outside the door to his offices. He saw Jacob and motioned him to come closer.

"It's madness," he said, his eyes wide with fear. "They're destroying the city."

Jacob nodded. "I ran across town, and there are fires everywhere. People are looting shops, grabbing whatever they can. I haven't seen any fights yet, but it can't be much longer."

"They're only attacking Jewish businesses, though," Wagner said. "Looks like Goebbels got exactly what he wanted."

"I can't believe this is a spontaneous reaction. Do you think it's the SS?"

"Maybe, or the Brownshirts, more likely. I saw some men in uniforms giving orders. Most of them are wearing normal clothes, though." An explosion on the next block rocked the ground, and they instinctively ducked.

A large group of men appeared from around the corner. They carried torches and jerry cans and shouted at people to get out of their way. Jacob counted at least twenty of them.

"Out with the Jews!"

Jacob looked at Wagner. He'd turned pale, his gaze fixed on the men.

"Trouble's here," Jacob said. The man across the street tightened his grip on the shovel. Jacob tried to get his attention, but the man was too focused on the group. The girl hid behind her mother, only her face peeking out.

The group reached the small family's house and stopped.

"Look at the brave one," one of the larger men in the front said. He flashed a sinister smile and held his arms out wide. "What do you think you're going to do ?"

The homeowner didn't respond but just looked at the brute and clenched his jaw.

"Get out of the way," the man said, stepping forward. "Don't give me a reason to hurt your little girl there."

Behind him, a man took a bottle from his backpack and filled it with gasoline from one of the jerry cans.

"You want to be a homeless *kike*?" The first man flashed a dirty, toothless grin "or a dead one?" He held up the bottle menacingly and struck the first match. The flame didn't hold, and the man cursed.

Jacob looked around the street—most people had fled into their houses.

We can't just leave them to fend for themselves.

He took a step toward the family across the street. Before he could take another, he felt a firm hand on his shoulder.

"You can't help them, Jacob." Wagner's eyes showed concern as he shook his head. "Look at those thugs—there's no reasoning with them."

Jacob tried to shake off the older man's grip, but Wagner was adamant.

"If you walk over there, they'll burn down the pharmacy as well. Not to mention what they'd do to you. You're a Jew, Jacob. Don't give them an excuse."

Jacob felt his eyes sting as he struggled to control his anger. *I can't just stand here and do nothing.* At the same time, he knew he couldn't take on twenty men on his own. *If only the man backs down, maybe it won't be that bad.*

The little girl started to cry. The sound pierced the evening sky, and her father looked over his shoulder. It was the first time he took his eyes off the group.

"It will be okay," he said softly as he put down his shovel to gently stroke her hair. "These angry men think we're going to hurt them, but you know that's not true, right?"

She sobbed and buried her face against her mother's skirts. The mother looked up at her husband with pleading eyes.

He shook his head. "I can't let them destroy our house. It's all we have."

The man grabbed his shovel and swung it at the man holding the bottle, smashing it to pieces on the street. The man roared with pain, and for a moment, everybody was too stunned to react as the sweet smell of gasoline spread.

The group recovered quickly and descended on the man like a pack of hyenas. He managed to get a few swings in, stepping back while they approached. He could only keep them from him for so long, and it was only a moment later he was pinned down on the ground.

Jacob saw the flash of a knife and looked away.

The leader of the group called out: "Stop, don't kill him!"

The man holding the knife paused and looked up at the leader in surprise. The man on the ground was a mess, his face bruised and bloodied. Despite this, defiance still shone in his eyes.

"Get him up," the leader said. "And get his wife and kid away from the house."

The man was dragged away; the girl left crying as her mother tried to comfort her. She shielded her daughter and clawed at the men approaching them. Outnumbered, the men pulled her and the child away from the house. They were left next to their husband and father, whose breathing was labored and shallow as he struggled to sit upright.

"I've decided it's better to have you see your house burned to the ground than to kill you here," the leader of the group said. "Besides, there's a better place to send you than kill you." He grinned and lit the rag hanging out of one of the bottles. The thugs smashed a window using the homeowner's shovel and stepped out of the way.

The leader threw the bottle into the house, which instantly engulfed the small front room in fire. The house turned into an inferno within seconds.

Jacob felt the heat on his face from the other side of the street. He could only watch as the small house crumbled in front of them.

"Okay, that's enough. Take him to the police station." The large man pointed at two strong men to pick up the homeowner, who'd passed out.

They dragged him away and left his wife and daughter in front of their now-smoldering house. They looked stunned.

"Where are you taking him?" the wife asked the group leader, who was walking away. She held her sobbing daughter close.

He looked at her with contempt. "He'll be in one of the jail cells nearby, along with the rest of you scum. You can go with him if you want—I don't care." He walked on, the group following him and ignoring the woman on the ground.

Jacob looked on in shock as the men passed him chanting Nazi anthems with outstretched arms. Most of them were in their early twenties, although he also spotted a few teenagers amongst them. Their eyes were full of menace, satisfied with the damage they'd wrought.

Wagner tugged at his shirt. "Keep your head down, Jacob," he whispered. "It looks like they're passing by our shops."

The men appeared to have sated their lust for blood for now and moved away. Relative peace returned to the street. Jacob stood in a daze. The pharmacy had survived this attack, but he felt the next wave of violence was just around the corner – would he suffer the same fate as the young father?

Wagner looked at him and took control. "I know it feels wrong, not doing anything just now. But we couldn't stop them. You know this, right?"

Jacob nodded absently.

"You need to get home and stay inside," Wagner said. "This can't go on forever, and you can't protect the pharmacy on your own. Keep yourself safe."

Jacob looked across the street, where the mother and child were wrapped in blankets.

He's right. I'm just as much a target.

He regained his senses and looked Wagner in the eye.

"Now go home, Jacob. I'm going to do the same. Avoid the main streets, and don't stop until you're inside."

Jacob shook Wagner's hand before turning back toward the city center, the dark sky overcast in smoke.

The Berlin streets were in pandemonium. People were dragged along by mobs of young men as trucks holding bound men zipped around the streets. This was no spontaneous uprising.

Jacob's only option was to keep moving and pray he wouldn't run into any of the groups he'd seen earlier. If he kept his head down, his chances were pretty good. So far, the people he'd seen hauled off were trying to defend their property. He pitied them; they didn't know what they were up against.

He suspected the Brownshirts were behind the attacks. They were the only group in Berlin that would exert themselves at these tasks with such zeal. The SS was just as despicable, but they were too organized and proud to plunder and loot.

Jacob avoided the main throughways, but he needed to cross Oranienburger Straße and pass the New Synagogue to get home. When he got there, the street was swamped, shattered glass lined the pavement.

He stepped over the large pieces of glass and hoped his boots would stop any smaller bits. Something was going on in front of the New Synagogue. He spotted a row of about twenty people who'd hooked arms and formed a human wall. Jacob was unsurprised to see Hans standing in the middle of the group.

Opposite them stood a much larger crowd, some armed with clubs and knives.

The groups were in a deadlock. Those people protecting the synagogue were content keeping the thugs at bay. Bystanders waited to see what would happen next. The sound of broken glass signaled that one of the ornate windows of the synagogue had been smashed.

A large man wearing a dark red coat stepped forward, Jacob could see a large scar on his cheek, his face blotted with rashes.

"We're burning down your synagogue," he said in a quiet, raspy voice.

Jacob couldn't place his accent, but he wasn't from Berlin.

"You can get outta the way or burn with your holy building," he continued.

A number of the younger men in front of him shuffled their feet. They looked to Hans, who stood tall in the middle of the group.

"You have no authority—you can't bully us," Hans said, his face hardening. "I've dealt with people like you all my life, and I'll be damned if I let you destroy our synagogue without a fight."

The man held Hans' gaze while he stepped toward him. "I was hopin' you'd say that." He leaned toward Hans, and their noses almost touched.

Hans was unfazed, and the men stood frozen for what felt like an eternity.

After everything Jacob had seen earlier today, he knew Hans wouldn't blink first.

"You'll have to go through me to get to the synagogue." Hans took a step toward the man, forcing him to step back. His courage emboldened the people around him, and they moved forward, too.

The man in red recovered quickly. Behind him, the larger group became restless as they clenched their weapons tighter.

Out of nowhere, the man lashed out at Hans, but Hans ducked, and the man hit nothing but air.

"You shoulda moved," the threatening man growled. The men behind him took this as their cue and poured forward.

The scene was horrific. The bloodthirsty crowd of thugs cut through the Jewish barrier with ease. Some of the younger men guarding the synagogue got a few punches in, but the fight was unfair. The men attacking knew what they were doing, expertly cutting and stabbing at essential spots on the defenders' bodies. Some of them were cut down and trampled as the men moved on to their next victims. Jacob watched on helplessly—there were too many people between him and the synagogue.

It ended as quickly as it started.

The coppery scent of blood hung in the air as Jacob searched for Hans amongst the fallen people. He was aghast to see him on the pavement, a large pool of blood forming around his body. Hans's breathing was shallow, his eyes rolled back in their sockets. Jacob instinctively began pushing through the crowd to help his friend, but hands clutched at him, and one voice came through sorrowfully: "Wait—or you'll end up just like them."

The thugs stepped over the bodies, ignoring the victims' pleas for help. They carried their jerry cans toward the New Synagogue, people nearby unable or unwilling to stop them.

"Just move the jerry cans into the place," the man with the scar said. "It'll burn faster, and they're not going to stop us anymore." He pointed at the heap of people sprawled on the ground.

Just as they opened the doors to the synagogue, there was a commotion in the crowd. A uniformed policeman marched straight to the entrance.

Jacob recognized Otto Belgardt, a well-known lieutenant he knew as a friendly and dedicated officer. He was the first uniformed policeman Jacob had seen all night.

Belgardt looked in horror at the scene. He stopped one of the men carrying a jerry can to the entrance of the synagogue.

"What do you think you're doing? Get that gasoline away from the building!"

Belgardt barked. The young man stopped, a flash of uncertainty crossing his face.

Jacob felt hopeful. *Is someone finally going to put a stop to this mayhem?*

Belgardt went up the steps, pushing past the other men. "All of you, stop this nonsense right now!" he shouted at the group drenching the New Synagogue in gasoline. "Don't you know this is a protected building? You're all breaking the law!"

The men turned to their leader, who stood in front of the main door holding an unlit torch.

"Move along, cop," said the man in red. "You got no power tonight. You know who we are, dontcha?" He struck a match and held it to the torch, which caught fire immediately, its hungry flames consuming the gasoline. That encouraged his men, who turned back to their work and ignored the police officer.

Belgardt looked unfazed. He calmly opened his jacket and unclipped his gun. Effortlessly, he cocked the hammer and aimed it at the man with the unsightly face—the scar now a deep shade of red, betraying his anxiety.

"Perhaps you'd like to reconsider my authority now?" Belgardt said. He moved closer to the door of the synagogue, keeping his pistol aimed at the leader.

Fear crossed the man's face and quickly spread to his companions, who put down their jerry cans.

A few of the younger attackers shirked away, trying to blend into the crowd. *Good.*

Belgardt reached the top of the stairs and was only a few steps away from the leader. His aim was fixed on the man's chest. "I suggest you get out of here now. You've done enough damage for one night."

The larger man looked angry, but Belgardt was the one with the gun.

"This isn't over," the man said, walking away from the synagogue. "You know we work under the Führer's own say, dontcha?" He spat on the ground.

Belgardt didn't budge, the barrel of his gun following the man down the stairs. "I must've missed the part about destroying national monuments."

The man snarled at him one last time and disappeared into the crowd.

Jacob rushed forward to check on the injured people, especially Hans, as the crowd dispersed now that the fight was over. He scanned the faces of the people on the ground; some of them no longer moving as he made his way up the steps. Fire trucks screeched to a stop in the street, the firemen quickly extinguishing the torches the men had left behind.

He found Hans propped up against the side of the synagogue. He was relieved to see his old teacher looking a little better than before.

"You see? We can stop them—we just need to have faith"—he burst into a violent cough, and a fireman handed him some water.

"Take it easy," Jacob said. Hans looked horrible, his face swollen and his left eye completely shut. Hans' clothes were stained with dark crimson patches of blood, but his good eye shone brightly.

The fireman gave them a thumbs-up. "You're going to be fine, but you need to get yourself checked by a doctor soon." He moved on to a young man next to Hans; hands gripped tightly to his side—it looked like they'd cracked a few of his ribs.

Jacob gently patted Hans on the shoulder. "That was both the bravest and most foolish thing I've ever seen you do."

Hans smiled. "Somebody had to stay here until the police finally showed up, no? You boys gave me practice in standing up to ruffians."

"I think Belgardt is one of the good ones—I haven't seen any other police out on the streets tonight."

"He IS a good one," answered Hans with a nod toward the policeman, who hadn't moved from his post, his eyes scanning the street. "He's checked on us a few times a day while we were out here the past two weeks. Even sent the Hitler Youth away on a few occasions. I'm sure he's not very popular with the brass."

Jacob looked around. "The streets have been taken over by gangs of thugs."

"It's the Brownshirts, no doubt. They might be wearing regular clothes, but I recognized a few of them."

"You saved the synagogue tonight, Hans. Don't you think you should see a doctor? There have to be plenty of them still willing to help you." Jacob looked around. "You're going to be okay here?"

Hans nodded. "Of course. It'll take more than a few cowards to get me down. Is the pharmacy okay?"

"It was when I was there a little earlier, but who knows?" Jacob shrugged. "Anything could happen tonight. I'm going to check on my parents."

Jacob walked wearily down the stairs. The Oranienburger Straße was a little less crowded, the shattered windows the remnants of the destructive wave that had passed through earlier. In the distance, the first rays of the rising sun struggled to make their way through the smoke.

–

Beyond The Tracks is available as ebook, paperback, hardcover, or audiobook from Amazon.

ABOUT THE AUTHOR

Michael Reit writes historical fiction based on true events. As an avid fan of history and historical fiction, and intrigued by WWII, he enjoys researching lesser-known events, locations, and people and bringing them to life in his novels. Born in the Netherlands, he now lives in beautiful Vienna, Austria, with his partner Esther, daughter Bibi, and Hungarian Vizsla Maggie.

You can connect through:
www.michaelreit.com
or
Facebook (MichaelReitAuthor)